HAUNTED

Also by Chuck Palahniuk

Chuck Palahniuk

DOUBLEDAY   NEW YORK LONDON TORONTO SYDNEY AUCKLAND

EVERY STORY IS A GHOST

HAUNTED

A Novel of Stories

PUBLISHED BY DOUBLEDAY
A division of Random House, Inc.

DOUBLEDAY and the portrayal of an anchor with a dolphin are
registered trademarks of Random House, Inc.

Book design by Michael Collica

Library of Congress Cataloging-in-Publication Data
Palahniuk, Chuck.
Haunted : a novel of stories / Chuck Palahniuk.— 1st ed.
p. cm.
ISBN 0-385-50948-0
1. Artists—Fiction. 2. Prisoners—Fiction. 3. Torture victims—
Fiction. 4. Social isolation—Fiction. I. Title.

PS3566.A4554H38 2005
813'.54—dc22
2004059380

PRINTED IN THE UNITED STATES OF AMERICA

June 2005
First Edition

1 3 5 7 9 10 8 6 4 2

There was much of the beautiful, much of the wanton, much of the *bizarre*, something of the terrible, and not a little of that which might have excited disgust.

"The Masque of the Red Death"
by Edgar Allan Poe

This was supposed to be a writers' retreat. It was supposed
   to be safe.
   An isolated writers' colony, where we could work,
   run by an old, old, dying man named Whittier,
   until it wasn't.
And we were supposed to write poetry. Pretty poetry.
   This crowd of us, his gifted students,
   locked away from the ordinary world for three months.

And we called each other the "Matchmaker." And the
   "Missing Link."
   Or "Mother Nature." Silly labels. Free-association names.
   The same way—when you were little—you invented
      names for the plants and
   animals in your world. You called peonies—sticky with
      nectar and crawling with
   ants—the "ant flower." You called collies: *Lassie Dogs.*
But even now, the same way you still call someone "that
   man with one leg."
   Or, "you know, the black girl . . ."

We called each other:
   The "Earl of Slander."

Or "Sister Vigilante."
The names we earned, based on our stories. The names
   we gave each other,
      based on our life instead of our family:
      "Lady Baglady."
      "Agent Tattletale."
Names based on our sins instead of our jobs:
      "Saint Gut-Free."
      And the "Duke of Vandals."
      Based on our faults and crimes. The opposite of
         superhero names.

Silly names for real people. As if you cut open a rag doll
   and found inside:
      Real intestines, real lungs, a beating heart, blood. A lot
         of hot, sticky blood.
And we were supposed to write short stories. Funny short
   stories.
      Too many of us, locked away from the world for one
         whole
      spring, summer, winter, autumn—one whole season of
         that year.

It doesn't matter who we were as people, not to old Mr.
   Whittier.
      But he didn't say this at first.
To Mr. Whittier, we were lab animals. An experiment.

But we didn't know.
   No, this was only a writers' retreat until it was too late for
      us to be anything,
   except his victims.

When the bus pulls to the corner where Comrade Snarky had agreed to wait, she stands there in an army-surplus flak jacket—dark olive-green—and baggy camouflage pants, the cuffs rolled up to show infantry boots. A suitcase on either side of her. With a black beret pulled down tight on her head, she could be anyone.

"The rule was . . . ," Saint Gut-Free says into the microphone that hangs above his steering wheel.

And Comrade Snarky says, "Fine." She leans down to unbuckle a luggage tag off one suitcase. Comrade Snarky tucks the luggage tag in her olive-green pocket, then lifts the second suitcase and steps up into the bus. With one suitcase still on the curb, abandoned, orphaned, alone, Comrade Snarky sits down and says, "Okay."

She says, "Drive."

We were all leaving notes, that morning. Before dawn. Sneaking out on tiptoe with our suitcase down dark stairs, then along dark streets with only garbage trucks for company. We never did see the sun come up.

Sitting next to Comrade Snarky, the Earl of Slander was writing something in a pocket notepad, his eyes flicking between her and his pen.

And, leaning over sideways to look, Comrade Snarky

says, "My eyes are *green,* not *brown,* and my hair is naturally this color *auburn."* She watches as he writes *green,* then says, "And I have a little red rose tattooed on my butt cheek." Her eyes settle on the silver tape recorder peeking out of his shirt pocket, the little-mesh microphone of it, and she says, "Don't write *dyed hair.* Women either *lift* or *tint* the color of their hair."

Near them sits Mr. Whittier, where his spotted, trembling hands can grip the folded chrome frame of his wheelchair. Beside him sits Mrs. Clark, her breasts so big they almost rest in her lap.

Eyeing them, Comrade Snarky leans into the gray flannel sleeve of the Earl of Slander. She says, "Purely ornamental, I assume. And of no nutritive value . . ."

That was the day we missed our last sunrise.

At the next dark street corner, where Sister Vigilante stands waiting, she holds up her thick black wristwatch, saying, "We agreed on four-thirty-five." She taps the watch face with her other hand, saying, "It is now four-thirty-nine . . ."

Sister Vigilante, she brought a fake-leather case with a strap handle, a flap that closed with a snap to protect the Bible inside. A purse handmade to lug around the Word of God.

All over the city, we waited for the bus. At street corners or bus-stop benches, until Saint Gut-Free drove up. Mr. Whittier sitting near the front with Mrs. Clark. The Earl of Slander. Comrade Snarky and Sister Vigilante.

Saint Gut-Free pulls the lever to fold open the door, and standing on the curb is little Miss Sneezy. The sleeves of her sweater lumpy with dirty tissues stuffed inside. She lifts her suitcase and it rattles loud as popcorn in a microwave oven. With every step up the stairs into the bus, the suitcase rattles loud as far-off machine-gun fire, and Miss Sneezy looks at us and says, "My pills." She gives the suitcase a loud shake and says, "A whole three months' supply . . ."

That's why the rule about only so much luggage. So we would all fit.

4

The only rule was one bag per person, but Mr. Whittier didn't say how big or what kind.

When Lady Baglady climbed on board, she wore a diamond ring the size of a popcorn kernel, her hand holding a leash, the leash dragging a leather suitcase on little wheels.

Waving her fingers to make her ring sparkle, Lady Baglady says, "It's my late husband, cremated and made into a three-carat diamond . . ."

At that, Comrade Snarky leans over the notepad where the Earl of Slander is writing, and she says, *"Facelift* is one word."

A few blocks later, after a couple traffic lights and around some corners waits Chef Assassin, carrying a molded aluminum suitcase with, inside, all his white elastic underpants and T-shirts and socks folded down to squares tight as origami. Plus a matched set of chef's knives. Under that, his aluminum suitcase is solid-packed with banded stacks of money, all of it hundred-dollar bills. All of it so heavy he used both hands to lift it into the bus.

Down another street, under a bridge and around the far side of a park, the bus pulled to the curb where no one seemed to wait. There the man we called the "Missing Link" stepped out of the bushes near the curb. Balled in his arms, he carried a black garbage bag, torn and leaking plaid flannel shirts.

Looking at the Missing Link, but talking sideways to the Earl of Slander, Comrade Snarky said, "His *beard* looks like something Hemingway might've shot . . ."

The dreaming world, they'd think we were crazy. Those people still in bed, they'd be asleep another hour, then washing their faces, under their arms, and between their legs, before going to the same work they did every day. Living that same life, every day.

Those people would cry to find us gone, but they would cry, too, if we were boarding a ship to start a new life across some ocean. Emigrating. Pioneers.

This morning, we were astronauts. Explorers. Awake while they slept.

These people would cry, but then they would go back to waiting tables, painting houses, programming computers.

At our next stop, Saint Gut-Free swung open the doors, and a cat ran up the steps and down the aisle between the seats of the bus. Behind the cat came Director Denial, saying, "His name is Cora." The cat's name was Cora Reynolds. "I didn't name him," said Director Denial, the tweed blazer and skirt she wore frosted with cat hair. One lapel swollen out from her chest.

"A shoulder holster," says Comrade Snarky, leaning close to tell the tape recorder in the Earl of Slander's shirt pocket.

All of this—whispering in the dark, leaving notes, keeping secret—it was our adventure.

If you were planning to be stranded on a desert island for three months, what would you bring along?

Let's say all your food and water would be provided, or so you think.

Let's say you can only bring along one suitcase because there will be a lot of you, and the bus taking you all to the desert island is only so big.

What would you pack in your suitcase?

Saint Gut-Free brought boxes of pork-rind snacks and dried cheese puffs, his fingers and chin orange with the salt dust. One bony hand gripping the steering wheel, he tilted each box to pour the snacks into his thin face.

Sister Vigilante brought a shopping bag of clothes with a satchel bag set in the top.

Leaning over her own huge breasts, holding them like a child in her arms, Mrs. Clark asked, did Sister Vigilante bring along a human head?

And Sister Vigilante opened the satchel far enough to show the three holes of a black bowling ball, saying, "My hobby . . ."

Comrade Snarky looks from the Earl of Slander scribbling into his notepad, then looks at Sister Vigilante's braided-tight black hair, not one strand pulling loose from its pins.

"That," Comrade Snarky says, *"is tinted hair."*

At our next stop, Agent Tattletale stood with a video camera held to one eye, filming the bus as it pulled to the curb. He brought a stack of business cards he passed out to prove he was a private detective. With his video camera held as a mask covering half his face, he filmed us, walking down the aisle to an empty seat at the back, blinding everyone with his spotlight.

A city block later, the Matchmaker climbed on board, tracking horse shit on his cowboy boots. A straw cowboy hat in his hands and a duffel bag hung over one shoulder, he sat and peeled back his window and spit brown tobacco juice down the brushed-steel side of the bus.

This is what we brought along for three months outside of the world. Agent Tattletale, his video camera. Sister Vigilante, her bowling ball. Lady Baglady, her diamond ring. This is what we'd need to write our stories. Miss Sneezy, her pills and tissues. Saint Gut-Free, his snack food. The Earl of Slander, his notebook and tape recorder.

Chef Assassin, his knives.

In the dim light of the bus, we all spied on Mr. Whittier, the workshop organizer. Our teacher. You could see the spotted shiny dome of his scalp under the few gray hairs combed across. The button-down collar of his shirt stood up, a starched white fence around his thin, spotted neck.

"The people you're sneaking away from," Mr. Whittier would say, "they don't want you enlightened. They want to know what to expect."

Mr. Whittier would tell you, "You cannot be the person they know and the great, glorious person you want to become. Not at the same time."

The people who really, actually loved us, Mr. Whittier said they'd beg us to go. To fulfill our dream. Practice our craft. And they would love us when we all came back.

In three months.

The little bit of life we'd each gamble.

We'd risk.

This much time, we'd bet on our own ability to create some masterpiece. A short story or poem or screenplay or memoir that would make sense of our life. A masterpiece that would buy our way out of slavery to a husband or a parent or a corporation. That would earn our freedom.

All of us, driving along the empty streets in the dark. Miss Sneezy fishes a damp tissue out of her sweater sleeve and blows her nose. She sniffs and says, "Sneaking out this way, I was so afraid of getting caught." Tucking the tissue back inside her cuff, she says, "I feel just like . . . Anne Frank."

Comrade Snarky digs the luggage tag out of her jacket pocket, the remains of her abandoned suitcase. Her abandoned life. And, turning the tag over and over in her hand, still looking at it, Comrade Snarky says, "The way I see it . . ." She says, "Anne Frank had life pretty good."

And Saint Gut-Free, his mouth full of corn chips, watching us all in the rearview mirror, chewing salt and fat, he says, "How's that?"

Director Denial pets her cat. Mrs. Clark pets her breasts. Mr. Whittier, his chrome wheelchair.

Under a streetlight, on a corner up ahead, the dark outline of another would-be writer waits.

"At least Anne Frank," Comrade Snarky said, "never had to tour with her book . . ."

And Saint Gut-Free hits the air brakes and cranks the steering wheel to pull over.

"Here's the job I left to come here," the Saint says. "And the
    life I gave up."
    He used to drive a tour bus.

Saint Gut-Free onstage, his arms folded across his chest—
    so skinny
    his hands can touch in the middle of his back
There stands Saint Gut-Free, with a single coat of skin
    painted on his skeleton.
    His collarbones loop out from his chest, big as grab
        handles.
His ribs show through his white T-shirt, and his belt—
    instead of his butt—keeps up his blue jeans.

Onstage, instead of a spotlight, a movie fragment:
    the colors of houses and sidewalks, street signs and
        parked cars,
    wipe sideways across his face. A mask of heavy traffic.
        Vans and trucks.

He says, "That job, driving tour bus . . ."
It was all Japanese, Germans, Koreans, all with English as
    a second language, with phrase

books clutched in one hand, nodding and smiling at
    whatever he told the
microphone as he steered the bus around corners, down
    streets, past the houses of
movie stars or extra-bloody murders, apartments where
    rock stars had overdosed.
Every day the same tour, the same mantra of murder,
    movie stars, accidents. Places
    where peace treaties got signed. Where presidents had
        slept.
Until that day Saint Gut-Free stops in front of a picket-fence
    ranch house, just a detour
        to see if his parents' four-door Buick is there, if this is
            still where they live,
    where pacing the front yard is a man, pushing a lawn
        mower.
There, into his microphone, the Saint tells his air-
    conditioned cargo:
    "You're looking at Saint Mel."
And, his father squinting at the wall of tinted bus
    windows,
    "The Patron Saint of Shame and Rage," says Gut-Free.

After that, every day, the tour includes "The Shrine of Saint
    Mel and Saint Betty."
    Saint Betty being the Patron Saint of Public Humiliation.
Parked in front of his sister's condo highrise, Saint Gut-Free
    points to
    some high-up floor. Up there, the shrine of Saint Wendy.
    "The Patron Saint of Therapeutic Abortion."

Parked in front of his own apartment,
    he tells the bus, "There's the shrine of Saint Gut-Free,"

the Saint himself, his pigeon shoulders, rubber-band lips,
    and baggy shirt,
reflected even smaller in the rearview mirror.
"The Patron Saint of Masturbation."
While each seat in his bus, nodding heads, craning their
    necks, they look to see
    something divine.

Guts

A Story by Saint Gut-Free

Inhale.

Take in as much air as you can.

This story should last about as long as you can hold your breath, and then just a little bit longer. So listen as fast as you can.

A friend of mine, when he was thirteen years old he heard about "pegging." This is when a guy gets banged up the butt with a dildo. Stimulate the prostate gland hard enough, and the rumor is you can have explosive hands-free orgasms. At that age, this friend's a little sex maniac. He's always jonesing for a better way to get his rocks off. He goes out to buy a carrot and some petroleum jelly. To conduct a little private research. Then he pictures how it's going to look at the supermarket checkstand, the lonely carrot and petroleum jelly rolling down the conveyor belt toward the grocery-store cashier. All the shoppers waiting in line, watching. Everyone seeing the big evening he has planned.

So, my friend, he buys milk and eggs and sugar and a carrot, all the ingredients for a carrot cake. And Vaseline.

Like he's going home to stick a carrot cake up his butt.

At home, he whittles the carrot into a blunt tool. He

slathers it with grease and grinds his ass down on it. Then—nothing. No orgasm. Nothing happens except it hurts.

Then this kid, his mom yells it's suppertime. She says to come down, right now.

He works the carrot out and stashes the slippery, filthy thing in the dirty clothes under his bed.

After dinner, he goes to find the carrot and it's gone. All his dirty clothes, while he ate dinner, his mom grabbed them all to do laundry. No way could she not find the carrot, carefully shaped with a paring knife from her kitchen, still shiny with lube and stinky.

This friend of mine, he waits months under a black cloud, waiting for his folks to confront him. And they never do. Ever. Even now he's grown up, that invisible carrot hangs over every Christmas dinner, every birthday party. Every Easter-egg hunt with his kids, his parents' grandkids, that ghost carrot is hovering over all of them.

That something too awful to name.

People in France have a phrase: "Spirit of the Stairway." In French: Esprit d'Escalier. It means that moment when you find the answer but it's too late. Say you're at a party and someone insults you. You have to say something. So, under pressure, with everybody watching, you say something lame. But the moment you leave the party . . .

As you start down the stairway, then—magic. You come up with the perfect thing you should've said. The perfect crippling put-down.

That's the Spirit of the Stairway.

The trouble is, even the French don't have a phrase for the stupid things you actually do say under pressure. Those stupid, desperate things you actually think or do.

Some deeds are too low to even get a name. Too low to even get talked about.

Looking back, kid-psych experts, school counselors now say that most of the last peak in teen suicide was kids trying to choke while they beat off. Their folks would find them, a towel twisted around the kid's neck, the towel tied to the rod in their bedroom closet, their kid dead. Dead sperm everywhere. Of course the folks cleaned up. They put some pants on their kid. They made it look . . . better. Intentional at least. The regular kind of sad, teen suicide.

Another friend of mine, a kid from school, his older brother in the navy said how guys in the Middle East jack off different than we do here. This brother was stationed in some camel country where the public market sells what could be fancy letter-openers. Each fancy tool is just a thin rod of polished brass or silver, maybe as long as your hand, with a big tip at one end, either a big metal ball or the kind of fancy carved handle you'd see on a sword. This navy brother says how Arab guys get their dick hard and then insert this metal rod inside the whole length of their boner. They jack off with the rod inside, and it makes getting off so much better. More intense.

It's this big brother who travels around the world, sending back French phrases. Russian phrases. Helpful jack-off tips.

After this, the little brother, one day he doesn't show up at school. That night, he calls to ask if I'll pick up his homework for the next couple weeks. Because he's in the hospital.

He's got to share a room with old people getting their guts worked on. He says how they all have to share the same television. All he's got for privacy is a curtain. His folks don't come and visit. On the phone, he says how right now his folks could just kill his big brother in the navy.

On the phone, the kid says how—the day before—he was just a little stoned. At home in his bedroom, he was flopped on the bed. He was lighting a candle and flipping through some old porno magazines, getting ready to beat off. This is after he's heard from his navy brother. That helpful hint about how Arabs beat off. The kid looks around for something that might do the job. A ballpoint pen's too big. A pencil's too big and rough. But, dripped down the side of the candle, there's a thin, smooth ridge of wax that just might work. With just the tip of one finger, this kid snaps the long ridge of wax off the candle. He rolls it smooth between the palms of his hands. Long and smooth and thin.

Stoned and horny, he slips it down inside, deeper and deeper into the piss slit of his boner. With a good hank of the wax still poking out the top, he gets to work.

Even now, he says those Arab guys are pretty damn smart. They've totally reinvented jacking off. Flat on his back in bed, things are getting so good this kid can't keep track of the wax. He's one good squeeze from shooting his wad when the wax isn't sticking out anymore.

The thin wax rod, it's slipped inside. All the way inside. So deep inside he can't even feel the lump of it inside his piss tube.

From downstairs, his mom shouts it's suppertime. She says to come down, right now. This wax kid and the carrot kid are different people, but we all live pretty much the same life.

It's after dinner when the kid's guts start to hurt. It's wax, so he figured maybe it would just melt inside him and he'd piss it out. Now his back hurts. His kidneys. He can't stand straight.

This kid talking on the phone from his hospital bed, in the background you can hear bells ding, people screaming. Game shows.

The X-rays show the truth, something long and thin, bent double inside his bladder. This long, thin V inside him, it's collecting all the minerals in his piss. It's getting bigger and more rough, coated with crystals of calcium, it's bumping around, ripping up the soft lining of his bladder, blocking his piss from getting out. His kidneys are backed up. What little that leaks out his dick is red with blood.

This kid, with his folks, his whole family, them looking at the black X-ray with the doctor and the nurses standing there, the big V of wax glowing white for everybody to see, he has to tell the truth. The way Arabs get off. What his big brother wrote him from the navy.

On the phone, right now, he starts to cry.

They paid for the bladder operation with his college fund. One stupid mistake, and now he'll never be a lawyer.

Sticking stuff inside yourself. Sticking yourself inside stuff. A candle in your dick or your head in a noose, we knew it was going to be big trouble.

What got me in trouble, I called it Pearl Diving. This meant whacking off underwater, sitting on the bottom at the deep end of my parents' swimming pool. With one deep breath, I'd kick my way to the bottom and slip off my swim trucks. I'd sit down there for two, three, four minutes.

Just from jacking off, I had huge lung capacity. If I had the house to myself, I'd do this all afternoon. After I'd finally pump out my stuff, my sperm, it would hang there in big, fat, milky gobs.

After that was more diving, to catch it all. To collect it and wipe each handful in a towel. That's why it was called Pearl Diving. Even with chlorine, there was my sister to worry about. Or, Christ Almighty, my mom.

That used to be my worst fear in the world: my teenage virgin sister, thinking she's just getting fat, then giving birth to a two-headed retard baby. Both the heads looking just like me. Me, the father AND the uncle.

In the end, it's never what you worry about that gets you.

The best part of Pearl Diving was the inlet port for the swimming-pool filter and the circulation pump. The best part was getting naked and sitting on it.

As the French would say: Who doesn't like getting their butt sucked?

Still, one minute you're just a kid getting off, and the next minute you'll never be a lawyer.

One minute, I'm settling on the pool bottom, and the sky is wavy, light blue through eight feet of water above my head. The world is silent except for the heartbeat in my ears. My yellow-striped swim trunks are looped around my neck for safe keeping, just in case a friend, a neighbor, anybody shows up to ask why I skipped football practice. The steady suck of the pool inlet hole is lapping at me, and I'm grinding my skinny white ass around on that feeling.

One minute, I've got enough air, and my dick's in my hand. My folks are gone at their work and my sister's got ballet. Nobody's supposed to be home for hours.

My hand brings me right to getting off, and I stop. I swim up to catch another big breath. I dive down and settle on the bottom.

I do this again and again.

This must be why girls want to sit on your face. The suction is like taking a dump that never ends. My dick hard and getting my butt eaten out, I do not need air. My heartbeat in my ears, I stay under until bright stars of light start worming around in my eyes. My legs straight out, the back of each knee rubbed raw against the concrete bottom. My toes are turning blue, my toes and fingers wrinkled from being so long in the water.

And then I let it happen. The big white gobs start spouting. The pearls.

It's then I need some air. But when I go to kick off against the bottom, I can't. I can't get my feet under me. My ass is stuck.

Emergency paramedics will tell you that every year about 150 people get stuck this way, sucked by a circulation pump. Get your long hair caught, or your ass, and you're going to drown. Every year, tons of people do. Most of them in Florida.

People just don't talk about it. Not even French people talk about EVERYTHING.

Getting one knee up, getting one foot tucked under me, I get to half standing when I feel the tug against my butt. Getting my other foot under me, I kick off against the bottom. I'm kicking free, not touching the concrete, but not getting to the air, either.

Still kicking water, thrashing with both arms, I'm maybe halfway to the surface but not going higher. The heartbeat inside my head getting loud and fast.

The bright sparks of light crossing and crisscrossing my eyes, I turn and look back . . . but it doesn't make sense. This thick rope, some kind of snake, blue-white and braided with veins, has come up out of the pool drain and it's holding on to my butt. Some of the veins are leaking blood, red blood that looks black underwater and drifts away from little rips in the pale skin of the snake. The blood trails away, disappearing in the water, and inside the snake's thin blue-white skin you can see lumps of some half-digested meal.

That's the only way this makes sense. Some horrible sea monster, a sea serpent, something that's never seen the light of day, it's been hiding in the dark bottom of the pool drain, waiting to eat me.

So . . . I kick at it, at the slippery, rubbery, knotted skin and veins of it, and more of it seems to pull out of the pool drain. It's maybe as long as my leg now, but still holding tight around my butthole. With another kick, I'm an inch closer to getting another breath. Still feeling the snake tug at my ass, I'm an incher closer to my escape.

Knotted inside the snake, you can see corn and peanuts. You can see a long bright-orange ball. It's the kind of horse-pill vitamin my dad makes me take, to help put on weight. To get a football scholarship. With extra iron and omega-3 fatty acids.

It's seeing that vitamin pill that saves my life.

It's not a snake. It's my large intestine, my colon pulled out of me. What doctors call "prolapsed." It's my guts sucked into the drain.

Paramedics will tell you a swimming-pool pump pulls eighty gallons of water every minute. That's about four hundred pounds of pressure. The big problem is, we're all connected together inside. Your ass is just the far end of your mouth. If I let go, the pump keeps working—unraveling my insides—until it's got my tongue. Imagine taking a four-hundred-pound shit, and you can see how this might turn you inside out.

What I can tell you is, your guts don't feel much pain. Not the way your skin feels pain. The stuff you're digesting, doctors call it fecal matter. Higher up is chyme, pockets of a thin runny mess studded with corn and peanuts and round green peas.

That's all this soup of blood and corn, shit and sperm and peanuts, floating around me. Even with my guts unraveling out my ass, me holding on to what's left, even then my first want is to somehow get my swimsuit back on.

God forbid my folks see my dick.

My one hand holding a fist around my ass, my other hand snags my yellow-striped swim trunks and pulls them from around my neck. Still, getting into them is impossible.

You want to feel your intestines, go buy a pack of those lambskin condoms. Take one out and unroll it. Pack it with peanut butter. Smear it with petroleum jelly and hold it underwater. Then try to tear it. Try to pull it in half. It's too tough and rubbery. It's so slimy you can't hold on.

A lambskin condom, that's just plain old intestine.

Now, you can see what I'm up against.

You let go for a second, and you're gutted.

You swim for the surface, for a breath, and you're gutted.

You don't swim, and you drown.

It's a choice between being dead right now or a minute from right now.

What my folks will find after work is a big naked fetus, curled in on itself. Floating in the cloudy water of their backyard pool. Tethered to the bottom by a thick rope of veins and twisted guts. The opposite of a kid hanging himself to death while he jacks off. This is the baby they brought home from the hospital thirteen years ago. Here's the kid they hoped would snag a football scholarship and get an M.B.A. Who'd care for them in their old age. Here's all their hopes and dreams. Floating here, naked and dead. All around him, big milky pearls of wasted sperm.

Either that or my folks will find me wrapped in a bloody towel, collapsed halfway from the pool to the kitchen telephone, the ragged, torn scrap of my guts still hanging out the leg of my yellow-striped swim trunks.

What even the French won't talk about.

That big brother in the navy, he taught us one other good phrase. A Russian phrase. The way we say, "I need that like I need a hole in my head," Russian people say, "I need that like I need teeth in my asshole."

Mnye etoh nadoh kahk zoobee v zadnetze.

Those stories you hear, about how animals caught in a trap will chew off their leg, well, any coyote would tell you a couple bites beats the hell out of being dead.

Hell . . . even if you're Russian, someday you just might want those teeth.

Otherwise, what you have to do is—you have to twist around. You hook one elbow behind your knee and pull that leg up into your face. You bite and snap at your own ass. You run out of air, and you will chew through anything to get that next breath.

It's not something you want to tell a girl on the first date. Not if you expect a kiss good night.

If I told you how it tasted, you would never, ever again eat calamari.

It's hard to say what my parents were more disgusted by: how I'd got in trouble or how I'd saved myself. After the hospital, my mom said, "You didn't know what you were doing, honey. You were in shock." And she learned how to cook poached eggs.

All those people grossed out or feeling sorry for me . . .

I need that like I need teeth in my asshole.

Nowadays, people always tell me I look too skinny. People at dinner parties get all quiet and pissed off when I don't eat the pot roast they cooked. Pot roast kills me. Baked ham. Anything that hangs around inside my guts for longer than a couple hours, it comes out still food. Home-cooked lima beans or chunk light tuna fish, I'll stand up and find it still sitting there in the toilet.

After you have a radical bowel resectioning, you don't digest meat so great. Most people, you have five feet of large intestine. I'm lucky to have my six inches. So I never got a football scholarship. Never got an M.B.A. Both my friends, the wax kid and the carrot kid, they grew up, got big, but I've never weighed a pound more than I did that day when I was thirteen.

Another big problem was, my folks paid a lot of good money for that swimming pool. In the end, my dad just told the pool guy it was a dog. The family dog fell in and drowned. The dead body got pulled into the pump. Even when the pool guy cracked open the filter casing and fished out a rubbery tube, a watery hank of intestine with a big orange vitamin pill still inside, even then, my dad just said, "That dog was fucking nuts."

Even from my upstairs bedroom window, you could hear my old man say, "We couldn't trust that dog alone for a second . . ."

Then my sister missed her period.

Even after they changed the pool water, after they sold the house and we moved to another state, after my sister's abortion, even then my folks never mentioned it again.

Ever.

That is my family's invisible carrot.

Now you can take a good, deep breath.

Because I still have not.

1.
2.
3.
4.
5.
6.
7.
8.
9.
10.
11.
12.
13.
14.
15.
16.
17.
18.
19.
20.
21.
22.
23.
24.

Under the next streetlight stands the Reverend Godless, next to him a square suitcase. It's still early morning enough that every color is black or gray. There, the black fabric of the suitcase is scarred with silver zippers running in every direction, a black Swiss cheese of little pockets and slots, sacks and compartments. Reverend Godless with his face—just red-raw meat around a nose and eyes, steak stitched together with thread and scars, his ears twisted and swollen—his eyebrows are shaved. Then, sketched on with black pencil in two surprised arcs that rise almost to his hairline.

Watching him climb up the bus steps, Comrade Snarky fingers open a button of her jacket. Closing the button, she leans close to the tape recorder tucked in the Earl of Slander's pocket.

Close into the little red RECORD light, Comrade Snarky says, The Reverend Godless is wearing a white blouse. A woman's blouse. With the buttons on the left.

In the dim streetlight, his rhinestone buttons sparkle.

Down the next stretch of road, around the next curve, standing outside the circle of a streetlight, standing back in the shadows, waits the Baroness Frostbite.

First her hand reaches in through the open door of the

bus, a normal hand, the fingers yellow where she's held her cigarettes. No wedding ring. The hand sets a plastic makeup case at the top of the steps. Then a knee appears, a thigh, the swell of a breast. A waist belted in a trench coat. Then everyone looks away.

We look at our watches. Or we look out the windows at parked cars and newspaper boxes. Fire hydrants.

Baroness Frostbite brought tubes and tubes of lip wax, she said, for the edges of her mouth. For when they cracked and bled in cold weather. Her mouth, it's just a grease-shiny hole she screws open and shut to talk. Her mouth, just a pink-lipstick pucker in the bottom half of her face.

Leaning in to the Earl of Slander, whispering close to his tape recorder, Comrade Snarky says, "Oh my God . . ."

As the Baroness Frostbite takes her seat, only Agent Tattletale watches her, from safe behind the lens of his video camera.

At the next stop, Miss America waits with her exercise wheel, a pink plastic wheel the size of a dinner plate with black rubber grips poking out each side of the hub. You'd hold each grip and kneel down on the floor. You'd lean forward to balance on the wheel, then roll forward and back by clenching your stomach. Miss America brought the wheel and some pink leotards, honey-blond hair coloring, and a home pregnancy test.

Walking down the aisle in the center of the bus—smiling at Mr. Whittier with his wheelchair, not smiling at the Missing Link—with every step, Miss America overlaps one foot a little in front of the other, making her hips look thin, always the forward leg hiding the one behind.

"The Fashion-Model Waddle," Comrade Snarky calls it. She leans over the Earl of Slander's notepad and says, "That color of blond is what women call *lifting the color.*"

Miss America had written in lipstick on the bathroom mirror, smeared there for her boyfriend to find in the motel room they'd shared, for him to find before his morning television appearance: "I am NOT fat."

We had all left some kind of note behind.

Director Denial, petting her cat, she told us she'd written a memo to her entire agency, telling them: "Find your own objects to fuck." That memo she left on every desk, last night, ready for her staff to find, this morning.

Even Miss Sneezy wrote a note, even if she had nobody to read it. In red spray paint on a bus-stop bench, she wrote, "Call me when you find a cure."

The Matchmaker left his note folded to stand on the kitchen table, so his wife wouldn't miss it. The note said: "It's been fourteen weeks since I had that head cold, and you still have not kissed me." He wrote, "This summer, you milk the cows."

The Countess Foresight had left a note telling her parole officer he could reach her by dialing 1-800-FUCK-OFF.

The Countess Foresight steps out of the shadows wearing a turban and wrapped in a lace shawl. Floating down the aisle of the bus, she stops a moment next to Comrade Snarky. "Since you're wondering," the Countess says, and dangles a limp hand, a plastic bracelet loose around the wrist. The Countess Foresight says, "It's a global-positioning sensor. A condition of my early release from prison . . ."

One, two, three steps, past the Comrade and the Earl, their mouths still hanging a little loose, without looking back, the Countess Foresight says, "Yes."

She touches her turban with the fingernails of one hand and says, "Yes, I did read your mind . . ."

Around the next corner, past the next shopping center and franchise motel, beyond another fast-food restaurant, Mother Nature sits on the curb in a perfect lotus position, her hands painted with dark henna vines and resting on each knee. A choker of brass temple bells tinkling around her neck.

Mother Nature brings on board a cardboard carton of clothes wrapped to protect bottles of thick oil. Candles. The box smelling of pine needles. The campfire smell of pine pitch. The salad-dressing smell of basil and coriander. The import-market smell of sandalwood. A long fringe sways along the hem of her sari.

Comrade Snarky's eyes roll up to show all white, and she fans the air with her floppy black felt beret, saying, "*Patch*ouli . . ."

Our writers' colony, our desert island, should be nicely heated and air-conditioned, or so we've been led to believe. We'll each have our own room. Lots of privacy, so we won't need a lot of clothes. Or so we've been told.

We have no reason to expect otherwise.

The borrowed tour bus would be found, but we wouldn't. Not for the three months we'd leave the world. Those three months we'd spend writing and reading our work. Getting our stories perfect.

Last on board, around another block and through another tunnel, waiting at our last pickup spot, was the Duke of Vandals. His fingers smudged and stained from pastel crayons and charcoal pencils. His hands blotched with silk-screen inks, and his clothes stiff with drabs and spatters of dried paint. All these colors still only gray or black, the Duke of Vandals is sitting, waiting there on a metal toolbox heavy with tubes of oil paint, brushes, watercolors, and acrylics.

He stands, making us wait while he shakes back his blond hair and twists a red bandana around to make a ponytail. Still standing in the doorway of the bus, the Duke of Vandals looks down the aisle at us all, spotlighted by Agent Tattletale's video camera, he says, "It's about time . . ."

No, we weren't idiots. We'd never agree to be stranded if we were really going to be cut off. None of us were so bored with this silly, below-average, watered-down, mediocre world that we'd sign our own death wish. Not us.

A living situation like this, of course, we expected fast access to emergency health care, just in case someone stumbled on the stairs or their appendix decided to burst.

So all we had to decide was: What to bring in our one suitcase.

This workshop, it's already supposed to have hot and cold running water. Soap. Toilet paper. Tampax. Toothpaste.

The Duke of Vandals left his landlord a note that said: Screw your lease.

Even more important was what we didn't bring. The Duke of Vandals didn't bring cigarettes, his mouth teeth-grinding wads of nicotine gum. Saint Gut-Free didn't bring pornography. Countess Foresight and the Matchmaker didn't bring their wedding rings.

As Mr. Whittier would say, "What stops you in the outside world, that will stop you in here."

The rest of the disaster wasn't our fault. We had no reason, none whatsoever, to bring a chainsaw. Or a sledgehammer or a stick of dynamite. Or a gun. No, on this desert island, we'd be completely, completely safe.

Before sunrise, on this sweet new day we won't ever see happen.

So we'd been led to believe. Maybe too safe.

It's because of all this, we brought nothing that could save us.

Around another corner, along another stretch of expressway, down an off-ramp, we drove, until Mr. Whittier said, "Turn here." Gripping the chrome frame of his wheelchair, he jabbed a beef-jerky finger. The skin withered and shrunk, the fingernail bone-yellow.

Comrade Snarky poked her nose up and sniffed, saying, "Am I going to have to live with that patchouli stink for the next twelve weeks?"

Miss Sneezy coughed into her fist.

And Saint Gut-Free steered the bus down a tight, dark alley. Between buildings so close they splashed back the brown spit of the Matchmaker, tobacco spattering the front of his bib overalls. Walls so close the concrete skinned the hairy elbow the Missing Link had resting on the sill of his open window.

Until the bus pulls to a stop and the door folds open to show another door—this second door steel, in a concrete wall. The alley so narrow you can't see down any length. Mrs. Clark slips out of her seat, down the steps, and jerks open a padlock.

Then she's gone, inside, and the bus door opens on a slot of pure nothing. Just black. The slot just wide enough to squeeze through.

From inside, you catch the needle-sharp smell of mouse urine. Mix in the same smell as opening an old, damp book half eaten by silverfish. Mix in the smell of dust.

And from the darkness, Mrs. Clark's voice says, "Hurry and get inside."

Saint Gut-Free will join us after he leaves the bus parked for the police to find.

Ditches the evidence. Blocks, maybe miles away. Where they'll find it, untraceable back to this steel doorway into concrete and dark. Our new home. Our desert island.

All of us crowded into that moment between the bus and the pitch-dark. At that last moment outside, Agent Tattletale tells us, "Smile."

What Mr. Whittier would call the camera behind the camera behind the camera.

That first moment of our new, secret life, the spotlight hits us, so bright and fast it leaves the dark more dark than black. That instant leaves us grabbing hold of each other by the coats and elbows, trying to stay upright, blinking-blind but trusting, while Mrs. Clark's voice leads us through that steel doorway.

That video moment: the truth about the truth.

"Smell is very important," Mother Nature says. Lugging her cardboard box, her brass bells tinkling, clutching the dark, she says, "Don't laugh, but in aromatherapy, they warn you never to light a sandalwood candle around bayberry incense . . ."

Under Cover

A Poem About Mother Nature

"I tried to become a nun," says Mother Nature, "because I
    needed to hide out."
  She didn't count on the drug test.

Mother Nature onstage, her arms are vined with red henna
    graffiti. From her fingertips
  to the shoulder straps of her tie-dyed, rainbow-colored
    cotton smock.
Around her neck, a choker of brass temple bells has turned
    the skin
  green. Her skin shining with patchouli oil.

"Who knew?" Mother Nature says. "And not just
    urinalysis."
  She says, "They test with hair and fingernail samples."
  She says, "That's plus the background check."
  The morals clause. The background check. The credit
    check. The dress code.

Standing onstage, barefoot, instead of a spotlight,
    instead of a smile or frown, a movie fragment of night
      sky washes across her face.
  A galaxy of stars and moons.

Her lips red with beet juice. Her eyelids smeared with
     yellow saffron dust.
     There, a shifting mask of pink nebulas. Of planets with
          rings and craters.

Mother Nature says, "They ask for too many letters of
     reference."
     Plus a polygraph test. Four pieces of picture ID.
"Four," Mother Nature says, holding up the hennaed fingers
     of one hand. Her
     bracelets of brass wire and dirty silver, rattling
          windchimes around her wrist.
     She says, "Nobody has four pieces of *picture ID . . .*"
To become a nun, she says, you have to take a sit-down
     test, worse than
     the SATs and the LSATs, put together. And full of story
          problems, such as:
     "How many angels *can* dance on the head of a pin?"
All of this, Mother Nature says, just to find out:
     "If you're marrying Christ on the rebound."

Her long hair pulled away from her face, braided and falling
     down her back,
     Mother Nature says,
     "Of course, I failed. Not just the drug test—I failed
          everything."
     Not just as a nun, but throughout most of her life . . .
She shrugs, her freckled shoulders under the tie-dyed
     straps,
     "So here I am."

The constellations shifting and crawling across her face,
     Mother Nature says,
     "I still needed someplace to hide."

Foot Work

A Story by Mother Nature

Don't laugh, but in aromatherapy, they warn you never to light a lemon-cinnamon candle at the same time you light a clove candle and a cedar-nutmeg candle. They just don't tell you why . . .

In feng shui, they never let on, but just by putting a bed in the wrong spot, you can focus enough chi to kill a person. You can give a late-term abortion with just acupuncture. You can use crystals or aura work to give people skin cancer.

Don't laugh, but there are back-alley ways you can turn anything New Age into a killing tool.

Your last week in massage school, they teach you never to work the transverse reflex zone at the heel of the foot. Never touch the arch of the left-foot dorsum. And especially not the outer-left-most aspect. But they don't tell you how come. This is the difference between therapists who work the light side versus the dark side of the industry.

You go to school to study reflexology. It's the science of manipulating the human foot to heal or stimulate certain parts of the body. It's based on the idea that your body is divided into ten different energy meridians. Your big toe, for example, it's connected straight to your head. To cure dandruff, you massage the little spot just behind your big toenail. To cure a sore throat, you massage the middle joint of the big toe. This isn't the kind of health care covered by any insurance plan. This is like being a doctor but without the income. The kind of people who want the space between each toe rubbed to cure brain cancer, they don't tend to have loads of money. Don't laugh, but even with years of experience manipulating people's feet, you'll still find yourself poor and rubbing the feet of people who never made income their top priority.

Don't laugh, but one day you see a girl you went to massage school with. This girl, she's your same age. You both wore beads together. You two braided dried sage and burned it to cleanse your energy field. The two of you were tie-dyed and barefoot and young enough to feel noble while you rubbed the feet of dirty homeless people who came into the school's free practice clinic.

That was years and years ago.

You, you're still poor. Your hair has started to break off at the scalp. From poor diet or gravity, people think you're frowning even when you're not.

This girl you went to school with, you see her coming out of a posh midtown hotel, the doorman holding the door open as she sweeps out swinging furs and wearing high heels that no reflexologist would ever strap her feet inside.

While the doorman is flagging her a cab, you go close enough to say, "Lentil?"

The woman turns, and it's her. Real diamonds sparkle at her throat. Her long hair shines, thick, heaving in waves of red and brown. The air around her smells soft as roses and lilac. Her fur coat. Her hands in leather gloves, the leather smooth and pale and nicer than the skin on your own face. The woman turns and lifts her sunglasses to rest on the crown of her hair. She looks at you and says, "Do I know you?"

You went to school together. When you were young—younger.

The doorman holds the cab's door open.

And the woman says, of course she remembers. She looks at a

wristwatch, blinding bright with diamonds in the afternoon sun, and says in twenty minutes she needs to be across town. She asks, can you ride along?

The two of you get into the back of the cab, and the woman hands the doorman a twenty-dollar bill. He touches his cap, and says it's always such a pleasure to see her.

The woman tells the cabdriver the next address, some place a little farther uptown, and the cab swings into traffic.

Don't laugh, but this woman—Lentil, your old friend—she loops one fur-coat arm out of the handle of her purse, she snaps the purse open, and inside is stuffed nothing but cash money. Layers of fifty- and hundred-dollar bills. With a gloved hand, she digs into these and finds a cell phone.

To you, she says, "This won't take a minute."

Next to her, your Indian-printed cotton wrap skirt, your flip-flop sandals and brass-bell necklace don't look chic and ethnic anymore. The kohl around your eyes and the faded henna designs on the back of your hands, they make you look like you never take a bath. Next to her diamond-stud earrings, your favorite dangling silver earrings could be thrift-store Christmas-tree ornaments.

Into the cell phone she says, "I'm en route." She says, "I can take the three o'clock, but only for a half-hour." She says good-bye and hangs up.

She touches your hand with a soft, smooth glove and says you look good. She asks what you're doing lately.

Oh, the same old same-old, you tell her. Manipulating feet. You've built a good list of repeat clients.

Lentil chews her bottom lip, looking at you, and she says, "So—you're still into reflexology?"

And you say, yeah. You don't see how you'll ever retire, but it pays the bills.

She looks at you as the cab goes a whole city block, not saying a word. Then she asks if you're free for the next hour. She asks if you'd

like to make some money, tax-free, doing a four-handed foot manipulation for her next client. All you'd have to do is one foot.

You've never done reflexology with a partner, you tell her.

"One hour," she says, "and we get two thousand dollars."

You ask, Is this legal?

And Lentil says, "Two thousand, each."

You ask, Just for a foot massage?

"Another thing," she says. "Don't call me Lentil." She says,
"When we get there, my name is Angelique."

Don't laugh, but this is real. The dark side of reflexology. Of
course we knew some aspect of it. We knew by working the plantar
surface of the big toe you could make someone constipated. By
working the ankle around the top of the foot, you could give them
diarrhea. By working the inside surface of the heel, you could make
someone impotent or give them a migraine headache. But none of
this would make you money, so why bother?

The cab pulls up to a carved pile of stone, the embassy of some
Middle Eastern oil economy. A uniformed guard opens the door, and
Lentil gets out. You get out. Inside the lobby, another guard wands
you with a metal detector, looking for guns, knives, whatever.
Another guard makes a phone call from a desk topped with a smooth
slab of white stone. Another guard looks inside Lentil's purse, pushing aside the paper money to find nothing but her cell phone.

The doors to an elevator open, and another guard waves you both
inside. Lentil says, "Just do what I do." She says, "This is the easi-
est money you'll ever make."

Don't laugh, but in school you'd hear the rumors. About how a
good reflexologist might be lured away to the dark side. To work
just certain pleasure centers on the sole of the foot. To give what
people only whispered about. What giggling people would call
"foot jobs."

The elevator opens onto a long corridor that leads to only one set
of double doors. The walls are polished white stone. The floor, stone.

The double doors are frosted glass and open to a room where a man sits at a white desk. He and Lentil kiss each other on the cheek.

The man behind the desk, he looks at you, but talks only to Lentil. He calls her Angelique. Behind him, another set of double doors open into a bedroom. The man waves the two of you to go through, but he stays behind, locking the doors. He locks you inside.

Inside the bedroom, a man lies facedown on a huge round bed with white silk sheets. He wears silk pajamas, shiny blue silk, and his bare feet hang off one edge of the bed. Angelique tugs off one of her gloves. She takes off the other glove, and you both kneel in the deep carpet and each take a foot.

Instead of a face, all you can see is his grease-combed black hair, his big ears fuzzed with tufts of black hair. The rest of his head has sunk into the white silk pillow.

Don't laugh, but those rumors are true. By pressing where Angelique pressed, by working the genital reflex zone on the plantar side of the heel, she had the man moaning, facedown in his pillow. Before your hands are even tired, the man is bellowing, soaked in sweat, the blue silk pasted to his back and legs. When he's silent, when you can't tell if he's even breathing, Angelique whispers it's time to go.

The man at the desk gives you each two thousand dollars, cash.

Outside, on the street, a guard flags a cab for Angelique.

Getting into the back seat, Angelique hands you a business card. It's the phone number for a holistic-healing clinic. Under the number, handwritten, it says: "Ask for Lenny."

The soft leather glove of her hand, the roses of her perfume, the sound of her voice, it all says, "Call me."

People have a lot of reasons they get into giving foot jobs. The idea that you can give your family a better life. You can give your mom and dad a little comfort and security. A car, maybe. A condo on the beach in Florida.

The day you gave your folks the keys to that condo, that was the happiest day of your life. That day they cried and admitted they never thought their baby would ever make a living just rubbing people's stinky feet. That's a day you'll pay for for the rest of your life.

Don't laugh, but it's not illegal. You're doing a simple foot manipulation. Nothing sexual happens except your client has an orgasm that leaves them too weak to walk for the next couple days. Men or women, it doesn't matter. You work the right spot on their feet, and they come hard as a seizure. So hard there's a smell when they lose control of their bowels. So hard most clients can only look at you, drool running out one corner of their mouth, and motion with a trembling finger for you to take the stack of hundred-dollar bills on the dresser or the coffee table.

Lenny calls from the clinic, and you get on a chartered jet to London. The clinic calls, and you fly to Hong Kong. The clinic is just Lenny, a guy with a Russian accent who lives in a suite in the Park Hampton Hotel, and who you give half your income to. It's Lenny's accent on the phone, telling you what flight to catch, what hotel room or private island where the next client's waiting.

Don't laugh, but the downside is, you never have time to go shopping. The money just piles up. Your uniform is a fur coat. To fit into this new world, you get good gold and platinum jewelry. You keep a head of perfect, glossy hair. Sitting in the lobby of the Ritz-Carlton, you might see a few kids you went to reflexology college with, now wearing Armani suits, Chanel cocktail dresses. Kids who used to be vegan bicycle-commuters, now you see them climbing in and out of limousines. You see them eating alone at small tables in hotel dining rooms. Drinking cocktails at the bar in private airports, waiting for the next chartered jet.

What used to be idealistic dreamers, now lured into professional footwork.

These hippie dreadlocked earth mothers and goateed skater-punks, you hear them on the telephone giving sell orders to their stockbrokers. Stashing money in offshore accounts and Swiss safety-deposit boxes. Haggling over uncut diamonds and Krugerrands.

Boys named Trout and Pony, Lizard and Oyster, now they're all called Dirk. Girls named Buttercup are all called Dominique.

This flood of people doing footwork, it brings the price down. Soon enough, instead of software billionaires and oil sheikhs, you're loitering in a hotel bar, wearing your last year's Prada and turning foot tricks for twenty bucks a pop. You're slipping under tables to manipulate the feet of conventioneers sitting at restaurant back booths. You're bursting out of big fake birthday cakes to do the feet of whole football teams, bachelor parties, just to keep up the payments on your parents' retirement home.

It's just a matter of time before you contract some incurable toenail fungus under your silk-wrapped French manicure.

You do all this just to pay the interest on money you borrowed from Lenny and his Russian Mafia. Money borrowed to buy stocks that tanked. Stocks recommended by Lenny. Or to buy the jewelry and shoes Lenny said you'd need to fit in.

You're in the lobby bar at the Park Hampton Hotel, trying to talk a drunk businessman into a ten-dollar foot job in the men's room. That's when you see her, Angelique, walking across the lobby, headed for the elevators. Her hair shining. Her furs dragging on the carpet behind her high-heeled feet. Angelique still looking great. Your eyes catch her, and with one gloved hand, she waves you over.

When the elevator comes, she says she's going up to Lenny's penthouse suite. The clinic.

She looks at you in your scuffed high heels, your fingernails chipped and jagged, and she says, "Come see what the next growth industry will be . . ."

The elevator stops on the fiftieth floor, the whole penthouse leased to Lenny, where two pin-striped suits full of muscle stand guarding a door. It's these goons you pay Lenny's cut to, half of everything you make. One guard says your names into a microphone pinned to his lapel, and the doors unlock with a loud buzz.

Inside, it's just you and Angelique and Lenny.

Don't laugh, but, lonely and isolated as your life is, doing footwork—Lenny's life looks worse. Locked up here on the penthouse floor, wearing a white terry-cloth bathrobe all day, counting his money, and talking on the telephone. The only furniture is a desk chair, the seat stained and dirty. A mattress is flopped near walls of glass that look out over the whole city. On a computer screen, stock prices scroll up without stopping.

Lenny comes to the both of you, his bathrobe hanging open, wearing wrinkled striped boxer shorts inside, white socks turned yellow on his feet. Lenny reaches both hands toward Angelique's face and says, "My Angel, my favorite." He cups her face in his hands and says, "How are you?"

In her high heels, Angelique must be a head taller than him. She smiles, saying, "Lenny . . ."

And Lenny smacks her, hard, one hand across her face, and he says, "You're cheating on me, that's how you are." He holds one hand up, the palm open and ready to smack her, again, and Lenny says, "You're taking outside assignments, aren't you?"

Holding one gloved hand to her cheek, hiding the red print of Lenny's hand, Angelique says, "Baby, no . . ."

And Lenny drops his hand. He turns his back to her. Lenny goes to look out the windows, the city spread out right next to his mattress.

"Baby," Angelique says. "Let me show you something new."

Angelique looks at me.

She goes to stand next to him, putting her gloved hands on his shoulders from behind, and Angelique says, "Let Mommy show you how much she still loves her baby . . ."

She steers Lenny to sit on the mattress. Then to lie back. She slips the yellowed sock off each of his feet.

"Come on, baby," she says. Taking off her gloves, she says, "You know I give *great* foot . . ."

Then Angelique does what you've never seen before. She gets down on her knees. She opens her mouth, her lips stretched wide and thin, and runs her tongue along the bottom of Lenny's sole.

Angelique cups her lips around Lenny's heel, and Lenny starts to moan.

Don't laugh, but there are jobs worse than the worst job you can imagine. A media mogul with no history of high blood pressure, he's found dead of a stroke in a room at the Four Seasons. A rock star in perfect health dies of kidney failure after a foot massage in the Chateau Marmot.

We have access to the feet of presidents and sultans. CEOs and movie stars. Kings and queens. We know how to make a paid hit look like natural causes.

This is what Angelique tells you on the way down in the elevator. After Lenny moaned and thrashed. After Angelique mouthed his foot until the one long moment Lenny sat up on the mattresses, clutching his chest in both hands and gaping his open mouth at her still sucking his heel. After his heart stopped, Angelique pulled the bedsheets up to his chin. She wiped the lipstick off his foot and smeared more around her mouth. She unplugged his phones and told the guards Lenny was taking a long nap.

On the way down in the elevator, Angelique tells you this was her last foot job. This kind of foot hit paid a million bucks, cash. A rival agency had hired her to bump off Lenny, and now she was out of the business for good.

In the lobby bar, the two of you have a cocktail to get the taste of Lenny's foot out of her mouth. Just one last, good-bye drink. Then Angelique says to look around the hotel lobby. The men in suits. The women in fur coats. They're all Rolfing killers, she says. Reiki killers. Colonic-irrigation assassins.

Angelique says, in gem therapy, just by putting a quartz crystal on someone's heart, then an amethyst on his liver and a turquoise on his forehead, you induce a coma that results in death. Just by sneaking into a room and rearranging someone's bedroom set, a feng-shui expert can trigger kidney disease.

"Moxibustion," she says, the science of burning cones of incense on someone's acupuncture points, "it can kill. So can shiatsu."

She drinks the last of her cocktail, and takes off the strand of pearls from around her neck.

All those cures and remedies that claim to be 100-percent natural ingredients, therefore 100-percent safe, Angelique laughs. She says, Cyanide is natural. So is arsenic.

She hands the pearls to you and says, "From now on, I'm back to being 'Lentil.' "

That's how you want to remember Angelique, not the way she looked in the newspaper the next day, fished out of the river in a soggy mink coat. Her earrings and diamond watch taken to make it look like a robbery. Not with her feet fondled to death, but dead the old-fashioned way, with a hollow-point bullet to the back of her perfect French braid. A warning to all the Dirks and Dominiques who might jump ship.

The clinic calls, not Lenny, but some other Russian accent, trying to send you to clients, but you don't trust them. The guards saw you with Lentil. Up at the penthouse. They must have another hollow-point ready for the back of your head.

Your folks call from Florida to say a black town car keeps following them, and somebody calls to ask if they know how to find you. By now, you're already running from flophouse to flophouse, giving back-alley foot jobs for enough cash to stay alive.

You tell your folks: Be careful. You tell them not to get massaged by anybody they don't know. Calling them from a pay phone, you tell them to never mess with aromatherapy. Auras. Reiki. Don't laugh, but you're going to be traveling for a long time, maybe the rest of your life.

You can't explain. By now, you've run out of quarters, so you tell your folks good-bye.

1.
2.
3.
4.
5.
6.
7.
8.
9.
10.
11.
12.
13.
14.
15.
16.
17.
18.
19.
20.
21.
22.
23.
24.

Our first week, we ate beef Wellington while Miss America knelt at every doorknob and tried to pick the lock with a palette knife borrowed from the Duke of Vandals.

We ate striped sea bass while Miss Sneezy ate pills and capsules from the rattling jars in her suitcase. While she coughed into her fist, and wiped her nose on her sweater sleeve.

We eat turkey Tetrazzini while Lady Baglady toys with her diamond ring. With the platinum band turned around, she talks to the big diamond that seems to sit cupped in her palm. "Packer?" she says. "This is *nothing* like I've been led to expect." Lady Baglady says, "How can I write anything profound if my environment isn't . . . ideal?"

Of course, Agent Tattletale's videotaping her. The Earl of Slander holds his tape recorder to catch every word.

A cough-cough, here. A cough-cough, there. Here, a gripe. There, a bitch. Everywhere, a complaint. Miss Sneezy says the air is swimming with toxic mold spores.

A rattle-rattle, here. A cough-cough, there. No one working. No writing getting done.

Skinny Saint Gut-Free, his face was always looking up, his mouth baby-bird gaped open as he poured in chili or apple pie or shepherd's pie from a silver Mylar bag. His

Adam's apple bobbed with each swallow, his tongue funneling the lukewarm mess past his teeth.

Chewing his tobacco, the Matchmaker spit on the stained carpet and said this dank building, these dim-dripping rooms, had nothing in common with the writers' colony he'd pictured: people writing longhand, looking down rolled green lawns; writers eating box lunches, each in their own private cottage. Orchards of apricot trees in a blizzard of white flower petals. Afternoon naps under chestnut trees. Croquet.

Even before she started to outline her screenplay, her life's masterpiece, Miss America said she couldn't. Her breasts were too sore to write. Her arms, too tired. She couldn't smell today's veal cutlets without vomiting a little of the crab cakes from the day before.

Her period was almost a week late.

"It's sick-building syndrome," Miss Sneezy told her. Her raw-red nose, already staying sideways, wiped in profile against one cheek.

Trailing her fingers along the railings and the carved backs of chairs, Lady Baglady showed us the dust. "Look," she told the fat diamond in her hand, she said, "Packer? Packer, this is not acceptable."

In our first week locked away, Miss Sneezy was coughing, breathing in the slow, deep notes a pipe organ would make.

Miss America was rattling locked doors. Yanking aside the green velvet drapes in the Italian Renaissance lounge to find windows bricked over. With the handle of her pink plastic exercise wheels, she broke a stained-glass window in the Gothic smoking room, only to find a cement wall wired with bulbs to fake daylight behind it.

In the French Louis XV lobby, the chairs and sofas all cornflower-blue velvet, the walls crowded and busy with plaster curls and scrolls painted gold, there, Miss America stood in her pink spandex active wear and asked for the key. Her hair, an ocean wave of blond breaking in curls and flips against the back of her head, she needed the key so she could go out, just for a few days.

"You're a novelist?" Mr. Whittier said. Even resting flat on the chrome arms of his wheelchair, his fingers tapped an invisible telegram. Veined and chased with wrinkles, the bones of his hands trembled in a constant blur.

"A screenwriter," Miss America said. A fist on each pink spandex hip.

Looking at her, tall and willowy, "Of course," Mr. Whittier said. "So write a movie script about being tired."

No, Miss America needed to see an obstetrician. She needed blood work done. She needed prenatal vitamins. "I need to see someone," she said. Her boyfriend.

And Mr. Whittier said, "This is why Moses led the tribes of Israel into the desert . . ." Because those people had lived for generations as slaves. They'd learned to be helpless.

To create a race of masters from a race of slaves, Mr. Whittier said, to teach a controlled group of people how to create their own lives, Moses had to be an asshole.

Sitting at the edge of a blue velvet chair, Miss America kept nodding her blond head. Her hair flip-flopping. She understood. She understood. Then she said, "The key?"

And Mr. Whittier told her, "No."

He balanced a silver Mylar bag of chicken Marsala on his knees, all around him the blue carpet patched and sticky with dark mold. Each soggy patch, a shadow branched with arms and legs. A mildewed ghost. Spooning up chicken Marsala, Mr. Whittier says, "Until you can ignore your circumstances, and just do as you promise," he says, "you'll always be controlled by the world."

"And what do you call this?" Miss America says, stirring the dusty air with her hands.

And Mr. Whittier says, for the first of a million times, "I'm only holding you to your word." And, "What stops you here is what stops your entire life."

The air will always be too filled with something. Your body too sore or tired. Your father too drunk. Your wife too cold. You will always have some excuse not to live your life.

"But what if something happened? What if we ran out of food?" Miss America says. "You'd open the door then, wouldn't you?"

"But we're not," Mr. Whittier says, his mouth full of chewed chicken and capers. "We're not running out of food."

And, no, we weren't. Not yet.

That first week inside, we ate vegetable curry over rice. We ate teriyaki salmon. All of it freeze-dried.

For food, we had green beans sealed in Mylar bags you couldn't tear with your bare hands. "Vermin-proof" was stenciled in black paint on each silver bag. We had vermin-proof green beans and chicken pot pie and golden-sweet whole-kernel corn. Inside each bag, something rattled, loose twigs and rocks and sand. Each bag inflated to a silver pillow with a puff of nitrogen to keep the contents dead. The lasagna with meat sauce or cheese ravioli.

Vermin-proof or not, our Missing Link could rip a bag open with his bare pubic-hairy hands.

To cook dinner, most people cut the bag open with scissors or a knife. You reached in and dug around until you found the little tea bag of iron oxide—added to absorb any trace of oxygen. You fished out the tea bag and dumped in so many cups of boiling water. We had a microwave. We had plastic forks and spoons. Paper plates. And running water.

You read ten pages in a vampire novel, and dinner was served. Instead of sticks and hot water, the silver pillow was full of home-style meatloaf or beef Stroganoff.

We'd sit on the blue carpet of the lobby stairs, a rippling blue waterfall, each step so wide we could all share the same one and our elbows not poke each other. This was the same beef Stroganoff the President and Congress would be eating deep underground during a nuclear war. It was from the same maker.

Other silver bags were stenciled "Chocolate Devil's Food Cake" and "Bananas Foster." Mashed potatoes. Macaroni and cheese. Freeze-dried French fries.

All of it, comfort food.

Every bag had a *good until* date that wouldn't come until we were dead. A shelf life until after most babies would be dead.

Strawberry cupcakes with a hundred-year life span.

We ate freeze-dried lamb with freeze-dried mint jelly while Lady Baglady discovered in her heart's own heart that she really did love her dead husband. She loved him, she cried into her hands. Her shoulders hunched and jerking with sobs inside her mink coat. Cradling the fat diamond in her palm, she needed to get out and bury her three-carat husband in their family plot.

We ate Denver omelets while the Duke of Vandals snapped and popped his nicotine gum and said this was a terrible time to give up smoking. And Saint Gut-Free lost the feeling in his left hand, a repetitive-motion injury, trying to climax without a picture.

The cat of Director Denial, the cat named Cora Reynolds, ate leftover striped sea bass while Countess Foresight and the Reverend Godless worried we weren't safe enough. We'd walked into a trap. They worried someone might find us and . . . They told Mr. Whittier they needed to keep moving, hiding, running to stay safe.

Reverend Godless, clutching a Barbra Streisand album, his split, blood-sausage lips moving as he read the lyrics in the liner notes, he told the Earl of Slander's tape recorder, "I just *assumed* we'd have a stereo, here."

In the viewfinder of Agent Tattletale's video camera, Chef Assassin lifted dripping green spoonsful of spinach soufflé into his fat face, saying, "I'm a professional chef. I'm *not* a food critic. But I can't go three months on *instant* coffee . . ."

Of course, everyone said they'd still write their work, their poems and stories. They'd complete their masterpiece. Just not here. Not now. Later, outside.

Our first week here, we got nothing done. Except complain.

"It's not an excuse," Miss America said, holding her flat stomach in both hands, "it's a human life."

Miss Sneezy coughed into her fist. She sniffed, her eyes bulging and bloodshot behind tears, and said, "My life's at stake, here." One hand digging in her pocket for another pill.

And, of course, Mr. Whittier shook his head no.

Sitting there in his blue velvet chair, the lobby scrolling gold and velvet around him, Mr. Whittier spooned clam chowder out of a Mylar bag and said, "Tell me a story about the baby's father." To Miss America, he said, "Write me the scene of how you met him."

And Agent Tattletale's camera zoomed in on Miss America's face for a close-up reaction shot.

Product Improvements

A Poem About Miss America

"I'm always looking," says Miss America, "for what's NOT
to like."
Every time she looks in a mirror.

Miss America onstage, her blond hair coils and spirals,
billows and looms,
to make her face look as small as possible.
One high-heeled foot, placed just a little in front of the
other
to make her legs overlap
so her hips look more
narrow.
Standing sideways, she twists her shoulders
to face the audience head-on.
All this breathless contortion to make her waist look
itty-bitty.

Onstage, instead of a spotlight, a movie fragment:
Her face veiled with exercise videos.
Her features, her eyes and lips, made up with hot-pink
leotards and leg warmers.
Her Miss America skin jumps and dances with a crowd of
women,

each of those women watching herself in a mirror.
The film: a shadow of a reflection of an image of an
    illusion.

She says, "My every glance in a mirror, it's a secret market
    survey."
She's her own test audience.
Rating her curb appeal on a scale of one to ten.
Every day, beta-testing a new upgraded version of
    herself-point-five.
Fine-tuning to follow market trends.

Her dress, swimsuit-tight, leotard-tight,
    her pantyhose run with women pedaling bicycles, going
        nowhere
    at a thousand calories an hour.
"For the Talent portion of my program," she says, "I'll show
    you how to unswallow."
    A bellyful of peach ice cream,
    a Halloween bag of miniature candy bars,
    six frosted doughnuts,
    two double cheeseburgers.
The usual stuff.
    And sometimes, sperm.

Her face swimming and flickering with aerobic work, her
    immediate ambition is
    to diminish initial buyer resistance.
With a long-term goal of becoming someone's long-term
    investment.
    As a durable consumer good.

Green Room

A Story by Miss America

It's nothing personal when bombs explode. Or when a gunman in a stadium takes a hostage. When the Net Monitor shows a special alert, any television station is going to toss to the talent on the national feed coming through.

If you're watching television, first the local booth producer and director will cut to the double-box format. A split screen to most people. Then the local talent says something like, "With the latest on the sinking ocean liner, here's Joe Blow in New York." That's what they call "the toss." Or "the kick."

The network feed takes over, and the local boys sit on their hands and wait for the network bump to signal the end of the special-alert feed.

No publicist thinks to explain all this to each newbie they send on the road, selling an investment video, a book, a new-fangled carrot peeler.

So, sitting in the green room, backstage at *Wake Up Chattanooga!,* a young guy with his hair slicked back, he explains some facts of life to this blonde.

She's super, way-too blond, he tells her. That kind of bleach blond, it drives the floor producer nuts, because you can't light it well without it flaring. Some floor producers, they call it "blowout." The blond head just looks on fire.

"Whatever you do," the slick guy tells the blonde, "if you got notes, don't reference them or the camera will be shooting the top of your head."

Floor producers, he says, they hate guests who bring notes. They hate guests who don't try to bury their agenda. Producers will tell you: "Be your product. Don't push it."

Ironical, but that same floor producer will call you "Fitness Wheel" because that's the slug written in your block on the schedule. It says "Investment Videos" for the slick guy's block. For the old man, the slug says: "Stain Remover."

The blonde and the slick guy, them sitting on the reject leather sofa in the green room, cups of old coffee abandoned on the table in front of them, hanging over them a couple video monitors flicker high on the walls, in the corners, mounted up near the ceiling. On one monitor, you see the national talent talking about the ocean liner, then tossing to video support that shows a ship belly-up and the specks of orange life vests floating around it. On the second monitor, the blonde says, there's something even sadder.

Up in that other corner, you see the A Block bozo, the old comb-over guy who got out of his Motel 6 bed at 5 a.m. to be here and pitch his special stain-removing brush he invented. Poor schmuck. He gets miked and put onstage, in the "living-room set" with its rain forest of fake plants. He sits under those hot lights while the on-air talent does their opening "chat."

The living-room set is different from the "kitchen set" and the "main set" because it has more fake plants and throw pillows.

This bozo thinks he's got a fat ten-minute segment because the station is playing the clock, not cutting to commercial until ten after the start. Most stations cut at eight or nine minutes. That way, we keep the audience from channel-surfing and get top ratings credit for the whole fifteen-minute block.

"Not pretty," the slick guy tells our blonde girl, and he crosses himself fast as a good Catholic, "but better him than either of us."

A heartbeat into his stain-removing demo, the A Block's cut off by the doomed ocean liner.

Sitting in this green room, on a ratty leather sofa in some double-digit ADI, the slick guy says he's got maybe seven minutes to teach an entire world to our Miss America.

ADI, that means Area of Direct Influence. Boston, for example, is the number-three ADI in the country because its media reach the third-largest market of consumers. New York is the number-one ADI. Los Angeles is number two. Dallas, number seven.

Where they're sitting is way down the list of ADIs. *Day Break Lincoln* or *New Day Tulsa*. Some media outlet that reaches a consumer market demographic totaling nobody.

Some other good advice is: Don't wear white. Never wear a black-and-white patterned anything because it will "shimmer" on camera. And always lose some weight.

"Just staying at this weight," our blonde tells the slick guy, "is a full-time job."

The on-air person, the talent here in Chattanooga, the slick guy says, the anchor here is a total straight pipe. Whatever they tell her over the IFD in her ear, those exact words will pop out her lipstick-red mouth. The director could feed her, ". . . Christ, we're going long! Toss to Adopt-a-Dog, and then we'll cut to commercial . . . ," and that's what she'd say on air.

A total straight pipe.

Our blonde girl, listening, she doesn't laugh. Not even a smile.

So the slick guy tells her, other talent he's seen, one time on a live feed to location, a warehouse fire roaring in the background, the on-air person fumbled with her hair, looking straight into a hot camera and going out live, she said, "Could you repeat the question? My IUD fell out . . ."

The reporter, she meant IFD. Internal Feedback Device, the slick guys says. He points at the anchor who appears on the monitor, and he says how one anchor will always have that kind of lopsided hairdo. The hair swooping down to hide one ear. It's because she's got a tiny radio stuck in her ear to take prompts and cues from the director. If the show is going long or they need to toss to a nuclear-reactor meltdown.

This blonde, she's on the road with some kind of exercise wheel you roll around on top of to lose weight. She wears a pink leotard and purple tights.

Yeah, she's thin and blonde, but the more ins and outs your face has, the slick guy tells her, the better you look on camera.

"That's why I have to keep my *before* picture," she says. Bending over in her chair, leaning over and over until her breasts press against her knees, she digs in a gym bag on the floor. She says, "This is the only real proof that I'm not just another skinny blonde girl." She takes something paper out of the bag, holding an edge between two fingers. It's a photograph, and the blonde tells the slick guy, "Unless people see this, they might think I was just born this way. They'd never know what I've done with my life."

Go on television with even a little baby fat, he tells her, and you look like nothing. A mask. A full moon. A big zero with no features for people to remember.

"Losing all that blubber is the only really *heroic* thing I've ever done," she says. "If I gain it back, then it'll be like I never lived."

You see, the slick guy says, television takes a three-dimensional thing—you—and turns it into a two-dimensional thing. That's why you look fat on camera. Flat and fat.

Holding the photo between two fingernails, looking at her old self, our blonde says, "I don't want to be just another skinny girl."

About her hair being too "hot," the slick guy tells her, "That's why you never see natural redheads in porn movies. You can't light them right, next to real people."

That's what this guy wants to be: the camera behind the camera behind the camera giving the last and final truth.

We all want to be the one standing farthest back. The one who gets to say what's good or bad. Right or wrong.

Our too-blonde girl, going to blow out the cameras, the slick guy tells her about how these local-produced shows are broken into six segments with commercials in between. The A Block, B Block, C Block, and so on. These shows like *Rise and Shine Fargo* or *Sun-Up Sedona,* they're a dying breed. Expensive to produce, compared to just buying some national talk-show product to fill the slot.

A promotion tour like this, it's the new vaudeville. Going from town to town, hotel to hotel, playing one-night stands on local television and radio. Selling your new and improved hair curler or stain remover or exercise wheel.

You get seven minutes to put your product across. That's if you're not slotted in the F Block—the last block, where in half the ADIs you get bumped off the program because an earlier block went too long. Some guest was so funny and charming they held him through the commercial. They "double-blocked" him. Or the network interrupted with a sinking ship.

That's why the A Block is so choice. The show starts, the anchors do their "chat" segment, and you're on.

No, pretty soon, all this hard-won know-how the slick guy's put together, it will be no good to anybody.

Maybe that's why he's teaching her for free. Really, he says, he should write a goddamn book. That's the American Dream: to make your life into something you can sell.

Still looking at her fat-self photograph, the blonde says, "It's pretty creepy, but this fatty-fat picture is worth more to me than anything," she says. "It used to make me sad, looking at it. But now it's the only thing that cheers me up."

She holds out her hand, saying, "I eat so much fish oil you can smell it." She wiggles the photo at the slick guy, saying, "Smell my hand."

Her hand smells like a hand, like skin, soap, her clear fingernail polish.

Smelling her hand, he takes the picture. Flattened out on paper, made into just height and width, she's a cow wearing a cropped top over low-rise jeans. Her old hair is a normal, average brown color.

If you look at what the slick guy's wearing, a pale-pink shirt with a robin's-egg-blue tie, a dark-blue sports coat, it's perfect. The pink warms up his flesh tones. The blue picks out his eyes. Before you even open your mouth, he says, you have to be presentable. Presentable, well-groomed broadcast content. You wear a wrinkled shirt, a stained tie, and you'll be the guest they cut if they run short of time.

Any television station just wants you to be clean, well-groomed, charming content. Camera-friendly content. A nice face, because a stain remover or an exercise wheel can't talk. Just happy, high-energy content.

On the monitor, the skin hanging off the old guy's neck, it's folded and pleated together where it has to tuck into his starched blue button-down collar. Even so, as he swallows, just sitting there, some extra skin spills out over the top of his collar, the way the *before*-photo girl's belly fat spills over the waist of her jeans.

This photo doesn't even look like the same girl. Mainly because in the picture she's smiling.

Looking at the green-room monitor, the slick guy points out how the hot camera never pans over the audience, never gives us a wide shot. That means the place is nothing but old ladies with bad teeth. The audience-recruitment person, he must've worked a deal. They drag these goobers in here at 7 a.m. and fill an audience, and the station will plug their Senior Craft Fair. That's how they stock these local shows with people to clap. Around Halloween, it will be all young people coming in, so the station will plug their haunted-house fund-raiser. Around Christmas, those bleachers are nothing but old folks who want their charity bazaars to get some attention. Fake applause traded for free advertising.

On the broadcast monitor, the national talent kicks the show back to the local anchor, who tosses to a pre-pro package tease about tomorrow's makeover show, then the bump: a beauty shot of the rain falling outside, a little fanfare, and we're into commercial.

The ship's sunk, with hundreds dead. Film at eleven.

The slick guy's investment pitch, he's rewriting it inside his head to include Acts of God. Disasters you can't predict. And how vitally important a good, sound investment plan can be to the people depending on you. Him, being his product. Hiding his agenda.

Him, the camera behind the camera.

Long as it took that ocean liner to sink, it looks as if our bleach blonde's hair will get her bounced off.

Before they come back from commercial, bumping with a traffic report, a voice-over and the live shot from some highway camera, before then the producer will escort the stain remover back to the green room. The floor producer, she'll hand the radio mike to the Investment Video. She'll tell the Fitness Wheel, "Thank you for coming down, but we're sorry. We overbooked and ran long . . ."

And she'll have Security escort our blonde out to the street.

All so they can wrap and meet the network feed—the soap operas and celebrity talk shows—at ten o'clock, sharp.

The old goober up on the monitor, he's got the same shirt and tie as the slick guy. The same blue eyes. He's got the right idea. Just the wrong timing's all.

"Let me do you a favor," the slick guy tells the blonde. Still holding the *before* fat picture of her, he says, "Will you take some good advice?"

Sure, she says, anything. And, listening, she picks up a cup of cold coffee with lipstick smeared on the paper rim that matches the pink lipstick on her mouth.

This blonde girl with her too-hot hair, she's the slick guy's own private personal ADI right now.

Especially, he tells her, don't let any of these daytime-talk-show Romeos get you into bed. He doesn't mean the on-air talent. It's the pitch guys you have to watch, these same guys you meet selling their miracle dust mops and get-rich schemes in city after city. You'll be thrown together in green rooms in ADIs all across the country. You and them lonely from your time stuck out on the road. Nothing but a motel room at the end of each day.

Speaking from personal experience, these green-room romances go nowhere.

"You remember the Nev-R-Run Pantyhose Girl?" he asks her.

And the blonde girl nods yes.

"She was my mom," the slick guy says. She met his dad while they were both on selling tours, meeting again and again in green rooms just like this. Truth is, he never married her. Ditched her as soon as he found out. Being pregnant, she lost the pantyhose pitchman contract. And the slick guy grew up watching shows like *Out-a-Bed Boulder* and *Wakey Wakey Tampa,* trying to figure out which of those smiling fast-talking men was his old man.

"It's why I'm in the business," he tells our blonde girl.

That's why: keep it business, is his first rule.

The blonde says, "Your mom is really, really pretty . . ."

His mom . . . He says, Those Nev-R-Run Pantyhose must've used asbestos. She caught cancer a couple months back.

"She was damn ugly," he says, "when she died."

At any second, the door into the green room will swing open, and the floor producer will come in, saying she's sorry but they might need to cut another guest. The producer, she'll look at the girl's bright-blond hair. The producer will look at the slick guy's navy-blue sports coat.

The F Block bailed out of here the moment the network broke in with the ocean liner. Then the E Block—Color Consultant, her slug said—bailed when the show looked doomed to run long. Then a Children's Book slotted for the D Block took off.

The sad truth is, even if you get your hair the right color blond and fake being funny and high-energy, good *content,* even then some terrorist with a box cutter might still walk off with your seven-minute segment. Sure, they can always tape you and run you packaged the next day, but chances are they won't. They've got content booked solid for this week, and running you on tape tomorrow means cutting someone else . . .

In their last minute alone, just them in the green room, the slick guy asks if he can do our blonde girl another favor.

"You want to give me your block?" she says. And she smiles, just like in the picture. And her teeth aren't too awful.

"No," he says. "But when somebody's being charming . . . when they tell you a joke . . . ," the slick guy says, and he tears her ugly *before* picture in half. The two halves he puts together and tears into quarters. Then eighths. Then whatever. Shreds. Little bits. Confetti. He says, "If you're going to succeed on television, you need to at least fake a smile."

At least pretend to like people.

There in the green room, the blonde's pink-lipstick mouth, it peels open and open and open until it hangs. Her lips go open and shut two, three times, the way a fish will gasp for breath, and she says, "You *ass* . . ."

It's then the floor producer walks in with the old goober.

The producer says, "Okay, I think we'll go with the investment video for this last segment . . ."

The old goober looks at the slick guy, the way you'd look at some department-store buyer who orders a half-million units, and he says, "Thomas . . ."

The blonde's just sitting there, holding her cup of cold black coffee.

The floor producer is unclipping the radio mike off the back of the man's belt. She's handing it to the slick guy.

And to the old goober, he says, "Good morning, Dad."

Grabbing the slick guy's hand and shaking it, the goober says, "How's your mom?"

The Nev-R-Run Pantyhose Girl. The girl you leave behind.

Our Miss Blonde stands. She gets to her feet, to give up, go home, fail.

And, taking the radio mike, checking the switch, to make sure it's not hot, the slick guy says, "She's dead."

She's dead and buried, and he'll never say where. Or, if he does, he'll lie about the city.

And, splash.

His hair and face, cold and wet.

He's covered all over in coffee. Cold coffee. His shirt and tie, ruined. His slick hair washed down across his face.

Our blonde reaches to take the radio mike, and she says, "Thanks for the advice." She says, "I think this makes me *next* . . ."

And tons worse than being too blonde, worse than wrecking his slick clothes and hair, our skinny girl has fallen in fucking love with him.

1.
2.
3.
4.
5.
6.
7.
8.
9.
10.
11.
12.
13.
14.
15.
16.
17.
18.
19.
20.
21.
22.
23.
24.

In the blue velvet lobby, something comes thudding down the stairs from the shadows of the first balcony. Step by step, the thudding gets louder until it's rumbling, round-dark, rolling down from the dim second floor. It's a bowling ball, thudding down the center of the staircase. Rolling black-silent across the lobby's blue carpet, Sister Vigilante's bowling ball passes Cora Reynolds where he licks his paws, then past Mr. Whittier drinking instant coffee in his wheelchair, then past Lady Baglady and her diamond husband, then the ball knocks, heavy-black, through the double doors, disappearing into the auditorium.

"Packer," Lady Baglady tells her diamond, "there's something locked in here with us." Making her voice low, almost a whisper, she asks the diamond, "Is it *you*?"

That little square of glass you're only supposed to break in the event of a fire, Miss America has already broken it. Every little window framed in red-painted metal with a little hammer hanging next to it on a chain, she breaks the glass and pulls the switch inside. Miss America does this in the lobby. Then in the red-lacquered, Chinese-restaurant-styled promenade with all its carved plaster Buddhas. Then in the Mayan-temple-styled foyer in the basement with its leering carved warrior faces. Then the Arabian Nights gallery behind the second-balcony boxes. Then in the projection booth tucked up against the roof.

Then nothing happens. No bells ring. No one comes to chop through the locked fire doors to rescue her. To rescue us.

Nothing happened, and nothing kept happening.

Mr. Whittier sits on a blue velvet sofa in the lobby, under the glass leaves of a chandelier big as a sparkling gray cloud above him.

Already, the Matchmaker was calling the chandeliers "trees." The row of them hanging down the center of each long salon or gallery or lounge. He called them orchards of glass grown out of chains wrapped in velvet and rooted in the ceiling.

Each of us seeing our own private at-home reality in these same big rooms.

The Earl of Slander is writing in his notepad. Agent Tattletale, videotaping. Countess Foresight, wearing her turban. Saint Gut-Free, eating.

With her whole arm, Director Denial tosses a fake mouse, and it lands halfway to the auditorium doors. With the other hand, she rubs the shoulder of her throwing arm while the cat, Cora Reynolds, brings the mouse back, his paws raising a rooster tail of boiling dust from the carpet.

Watching them, one arm folded across her chest to support her breasts, one hand twisted around to rub the back of her neck, Mrs. Clark says, "In the Villa Diodati, they had five cats."

Saint Gut-Free eats instant crêpe Suzette out of a Mylar bag with a plastic spoon.

Shaping her fingernails with an emery board, Lady Baglady watches every dripping pink spoonful move from the bag to his mouth, and she says, "That *can't* be any good."

And nothing more happens. More nothing happens.

That's until Miss America comes to stand in the middle of us, saying, "This is illegal." What Mr. Whittier has done is kidnapping. He's holding people against their will, and that's a felony.

"The sooner you do as you promised," Mr. Whittier says, "the sooner these three months will go by."

Throwing the fake mouse, Director Denial says, *"What* is the Villa Diodati?"

"It's a house on Lake Como," Lady Baglady tells her fat diamond.

"Lake *Geneva*," Mrs. Clark says.

Looking back, it was Mr. Whittier's stand that we're always right.

"It's not a matter of right and wrong," Mr. Whittier would say.

Really, there is no wrong. Not in our own minds. Our own reality.

You can never set off to do the *wrong* thing.

You can never say the *wrong* thing.

In your own mind, you are always right. Every action you take—what you do or say or how you choose to appear—is automatically right the moment you act.

His hand shaking as he lifts his cup, Mr. Whittier says, "Even if you were to tell yourself, 'Today, I'm going to drink coffee the *wrong* way . . . from a dirty boot.' Even that would be right, because you chose to drink coffee from that boot."

Because you can do nothing wrong. You are always right.

Even when you say, "I'm such an idiot, I'm so wrong . . ." you're right. You're right about being wrong. You're right even when you're an idiot.

"No matter how stupid your idea," Mr. Whittier would say, "you're doomed to be right because it's yours."

"Lake Geneva?" Lady Baglady says with her eyes closed. Pinching her temples, rubbing them between the thumb and index finger of one hand, she says, "The Villa Diodati is where Lord Byron raped Mary Shelley . . ."

And Mrs. Clark says, "It was *not*."

We're all condemned to be right. About everything we can consider.

In this shifting, liquid world where everyone is right and any idea is right the moment you act on it, Mr. Whittier would say, the only sure thing is what you promise.

"Three months, you promised," Mr. Whittier says through the steam of his coffee.

It's then something happens, but not much.

In that next look, you feel your asshole get tight. Your fingers fly to cover your mouth.

Miss America is holding a knife in one hand. With her other hand, she grips the knot of Mr. Whittier's necktie, pulling his face up toward her own. Mr. Whittier's coffee, dropped, spilled steaming-hot on the floor. His hands hang, shaking, swirling the dusty air at each side.

Saint Gut-Free's silver bag of instant crêpe Suzette drops, spilled out on the cornflower-blue carpet, the sticky red cherries and reconstituted whipped cream.

And the cat runs over for a taste.

Her eyes almost touching Mr. Whittier's, Miss America says, "So I'm right if I kill you?"

The knife, one of the set that Chef Assassin brought in his aluminum suitcase.

And Mr. Whittier looks back into her eyes, so close their lashes touch when they blink. "But you'll still be trapped," he says, his few gray hairs hanging loose from the back of his skull. His voice choked to a croak by his necktie.

Miss America waves the knife at Mrs. Clark, saying, "What about her? Does she have a key?"

And Mrs. Clark shakes her head, No. Her eyes popped-open wide, but her baby-doll pout still silicone-frozen.

No, the key is hidden somewhere in the building. A place only Mr. Whittier would look.

Still, even if she kills him she's right.

If she sets fire to the building and hopes the firemen will see the smoke and rescue her before we all suffocate—she's right, again.

If she sticks the knife point in Mr. Whittier's milky-cataract eyeball and pops it out on the floor for the cat to bat around—she's still right.

"In the face of that," Mr. Whittier says, his necktie pulled tight in her fist, his face turning dark red, his voice a whisper, "let's start by doing what we promised."

The three months. Write your masterpiece. The end.

The chrome wheelchair clatters when he lands, dropped by Miss America's hand. Carpet dust fills the air, and the chair's two front wheels lift off the carpet when he lands so hard. Both Mr. Whittier's hands go to his collar, to pull his tie loose. He leans down to take his coffee cup off the floor. His gray comb-over hairs, hanging straight down, fringe around the sides of his spotted bald head.

Cora Reynolds keeps eating the cherries and cream off the dusty carpet beside Saint Gut-Free's chair.

Miss America says, "This is *so not* over . . ." And she shakes the blade of the knife at everyone in the lobby. One fast sweep of her arm, a shudder and twitch of her muscles, and the knife is now stuck in the back of a palace chair across the room. The blade buried and humming in blue velvet, the handle still shivers.

From behind his video camera, Agent Tattletale says, *"Print* it."

Cora Reynolds, his pink suede tongue still lick-lick-licking the sticky carpet.

The Earl of Slander writes something in his notebook.

"So, Mrs. Clark," Lady Baglady says, "the Villa Diodati?"

"They had *five* cats there," Mr. Whittier says.

"Five cats and eight big dogs," Mrs. Clark says, "three monkeys, an eagle, a crow, and a falcon."

It was a summer house party in 1816, where a group of young people spent most days trapped in a house because of rain. Some of them were married, some not. Men and women. They read ghost stories to each other, but the books they had were terrible. After that, they all agreed to write a story. Any sort of scary story. To entertain each other.

"Like the Algonquin Round Table?" Lady Baglady asks the diamond on the back of her hand.

Just a group of friends sitting around, trying to scare each other.

"So what did they write?" Miss Sneezy says.

Those middle-class, bored people just trying to kill time. People trapped together in their moldy-damp summer house.

"Not much," Mr. Whittier says. "Just the legend of *Frankenstein*."

Mrs. Clark says, "And *Dracula* . . ."

Sister Vigilante comes down the stairs from the second floor. Crossing the lobby, she's looking under tables, behind chairs.

"It's in *there*," Mr. Whittier says, lifting a blurred finger to point at the auditorium double doors.

Lady Baglady looks off, sideways, to the auditorium doors where Miss America and the bowling ball have both disappeared. "My late husband and I were experts at being bored," says Lady Baglady, and she makes us wait as she takes three, four, five steps across the lobby to pull the knife out of the chair back.

Holding the knife, looking at the blade, feeling how sharp with her finger, she says, "I could tell you all about how rich, bored people kill time . . ."

Think Tank

A Poem About Lady Baglady

"It only takes three doctors," says Lady Baglady, "to make
  you disappear."
  For the rest of your natural life.

Lady Baglady onstage, her legs are waxed smooth. Her
  eyelashes, dyed thick-black.
    Her teeth bleached bright as her pearls. Her skin,
      massaged.
    Her diamond ring flashes, lighthouse-bright.
    Her linen suit, first pinned and chalked, then tucked and
      trimmed
    until it will fit no one else in the world.
All of her, a monument to sitting still
    while a team of trained experts toiled long and hard,
    for a lot of money.

Onstage, instead of a spotlight, a movie fragment:
    A veil of women dragging fur coats. The feeling of silk
      settles over her face.
On film, the armor of gold and platinum jewelry, warning
  you
    with the red flash of rubies and canary-yellow sapphires.

Lady Baglady says, "It's no fun, having a genius for a
    father."
    Or a mother or husband or wife, ask anyone. Anyone
        rich.
Still, she says, it only takes three doctors . . .
    Thanks to the Think Tank Sanitarium.

"Really brilliant people," she says, "they're really most-
    happy, being . . .
    fully committed."
If Thomas Edison were alive. Madame Curie. Albert
Einstein.
    Their husbands, wives, sons, daughters would all sign
        the necessary paperwork.
    In an instant.
"To protect their income stream," says Lady Baglady.
    That flow of money from fees and royalties for patents
        and inventions.

The veil of spa treatments and pedicures, charity balls and
    opera boxes, wiping
    Lady Baglady's smooth face,
    she says, "My own father included. For his own good."

"He was . . . acting out," she says. "Seeing a younger
    woman. Wearing a toupee."
    Not sharing the income from his product line. Neglecting
        his work.
So—three doctors later—there he is:
    With all the other genius inventors. Behind locked
        doors.
    Without telephones.
    For the rest of his natural life.

From inside her veil of private islands . . . horse shows . . .
  estate auctions,
    Lady Baglady says, "The acorn never does fall far."
    She says, "We're all . . . some kind of genius.
    "Just," she says, "some of us in other ways."

After you give up television and newspapers, the mornings are the worst part: that first cup of coffee. It's true, that first hour awake, you want to catch up with the rest of the world. But her new rule is: No radio. No television. No newspaper. Cold turkey.

Show her a copy of *Vogue* magazine, and Mrs. Keyes still gets choked up.

The newspaper comes, and she just recycles it. She doesn't even take off the rubber band. You never know when the headline will be:

"Killer Continues to Stalk the Homeless"

Or: "Bag Lady Found Butchered"

Most mornings over breakfast, Mrs. Keyes reads catalogues. You order just one single miracle shoe-tree over the telephone, and every week, for the rest of your life, you'll get a stack of catalogues. Items for your home. Your garden. Time-saving. Space-saving gadgets. Tools and new inventions.

Where the television used to be, there on the kitchen counter, she put an aquarium with the kind of lizard that changes color to match your decor. An aquarium, you flip the switch for the heat lamp and it's not going to tell you another transient wino was shot to death, his body dropped in the river, the fifteenth victim in a killing spree targeting the city's homeless, their bodies found stabbed and shot and set on fire with lighter fluid, the street people panicked and fighting their way into the shelters at night, despite the new tuberculosis. The outbound boxcars packed full. The social advocates claiming the city has put out a hit on panhandlers. You get all this just glancing at a newsstand. Or getting into a cab with the radio turned up loud.

You get a glass tank, put it where the TV used to be, and all you get is a lizard—something so stupid that every time the maid moves a rock the lizard thinks it's been relocated miles away.

It's called Cocooning, when your home becomes your whole world.

Mr. and Mrs. Keyes—Packer and Evelyn—they didn't use to be this way. It used to be not a dolphin died in a tuna net without them rushing out to write a check. To throw a party. They hosted a banquet for people blown apart by land mines. They threw a dinner dance for massive head trauma. Fibromyalgia. Bulimia. A cocktail party and silent auction for irritable bowel syndrome.

Every night had its theme:

"Universal Peace for All Peoples."

Or: "Hope for Our Unborn Future."

Imagine going to your senior prom every night for the rest of your life. Every night, another stage set made of South American cut flowers and zillions of white twinkle lights. An ice sculpture and a champagne fountain and a band in white dinner jackets playing some Cole Porter tune. Every stage set built to parade Arab royalty and Internet boy wonders. Too many people made rich fast by venture capital. Those people who never linger on any landmass longer than it takes to service their jet. These people with no imagination, they just flop open *Town & Country* and say:

I want that.

At every benefit for child abuse, everyone walked around on two legs and ate crème brûlée with a mouth, their lips plumped with the same derma fillers. Looking at the same Cartier watch, the same time surrounded with the same diamonds. The same Harry Winston necklace around a neck sculpted long and thin with hatha yoga.

Everyone climbed in or out different colors of the same Lexus sedan.

No one was impressed. Every night was a complete and utter social stalemate.

Mrs. Keyes's best friend, Elizabeth Ethbridge Fulton Whelps, "Inky," used to say there's only one "best" of anything. One night, Inky said, "When everyone can afford the best, the truth is, it does look a little—common."

All the Old Society had gone missing. The more newly minted media barons showed up at any event, the fewer old-money railroad or ocean-liner crowd would.

Inky always said being absent is the new being present.

It's after some cocktail reception for victims of gun violence that the Keyeses walk out to the street. Packer and Evelyn are coming down the art-museum steps, and there's the usual long line of nobodies waiting in fur coats for the parking valets. This is right on the sidewalk, near a bus-stop bench. Sitting on the bench are a wino and a bag lady everyone's trying not to see.

Or smell.

These two, they're not young, dressed in clothes you might find in the trash. Bits of thread showing at every seam, the fabric stiff and blotchy with stains. The bag lady has on tennis shoes flopping open with no laces. Her hair shows through, matted and crushed inside the webbing of a wig, the fake plastic hair as rough and gray as steel wool.

The wino has a knitted brown stocking cap pulled down on his head. He's pawing the bag lady, shoving one hand down the front of her stretch-polyester pants and crawling his other hand up under her sweatshirt. The bag lady, she's twisting inside her clothes, moaning, her tongue rolling around her open lips.

The bag lady, where her sweatshirt is pulled up, her stomach looks flat and tight, her skin massaged pink.

The wino, his baggy sweatpants are tented in front with an erection. The peak of his tent shows a dark spot of wet leaked through.

Packer and Evelyn, they must be the only ones watching these two grope each other. The parking valets run between here and the parking garage down the block. The mob of new money looks at the sweep-second hand go around and around on their diamond watches.

The wino pulls the bag lady's face against the outline in his pants. The bag lady's lips, they crawl around on the dark stain growing there.

The bag lady's lips, Evelyn tells Packer, she knows those lips.

You hear a little sound, the kind of shrill ring that makes everyone waiting for a valet reach into a fur-coat pocket for their cell phone.

Oh my God, Mrs. Keyes says. She tells Packer, That bag lady getting pawed by the wino, that could almost be Inky. Elizabeth Ethbridge Fulton Whelps.

The shrill little ring sounds again, and the bag lady reaches down. She pulls up the bottom of one pant leg, unhemmed and unraveling beige polyester, to show her leg wrapped thick with a dirty elastic bandage. Her lips still on the wino's crotch, from between layers of bandages her fingers take a little black handful.

The shrill ring comes again.

The last Evelyn heard, Inky ran a magazine. Maybe *Vogue* magazine. She spent half of each year in France, deciding the hemline for next season. She sat ringside at the shows in Milan, and taped a fashion commentary that ran on some cable news network. She stood on red carpets and talked about who wore what to the Academy Awards.

This bag lady on the bus-stop bench, she holds the black object to the side of her gray plastic wig. She fingers it and says, "Hello?" She takes her mouth off the wet bulge in the wino's pants, and she says, "Are you writing this down?" She says, "Lime is the new pink."

The bag lady's voice, Mrs. Keyes tells her husband, she knows that voice.

She says, "Inky?"

The bag lady slips the little phone back between the bandages around her leg.

"That stinky wino," Packer says, "that's the president of Global Airlines."

It's then the bag lady looks up and says, "Muffy? Packer?" The wino's hand still feeling around deep in the front of her stretch pants, she pats the bench beside her and says, "What a nice surprise."

The bum pulls back his fingers, shiny wet in the streetlight, and he says, "Packer! Come say hello."

And of course Packer is always right.

Poverty, Inky says, is the new wealth. Anonymity is the new fame.

"Social divers," Inky says, "are the new social climbers."

The Jet Set are the original homeless people, Inky says. We may have a dozen homes—each in a different city—but we still live out of a suitcase.

This makes sense, if only because Packer and Evelyn are never on the cutting edge of anything. This whole social season, they've been going to horse shows, gallery openings, and auctions, telling each other all the Old Guard socialites were in detox or having cosmetic surgery.

Inky says, "Whether you do it with a shopping cart or a Gulfstream G550, it's the same instinct. To always be on the move. To not be tied down."

Anymore, she says, all you need is cash money, and you're sitting on the Opera Steering Committee. You make a hefty donation, and you get a place on the Museum Foundation Board.

You write a check, and that makes you a celebrity.

You get stabbed to death in a hit movie, and you're famous.

In other words: tied down.

Inky says, "Nobodies are the new celebrity."

The Global Airlines wino, he has a bottle of wine, wrapped in a brown paper bag. The wine, he says, is mixed with equal parts of mouthwash, cough syrup, and Old Spice cologne, and after one drink the four of them go strolling through the dark, through the park, where you'd never go at night.

What you have to love about drinking is, every swallow is an irrevocable decision. You charging ahead, in control of the game. It's the same with pills, sedatives and painkillers, every swallow is a definite first step down some road.

Inky says, "Public is the new private." She says, if you check into even the most boutique hotel—one of those white-robe places with orchids trembling next to the bidet in a white marble bathroom— even then, chances are a tiny camera is wired to watch you. She says the only place left to have sex is out in the open. The sidewalk. The subway. People only want to watch if they think they can't.

Besides, she says, the entire champagne-and-caviar lifestyle had lost its zap. Taking the Lear jet from here to Rome in six hours, it's made escaping too easy. The world feels so small and played out. Globe-trotting is just the chance to feel bored more places, faster. A boring breakfast in Bali. A predictable lunch in Paris. A tedious dinner in New York, and falling asleep, drunk, during just another blow job in L.A.

Too many peak experiences, too close together. "Like the Getty Museum," Inky says.

"Lather, rinse, and repeat," says the Global Airlines wino.

In the boring new world of everyone in the upper-middle class, Inky says nothing helps you enjoy your bidet like peeing in the street for a few hours. Give up bathing until you stink, and just a hot shower feels as good as a trip to Sonoma for a detoxifying mud enema.

"Think of it," Inky says, "as a kind of poverty sorbet."

A nice little window of misery that helps you enjoy your real life.

"Join us," Inky says. The sticky green stain of cough syrup

smeared around her mouth, strands of her plastic wig hair sticking to it, she says, "This next Friday night."

Looking bad, she says, is the new looking good.

She says all the right people will be there. The Old Guard. The best parts of the Social Register. Ten in the evening, under the westside ramps to the bridge.

They can't, Evelyn says. Packer and her, Wednesday night they're committed to attend the Waltz to End Hunger in Latin America. Thursday is the Aboriginals in Need Banquet. Friday is a silent auction for runaway teen sex workers. These events, with all the polished acrylic awards they hand out, it makes you long for the day when the number-one fear of Americans was public speaking.

"Just go to the midtown Sheraton," Inky says. "Check into a room."

Evelyn must make a pug-dog face, because then Inky tells her, "Relax."

She says, "Of course we don't *stay* there. Not at a *Sheraton*. It's only a place to change clothes."

Anytime after ten on Friday night, she says, under the ramps of the bridge.

Packer and Evelyn Keyes, their first problem is always what to wear. For a man, it looks easy. All he has to do is put on his dinner jacket and his trousers inside out. Put your shoes on the wrong feet. *Voilà*—you look crippled and crazy.

"Insanity," Inky would say, "is the new sanity."

Wednesday, after the hunger waltz, Packer and Evelyn come out of the hotel ballroom and you can hear someone on the street singing "Oh Amherst, Brave Amherst." In the street, Frances "Frizzi" Dunlop Colgate Nelson is drinking oversized cans of malt liquor with Schuster "Shoe" Frasier and Weaver "Bones" Pullman, the three of them sitting with their dirty pants rolled up and their bare feet in a fountain. Frizzi is wearing her bra on the outside.

Dressing down, Inky says, is the new dressing up.

At home, Evelyn tries on a dozen garbage bags, green and black plastic bags big enough for yard debris, but they all make her look fat. To look good, she settles on a narrow white bag made for upright kitchen trash. It looks elegant, even, snug as a Diane von Furstenberg wrap dress, belted with a melted old electrical cord, a dash of bright safety orange, with the loose wires and plug hanging loose down one side.

This season, Inky says everyone is wearing their wigs backward. Mismatched shoes. Cut a hole in the center of a soiled blanket, she says, wear it as a poncho, and you're ready for a night of fun on the street.

To be safe, the evening they check into the midtown Sheraton, Evelyn takes three suitcases full of army surplus. Yellowed, stretched-out bras. Sweaters thick with balls of lint. She takes a jar of clay facial mask to dirty them up. They sneak down the hotel fire stairs, fourteen flights to a door that opens on a back alley, and they're free. They're nobody. Anonymous. Without the responsibility to run anything.

No one's looking at them, asking for money, trying to sell them something.

Walking to the bridge, they're invisible. Safe in their poverty.

Packer starts to limp a little, from his shoes being on the wrong feet. Evelyn lets her mouth hang open. Then she spits. Yes, the girl taught to never even scratch an itch in public, she spits in the street. Packer sways, bumping against her, and she clutches his arm. He swings her around, and they kiss, reduced to just two wet mouths while the city around them, it disappears.

That first night on the street, Inky comes over with something reeking inside a black patent-leather purse webbed with cracks. It's the smell of low tide on a hot day at the shore. The smell, "It's the new anti-status symbol," she says. Inside the purse is a cardboard takeout box from Chez Héloise. Inside the box is a fist-sized lump of orange roughy. "Four days old," Inky says. "Swing it around. The smell beats a bodyguard for keeping people away."

Stink for privacy, the new way to protect personal space. Intimidation by odor.

You can get used to any smell, she says, no matter how bad. Inky says, "You got used to Calvin Klein's Eternity . . . ?"

The two of them, Inky and Evelyn, walk around the block, getting a little chill time away from the party. Up ahead, the entourage of some miniskirt statue is piling out of a limousine, thin people with headsets wired between their mouth and ear, each person holding a conversation with someone far away. As the two waddle past, Inky stumbles, brushing the purse full of rotten fish, pressing it against the sleeves of leather and fur coats. The bodyguards in dark suits. Personal assistants in tailored black.

The entourage crowds together, pulling away, all of them moaning and pressing a manicured hand over their nose and mouth.

Inky, she keeps on walking. She says, "I love doing that."

In the face of this new money, Inky says it's time to change the rules. She says, "Poverty is the new nobility."

Up ahead is a herd of Internet millionaires and Arab oil sheikhs, all of them smoking outside an art gallery, and Inky says, "Let's go pester them for pocket change . . ."

This is their vacation from being Packer and Muffy Keyes, the textile CEO and the tobacco-products heiress. Their little weekend retreat into the social safety net.

The Global Airlines wino happens to be Webster "Scout" Banners. Him, Inky, and Muffy, they meet up with Skinny and Frizzi. Then Packer and Boater come join them. Then Shoe and Bones. They're all drunk and playing charades, and at one point Packer shouts out, "Is there anyone under this bridge *not* worth at least forty million dollars?"

And, of course, you only hear the traffic passing by above.

Later, they're pushing shopping carts someplace *industrial*. Inky and Muffy pushing one cart, Packer and Scout walking a ways behind. And Inky says, "You know, I used to think the only thing worse than losing at love was winning . . ." She says, "I used to be so in love with Scout, ever since school, but you know how events . . . disappoint us."

Inky and Muffy, their hands wearing those gloves without fingers so they can sort old cans better, Inky says, "I used to think the secret to a happy ending was to bring down the curtain at the exact right time. A moment after happiness, then everything's all wrong, again."

Those social climbers who think they have it tough—their fear of using the wrong fork, or panicking when the fingerbowls are passed—the homeless have so much more to fret about. There's botulism. There's frostbite. A flash of capped tooth could expose you. A whiff of Chanel No. 5.

Any of a million little details could give you away.

They've become what Inky calls the "Commuting Homeless."

She says, "Now? Now I love Scout. I love him as if I'd never married him." On the streets like this, it feels like they're pioneers starting a new life in some wilderness. But instead of bears or wolves to worry about, they have—Inky shrugs and says—drug dealers and drive-by shootings.

"This is still the best part of my life," she says, "but I know it can't last forever . . ."

Already her new social calendar was filling up. All this social diving. Doing anything on Tuesday is out of the question, because she plans to go rag-picking with Dinky and Cheetah. After that, Packer and Scout are meeting to sort aluminum cans. After that, everyone's stopping by the free clinic to have our feet looked at by some young, dark-eyed doctor with a vampire accent.

Packer says the aluminum can is the Krugerrand of the street.

Standing at the top of a ramp, where cars come off the freeway, Inky says, "Think *high concept*. Pretend you're doing a single-line movie pitch to network television."

On a sheet of brown cardboard, using a black felt-tipped marker, Inky writes: Single Mom. Ten Kids. Breast Cancer.

"You do this—right?—" she says, "and people just *give you money . . .*"

Muffy writes: Crippled War Vet. Starving. Need to get home.

And Inky says, "Perfect." She says, "You just pitched *Cold Mountain.*"

This is their little urban campout.

This hiding out in the open. This hiding in plain sight.

No one's easier to ignore than the homeless. You could be Jane Fonda or Robert Redford, but if you're pushing a shopping cart down the avenue at high noon, wearing three layers of soiled clothing and muttering cusswords under your breath—nobody's going to notice you.

They could do this for the rest of their lives. Scout and Inky, they plan to get on a list for a low-income apartment. They want to sit in waiting rooms and get free dental care from attractive young medical students. They'll apply for free methadone, then work their way up to heroin. Adult vocational training. Fry hamburgers. Learn to drive and do laundry, then work their way up into the lower-middle class.

At night, when Packer and Evelyn hold each other, under some bridge or on cardboard laid across a steaming, warm manhole cover, his hands inside her clothing, bringing her to climax as strangers walk past, the two have never been so in love.

But Inky's right. It can't last forever. The end comes so fast, no one's sure what happened until it's in the newspaper the next day.

They're asleep in the doorway of some warehouse, feeling more at home than they ever have in Banff or Hong Kong. By now their blankets smell like each other. Their clothes—their bodies—feel like a house. Just Packer's arms around his wife could be a duplex on Park Avenue. A villa in Crete.

It's that night a black town car hits the curb, brakes squealing and one tire bumping up onto the sidewalk. The headlights, two circles of bright high-beams, shine right on Mr. and Mrs. Keyes, waking them up. The back door falls open and screams spill out from the back seat. Headfirst, her hands and arms flying, a girl falls out onto the sidewalk. Her long dark hair hiding her face, she's naked and scrambling on hands and knees away from the car.

Packer and Evelyn, buried in their house of old rags and damp blankets, the naked girl is scrambling toward them.

Behind her, a man's black shoe steps out of the car's open door. A dark pant leg follows. A man wearing black leather gloves climbs out of the car's back seat while the girl gets to her feet, screaming. Screaming, Please. Screaming for help. So close you can see one, two, three gold hoops pierced through one of her ears. Her other ear is gone.

What looks like a long braid of dark hair is really blood running down the side of her neck. Where the ear was, you see just a jagged ridge of flesh.

The girl gets to the Keyeses, just their eyes showing from under the blankets.

As the man grabs her by the hair, the girl grabs at their rags. As the man lifts her, kicking and weeping, into the car, the girl tugs the blankets, showing them here, still half asleep, blinking in the car's bright headlights.

The man has to see them. Anyone driving the car must see.

The girl screams, "Please." She screams, "The license plate . . . ," and she's pulled back inside. The car door slams shut and the tires squeal, leaving just the girl's blood and skidmarks of black rubber. In the gutter with the fast-food paper cups, dropped or knocked out in the struggle, a torn, pale ear sparkles with two gold hoop earrings still looped through it.

It's over breakfast, a room-service omelet of greasy mushrooms, English muffins, lukewarm coffee, and cold bacon in their suite at the Sheraton, it's there they see the newspaper. In local news, a Brazilian oil heiress was kidnapped. The picture of her is the naked girl with long dark hair from the night before, but smiling and holding a trophy with a little gold tennis player on top.

According to the newspaper, the police haven't a single witness.

Of course, the Keyeses could send a note, but they really didn't see anyone's face. They didn't see the license plate. All they saw was the girl. The blood. Packer and Evelyn, they can't offer any real help. Going to the police, all they could do is humiliate themselves. Already, you could imagine the headlines:

"Society Couple Goes Slumming for Kicks"

Or: "Billionaires Playing Poor"

God forbid if they told about Inky and Scout, Skinny and Shoe and Bones.

Packer and Evelyn putting themselves up for public ridicule was not going to save this poor girl. Their suffering wouldn't lessen a moment of hers.

In the newspaper the next week, the kidnapped heiress was found dead.

Still, Inky wasn't worried. Poor, dirty people have nothing to worry about on the street. The girl who got killed was young. She looked clean and pretty and rich. "Having nothing to lose," Inky said, "is the new wealth."

And Packer said, "Lather, rinse, and repeat."

No, Inky wasn't about to give up her happiness and go back to being rich and famous. And more and more, those nights, Packer went with her. To protect her, he said.

One of those nights, Evelyn's at the Charity Dinner Dance Against Colon Cancer when her cell phone rings. It's Inky, and in the background a man is shouting. Packer's voice. In the phone, Inky is breathing hard, saying, "Muffy, please. Muffy, please, we're lost and someone is chasing us." She says, "We've tried the police, but . . ." And the call cuts off.

As if she's run into a tunnel. Under an overpass.

The headline in the next day's newspaper says:

"Publisher and Textile CEO Found Stabbed to Death"

Now, almost every morning, there's a new headline to avoid:

"Bag Lady Found Butchered"

Or: "Killer Continues to Stalk the Homeless"

Somewhere, every night, that black town car is looking for Mrs. Keyes, the only witness to a crime. Someone is killing anyone on the street who might be her. Anyone dressed in rags and asleep under a pile of blankets.

It's after that Evelyn goes cold turkey. She cancels the newspaper. To replace the television, she buys the glass tank with a lizard that changes color to match any paint scheme.

Nowadays, Mrs. Keyes, she's the opposite of homeless. She has too much home. She's burdened with home. Buried in home. She reads her catalogues. Looking at the glossy pictures of garden ornaments. Diamond jewelry made from the cremains of your dead loved ones.

Of course, she still misses her friends. Her husband. But it's like Inky would say: Being absent is the new being present.

And she still buys tickets for the charity events. The silent auctions and dance recitals. It's important to know she's doing something to make the world a little bit better. Next, she'd like to go swimming with endangered gray whales.

Sleep in the canopy of some dwindling rain forest.

Photograph some vanishing zebras. Eco-slumming.

It's important to be aware. She still wants to make a difference.

5.

6.
7.
8.
9.
10.
11.
12.
13.
14.
15.
16.
17.
18.
19.
20.
21.
22.
23.
24.

That summer at the Villa Diodati, Mrs. Clark tells us, it was just five people:

The poet, Lord Byron.

Percy Bysshe Shelley and his lover, Mary Godwin.

Mary's half-sister, Claire Claremont, who was pregnant by Byron.

And Byron's doctor, John Polidori.

Listening, we're sitting around the electric fireplace in the second-balcony smoking room. The Gothic smoking room. Each of us pulled up in a yellow leather wing chair or a needlepoint sofa or tapestry loveseat we'd dragged from somewhere, the carved, pointed legs leaving ruffled trails in the dusty, matted carpets.

All of us, here, except for Lady Baglady, who went to bed early. And Miss America, off picking locks.

The electric fireplace is just a rotating light under a bed of red and yellow glass chunks glued together. Light without heat. All our hanging crystal trees turned off, and the red-and-yellow light dancing across our faces, shapes of red-and-yellow light move across the wood paneling and the floor of flat stones fit together.

Just those five people, Mrs. Clark says, bored and trapped indoors by the rain. Shelley and company. They took turns reading to each other from a collection of German ghost stories called *Fantasmagoriana.*

"Lord Byron," Mrs. Clark says, "couldn't stand the book."

Byron said there was more talent in the room than in the book they were reading. He said they could each write a better horror story. They should, each of them. Write a story.

This was almost a century before Bram Stoker's *Dracula,* but out of that summer came Dr. John Polidori's book *The Vampyre,* and our modern idea of a bloodsucking demon.

On one of those rainy nights, with the thunder and lightning over Lake Geneva, eighteen-year-old Mary Godwin had the dream which would become the Frankenstein legend. Both monsters the basis for countless books and movies that followed.

Even the house party itself had become a legend. Around the shores of Lake Geneva, the vacation hotels set up telescopes in their lakeside windows so guests could watch what everyone said was an orgy of incest at the villa. Middle-class tourists, bored on their summer tour, they put their worst fears under Lord Byron's roof. Just that handful of young people, trying to live outside the million rules of their culture, and people spied on them through telescopes, expecting to see monsters.

Here, we were the modern equivalent of the people at Villa Diodati.

We were the modern version of the Algonquin Round Table.

Just people telling stories out loud to each other.

People looking for one idea that would echo for the rest of time. Echo into books, movies, plays, songs, television, T-shirts, money.

It was these same faces—among three times as many, a mob—when we first met in person, in the back of a coffeehouse. Us: the faces who made the final cut. Even then, Countess Foresight wore her signature turban. The Duke of Vandals, his blond ponytail. The Missing Link, his long-hanging nose and dark wilderness of beard.

The way people gossip about the Villa Diodati today, in time people will talk about that coffee shop. People who never saw the advertisement will swear they were there. They were smart and didn't agree to go along on the retreat. Otherwise, they might be dead. Or rich. Over time, that coffeehouse, with its racks of free newspapers and bulletin board pinned full of business cards offering colonic irrigation and holistic pet counseling, that shop would have to be the size of a stadium to hold the people who will claim to have been there that night.

That night will become a legend.

The Mythology of Us.

The hemp people and poets and housewives and us, standing with paper cups of coffee, we listened while Mrs. Clark talked. Her out-there breasts and that silicone pout making some people giggle. When someone asked about a phone number for the outside world to reach people on retreat, Mrs. Clark said, yes. She said, "It's 1-800-FUCK-OFF."

It's that moment, some people walked away.

Meaning, No. No contact with the outside world. No television or radio or telephone or Internet. Just you and what you bring in your one suitcase.

Meaning more people walked away.

The people who walked away, the first-round survivors. The smart ones who get to tell their own story. The camera behind the camera behind the camera, Mr. Whittier would say. They'll have their ultimate truth—but just about that night.

Those poor idiots sold short.

We all saw the advertisement, just in different ways. On different bulletin boards around town, it said:

WRITERS' RETREAT:
ABANDON YOUR LIFE FOR THREE MONTHS.

Just disappear. Leave behind everything that keeps you from creating your masterpiece. Your job and family and home, all those obligations and distractions—put them on hold *for three months.* Live with like-minded people in a setting that supports total immersion in your work. Food and lodging included free for those who qualify. Gamble a small fraction of your life on the chance to create a new future as a professional poet, novelist, screenwriter. Before it's too late, live the life you dream about. Spaces very limited.

The advertisement was printed on an index card. A recipe card. Boxed inside a dashed line, like a coupon you'd cut out. And at the bottom was a phone number. It was Mrs. Clark's number, stapled to the cork bulletin board in the library foyer. By the restrooms in the back of the supermarket. In the Laundromat. That advertisement on an index card, one week it was everywhere. The next week, it was nowhere.

All the cards had disappeared.

People who saw it, if they called the phone number, they got a recording of Mrs. Clark saying the coffeehouse, the time and date we should all meet.

Already, in our minds, here in the red-and-yellow fake firelight, we could picture the future: the scene of us telling people how we'd taken this little adventure and a crazy man had kept us trapped in an old theater for three months. Already, we were making matters worse. Exaggerating. We'd say how the place was freezing-cold. There was no running water. We had to ration the food.

None of that was true, but it does make a better story. No, we'd warp the truth. Blow it up. Stretch it out. For effect.

We'd create our own incestuous orgy of people and animals for the world to gossip about.

The little backstage dressing room we each got, talking about it, we'd load it with poisonous spiders. Hungry rats. Not just Director Denial's cat hair sticking everywhere.

A ghost. We'd put a ghost in the old theater to build the story, make room for special effects. Oh, we'd haunt this place ourselves, pack it with lost souls.

We'd turn our lives into a terrible adventure. A true-life horror story with a happy ending. A trial we'd survive to talk about.

Except for Lady Baglady with her handful of dead husband. Miss America with her fetus, snowballing bigger and bigger, cell by cell, inside her. And Miss Sneezy with her mold allergy, the rest of us wanted more. More pain and suffering to dredge up, later, on national talk shows. Those television shows Miss America talked about. Even if we never sparked a good idea, never wrote our masterpiece novel, this three months trapped together could be enough to make a memoir. A movie. A future of not working a regular job. Just being famous.

A story worth selling.

For now, sitting around the glass fireplace, we're ticking off the details we need to remember to create this scene on national television. So we could advise "on the set" in making the movie "authentic." The story of how we were kidnapped and held hostage and every day Miss Sneezy got more sick and the baby inside Miss America got bigger.

No one will say it, but Miss Sneezy's death would make a perfect third-act climax. Our darkest moment.

The perfect ending would be the landlord stumbling in after the lease has expired, just in time to rescue the fragile Miss America. The demented Lady Baglady. A few of us would come limping out, squinting and weeping, into the sunlight. The rest of us would be carried out on stretchers and slid into ambulances for a siren's trip to the hospital. The movie could jump ahead a little to show us all standing bedside as Miss America gives birth. Then jump again, to show us at the funeral for Miss Sneezy. The ghost of poor Miss Sneezy, sacrificed to juice the plot.

We'd have Agent Tattletale's camera for video support. The Earl of Slander's audiocassettes for voice-over.

Then, as completion, Miss America would name her new child Miss Sneezy, or whatever her first name had been. A sense of the circle mended. Of life going on, renewed. Poor, frail Miss Sneezy.

In the movie–book–T-shirt story, we'd all love Miss Sneezy . . . her deep courage . . . her sunny humor.

Sigh.

No, unless one of us coughs up a new-fangled Frankenstein or Dracula, our own story will have to get a lot more dramatic before it would be worth selling. We need everything to get much, much worse before it's all over.

Screw the idea of creating anything original. It's no use, writing some let's-pretend piece of fiction. That takes so much effort for what little you get in cash money.

Especially split seventeen ways. Royalty-wise. Sixteen ways, if you subtract the doomed Miss Sneezy.

All of us silent, but commanding her: *Cough.*

Hurry up and die, already.

No, when everyone else walked out of that coffeehouse meeting, we were the smart ones. Yes, it looked like a crackpot venture that would lead to big trouble, but, hey—*it looked like a crackpot adventure that could lead to big money.*

All of us sitting here silent, but commanding Miss Sneezy: *Cough.*

All of us, we're aching for her to help make us famous.

That's why the Reverend Godless botched the wiring to all the fire alarms. The very first hour we were inside. At least, that's what he told the Matchmaker. Godless learned wiring in the military, and the Missing Link helped by holding the flashlight. For good measure, they checked all the phone lines. The one line they found still working, the Missing Link with his hairy muscles yanked it out of the wall.

That's why Countess Foresight stuck the tines of plastic forks in every door lock and snapped them off. No way could anyone use a key. Just in case her parole officer could track her by that bracelet. No, none of us wanted to be rescued—not just yet.

Just all of us hedging our bets. Scenes that won't be in the movie.

This will all look like Mr. Whittier's doing. Evil, sadistic old Mr. Whittier.

Already, our team is forming up against the team of Mrs. Clark and Mr. Whittier.

Miss America and Miss Sneezy already just plot points. Our sacrifice. Doomed.

In the red and yellow shapes of electric firelight, in the carved wood paneling of the Gothic smoking room, sunk in the cushion of her leather wing chair, Mrs. Clark's chin nods lower and lower, almost settling into her cleavage. She asks, did Sister Vigilante find the bowling ball?

And the Sister shakes her head, No. She taps the face of her wristwatch and says, "Civil twilight comes in forty-five . . . forty-four minutes."

Miss Sneezy coughs—a long, rumbling, wet-gravel cough—and it's all we can do *not* to cheer. She digs in her pocket for a pill, a capsule, but her hand comes back empty.

Sister Vigilante excuses herself and starts down the stairs toward the lobby, toward bed, disappearing step by step, growing shorter, until the top of her black-tinted hair is gone.

Our Miss America is somewhere else, kneeling at a doorknob, trying to pick the lock. Or pulling a fire alarm we know won't work.

Thanks to the Reverend Godless.

The red light glows on the Earl of Slander's tape recorder. Agent Tattletale shifts his video camera from one eye to the other.

And from down the stairs comes up a scream. A woman's long wail. The voice of Sister Vigilante, telling us to come quick. She's stumbled over something.

The Lady Baglady. A new stain. A knife wrapped in the fingers of one hand. All around her, a dark lake of her blood melting into the lobby's blue carpet.

Long dark hair seems to twine down one side of her face and disappear into the collar of her fur coat. But at the bottom step, when she's life-sized, the braided dark hair is blood. Under the sculpted hair on that side of her face, her ear is gone. Sprawled there, she holds out one hand filled with red and pink, a shining pearl earring in the center of the oyster-mess, catching the fake firelight. In her palm, cupped next to the pink ear, the diamond of her dead husband.

With all of us looking down the stairs at her, the Lady Baglady smiles. Her head rolls to one side, to look up at us, and she says, "I'm bleeding . . . so heavily . . ." Beyond her pale face and hands, a path of blood seems to trail off forever. Her fingers relax, and the knife slips to the carpet, and she says, "Now, Mr. Whittier, you must let me go home . . ."

Elbowing the Earl of Slander, Comrade Snarky says, "What did I tell you? Look." She nods toward the top of the bloody braid and says, "Now you can see the facelift scar."

And Lady Baglady is dead. Sister Vigilante says this, holding a finger to her neck. Blood smeared on the Sister's finger.

At this point, our future is set. Done. This will be our meal ticket, telling people how we witnessed an innocent human being driven to commit suicide, plus adding the story of Lady Baglady slumming. The tragedy of her husband. The Brazilian oil heiress, kidnapped. Screw the idea of inventing monsters. Here, we just had to look around. Pay attention.

In the viewfinder of his camera, Agent Tattletale rewinds and watches as Lady Baglady tells her story onstage. Telling and retelling it.

Our puppet. Our plot event.

The Earl of Slander rewinds his tape recorder and we hear Sister Vigilante's scream, over and over.

Our parrot.

And in the red-and-yellow light from the glass fire, Mr. Whittier says, "So it's started already . . ."

"Mr. Whittier?" Mrs. Clark says.

Mr. Whittier, our villain, our master, our devil, whom we love and adore for torturing us, he sighs. Watching Lady Baglady's dead body, one of his shaking, quivering, trembling hands rises to cup his mouth, and he yawns.

Watching the dead body, Director Denial is petting the cat in her arms, tabby-orange cat hair drifting to settle everywhere.

The Baroness Frostbite and Countess Foresight kneel over the body. Not crying, but their eyes so open you can see white all around the iris, the way your eyes would look at a winning lottery ticket.

Watching the body, Saint Gut-Free is spooning cold spaghetti out of a silver bag. Bits of cat hair in every dripping red bite.

This is us against us against us for the next three months.

From the top of the stairs, sitting in his wheelchair, Mr. Whittier watches. Beside him, the Earl of Slander fiddles with his pen and pad, still taking notes.

Pointing a blurred finger, Mr. Whittier says, "You, you're writing this down?"

Not looking up from his version of the truth, the Earl nods, yes.

"So—tell us a story," Mr. Whittier says. "Come back to the fire," he says, and, with a twist of his trembling hand, "Please."

And the Earl of Slander smiles. He flips to the next clean page in his notepad and caps his pen. Looking up, he says, "Does anybody remember that old TV show *Danny-Next-Door?*" Making his voice slow and rumbling-deep, he says, "One day . . ." He says, "One day, my dog ate some garbage wrapped in aluminum foil . . ."

Trade Secrets

A Poem About the Earl of Slander

"Those people in line," the Earl says, "a week early for the
    opening of some movie . . ."
Those people are paid to wait in line.

The Earl of Slander onstage, he stands with one hand
    raised, holding a sheet of paper,
    the white paper, blocking his face.
The rest of him in a blue suit, a red necktie. Buffed
        brown shoes.
    On the wrist of his raised hand, a gold watch,
    engraved with: "Congratulations"

Onstage, instead of a spotlight, instead of a face,
    projected on the paper is the 72-point headline:
    Local Reporter Wins Pulitzer Prize

Behind this headline, the Earl says, "Those people live their
    lives standing in line . . ."
For one summer blockbuster after another.
The movie studios bus those supposed fan-kids from
        town to town.
From sci-fi film to superhero fantasy.

Each week, a new town, a new motel, a new PG-13 to
pretend they adore.
Those cardboard and tinfoil costumes, so obviously
homemade,
the Wardrobe Department makes them and ships them
ahead.
All this effort to fool the local media into running a real
news story, for free publicity.
To build a credible buzz about how much folks will love
this film.
All this time and money, it's called "seeding the audience."

In his shirt pocket blinks the small red light of a tape
recorder taking down every word.
As the Earl asks, "Who's the bigger fool?"
The reporter who refuses to invent a meaning for life?
Or the reader who wants it?
And stands ready to accept this meaning presented in
the words of a stranger?

His voice from behind the paper, the Earl of Slander says,
"A journalist has a right . . .
. . . and a duty, to destroy
those golden calves he helps create."

Swan Song

A Story by the Earl of Slander

One day, my dog eats some garbage wrapped in aluminum foil and has to get a thousand bucks' worth of X-rays. The yard behind my apartment building is full of garbage and broken glass. Where people park their cars, puddles of antifreeze wait to poison any dog or cat.

Even with a bald head, the veterinarian looks like some old best friend. Like a kid I grew up with. A smile I saw every day of my childhood. The dimple in his chin and every freckle on his nose, I know them all. The gap between his two front teeth, I know how he could use it to whistle.

Here and now, he's giving my dog an injection. Standing at a silvery steel table in a cold, white tile room, holding the dog by the skin of its neck, he says something about heartworm.

In the phone book, when I found him, I was blind with crying, afraid my dog might die. Still, there was his listing: Kenneth Wilcox, D.V.M. A name I loved, somehow. For some reason. My savior.

Now, pulling back each of the dog's ears and looking inside, he says something about distemper. Embroidered on the chest pocket of his white coat, it says "Dr. Ken."

Even the sound of his voice echoes from a long time

back. I've heard him sing "Happy Birthday." Shouting "Strike one!" at baseball games.

This is him, some old friend of mine, but too tall, the skin of his eyelids baggy-dark and hanging down. Too fleshy under his chin. His teeth look a little yellow, and his eyes aren't as bright blue as they should be. He says, "She looks good."

I say, Who does?

"Your dog," he says.

Still looking at him, his bald head and blue eyes, I ask, "Where did you go to school?"

He says some college in California. Someplace I never heard of.

He was little when I was little, and somehow we grew up together. He had a dog named Skip and walked around barefoot all summer, always going fishing or building a tree house. Looking at him, I can picture one cold afternoon building the perfect snowman while his grandma watches from the kitchen window. I say, "Danny?"

And he laughs.

That same week, I'm pitching a story about him to an editor. About how I found him, found little Kenny Wilcox, the child actor who played Danny on the television show *Danny-Next-Door* a million years ago. Little Danny, the kid we all grew up with, he's a vet now. He lives in a tract house in some suburban development. Mows his own lawn. This is him, bald and middle-aged, a little fat and ignored.

This faded star. He's happy and living in a two-bedroom house. Branching out from each eye, he has laugh lines. He takes pills to control his cholesterol. He's the first to admit, after those years as the center of attention, he's a bit of a loner. But he's happy.

What's important is, Dr. Ken has agreed. Sure, he'll do an interview. A little profile for the Sunday Entertainment Section of the newspaper.

The editor I'm pitching to, he twists the end of a ballpoint pen in his ear, digging out wax. Looking worse than bored.

This editor tells me readers don't want a story about somebody born cute and talented, getting paid a fortune to appear on television, then living happily ever after.

No, people don't want a happy ending.

People want to read about Rusty Hamer, the little boy on *Make Room for Daddy* who shot himself. Or Trent Lehman, the cute kid from *Nanny and the Professor* who hanged himself on a playground fence. Little Anissa Jones, who played Buffy on *Family Affair,* clutching a doll named Mrs. Beasley, then swallowing the biggest overdose of barbiturates in the history of Los Angeles County.

This is what people want. The same reason we go to racetracks to watch the cars crash. Why the Germans say, *"Die reinste Freude ist die Schadenfreude."* Our purest joy comes when people we envy get hurt. That most genuine form of joy. The joy you feel when a limousine turns the wrong way down a one-way street.

Or when Jay Smith, the "Little Rascal" known as Pinky, was found stabbed to death in the desert outside Las Vegas.

It's the kind of joy we felt when Dana Plato, the little girl on *Diff'rent Strokes,* got arrested, posed naked in *Playboy,* and took too many sleeping pills.

People standing in line at the supermarket, clipping coupons, getting old, those are the headlines that sell these people a newspaper.

Most people, they want to read about Lani O'Grady, the pretty daughter on *Eight Is Enough,* found dead in a trailer house with her belly full of Vicodin and Prozac.

No crack-up, the editor tells me, no story.

Happy Kenny Wilcox with his laugh lines, he wouldn't sell.

The editor tells me, "Find Wilcox with kiddie porn on his computer. Find him with dead bodies under his house. Then you got a story."

This editor says, "Better yet, find him with all the above, but find him dead."

The next week, my dog drinks a puddle of antifreeze. My dog's named Skip after the dog on *Danny-Next-Door,* the dog little Danny used to have. My Skip, my baby's white with big black spots and a red collar just like on television.

The only cure for antifreeze is to pump the dog's stomach. Then fill her tummy with activated charcoal. Find a vein and start the dog on an ethanol drip. Pure grain alcohol to flush out the kidneys. To save my dog, my baby, I need to get her dead drunk. This means another trip to see Dr. Ken, who says, Sure, next week is fine for an interview. But he warns me, his life's not very exciting.

I tell him, Trust me. Good writing means you take the regular facts and deliver them in a sexy way. Don't worry about your life story, I tell him, that's my job.

These days, I could use a good story assignment. Me, I've been writing freelance for a couple years. Since I got canned from doing entertainment features. That was good money, the press-junket stuff, puffing up quotes for movie launches, sharing a movie star with a tableful of media people for ten minutes, all of them trying not to yawn.

Movie premiers. Album releases. Book launches. It was a steady stream of work, but give the wrong opinion and you're off the gravy train. A movie studio threatens to pull their retail display advertising, and—abracadabra—your byline disappears.

Me, I'm broke because one time I tried to warn people. One movie, I wrote that people might do better to spend their money somewhere else, and since then I'm out of the loop. Just one summer slasher movie and the power behind it, and I'm begging to write obituaries. To write photo captions. Anything.

It's a bald cheat, building a house of cards you don't get to knock down. You spend all those years piling up nothing, creating an illusion. Turning a human being into a movie star. Your real payday is at the back end of the deal. Then you get to pull out the rug. Knock down the cards. Show the handsome ladies' man cramming a gerbil up his ass. Reveal the girl-next-door shoplifting and stoned on painkillers. The goddess beating her kids with a wire hanger.

The editor's right. So is Ken Wilcox. His life is an interview no one will ever buy.

For prep, the whole week before we talk, I surf the Internet. I download files from the former Soviet Union. Here's a different kind of child star: Russian schoolboys without pubic hair, sucking off fat old men. Czech girls still waiting for their first period, getting butt-fucked by monkeys. I save all these files to one thin compact disk.

Another night, I clip a leash on Skip and risk a long walk through my neighborhood. Coming back to my apartment, my pockets are stuffed with plastic sandwich bags and little paper envelopes. Squares of folded aluminum foil. Percodans. OxyContins. Vicodins. Glass vials of crack and heroin.

The interview, I write all fourteen thousand words before Ken Wilcox even opens his mouth. Before we even sit down together.

Still, to keep up appearances, I bring my tape recorder. I bring a notepad and pretend to take notes with a couple dried-out pens. I bring a bottle of red wine spiked with Vicodin and Prozac.

At Ken's little house in the suburbs, you'd expect a glass case crammed with dusty trophies, glossy photos, civic awards. A memorial to his childhood. There's nothing like that. Any money he's got, it's in the bank, drawing interest. His house is just brown rugs and painted walls, striped curtains on each window. A bathroom with pink tile.

I pour him red wine and just let him talk. I ask him to pause, then act like I'm getting every quote perfect.

And he's right. His life is more boring than a black-and-white summer rerun.

On the other hand, the story I already wrote is great. My version is all about little Kenny's long slide from the spotlight to the autopsy table. How he lost his innocence to a long list of network executives in his campaign to become Danny. To keep the sponsors happy, he was farmed out as a sexual plaything. He took drugs to stay thin. To delay the onset of puberty. To stay up all night, shooting scene after scene. No one, not even his friends and family, nobody knew the depths of his drug habit and perverted need for attention. Even after his career collapsed. Even becoming a D.V.M. was just to get access to good drugs and sex with small animals.

The more wine Ken Wilcox drinks, the more he says his life didn't start until *Danny-Next-Door* was canceled. Being little Danny Bright for eight seasons, that's only real the way your memories of second grade might seem real. Only blurry moments not connected. Each day, each line of dialogue was just something you learned long enough to pass a test. The pretty farmhouse in Heartland, Iowa, was just a false front. Inside the windows, behind the lace curtains, was bare dirt scattered with cigarette butts. The actor who played Danny's grandma, if they were speaking in the same shot, she used to spray spit. Her spit sterilized: more gin than saliva.

Sipping red wine, Ken Wilcox says his life now is so much more important. Healing animals. Saving dogs. With every swallow, his talking breaks up into single words spread wider and wider apart. Just before his eyes close, he asks how Skip is doing.

My dog, Skip.

And I tell him, Good, Skip is doing great.

And Kenny Wilcox, he says, "Good. I'm happy to hear it . . ."

He's asleep, still smiling, when I slip the gun into his mouth.

"Happy" doesn't do anybody any good.

A gun not registered to anybody. My hand in a glove, the gun in his mouth with his finger wrapped around the trigger. Little Kenny's on his sofa, stripped of his clothes, his dick smeared with cooking grease, and a video of his old show playing on the television. The real clincher is the kiddie porn downloaded to his computer hard drive. The hard-copy pictures of kids getting screwed, they're printed and taped to the walls of his bedroom.

The bags of painkillers are stashed under his bed. The heroin and crack buried in his sugar canister.

Inside of one day, the world will go from loving Kenny Wilcox to hating him. Little Danny-Next-Door will go from a childhood icon to a monster.

In my version of that last evening, Kenneth Wilcox waved the gun around. He bellowed about how no one cared. The world had used and rejected him. He drank and popped pills all evening and said he wasn't afraid to die. In my version, he died after I'd gone home.

That next week, I sold the story. The last interview with a child star loved by millions of people all over the world. An interview done just hours before his neighbor found him dead, the victim of suicide.

The week after, I'm nominated for the Pulitzer Prize.

A few weeks later, I win. That's only two thousand dollars, but the real payoff is long-term. Anymore, not a day goes by when I'm not turning work down. When my agent's fielding offers for me. No, I only do high-profile, big-money work. Big magazine cover stories. National audiences.

Anymore, my name means Quality. My byline means The Truth.

You look in my address book, and it's all names you know from movie posters. Rock stars. Best-selling authors. Everything I touch, I turn to Famous. I move from my apartment to a house with a yard for Skip to run around. We have a garden and a swimming pool. A tennis court. Cable television. We pay off the thousand-plus bucks we owe for the X-rays and the activated charcoal.

Of course, you can still turn on some cable network and see Kenneth Wilcox, the little boy he used to be, whistling and pitching baseballs, before he turned into a monster with gin spit on his face. Little Danny and his dog, walking barefoot through Heartland, Iowa. His syndicated ghost keeps my story alive, the contrast. People love knowing my truth about that little boy who seemed so happy.

"Die reinste Freude ist die Schadenfreude."

This week, my dog digs up an onion and eats it.

Me, I'm calling vet after vet, trying to find someone who'll save her. At this point, money's no problem. I can pay anything.

Me and my dog, we have a great life. We're so happy. It's while I'm still on the phone, flipping through the telephone book, when my Skip, my baby, she stops breathing.

1.
2.
3.
4.
5.

6.

7.
8.
9.
10.
11.
12.
13.
14.
15.
16.
17.
18.
19.
20.
21.
22.
23.
24.

"Let's start with the end," Mr. Whittier would say.

He'd say, "Let's start with a plot spoiler."

The meaning of life. A unified field theory. The big reason why.

We'd all be sitting in the Arabian Nights gallery, sitting cross-legged on silk pillows and cushions stained with spots of mildew. Chairs and sofas that stunk of dirty laundry when you sat down and pushed the air out of them. There, under the high-up, echoing dome, painted in jewel colors that would never see daylight, never fade, among the brass lamps hanging down, each with a red or blue or orange lightbulb shining through the cage of patterns cut out of the brass, Mr. Whittier would sit there, eating dried something in crunching handfuls from a Mylar bag.

He'd say, "Let's get the big, big surprise over and done with."

The earth, he'd say, is just a big machine. A big processing plant. A factory. That's your big answer. The big truth.

Think of a rock polisher, one of those drums, goes round and round, rolls twenty-four/seven, full of water and rocks and gravel. Grinding it all up. Round and round. Polishing those ugly rocks into gemstones. That's the earth. Why it goes around. We're the rocks. And what happens to us—

the drama and pain and joy and war and sickness and victory and abuse—why, that's just the water and sand to erode us. Grind us down. To polish us up, nice and bright.

That's what Mr. Whittier would tell you.

Smooth as glass, that's our Mr. Whittier. Buffed by pain. Polished and shining.

That's why we love conflict, he says. We love to hate. To stop a war, we declare war on it. We must wipe out poverty. We must fight hunger. We campaign and challenge and defeat and destroy.

As human beings, our first commandment is:

Something needs to happen.

Mr. Whittier had no idea he was so right.

The more Mrs. Clark talked, the more we could see this wouldn't be the Villa Diodati. The babe who wrote *Frankenstein,* she was the kid of two writers: professors famous for think-tank books called *Political Justice* and *A Vindication of the Rights of Women.* They had famous smart people crashing at their house all the time.

We were no summer-house party of brainy bookworms.

No, the best story we'd bring out of this building would be just how we survived. How crazy Lady Baglady died cradled in our weeping arms. Still, that story would have to be good enough. Exciting enough. Scary and dangerous enough. We'd have to make sure it was.

Mr. Whittier and Mrs. Clark were too busy droning on. We needed them to get rough with us. Our story needed them to flog and beat us.

Not bore us to death.

"Any call for world peace," Mr. Whittier would say, "is a lie. A pretty, pretty lie." Just another excuse to fight.

No, we love war.

War. Starvation. Plague. They fast-track us to enlightenment.

"It's the mark of a very, very young soul," Mr. Whittier used to say, "to try and fix the world. To try and save anyone from their ration of misery."

We have always loved war. We are born knowing that war is why we're here. And we love disease. Cancer. We love earthquakes. In this amusement-park fun house we call the planet earth, Mr. Whittier says we adore forest fires. Oil spills. Serial killers.

We love terrorists. Hijackers. Dictators. Pedophiles.

God, how we love the television news. The pictures of people lining up beside a long, open grave, waiting to be shot by another new firing squad. The glossy newsmagazine photos of more everyday people torn to bloody shreds by suicide bombers. The radio bulletins about freeway pile-ups. The mud slides. The sinking ships.

His quivering hands telegraphing the air, Mr. Whittier would say, "We love when airplanes crash."

We adore pollution. Acid rain. Global warming. Famine.

No, Mr. Whittier had no idea . . .

The Duke of Vandals found every bag of anything that included beets. Any silver Mylar pillows rattling with the sliced beets inside, dry as poker chips.

Saint Gut-Free poked a hole in every bag that held any kind of pork or chicken or beef. Meat being something he can never digest.

All the Mylar bags puffed full of nitrogen gas, they were arranged by food, stuffed into brown boxes of corrugated cardboard. In the boxes stenciled "Dessert" were bags of dried cookies, rattling the way seeds would inside a dried gourd. Inside the boxes stenciled "Appetizers," freeze-dried chicken wings rattled like old bones.

Out of her fear of getting fat, Miss America found every box stenciled "Desserts" and used Chef Assassin's carving knife to poke holes in every bag.

Just to speed up our suffering. Fast-track us to enlightenment.

One hole, and the nitrogen would leak out. Bacteria and air would leak in. All the mold spores that were killing Miss Sneezy, carried on the warm damp air, they'd be eating and breeding in each silver pocket of sweet-and-sour pork, breaded halibut, pasta salad.

Before Agent Tattletale snuck into the lobby to ruin every crêpe Suzette, he'd make sure no one was around.

Before Countess Foresight crept into the lobby to stab every silver bag that might contain even trace amounts of cilantro, she made sure Agent Tattletale was gone.

We each only ruined the food we hated.

Cross-legged in the Arabian Nights gallery, among the plaster pillars carved to look like elephants standing on their back legs, rearing up to support the ceiling with their front feet, his teeth crunching another handful of dried sticks and rocks, Mr. Whittier would say, "In our secret heart's heart, we love to root against the home team."

Against humanity. It's us against us. You, the victim of yourself.

We love war because it's the only way we'll finish our work here. The only way we'll finish our souls, here on earth: The big processing station. The rock tumbler. Through pain and anger and conflict, it's the only path. To what, we don't know.

"But we forget so much when we're born," he says.

Being born, it's as if you go inside a building. You lock yourself inside a building with no windows to see out. And after you're inside any building long enough, you forget how the outside looked. Without a mirror, you'd forget your own face.

He never seemed to notice how one of us was always missing from the gallery. No, Mr. Whittier just talked and talked, while somebody was always sneaking downstairs to destroy any Mylar bag that listed green peppers as an ingredient.

That's how it happened. How no one knew everyone else had the same plan. We each just wanted to raise the stakes a little. To make sure our rescue team wouldn't find us pillowed in silver bags of rich food, suffering from nothing but boredom and gout. Each suffering survivor, fifty pounds heavier than when Mr. Whittier took us hostage.

Of course, we each wanted to leave enough food to last until we were *almost* rescued. Those last couple days, when we were really fasting, hungry and suffering—we could stretch that to a couple weeks in the retelling.

The book. The movie. The television miniseries.

We'd starve just long enough to get what Comrade Snarky called "Death Camp Cheekbones." The more ins and outs your face has, the better Miss America says you'll look on television.

Those vermin-proof bags were so tough, we'd each begged to borrow a knife from Chef Assassin, from his beautiful set of paring knives, chef's knives, cleavers, filleting knives and kitchen shears. Except for the Missing Link with his bear-trap jaw; he'd just use his teeth.

"You are permanent, but this life is not," Mr. Whittier would say. "You don't expect to visit an amusement park, then stay forever."

No, we're only visiting, and Mr. Whittier knows that. And we're born here to suffer.

"If you can accept that," he says, "you can accept anything that happens in the world."

The irony is, if you can accept that—you'll never again suffer.

Instead, you'll run toward torture. You'll enjoy pain.

Mr. Whittier had no idea he was so right.

At one point, that evening, Chef Assassin walked into the salon, still holding a boning knife in one hand. He looked at Whittier and said, "The washing machine is broke. Now you have to let us go . . ."

Mr. Whittier looked up, still crunching a mouthful of dried turkey Tetrazzini, he said, "What's wrong with the washer?"

And Chef Assassin held up something in his other hand, not the knife, something loose and dangling. He said, "Some desperate, hostage cook cut off the plug-in . . ."

The object dangling from his hand.

It's after that we couldn't wash clothes, another plot point for the story that would be our cash cow.

At that point, Mr. Whittier groaned and slipped the fingers of one hand inside the top of his pants. He said, "Mrs. Clark?" His fingers pressed the spot inside his belt, and he said, "Now, *that* hurts . . ."

Watching him, twirling his rope of cut-off plug-in, Chef Assassin said, "I hope it's cancer."

His fingers still in his pants, sunk in his Arabian cushions, Mr. Whittier bends double to put his head between his knees.

Mrs. Clark steps forward, saying, "Brandon?"

And Mr. Whittier slips to the floor, his knees pulled to his chest, moaning.

In our heads, for the scene in the movie, this scene only with a movie star twisting in fake pain on the red-and-blue Oriental carpet, in our heads, we're all writing down: "Brandon!"

Mrs. Clark squats down to lift the empty Mylar bag from where he's dropped it among the silk cushions. Her eyes twitch across the words stenciled there, and she says, "Oh, Brandon."

All of us trying to be the camera behind the camera behind the camera. The last story in line. The truth.

In the future movie and TV miniseries version of this scene, we're all coaching a famous beauty-queen actress to say: "Oh my God, Brandon! Oh, dear sweet suffering Jesus!"

Mrs. Clark holds the bag for him to see, and she says, "You just ate the equivalent of ten turkey dinners . . ." She says, "Why?"

And Mr. Whittier moans. "Because," he says, "I'm still a growing boy . . ."

In the future version, the beauty queen cries: "You're splitting apart inside! You're going to explode like a burst appendix!"

In the movie version, Mr. Whittier is screaming, his shirt stretched tight over his swelling belly, his fingernails claw the buttons open. Just then the tight skin starts to tear, the way a nylon stocking gaps open. Red blood spouts straight out, the way a whale clears its blowhole. A blood fountain that makes the audience scream.

In reality, his shirt looks a little tight. His hands unbuckle his belt. They pop open the top button of his pants. Mr. Whittier cuts a fart.

Mrs. Clark holds out a glass of water, saying, "Here, Brandon. Drink something."

And Saint Gut-Free says, "No water. He'll only bloat more."

Mr. Whittier, his body twists until he's stretched out on his stomach against the red-and-blue carpet. Each breath comes fast and short as a dog panting.

"It's his diaphragm," Saint Gut-Free says. The food expanding in his stomach, it's already absorbing moisture and blocking the duodenum at the bottom. The ten turkey Tetrazzini dinners are expanding upward, compressing his diaphragm, making it so his lungs can't inhale.

Saying this, Saint Gut-Free is still eating handfuls of dried something from his own silver bag. Chewing and talking at the same time.

Another happening inside could be the stomach splitting, fouling the abdominal cavity with blood and bile and growing bits of turkey meat. Bacteria spilling from the small intestine. Leading to peritonitis, Saint Gut-Free says, an infection of the cavity wall.

In our movie version, Saint Gut-Free is tall with a straight nose and thick-framed glasses. He has a shock of thick, wild hair. A stethoscope hangs on his chest as he says *duodenum* and *peritoneum*. *Not* with his mouth full. In the movie, he holds out one hand, palm-up, and demands: "Scalpel!"

In the version based-on-a-true-story, we boil water. We give Mr. Whittier shots of brandy and a bullet to bite. We mop Saint Gut-Free's forehead with a little sponge while a clock tick-tocks, tick-tocks, tick-tocks, loud.

The noble victims saving their villain. The way we helped comfort poor Lady Baglady.

In reality, we just stand here. Our hands, waving away his fart smell. We're maybe wondering how Whittier will play this scene, if he'll live or die. We really need a director. Someone to tell each one of us what our character would do.

Mr. Whittier just moans, stroking his sides with his hands.

Mrs. Clark just leans over him. Her breasts looming, she says, "Here, someone help me get him to his room . . ."

Still nobody moves to help. We need for him to die. We can still make Mrs. Clark the evil villain.

Then Miss America says it. She steps up beside his bloated stomach, face-down, his shirttails pulled out of his pants, the elastic of his underwear showing as his waistband rides down. Miss America steps up and—oomph!—her shoe kicks into the stretched-tight side of his belly. It's then she says, "Now, where's the goddamn key?"

And Mrs. Clark bends an arm and elbows her back, away from the body. Mrs. Clark says, "Yes, Brandon. We need to get you to a hospital."

In his own way, Mr. Whittier did. He gave us the key. His stomach pulling apart on the inside, the cavities of him filling with blood, the dried chips of turkey still expanding, soaking up blood and water and bile, getting bigger until the skin of his belly looks pregnant. Until his bellybutton pops out, poked out stiff as a little finger.

All of this, it takes place in the spotlight of Agent Tattletale's camera, him taping over the death of Lady Baglady. Replacing yesterday's tragic scene with today's.

The Earl of Slander holds his tape recorder close, using the same cassette, betting this horror will be worse than the last.

This moment, it's a plot point we've never dared dream. The first-act climax that would make our lives worth cash money. Mr. Whittier's busting open, the event we could witness to become someone famous, a famous authority. Like Lady Baglady's ear, Mr. Whittier's belly splitting open was our ticket. A blank check. A free pass.

We were all soaking it up. Absorbing the event. Digesting the experience into a story. A screenplay. Something we could sell.

The way his pumpkin belly subsided a little, going a bit flat when the pressure collapsed his diaphragm. We studied how his face, his mouth stretched open, his teeth biting for more air. More air.

"An inguinal hernia," Saint Gut-Free said. And we all said those words under our breath to better remember.

"To the stage . . . ," Mr. Whittier says, his face buried in the dusty carpet. He says, "I'm ready to recite . . ."

An inguinal hernia . . . , we all echo in our heads. What's happened so far wouldn't make a good joke. All these idiots fooled into a building and trapped. The ringleader gets gas, and we escape. That's just NOT going to play.

Already, Mother Nature is planning to take off her choker of brass bells and sneak him some water.

Director Denial is planning to walk Cora Reynolds past his room and smuggle in a big pitcher of water.

The Missing Link sees himself tiptoeing to Mr. Whittier's dressing room all night long, ladling water down his throat until the man goes: ka-boom.

"Please, Tess?" Mr. Whittier says. He says, "Would you help me to bed?"

And we all jot a note in our heads: *Tess and Brandon, our jailers.*

"Hurry, to the stage . . . I'm cold," Mr. Whittier says while Mother Nature helps him to his feet.

"Probably shock," Saint Gut-Free says.

In the version we'll sell, he's already a goner. One villain will die, and his she-villain will torment the rest of us in her rage. Mistress Tess, holding us captive. Depriving us of food. Forcing us to wear dirty rags. We, being her innocent victims.

Saint Gut-Free stands to put an arm around Mr. Whittier. Mother Nature helps. Mrs. Clark follows with her glass of water. The Earl of Slander with his tape recorder. Agent Tattletale, his video camera.

"Trust me," Saint Gut-Free says. "I happen to know a lot about human insides."

As if we still needed her to die, Miss Sneezy sneezes into her fist. Miss Sneezy, the future ghost of here.

Wiping the spray from her arm, Comrade Snarky says, "Gross!" She says, "Were you raised in a plastic bubble or what?"

And Miss Sneezy says, "Yeah, pretty much."

The Matchmaker excuses himself, saying he's tired and needs some sleep. And he sneaks down to the subbasement to sabotage the furnace.

He couldn't guess, but the Duke of Vandals has already beat him to that punch.

This leaves the rest of us sitting on the silk cushions and pillows spotted with mildew under the Arabian Nights dome. The silver bag of turkey Tetrazzini empty on the carpet. The carved elephant pillars.

In our heads, we're all jotting down the line: *I happen to know a lot about human insides . . .*

And nothing more happens. More nothing happens.

Until the rest of us unfold our legs and slap the dust from our clothes. We head for the auditorium, our fingers crossed we'll hear Mr. Whittier's last words.

"The same mistakes we made as cavemen," says Mr.
    Whittier, "we still make."
    So maybe we're supposed to fight and hate and torture
        each other . . .

Mr. Whittier rolls his wheelchair to the edge of the stage,
    with his spotted hands, his bald head.
    The folds of his slack face seem to hang
    from his too-big eyes, his cloudy, watery-gray eyes.
The ring looped through one of his nostrils, the earphones
    of his CD player looped around the wrinkles and folds of
    his beef-jerky neck.

Onstage, instead of a spotlight, a black-and-white movie
    fragment:
    Mr. Whittier's head is wallpapered with newsreel armies
        marching.
    His mouth and eyes lost in the shadow boots and
        bayonets that worm across his cheeks.

He says, "Maybe suffering and misery is the point of life."
    Consider that the earth is a processing plant, a factory.
Picture a tumbler used to polish rocks:

A rolling drum filled with water and sand.
Consider that your soul is dropped in as an ugly rock,
some raw material or a natural resource, crude oil,
   mineral ore.
And all conflict and pain is just the abrasive that rubs us,
polishes our souls, refines us,
teaches and finishes us over lifetime after lifetime.
Then consider that you've chosen to jump in, again and
   again,
knowing this suffering is your entire reason for coming to
   earth.
Mr. Whittier, his teeth crowded too many in his narrow
   jawbone,
his dead-tumbleweed eyebrows, Mr. Whittier's bat-wing
   ears spread wide
with the shadow armies marching across,
he says,
"The only alternative is, we're all just eternally stupid."

We fight wars. We fight for peace. We fight hunger. We love
   to fight.
We fight and fight and fight, with our guns or mouths or
   money.
And the planet is never one lick better than it was before
   us.

Leaning forward, both his hands clawed on the arms of his
   wheelchair,
as the newsreel armies march over his face, those
   moving tattoos
of their machine guns and tanks and artillery,
Mr. Whittier says: "Maybe we're living the exact way we're
   meant to live."
Maybe our factory planet is processing our souls . . . just
   fine.

Dog Years

A Story by Brandon Whittier

These angels, they see themselves being. These agents of mercy.

Put together so much more nice than God had planned, with their rich husbands and good genetics and orthodontia and dermatology. These stay-at-home mothers with teenaged kids in school. At-home, but not homemakers. Not housewives.

Educated, sure, but not too smart.

They have help for all the rough work. Hired experts. They use the wrong scouring powder, and their granite countertops or limestone tile is worthless. The wrong fertilizer, and their landscaping gets burned. The wrong color paint, and all their careful effort, their investment, suffers. With the kids in school, and God at his office, the angels have all day to kill.

So here they are. Volunteers.

Where they can't screw up anything too important. Pushing the library cart around a retirement center. Between yoga and their book group. Hanging the Halloween decorations at an old-folks' home. Any old-age hospice, you'll find them, these angels of boredom.

These angels with their flat-soled shoes handmade in Italy. Their good intentions and art-history degrees and long afternoons to kill until the kids get home from soccer or ballet after school. These angels, pretty in their flower-print sundresses, their clean hair tied back. And smiling. Smiling. Every time you sneak a look.

With a nice word to say for every patient. A comment about what a nice collection of get-well cards you've arranged on the dresser. What nice African violets you grow in pots on your windowsill.

Mr. Whittier loves these angel women.

Always, for Mr. Whittier, the spotted, bald old man at the end of the hall, they say: What nice black-light, butt-rock concert posters he has taped above his bed. What a colorful skateboard he has propped beside the door.

Old Mr. Whittier, bug-eyed dwarf Mr. Whittier, he asks, "What's shaking, ladies?"

And the angels, they laugh.

At this old man who still plays at being so young. It's so sweet, his being so young at heart.

Sweet, goofy Mr. Whittier with his Internet surfing and snow-boarder magazines. His CDs of hip-hop music. A brimmed cap, turned around backward on his head. Just like a high-school kid.

An ancient version of their own teenagers in school. They can't not flirt back. They can't not like him a little, with his spotted, backward-capped head between earphones, listening to head-banger rock so loud it leaks out.

Mr. Whittier in the hallway, parked in his wheelchair with one hand open, palm-up, he says, "Gimme five . . ."

And all the volunteer ladies slap his hand as they walk past.

Yes, please. That's how the angels want to turn ninety years old: Still with-it. Still hip to new trends. Not fossilized, the way they feel now . . .

In so many ways, this old man seems younger than any of the vol-unteers in their thirties or forties. These middle-aged angels a half or a third his age.

Mr. Whittier with his fingernails painted black. A silver ring looped through one honking-big, old-man nostril. Around his ankle, a tattoo of barbed wire shows above his cardboard bedroom slipper.

A clunky skull-face ring rattles loose around one stiff, little-stick finger.

Mr. Whittier blinking his milky-cataract eyes, saying, "How about you be my date for the high-school prom . . . ?"

All the angels, they blush. Giggling at this safe, funny old man. They sit on his wheelchair lap, their muscle-toned, personal-trained thighs perched on his sharp, bony knees.

It's only normal that, someday, an angel will gush. To the head nurse or an orderly, a volunteer will gush about what a wonderful youthful spirit Mr. Whittier has. How he's still so full of life.

At that, the nurse will look back, eyes not blinking, mouth open a moment, quiet a moment, before the nurse says, "Of course he acts young . . ."

The angel says, "We should all stay so full of life."

So filled with high spirits. Such pep. So perky.

Mr. Whittier is just so inspirational. They say that a lot.

These angels of mercy. These angels of charity.

Those foolish, foolish angels.

And the nurse or orderly will say, "Most of us did . . . have that kind of pep." Walking away, the nurse will say, "When we were his age."

He's not old.

Here's how the truth always leaks out.

Mr. Whittier, he suffers from progeria. The truth is, he's eighteen years old, a teenager about to die of old age.

One out of eight million kids develops Hutchinson-Gilford progeria syndrome. A genetic defect in the protein lamin A will make their cells fall apart. Aging them at seven times the normal rate. Making teenaged Mr. Whittier, with his crowded teeth and big ears, his veined skull and bulging eyes, making his body 126 years old.

"You could say . . . ," he always tells the angels, waving away their concern with one wrinkled hand, "you could say I'm aging in dog years,"

In another year, he'll be dead of heart disease. Of old age, before he's twenty.

After this, the angel doesn't turn up for a while. The truth is, it's just too sad. Here's a kid, maybe younger than one of her own teenagers, dying alone in a nursing home. This kid, still so full of life and reaching out for help, to the only people around—to her— before it's too late.

This is too much.

Still, every yoga class, every PTA meeting, each time she looks at a teenager, this angel wants to cry.

She has to do something.

So she goes back, with her smile toned down a little. She tells him, "I understand."

She smuggles in a pizza. A new video game. She says, "Make a wish, and I'll help make it come true."

This angel, she wheels him out a fire exit for a day riding roller-coasters. Or hanging out at the mall. This teenaged geezer and a beautiful woman, old enough to be his mother. She lets him slaughter her at paintball, the colors wrecking her hair. His wheelchair. She takes a dive at laser tag. She half carries his wrinkled half-naked carcass to the top of a waterslide, again and again, all of one hot, sunny afternoon.

Because he's never been high, the angel steals dope from her kid's stash box and teaches Mr. Whittier how to use a bong. They talk. Eat potato chips.

The angel, she says her husband has become his career. Her kids are growing away from her. Their family is falling apart.

Mr. W., he says his own folks, they couldn't cope. They have four other kids to raise. It's the only way they could afford the nursing home, by making him a ward of the court. After that, they'd show up and visit less and less.

And telling that, with some soft guitar ballad playing, Mr. W. will start to cry.

The one wish he wanted most was to love someone. To really make love. Not die a virgin.

Right then, the tears still rolling down from his stoner-red eyes, he'd say, "Please . . ."

This wrinkled old kid, he'd sniff and say, "Please, stop calling me *Mister*."

The angel stroking his bald, spotted head, he'd tell her, "My name is Brandon."

And he'd wait.

And she'd say it:

Brandon.

Of course, after that, they'd fuck.

Her, gentle and patient. The Madonna and the whore. Her long, yoga-trained legs spread to this naked, wrinkled goblin.

Her, the altar and the sacrifice.

Never as beautiful as she looked, next to his spotted, veined old skin. Never as powerful as she felt, as he drooled and trembled over her.

And, damn—for a virgin—if he didn't take his own sweet time. He'd started missionary-style, then had one of her legs in the air, splitting the reed. Then both her feet, gripped tight around the ankles and framing his panting face.

Thank God for the yoga.

Viagra-hard, he rode her on all fours, doggy-style, even taking himself out and poking at her ass until she said to stop. She was sore and stoned, and as he bent her legs to force her feet up, behind her head, by then her bright, fake angel's smile had come back.

After all that, he came. In her eyes. In her hair. He asked her for a cigarette she didn't have. Taking the bong off the floor beside the bed, he torched another bowl and didn't offer her a hit.

The angel, she got dressed and tucked her kid's bong under her coat. She knotted a scarf around her sticky hair and started to leave.

Behind her, as she opened the door to the hallway, Mr. Whittier was saying, "You know, I ain't ever had a blow job before, neither . . ."

As she stepped out of the room, he was laughing. Laughing.

After that, she'd be driving, and her cell phone would ring. It would be Whittier suggesting bondage, better drugs, blow jobs. And when the angel finally told him, "I can't . . ."

"Brandon . . ." he'd tell her. "The name's Brandon."

Brandon, she'd say. She couldn't see him, not anymore.

It's then he'd tell her—he lied. About his age.

Over the phone, she'd say, "You don't have progeria?"

And Brandon Whittier would say, "I'm not eighteen years old."

He wasn't eighteen, and he had the birth certificate to prove it. He was thirteen years old. Now a victim of statutory rape.

But, for enough cash money, he wouldn't squeal to the cops. Ten grand, and she wouldn't suffer through an ugly courtroom drama. Front-page headlines. All her lifetime of good works and investments reduced to nothing. All for a quick fuck with a little kid. Worse than nothing—her the pedophile, now a sex criminal who would need to register her whereabouts for the rest of her life. Maybe get divorced and lose her kids. Sex with a minor carried a mandatory five-year prison sentence.

On the other hand, in another year he'd be dead of old age. Ten grand was a small price to pay for the rest of her life.

Ten grand and maybe just one little knob job for old times' sake . . .

So of course she paid. They all paid. All the volunteers. The angels.

None of them ever went back to the old-folks' home, so they never met each other. To each angel, she was the only one. Really, there were a dozen or more.

And the money? It just kept piling up. Until Mr. Whittier was too old and tired and bored to just fuck.

"Look at the stains in the lobby carpet," he said. "See how those stains have arms and legs?"

The same as the volunteer ladies, we were trapped by a boy in the body of an old man. A thirteen-year-old kid dying of old age. The part about his family abandoning him, that much was true. But Brandon Whittier was no longer dying ignored and alone.

And, the same way he'd bagged one angel after another, this wasn't his first experiment. We weren't his first batch of guinea pigs. And—until one of those stains came back to haunt him—he told us, we would not be his last.

1.
2.
3.
4.
5.
6.
7.
8.
9.
10.
11.
12.
13.
14.
15.
16.
17.
18.
19.
20.
21.
22.
23.
24.

Morning starts with a woman yelling. The woman's voice, the shouting, is Sister Vigilante. Between each shout, you can hear the butt of a fist pound on wood. You can hear a wooden door boom and bounce in its frame. Then the yelling again.

Sister Vigilante yells, "Hey, Whittier!" Sister Vigilante shouts, "You're late with the fucking sunrise . . . !"

Then the fist, pounding.

Outside our rooms, our backstage dressing rooms, the hallway is dark. Beyond that, the stage and auditorium are dark. Pitch-dark except for the ghost light.

We're each getting up, grabbing some clothes, not sure if we've been asleep an hour or a night.

The ghost light is a single bare bulb on a pole that stands center stage. Tradition says it keeps any ghost from moving in when a theater is empty and dark.

In theaters before electricity, Mr. Whittier would say, the ghost light acted as a pressure-relief valve. It would flare and burn brighter, to keep the place from exploding if there was a surge in the gas lines.

Either way, the ghost light meant good luck.

Until this morning.

First it's the yelling that wakes us. Then it's the smell.

Here's the sweet smell of the black muck Lady Baglady might find slumming in the bottom of a Dumpster. It's the smell of a garbage truck's gummy, sticky back mouth. The smell of swallowed dog mess and old meat. Chewed and swallowed and packed tight together. The smell of old potatoes melting into a black puddle under the kitchen sink.

Holding our breath, trying not to smell, we're feeling our way out our doors and down the black hallway, through the dark, toward all the yelling.

Here, night and day are a matter of opinion. Until now, we just agreed to trust Mr. Whittier. Without him, whether it's a.m. or p.m. is a matter for debate. No light comes from the outside. No telephone signals. No sounds.

Still pounding the door, Sister Vigilante shouts, "Civil dawn was eight minutes ago!"

No, a theater is built to exclude the outside reality and allow actors to build their own. The walls are double layers of concrete with sawdust packed between them. So no police siren or subway rumble can wreck the spell of someone's fake death onstage. No car alarms or jackhammer can turn a romantic kiss into a belly laugh.

Each sunset is just when Mr. Whittier looks at his watch and says good night. He climbs up to the projection booth and throws the breakers, blacking out the lights in the lobby, the foyers, the salons, then the galleries and lounges. The darkness herds us toward the main auditorium. This twilight, it falls room by room until the only light left is in the dressing rooms, backstage. There, each of us sleeps. Each room with one bed, one bathroom, a shower, and a toilet. Room enough for one person and one suitcase. Or wicker hamper. Or cardboard box.

Morning is when we hear Mr. Whittier in the hallway outside our rooms, shouting good morning. A new day is when the lights come back on.

Until this morning.

Sister Vigilante shouts, "This is a law of *nature* you're violating . . ."

Here, with no windows or daylight, the Duke of Vandals says we could be trapped in an Italian Renaissance space station. We could be deep underwater in an ancient Mayan submarine. Or what the Duke calls a Louis XV coal mine or bomb shelter.

Here, in the middle of some city, inches away from the millions of people walking and working and eating hot dogs, we're cut off.

Here, anything that looks like a window, draped with velvet and tapestry, or fitted with stained glass, it's fake. It's a mirror. Or the dim sunlight behind the stained glass is lightbulbs small enough to make it always dusk in the tall arched windows of the Gothic smoking room.

We still hunt for ways out. We still stand at the locked doors and scream for help. Just not too hard or too loud. Not until our story would make a good movie. Until each of us becomes a character skinny enough for a movie star to play.

A story to save us from all the stories of our past.

In the hallway outside Mr. Whittier's dressing room, Sister Vigilante slams a fist on the door, shouting, "Hey, Whittier! You got a lot to answer for this morning," and you can see the Sister's breath puffing steam with every word.

The sun hasn't come up.

The air is cold and stinks.

The food is gone.

The rest of us, together, we tell Sister Vigilante: Shush. People *outside* might hear and come to our rescue.

A lock clicks, and the dressing-room door swings open to show Mrs. Clark in her stretched terry-cloth bathrobe. Her eyelids red and half open, she steps out, into the hallways, and shuts the door behind her back.

"Listen, lady," Sister Vigilante says. "You need to treat your hostages better."

The Duke of Vandals stands beside her. The same Duke of Vandals who went to the basement last night and sawed a bread knife through all the wires feeding into the furnace blower.

Mrs. Clark rubs her eyes with one hand.

From behind his camera, Agent Tattletale says, "Do you realize what time it is?"

Into the Earl of Slander's tape recorder, Comrade Snarky says, "Do you know there's no hot water?"

Comrade Snarky, the one who traced the copper pipes along the basement ceiling, following them back to the boiler for heating water, where she shut off the gas. She should know. She pried the handle off the gas valve and dropped the handle through a drain in the concrete floor.

"We're going on strike," skinny Saint Gut-Free says. "We're not writing any brilliant, amazing *Frankenstein* shit unless we get some heat."

This morning: No heat. No hot water. No food.

"Listen, lady," the Missing Link says. His beard almost scours Mrs. Clark in the forehead, he stands so close in the narrow hallway outside the dressing rooms. He slides the fingers of one hand under the lapel of her bathrobe. Leaning to press her chest flat with his, the Missing Link's hand makes a fist, and he bends his elbow to lift her off the floor by that fistful of flannel.

Mrs. Clark, her slipper feet kicking in air, her hands grabbing around the hairy wrist that holds her, her eyes bug out, driving her head backward until her hair hits the closed door. Her head hits the door with a boom.

Shaking her in his fist, the Missing Link says, "You tell old man Whittier he needs to get us some food. And get us some heat. Or get us out of here—now."

Us: the innocent victims of that oversleeping, evil, kidnapping madman.

In the blue velvet lobby, we'll have nothing for breakfast.

Bags holding anything made with liver, they were pincushioned with ten or fifteen holes. Everyone had to punch that ballot.

Out in the lobby, every silver Mylar pillow, it's gone flat. All of us with the same idea.

Even with the furnace not working, the air already cold, the food's gone bad.

"We need to wrap him," Mrs. Clark says. To wrap him and carry the body to the deepest subbasement with Lady Baglady.

"That smell," she says, "it's not the food."

We don't ask the details of how he died.

It's better Mr. Whittier died offstage. This way leaves us to script the worst: His eyes rolling to watch his belly swell bigger and bigger in the night, until he can't see his feet. Until some membrane or muscle splits, inside, and he feels the rush of warm food flood against his lungs. Against his liver and heart. Next, he'd feel the chills of shock. The gray hair on his chest would turn swampy with cold sweat. His face, running with sweat. His arms and legs shake with the cold. The first signs of coma.

No one will believe Mrs. Clark, now that she's the new villain. Our new evil supervixen oppressor.

No, we get to stage this scene. We'll have him screaming with delirium. Mr. Whittier will be bleached pale and hiding behind his spread fingers, saying the devil is after him. He'll be screaming for help.

He'll lapse into his coma. And die.

Saint Gut-Free with his complicated words about the peritoneum, the duodenum, the esophagus, he'll know the official term for what went wrong.

In our version, we'll kneel at Whittier's bedside, to pray for him. Poor, innocent us, starving and trapped here but still praying for our devil's eternal soul. Then a soft-focus dissolve and toss to commercial.

That's a scene from a hit movie. A scene with *Emmy nomination* written all over it.

"That's the nicest thing about dead people," says the Baroness

Frostbite, putting lipstick on top of her lipstick. "They can't correct you."

Still, a good story means no heat. Slow starvation means no breakfast. Dirty clothes. Maybe we're not as brainy-smart as Lord Byron and Mary Shelley, but we can tolerate some shit to make our story work.

Mr. Whittier, our old, dead monster.

Mrs. Clark, our new monster.

"Today," the Matchmaker says, "is going to be a long, long day."

And Sister Vigilante holds up one hand, her wristwatch glowing radium-green in the dim hallway. Sister Vigilante shakes the watch to make it flash, and she says, "Today is going to be as long as *I say it will be* . . ."

To Mrs. Clark, she says, "Now show me how to turn on the damned lights."

And the Missing Link drops her slipper feet to the floor.

Clark and the Sister, they feel their way off into the darkness, patting the damp hallway walls, moving toward the gray of the ghost light onstage.

Mr. Whittier, our new ghost.

Even Saint Gut-Free's stomach growls.

To shrink their stomachs, Miss America says some women will drink vinegar. That's how bad hunger pangs can hurt.

"Tell me a story," Mother Nature says. She's lit an apple-cinnamon candle with bite marks in the wax. "Anybody," she says. "Tell me a story to make me never want to eat, ever again . . ."

Director Denial hugs her cat, saying, "A story might ruin *your* appetite, but Cora is still hungry."

And Miss America says, "Tell that cat, in a couple days he'll qualify as food." Already, her pink spandex boobs look bigger.

And Saint Gut-Free says, "Please, can anybody please take my mind off my stomach." His voice different, smooth and dry, for the first time without food in his mouth.

The stink is thick as fog. That smell no one wants to breathe.

And, walking toward the stage, toward the circle around the ghost light, the Duke of Vandals says, "Before I ever sold a painting . . ." He looks back to make sure we'll follow, and the Duke says, "I used to be the opposite of an art thief . . ."

While, room by room, the sun starts to come up.

And in our heads, we all write this down: *The opposite of an art thief . . .*

For Hire

A Poem About the Duke of Vandals

"Nobody calls Michelangelo the Vatican's bitch," says the
    Duke of Vandals,
        just because he begged Pope Julius for work.

The Duke onstage, his scruffy jaw, scrub brush with pale
    stubble,
        it goes round and round, kneading and grinding
        a wad of nicotine gum.
His gray sweatshirt and canvas pants are flecked with dried
    raisins of red, dark-red,
        yellow, blue and green, brown, black and white paint.
His hair tumbles behind him, a tangle of brass wire,
    tarnished dark with oil
        and dusted with sticky flakes of dandruff.

Onstage, instead of a spotlight, a movie fragment:
    a slide show of portraits and allegories, still lifes and
        landscapes.
All of this ancient art, it uses his face, his chest, his
    stocking feet in sandals
        as a gallery wall.

The Duke of Vandals, he says, "No one calls Mozart a
    corporate whore"

because he worked for the Archbishop of Salzburg.
After that, then wrote *The Magic Flute,*
wrote *Eine kleine Nachtmusik,*
paid by trickle-down cash from Giuseppe Bridi and his
  big-money silk industry.
Nor do we call Leonardo da Vinci a sellout,
  a tool,
  because he slopped paint for gold from Pope Leo X and
    Lorenzo de' Medici.

"No," says the Duke, "We look at *The Last Supper* and the
  Mona Lisa
and never know who paid the bills to create them."
What matters, he says, is what the artist leaves behind, the
  artwork.
  Not how you paid the rent.

One judge called it "malicious mischief." Another judge called it "destruction of public property."

In New York City, after the guards caught him in the Museum of Modern Art, the judge reduced the charge to "littering" as a final insult. After the Getty Museum in Los Angeles, the judge called what Terry Fletcher did "graffiti."

At the Getty or the Frick or the National Gallery, Terry's crime was always the same. People just couldn't agree on what to call it.

None of these judges should be confused with the Honorable Lester G. Myers of the Los Angeles County District Court, art collector and downright nice guy. The art critic is not Tannity Brewster, writer and knower of all things cultural. And relax, no way is the gallery owner Dennis Bradshaw, famous for his Pell/Mell Gallery, where just by coincidence people get shot in the back. Every once in a while.

No, any resemblance between these characters and anyone living or dead is a complete accident.

What happens here is all made up. No one is anyone except Mr. Terry Fletcher.

Just keep telling yourself this is a story. None of this is for real.

The basic idea came from England, where art students go to the post office and take stacks of the cheap address labels available at no charge. Every post office has stacks and stacks of these labels, each one the size of your hand with the fingers straight but held tight together. A size easy to hide in your palm. The labels had a peel-off backing of waxed paper. Under that was a layer of glue designed to stick to anything, forever.

That was their real charm. Young artists—nobodies, really—they could sit in their studio and paint a perfect miniature. Or sketch a charcoal study after painting the sticker with a base coat of white.

Then, sticker in hand, they'd go out to hang their own little show. In pubs. In train carriages. The back seats of taxicabs. And their work would "hang" there for longer than you'd guess.

The post office made the stickers with such cheap paper that you could never peel them away. The paper tore in specks and flakes at the edge, but even there, the glue would stay. The raw glue, looking lumpy and yellow as snot, it collected dust and smoke until it was a black smear so much worse than the little art-school painting it had been. Folks found that any artwork was better than the ugly glue it left behind.

So—people let the art hang. In elevators and toilet stalls. In church confessionals and department-store fitting rooms. Most of these, places where a few paintings might help. Most of the painters just happy to have their work seen. Forever.

Still—leave it to an American to take something too far.

For Terry Fletcher, the big idea came while he stood in line to see the *Mona Lisa.* The closer he got, the painting never got any bigger. He had art textbooks that were bigger. Here was the most famous painting in the world, and it was smaller than a sofa cushion.

Anywhere else, it would be so easy to slip inside your coat and cross your arms over. To steal.

As the line crept closer to the painting, it didn't look like such a miracle, either. Here was the masterwork of Leonardo da Vinci, and it didn't look worth wasting a whole day on his hind legs in Paris, France.

It was the same letdown that Terry Fletcher felt after seeing that ancient petroglyph of the dancing flute player, Kokopelli, after seeing it painted on neckties and glazed on dog-food bowls. Hooked into bathmats and toilet-seat covers. When, at last, he'd gone to New Mexico and seen the original, hammered and painted into a cliff face—his first thought was: *How trite . . .*

All the dinky old masterpiece paintings with their puffed-up reputations, the British post-office stickers, what it meant was, he could do better. He could paint better and sneak his work into museums, framed and wrapped inside his coat. Nothing too big, but he could put double-sided mounting tape on the back, and when the right moment came . . . just stick the painting on the wall. Right there for the world to see, between the Rubens and the Picasso . . . an original work by Terry Fletcher.

In the Tate Gallery, crowding the Turner painting of *Snow Storm: Hannibal and His Army Crossing the Alps,* there would be Terry's mom, smiling. She'd be drying her hands in a red-and-white-striped dishtowel. In the Prado Museum, butted up against the Velázquez portrait of the Infanta would be his girlfriend, Rudy. Or his dog, Boner.

Sure, it was his work, his signature, but this would be about heaping glory on the people he loved.

It's too bad that most of his work would end up hung in a museum's bathroom. It was the only space without a guard or security camera. During slow hours, he could even step into the ladies' room and hang a picture.

Not every tourist went into every gallery of a museum, but they all went to the bathroom.

It almost didn't seem to matter, how the picture looked. What made it art, a masterpiece, that seemed to depend on where it hung . . . how rich the frame looked . . . and what other work it hung beside. If he did his research, found the right antique frame, and hung his picture in the center of a crowded wall, it would be there for days, maybe weeks, before he got a call from the museum staff. Or the police.

Then came the charges: malicious mischief, destruction of public property, graffiti.

"Litter," a judge called his art, and slapped Terry with a fine and a night in jail.

In the cell the police give Terry Fletcher, everybody before him had been an artist, scratching away the green paint to make pictures on each wall. Then to sign their name. Petroglyphs more original than Kokopelli. The *Mona Lisa*. By names that weren't Pablo Picasso. It was that night, looking at those pictures, Terry almost gave up.

Almost.

The next day, a man came to his studio, where black flies circled a pile of fruit Terry had been trying to paint when he was arrested. This was the lead art critic for a chain of newspapers. He was a friend of the judge from the night before, and this critic said, yes, he found the whole story funny as hell. A perfect story for his syndicated column about the art world. Even with the sweet smell of the rotting fruit, the flies buzzing, this man said he'd love to see Terry's work.

"Very good," the critic said, looking at canvas after canvas, each of them small enough to fit inside a trench coat. "Very, very good."

The black flies kept circling, landing on the spotted apples and black bananas, then buzzing around the two men.

The critic wore eyeglasses with each lens as thick as the porthole on a ship. Talking to him, you'd want to shout, the way you'd yell to someone behind an upstairs window, inside a big house and not coming to answer the locked door.

Still, he was absolutely, positively, undeniably NOT Tannity Brewster.

Most of the best pictures, Terry told him, they were still in lockup as evidence in future trials.

But the critic said that didn't matter. The day after, he brought a gallery owner and a collector, both of them famous from their opinions being in national magazines all the time. The group of them look at his work. They keep repeating the name of an artist famous for his messy prints of dead celebrities and signing his work huge with a can of red spray paint.

Again, this gallery owner was not Dennis Bradshaw. And when she spoke, this art collector had a Texan accent. Her red-blond hair was the exact creepy orange-peel color as her tanned shoulders and neck, but she was not Bret Hillary Beales.

She's a totally made-up character. But as she looked at his painting, she kept using the word "bankable."

She even had a little tattoo that said "Sugar" in lacy script on her ankle, just above her sandaled foot, but she was in no way, absolutely not, nope, NOT Miss Bret Hillary Beales.

No, this fake, made-up critic, art collector, and gallery owner, at last, they tell our artist: Here's the deal. They have millions invested in the work of this messy printmaker, but his current output was flooding the art market. He was making money with volume, but driving down the value of his earlier work. The value of their investment.

The deal was, if Terry Fletcher will kill the printmaker—then the art critic, the gallery owner, and the collector will make Terry famous. They'll turn him into a good investment. His work will sell for a fortune. The pictures of his mother and girlfriend, his dog and hamster, they'll get the buildup they need to become as classic as the *Mona Lisa*. As the Kokopelli, that Hopi god of mischief.

In his studio, the black flies still circled the same heap of soft apples and limp bananas.

And if it helps, they tell Fletcher, the printmaker only got famous because he murdered a lazy sculptor, who in turn had murdered a pushy painter, who had murdered a sell-out collage maker.

All those people are still dead while their work sits in a museum, like a bank account every minute snowballing in value. And not even pretty value, as the colors go brown as a van Gogh sunflower, the paint and varnish cracking and turning yellow. Always so much smaller than people would expect after waiting all day in line.

The art market had worked this way for centuries, the critic said. If Terry chose not to take this, his first real "commission," it was no problem. But he still had a long future of unsettled court cases, charges still outstanding against him. These art people could wipe out all that with a phone call. Or they could make it worse. Even if he did nothing, Terry Fletcher could still go to jail for a long, long time. That scratched green cell.

After that, who would believe the word of a jailbird?

So Terry Fletcher, he says: Yes.

It helps that he's never met the printmaker. The gallery owner gives him a gun and tells him to wear a nylon stocking over his head. The gun is only the size of your hand with the fingers straight but held tight together. A tool easy to hide in your palm, it's only the size of a package label, but does a job just as forever. The sloppy printmaker will be in the gallery until it closes. After that, he'll walk home.

That night, Terry Fletcher shoots him, three times—pop, pop, pop—in the back. A job faster than hanging his dog, Boner, in the Guggenheim Museum.

A month later, Fletcher has his first real show in a gallery.

This is NOT the Pell/Mell Gallery. It has the same black and pink checkerboard tiles on the floor, and a matching striped canopy over the door, and oodles of smart people go there to invest in art, but this is some other, let's-pretend kind of gallery. Filled with *fake* smart people.

It's after that Terry's career gets complicated. You might say he did his job too well, because the art critic sends him off to kill a conceptual artist in Germany. A performance artist in San Francisco. A kinetic sculptor in Barcelona. Everyone thinks Andy Warhol died from gallbladder surgery. You think Jean-Michel Basquiat died of a heroin overdose. That Keith Haring and Robert Mapplethorpe died from AIDS.

The truth is . . . you think what people want you to think.

This whole time, the critic says if Fletcher backs down the art world will frame him for the first murder. Or worse.

Terry asks, What's worse?

And they don't say.

Leave it to an American to take something too far.

Between killing every sell-out artist, every lazy, sloppy artist, Terry Fletcher has no time to do his own art well. Even the pictures of Rudy and his mom, they look rushed, messy, as if he couldn't care less. More and more, he's knocking out different versions of the dancing, flute-playing Kokopelli. He's blowing up photos of the *Mona Lisa* to wall-sized, then hand-coloring the photos in colors popular for room decoration that year. Still, if his signature is at the bottom, people buy it. Museums buy it.

And after this year of being famous . . .

After that year, he's in an art gallery, talking to the owner. The same man who lent him a gun the year before. NOT Dennis Bradshaw. The street outside is dark. His wristwatch says eleven o'clock. The galley owner says he needs to close up and get home himself. Whatever happened to that gun, Terry doesn't know.

The owner opens the front door, and outside is the dark sidewalk. The black-and-pink-striped canopy. The long walk home.

Outside, the lampposts are glued with the little paintings of people you'll never know. The street is pasted with their unsigned artwork. It's this long walk into the dark that will happen, if not tonight, then some night. With this next step, every night will be a walk into the world where every artist wants a chance to be known.

We're in the Mayan foyer, the walls covered with plaster, pitted to look like lava rock. The fake lava rock is carved to look like warriors wearing loincloths and feather head-dresses. The warriors wearing capes of spotted fur to look like leopards. The whole room telling the story it wants you to accept as the truth.

Carved plaster parrots trail tailfeathers in rainbows of orange and red.

From fake cracks and crumbling places in the plaster stone, made to look ancient, high above our heads sprout chains of fat purple orchids made of paper.

"Mr. Whittier was right," says Mrs. Clark, looking around. "We do create the drama that fills up our life."

Only dust dulls the orange feathers and purple flowers. Fake-leopard-spot fur covers the black wood sofas. The sofas and leering warrior faces and fake lava rock, they're all cob-webbed together with strands of gray.

Mrs. Clark says, Sometimes it seems that we spend the first half of our lives looking for some disaster. And she looks down at her straight-out chest—a look made almost impossible by her enhanced lips. As young people, she says, we want something to slow us down and keep us trapped in one place long enough to look below the surface of the world. That disaster is a car crash or a war. To make us sit still. It can be getting cancer or getting pregnant. The important part is how it seems to catch us by surprise. That disaster stops us from living the life we'd planned as children—a life of constant dashing around.

"We still create the drama and pain we need," says Mrs. Clark. "But this first disaster is a vaccination, an inoculation."

Your whole life, she says, you're searching for disaster—you're auditioning disasters—so you'll be well rehearsed when the ultimate disaster finally arrives.

"For when you die," Mrs. Clark says.

Here in the Mayan foyer, the black wood sofas and chairs are carved to look like the altars on top of pyramids where human sacrifices would go to get their hearts torn out.

The carpet is some lunar calendar, circles inside circles, patterned black-on-orange and sticky with spilled sodas. At our feet spreads a moldy stain branching arms and legs.

Sitting down on the fake-fur cushions, you can still smell popcorn.

That's her theory. The Mrs. Clark extension to the theory of Mr. Whittier.

We have pain and hate and love and joy and war in the world because we want them. And we want all that drama to prepare us for the test of facing death, someday.

Mother Nature, sitting with both arms out straight in front of her, sleepwalker-style, she spreads her fingers and looks at the smudged dark henna designs painted on her skin. With the fingers of one hand, she feels around the base of each finger on her other hand. Feeling the bone, for how thick, Mother Nature says, "Do you think Lady Baglady was ready?" She says, "Do you think Mr. Whittier was?"

And Mrs. Clark shrugs. She says, "Does that matter?"

Sitting on the fake fur next to Mother Nature, Director Denial has twisted a nylon stocking around the wrist of her left hand. With her right hand, she twists the stocking tighter as the fingers of her left hand turn white. So white, even the pale cat hair looks dark against her blue-white skin. Until those white feeling-nothing fingers wilt and hang, limp from her wrist.

In his lap, Saint Gut-Free works the thumb of his right hand, stroking the thumb up and down with the fist of his left hand. Feeling the bumps and knuckles of his thumb so he'll never forget. For after it's gone.

We all sit here, watching each other. Waiting for the next plot point or bit of dialogue to catch and squirrel away for our marketable version of the truth.

Agent Tattletale moves his camera spotlight from person to person. The Earl of Slander's little-mesh microphone peeks out of his shirt pocket.

This moment foreshadowing the real horror of the next. This moment's already taping over the death of Mr. Whittier, which taped over the death of Lady Baglady, which taped over Miss America holding a knife to Mr. Whittier's throat.

To Mrs. Clark, Mother Nature says, "So why did you love him?"

"I didn't come here because I loved *him*," Mrs. Clark says. To Agent Tattletale, she says, "Do *not* point that camera at me. I look terrible on video . . ." Still, in the heat of the camera's spotlight, Mrs. Clark smiles with her teeth clenched, a clown's smile with her water-balloon lips, saying, "I came here because I saw an advertisement . . ."

And she trusted herself to this man she didn't know? She followed him and helped him? Even knowing he'd trap her behind a locked door? It doesn't make sense.

The Reverend Godless, with his stitched-meat face, his eyebrows shaved off, his fingernails so long he can't make a fist, he says, "But you cried . . ."

"Every apostle or disciple," Mrs. Clark says, "as much as they're running to follow their savior—they're running just as hard to escape something else."

With the warriors carved to watch us, the paper orchids dyed and folded to look natural, Mrs. Clark says how she used to have a daughter. A husband.

"Cassie was fifteen," she says.

She says, "Her name was Cassandra."

Mrs. Clark says, sometimes when the police find a shallow grave or the dumped body of a murder victim, the detectives will hide a microphone there. It's standard procedure.

She nods at the Earl of Slander, at the tape recorder in his pocket.

The police will hide nearby, and listen for days or weeks. Because almost always the killer will come back and talk to the victim. Pretty much always. We need to tell the story of our life to someone, and the killer can only discuss his crime with a person who won't punish him. His prey.

Even a killer needs to talk, to tell his life story, so bad he'll come and sit beside a grave or a rotting body and just blab, blab, blab at it for hours. Until he makes sense. Until the killer can convince himself with the story of his new reality. The reality that—he was right.

That's why the police wait.

Still smiling, she says, "And that's why I'm here." Mrs. Clark says, "Like the rest of you, I only wanted some way to tell my story . . ."

Still in the warm circle of Agent Tattletale's spotlight, Mrs. Clark says, "Please." She cups both hands to cover her face, and through her fingers tight together, she says, "It was a video camera that wrecked my marriage . . ."

Looking Back

A Poem About Mrs. Clark

"You're training a new employee," says Mrs. Clark, "to take
   over your boring old job."
   When you raise a child.

Mrs. Clark onstage, her arms wrap across the front of her,
   each hand cupping the other elbow
   to cradle breasts chosen by a much braver woman.
   With a much stronger back.
   This chest, now a reminder of every mistake she hoped
      would save her.
Her eyelids are tattooed the orange that looked so chic
   two decades ago,
   her lips siliconed to the size and shape of suction cups,
   then tattooed a forgotten shade of frosty peach.
Her Mrs. Clark hairdo and clothes, frozen from a time
   when she lost her nerve, and stopped taking any new
      risk.

Onstage, instead of a spotlight, a movie fragment:
   Home movies show a little girl wearing a party hat of
      paper, strapped
   under her chin with a string of elastic,
   blowing out five birthday candles.

"Before you get fired," Mrs. Clark says, "you train this new
   person by telling her . . ."
   Don't touch. Hot!
   Feet off the sofa!
   And—never buy *anything* with a nylon zipper.
With every lecture, you're forced to look again at every
   choice you've made
   over the lesson-by-lesson chain of your entire life.
And after all these years, you see how little you have to
   work with,
   how limited your life and education have been.
   How scant was your courage and curiosity.
   Not to mention your expectations.

Mrs. Clark onstage, she sighs, her breasts rising big as
   soufflés
   or loaves of bread, then falling, settling, resting.
She says how maybe the best advice is what you can't tell
   her at all:
   To preserve yourself as the center of the world,
   to stay your own best authority on everything,
   your own expert on all topics,
   infallible,
   omniscient.
   Always, every time of the month, forever:
   Use birth control.

Post-Production
A Story by Mrs. Clark

Tess and Nelson Clark, the first couple of days, they lived as if nothing had happened. This meant getting into work clothes and unlocking the door of their car. They'd drive to the office. That night, they'd sit not-talking at the kitchen table. They'd eat some food.

So what.

The rental place would call about needing their camera equipment back.

Nelson was home, with Tess, or he wasn't.

By the third day, she only got out of bed to use the toilet. She didn't bother to call in sick to work. Her heart would just beat and beat, no matter what she tried. That's not to say she tried anything.

It wasn't worth the effort to start drinking or start measuring the car for a hose long enough to connect the exhaust pipe with the driver's-side window. No way was it worth the effort to go see a doctor at her HMO and lie hard enough he'd prescribe a good sleeping pill. Anything else she might do, like pushing a razor blade into her wrist, taking that kind of action just looked like another stupid plan to solve all her problems one more time.

The lights and camera were still crowded around the Clarks' bed.

Committing suicide just seemed to be another aggressive plan to fix her life. If she turned on the movie lights and camera, they could get the death on tape. A snuff movie in two parts. A miniseries. Another Big Project. Killing herself would just be: Tess Clark, getting the job overdone. Another beginning, middle, and end.

Going to work just looked crazy. Eating another meal, ever, made about as much sense as planting tulip bulbs in the shadow of a falling atom bomb.

This is all a flashback now, but it was Nelson who'd looked at their savings account. It was him who said the only way they could afford to have a baby is by making an adult video.

"One day," Mrs. Clark says, "this will happen to you, and in just that one second your life will feel about one hundred years too long . . ."

On their fifth day of lying in bed, they'd swear they'd been alive forever. Lying in bed day after day is probably how it feels to be a vampire. Imagine being alive for thousands of years and you keep making the same stupid mistake. Just for thousands of years you keep going to bars and clubs and you think you're having a great time. You imagine you're the center of attention. You have a husband you think is handsome. You think you're both such entirely hot shit.

The Clarks thought a lot of couples got rich by making adult movies. The home-video industry is only popular because video porn created the demand. Couples all except them were making extra money in their spare time. Other married couples weren't just wasting their sex, unwatched, unappreciated by strangers. First, they'd rent a camera and the editing deck. They'd find a distributor for the movie. Since they were married, Nelson said, it wouldn't even be a sin.

Now, it doesn't make any sense to get out of bed and erase the videotape. That would be like breaking a mirror for showing you the truth. Like killing the bearer of bad news.

"Just laying in bed day after day," Mrs. Clark says, "you realize it's not wooden stakes that kill vampires." It's all the emotional baggage and letdowns they have to carry around for century after century.

You want to think you're getting funnier and smarter all the time. As long as you're making an effort, you're headed for that Big Win. That's how you'd feel as a vampire for maybe the first couple hundred years. After that, all you have is the same failed relationship multiplied by two hundred.

So what.

The trouble with eternal youth is, you do tend to procrastinate. So the Clarks taught themselves how to make a video. This included Nelson shaving away the hair around the base of his dick, to make it look bigger. Tess got breast implants as big as her spine would support. During just an afternoon nap, she got the kind of stand-alone bustline you only see in adult movies. Her lips she got threaded inside with tubes of puffed-foam fillers, giving her a blow-job pout for the rest of her life. Both the Clarks, they signed up for tanning sessions, twenty minutes, twice a day. They read out loud to each other, how editing a video is done by the exact time code given to each moment of tape.

Every moment is coded with the hour, the minutes, the second, and the exact frame number. The code 01:34:14:25 would mean the first hour, thirty-fourth minute, fourteenth second, and twenty-fifth frame of a video tape. Editing even an adult video, you have to create a false reality. You have to imply a relationship by putting events next to each other. This path of images, it has to lead the viewer from one sex act to the next. You have to fake a continuity. The illusion has to make sense.

They got most of the oral coverage shot before 10:22:19:02.

Then they did a lot of genital footage until 25:44:15:17.

They shot some perianal and then perivaginal footage until 31:25:21:09.

And they finished off with the anal stuff at 46:34:07:15.

Since these movies always end the same way, the story about getting there, the journey to the big orgasm, is what's most important. The orgasm, just a formality. Stock footage.

Something else to keep in mind is, the average shot in a video is eight to fifteen seconds long. Tess and Nelson would have to work together for about twenty seconds at a time. After that long, they'd get up and hit the PAUSE button. They'd move the camera to a new angle and relight the shot. They'd film for another twenty seconds. Their marriage was still where sex was fun, but after that first day of filming, the only thing that kept them going was the money they'd make. The money and the baby.

"We were both," Mrs. Clark says, "full of that energy that makes dogs dance just before they get fed."

Tess and Nelson, they'd never looked better than they did going into that movie. That was the worst part. For most of a week, they kept going back to the bedroom. Even linked together just twenty seconds at a time, they must've had sex for a total of some forty-eight hours. The hot lights sucking the sweat out of their tanned skin.

To keep excited, they set up a television just outside the shot and ran adult movies they could watch while being taped. These became their cue cards or TelePrompTer they could mimic. The same as the Clarks, the people in each movie seemed to be looking off camera at a movie of their own. This chain of voyeurism, the Clarks watching someone watch someone watch someone, it felt good. The video that Tess and Nelson watched, it was at least five years old. The men had long sideburns and the women wore dangle earrings and blue-sparkle eye shadow. How old the movie *those* people were watching, it was anybody's guess, but it felt better, knowing that all of them were daisy-chained throughout history.

Those video people, they looked the Clarks' age in front of their camera, but now they'd be sliding into middle age. They looked young, with muscles in their legs and arms, long and standing out, but they moved fast, as if what they watched off camera was a clock.

To help each other smile, Tess and Nelson took turns saying what they'd do with their money.

They'd buy a house.

They'd travel to Mexico.

They'd make real movies. Feature films. They'd start their own independent production company, and never work for other people, ever again.

They'd name their child Cassie, if it was a girl.

Baxter, if it was a boy. Instead of some old birthing video, someday they'd show their child his conception. Baxter would see just how hot and with-it his old folks had been. It seemed so progressive.

And after that, they'd never, ever have to have sex, ever again.

The worse the job got, the more they expected to earn. The more it hurt to touch their chapped skin, or to lie back against the cold, sweat-soaked mattress, the brighter they had to make their future. Their faces ached from smiling. Their skin burned red from being caressed. As the marathon went on, their reward had to grow more and more impossible.

Then, quick as a doctor saying your disease is fatal, quick as a judge handing down a death sentence, they were done.

The Clarks had done everything they could imagine to each other. All they had left to do was edit the tape.

That was supposed to be the fun part.

The difference between how you look and how you see yourself is enough to kill most people.

And maybe the reason vampires don't die is because they can never see themselves in photographs or mirrors.

"No amount of editing," Mrs. Clark says, "was going to save us."

No amount of aerobic exercise or plastic surgery would ever make them look the way they'd imagined they looked before they watched that tape. All they saw were two almost hairless animals, hairless and dark pink and proportioned all wrong, the way mongrel crossbreed dogs look, with short legs and long necks and thick torsos with no definite waist. They were grinning big bear-trap smiles at each other while their eyes darted at the camera to make sure someone was still paying attention. They sucked their stomachs flat.

Worse than their everyday ugliness was the proof they were getting old. Their lips suction-cupped each other, and their loose skin looked baggy and wadded around every orifice. Their bodies rocked together as if they were some terrible old machine forced to work at top speed until it would break apart.

Nelson's erection looked twisted and dirt-dark, something from a bin in the back of a Chinese grocery. Tess's lips and her chest looked sideshow-too-big, the scars still burning-red.

So what.

Tess Clark cried as they watched themselves from every angle, in every position. Every part of them, from the soles of their feet to their scalps, the secrets they kept between their legs, the hair they hid under their arms, they watched it all, until the tape ran out and left them sitting in the dark.

That was all they were.

After that, even crying seemed like another doomed way to get through the moment. Any emotion seemed a silly and useless way to deny what they'd both seen. Any action meant starting over with another doomed, stupid dream.

They could make another movie. Start their production company. Only now, whatever they did, they would know it wasn't real. They'd never be the way they imagined they were.

And no matter how hard they tried, no matter how much money they made, they were both going to die.

In two days with a rented camera, they'd used up their lifetime allowance of interest in each other. Neither of them held any mystery.

The lights and camera, ABC Rentals kept calling to get them back. The rental company kept charging their credit card until the Clarks owed more money than they'd ever put in savings.

The day Nelson Clark rolled out of bed, to pack the camera and lights, to take them back, that day he didn't come home.

That next week, Mrs. Clark's period didn't come, either.

"These two huge breasts," Mrs. Clark says, "they were supposed to be a tax deduction." Just the appearance of something big and mothery. And now a baby was on the way.

Nelson Clark never did come home. In a city this size, every year, hundreds of husbands walk away. Kids leave home. Wives escape. People disappear.

So what.

Tess Clark burned the videotape, but it plays every time her eyes close. Even now, almost sixteen years later. Even now that her child is born and grown and dead.

That baby, she named: Cassandra.

1.
2.
3.
4.
5.
6.
7.
8.
9.
10.
11.
12.
13.
14.
15.
16.
17.
18.
19.
20.
21.
22.
23.
24.

It's in the Italian Renaissance lounge that Mrs. Clark finds Director Denial slumped over a heavy, dark wood table. The table dripping with blood from every edge. The sticky blood already flocked with a layer of cat hair. Director Denial with a rope of twisted nylon stocking tied around her wrist. A meat cleaver is sunk in the table. Above the nylon stocking, the Director's hand lies pale in a puddle of dark red.

On the floor under the table, Cora Reynolds chews on a severed index finger.

"My dear," Mrs. Clark says, looking at the crusted, bloody stump as the Director wraps a scrap of yellow silk around and around to cover it. The blood soaking through the yellow. Mrs. Clark steps forward to help, to wrap the silk tighter, and she says, "Who did this to you?"

Director Denial twists her nylon tourniquet tighter, saying, "You did."

At this point, everyone is looking for an edge.

We all want some way to pad our role. To put our character into the spotlight after we're rescued.

Plus, it's a way to feed the cat.

Whoever can show the worst suffering, the most scars, they'll play the lead in the public mind. If the outside world broke in to rescue us right now, Director Denial would be our biggest victim—flashing the stubs of her severed toes and fingers, flaunting them for sympathy. Making herself the lead character. The A Block on any television talk show.

Making us her supporting cast.

Not to be outdone, skinny Saint Gut-Free borrowed a cleaver from Chef Assassin and lopped the thumb off his right hand. A radical thumb-ectomy.

Not to be upstaged, Reverend Godless asked to borrow the cleaver and hacked the smallest toe off each his feet. "To be famous," he said, "and after that, wear really *narrow* high heels."

The green wallpaper and silk drapes of the Italian Renaissance lounge, the green is spattered and sprayed with blood that looks black under electric light. The floor feels so sticky, the carpet, that every step tries to pull off your shoes.

The Missing Link says losing a finger does take your mind off being hungry. The Missing Link, he's wearing a bishop's vestments, sprouting black chest hair at the collar, all white brocade embroidered with gold thread along the edges. He's wearing a powdered wig that makes his square head and shaggy beard look twice as big.

With his ponytail, the Duke of Vandals wears a buckskin shirt and pants with long fringe flapping from every seam. Chewing his nicotine gum. Mother Nature limps around, hobbling in high-heeled sandals that show off her own severed toes, her choker of brass bells jingling with every limp. Nibbling a clove-nutmeg aromatherapy candle.

We're all keeping warm in frilly Lord Byron poet blouses. Or Mary Shelley long skirts filled with petticoats. Dracula capes lined with red satin. Heavy Frankenstein boots.

About this time, Saint Gut-Free asks if he can be the one to fall in love.

Every epic needs a romantic subplot, he says, holding his pants up with one hand. To cover all the marketing bases, we need two young people deep and desperately in love—but kept apart by a cruel villain.

Saint Gut-Free and Miss Sneezy, talking in the Italian Renaissance lounge with its embroidered chairs and banners of green silk between tall windows of mirror, here was the place to hatch a romance.

"I was thinking I'd be in love with Comrade Snarky," Saint Gut-Free says.

Next to them, the meat cleaver's stuck in the long wood table: Mr. Whittier's ghost waiting for its next victim.

Wiping her nose sideways, Miss Sneezy asks, has the Saint talked to Comrade Snarky about her being in love, too? After we're rescued, during the marketing-and-media-promotion part, any two people who fought to be together, they'll have to at least fake being in love. How they act inside here, it won't matter, but once those doors come open they'll need to be kissing and hugging every time a camera turns their way. People will expect a wedding. Maybe even children.

Batting her bloodshot eyes, Miss Sneezy says, "Pick a girl you can fake loving for the rest of your life . . ."

Saint Gut-Free says, "How about me and the Countess Foresight?"

The way Saint Gut-Free sees it, being fake married to him has got to beat hacking off fingers. Any woman here should jump at the chance.

And, smiling, her face close-up into his, Miss Sneezy says, "How about you and *me*?"

And Saint Gut-Free says, "How about Baroness Frostbite?"

"She has no lips," Miss Sneezy says. "I mean, she *really* has no lips."

How about Miss America?

"She'll already get famous for being pregnant," Miss Sneezy says. She says, "I'm not pregnant, *and I have lips* . . ."

Director Denial has already hacked off fingers. So has Sister Vigilante—plus some toes, using the same paring knife that Lady Baglady borrowed from Chef Assassin to slice off her ear. Their plan, after we're rescued, is to tell the world how Mr. Whittier tortured them by hacking off a little bit for every day they didn't produce a great work of art. Or—Mrs. Clark did the cutting while Mr. Whittier held the victim down, screaming, on the long, dark wood table in the Italian Renaissance lounge.

The table is already scarred from practice chops and nervous chops and successful chops with Chef Assassin's meat cleaver.

"Okay," Saint Gut-Free says. "How about Mother Nature?"

It's clear, he just wants his feet rubbed, some new way to get his rocks off. A foot job. Another hands-free method beyond the invisible carrot, the candle wax, and the swimming pool. Not so much a romantic subplot as sexual need.

Better, Miss Sneezy says. She says, "You know what Mother did with her nose, don't you?"

Poor Miss Sneezy, she still coughed and coughed from the mold spores we had to breathe, but her suffering looked like nothing compared to Mother Nature, who borrowed a filleting knife to slit each of her nostrils, straight up to the bridge of her nose—her brass bells jingling and scabs spraying everywhere each time she had to laugh.

Still, we needed the romantic subplot. *Any* romantic storyline.

Really, it was Mr. Whittier who slit Mother Nature's nose.

"But he's dead," Mrs. Clark says.

Mr. Whittier did it before he died, the Missing Link says. With everyone hacking off fingers and toes and ears, no way is anyone going to walk out of here without a good scar. A stump they can flash in close-up on television. Mr. Whittier did it to keep Saint Gut-Free and Mother Nature apart. To punish them for falling in love.

In our version of what happened, every toe or finger, it was eaten by the villains whom no one will believe.

The Matchmaker has been asking around, trying to find someone willing to lop off his penis. Because it's perfect—how that torture fits with some old family joke.

One slice, he says, and all your problems are solved. Just a severed penis in the dirt.

"Besides, I'm not using it for anything," the Matchmaker says, and smiles. Wink, wink.

So far, no one's volunteered to swing the cleaver. Not because it's too disgusting, too awful, but because it would so put him in the driver's seat. A chopped-off penis is something none of us could top.

Still, if he did it—and bled to death—it would mean the royalties would only get split fifteen ways. Fourteen ways if Miss Sneezy would hurry up and suffocate on the mold. Thirteen ways if Miss America is considerate enough to die in childbirth.

Everyone feeding their bits and pieces to the cat, Cora Reynolds is getting huge.

"If you do chop your dick," says Director Denial, "do not feed it to my cat."

She says, "That's not something I want to know every time Cora licks my face . . ."

It was looking for bandages that we found the costumes. Backstage, we were hunting for clean cloth to tear into bandage strips, and here were gowns and coats left over from vaudeville and light opera. Folded away with tissue paper and mothballs, in trunks and garment bags, here were hoop skirts and togas. Kimonos and kilts. Boots and wigs and armor.

Thanks to Mrs. Clark cutting the plug off the washing machine, any clothes we'd brought were stinking with dirt and sweat. Thanks to Mr. Whittier wrecking the furnace, the building was colder every day. So we started to wear these tunics and sarongs and waistcoats. These velvets and satin brocades. Pilgrim hats with silver buckles. Elbow-long gloves of white leather.

"These rooms . . . ," the Countess Foresight says, stumbling in her turban, hacking off her toes, but not the security tracking bracelet around her wrist. "These clothes . . . all this blood . . . ," she says, "I feel as if I'm in a very creepy Grimm's fairy tale."

We wore fur stoles made of small animals biting each other in the ass. Minks and ferrets and weasels. Dead, but their teeth still sunk in, deep.

Here, in the Italian Renaissance lounge, down on one knee, holding her bloody hand and looking up her slit nose, Saint Gut-Free said to Mother Nature, "Can you pretend to love me for the rest of your life?"

And, kneeling there, he slipped the sticky-red three-carat diamond he'd hacked off Lady Baglady's hand, Saint Gut-Free slipped sparkling-dead Lord Baglady onto Mother Nature's red-hennaed finger.

And his stomach growled.

And she laughed, blood and scabs—everywhere.

By now even these silk shirts and linens are stiff and matted with blood. The fingers of gloves hanging empty. Shoes and boots stuffed with balled-up socks to replace missing toes.

The fur stoles, the weasels and ferrets, soft as the fur on the cat.

"Keep feeding that cat," says Miss America. "And he can be our Thanksgiving turkey."

"Don't even joke," Director Denial tells her, scratching the cat's fat stomach. "Little Cora is *my baby . . .*"

With the roots of her bleached hair grown out, brown, a kind of measuring stick to show how long we've been trapped, Miss America watches the cat pick the meat off another finger. Looking up, at Director Denial, she says, "If it was you who took my exercise wheel, I want it back." Holding her hands a little ways apart, Miss America says, "It's pink plastic, about *so* big. You remember."

Brushing the layer of cat hair from her sticky, yellow silk bandages, the Director says, "What about your unborn child?"

And, stroking her own little belly, Miss America says, "The Matchmaker should feed *me* his penis." She says, "I'm the one *not eating* for two . . ."

Job Description

A Poem About Director Denial

"A police officer," says Director Denial, "has to protect a
   Satan worshiper."
   You don't get to pick and choose.

Director Denial onstage, the tweed sleeves of her blazer
   disappear around her back,
      where her hands are holding each other
      hidden, the way you'd stand for a firing squad.
Her hair, salted with gray and cut short to look bristling
   on purpose.

Onstage, instead of a spotlight, a movie fragment:
   A security video, grainy black and white,
      of suspects under arrest, standing in lineups for
         identification by a witness.
      Suspects wrestling with handcuffs, or their coats pulled
         up in back
      to hood their faces as they go into court.

Onstage stands Director Denial, with the bulge of her
   shoulder holster
      swelling one lapel of her blazer.

Her tweed skirt hemmed above cuffed white running shoes,
the shoelaces double knotted.

She says, "An officer of the law has to die for pretty much
everybody."
You die for people who kick dogs.
Drug addicts. Communists. Lutherans.
You die to protect and serve rich kids with trust funds.
Child molesters. Pornographers. Prostitutes.
If that next bullet has your name on it.

Her face crowded with victims and criminals, black and
white,
Director Denial says, "You might die for welfare
queens . . ."
Or drag queens.
For folks who hate you, or folks who'd call you a hero.
You don't get to discriminate when your number comes up.

"And if you're really stupid," Director Denial says, "you die
still hoping."
You made the world just a little bit better place.
And maybe, just maybe, your death
will be the last.

Please understand.

Nobody here is defending what Cora did.

Maybe two years ago was the only time anything like this had ever happened. Spring and fall, the county staff has to take a refresher in mouth-to-mouth. Cardiopulmonary resuscitation. Each group meets in the health room to practice heart massage on the dummy. They partner up, the agency director pumping the chest, the other person kneeling down, pinching the nose shut, and blowing air into the mouth. The dummy is a Breather Betty model, just a torso with a head. No arms or legs. Rubbery blue lips. Eyes molded open, staring. Green eyes. Still, whoever makes these dummies, they glued long eyelashes on her. They glued on a glamour-girl wig, the red hair so smooth you don't feel your fingers combing it until someone else says, "Easy there . . ."

While she knelt next to the dummy and spread her red-painted fingernails against its chest, the agency director, Director Sedlak, said how all Breather Betty dolls are molded from the death mask of a single French girl.

"True story," she told the group of them.

This face on the floor, it's the face of a suicide pulled from the water over a century ago. Those same blue lips.

The same staring dull eyes. All Breather Betty dolls are molded from the face of this same young woman who threw herself into the Seine River.

If the girl died because of love or loneliness, we'll never find out. But police detectives used plaster to cast a mask of her dead face, to help find her name, and decades later a toymaker owned that death mask and used it to cast the face of the first Breather Betty.

Despite the risk that somebody in a school or factory or Army unit might someday lean down and recognize the long-dead body of their sister, mother, daughter, wife, this exact dead girl is kissed by millions of people. For generations, millions of strangers have pressed their mouths over hers, those lips her exact drowned lips. For the rest of history, all over the world, people will be trying to save this same dead woman.

This woman who just wanted to die.

The girl who turned herself into an object.

Nobody said that last part. But nobody had to say it.

So, last year, Cora Reynolds was in a group that goes to the health room and takes the Breather Betty out of her blue plastic suitcase. They lay her out on the linoleum tile. Swab her mouth with hydrogen peroxide. It's standard hygiene procedure. Another county policy. Director Sedlak bends to put both her palms on the middle of Betty's chest. On her sternum. Someone kneels close to pinch Betty's nose. The director shoves down on the plastic chest. And the kneeling guy, with his mouth on Betty's rubber mouth, he starts to cough.

He leans back, coughing, sitting on his heels. Then he spits. Splat, there on the health-room linoleum tile, he spits. The mouth guy wipes the back of one hand across his lips and says, "Damn, that stinks."

The people crowded around, Cora Reynolds among them, the rest of the class, they lean closer.

Still squatting there, the mouth guy says, "There's something inside her." He covers his mouth and nose with one cupped hand.

His face twisted sideways, away from the rubber mouth but still watching it, he says, "Go ahead. Hit her, again. Hit her hard."

The director, bent over with the heels of both hands on Betty's chest, her fingernails painted dark red, she shoves down.

And a fat bubble swells between Betty's blue rubber lips. Some liquid, some salad dressing, thin and milky white, the bubble swells big. A greasy gray pearl. Then a Ping-Pong ball. A baseball. Until it pops. Spattering the greasy off-white soup everywhere. This thin, watery culture, puffing a cloud of stink into the room.

Until that day, anybody could use the Health Room. Lock the door. Unfold the rollaway cot and take a nap during their lunch hour. If they got a headache. Or cramps. The first-aid kit, that's where they'd find it. All the bandages and aspirin. You didn't need anybody's permission. All that's in there is the rollaway cot, a little cabinet with a metal sink for hand-washing, a switch on the wall for the light. The blue plastic suitcase that Breather Betty comes in, it has no lock.

The group, they roll the dummy onto her side, and from the corner of her soft rubber mouth, first a drip, drip, drip, then a thin stream of creamy gruel runs out. Some of the watery mess washes down her pink rubber cheek. Some of it webs between her lips and plastic teeth. Most of it pools on the linoleum tile.

This dummy, now a French person. A girl who drowned. A victim of herself.

Everyone standing there, breathing behind a cupped hand or a handkerchief. Blinking back the smell that makes their eyes water. Their throats slide up and down inside their neck skin as they swallow and swallow to keep their scrambled eggs and bacon and coffee and oatmeal with skim milk and peach yogurt and English muffins and cottage cheese down, deep in their gut.

The mouth guy grabs the bottle of hydrogen peroxide and throws his head back. Dumping a double swig into his mouth, he puffs his cheeks. He stares at the ceiling, eyes closed, mouth open, gargling the peroxide. Then he snaps forward to spit his mouthful into the little metal sink.

The room, everybody breathing the laundry-bleach smell of the peroxide, underneath that the toilet smell from the Breather Betty's lungs. The director, she says for somebody to grab a sex-crime investigation kit. The swabs and slides and gloves.

Cora Reynolds, she was among that group, standing so close that she tracked some of the slippery muck all the way back to her desk. It's after that day County Facilities put a lock on the door and gave Cora the key. Since then, you get cramps and you put your name on a list, with the date and time, before you get that key. You get a headache, and you ask Cora for two aspirin.

The team at the state labs, when they got the swabs and they ran the slides and cultures, they asked: Was this a joke?

Yeah, the lab team said, the ooze was sperm. Some of it maybe six months old. Dating back to the last mouth-to-mouth class session. But, hey, there was so much of it. Besides, running it for DNA, the genetic signifiers showed this was the work of twelve, maybe fifteen different men.

The county guys on this end, they said, Yeah. A bad joke. Now forget it.

This is just what human beings do—turn objects into people, people into objects.

Nobody's saying it's the county team that screwed up. Screwed up big-time.

The Breather Betty dummy, it's no surprise Cora took it home. Rinsed out its lungs, somehow. Washed and set its red glamour-girl hair. Cora bought a new dress for its armless, legless torso. A string of fake pearls for around its neck. Anything that helpless, Cora could never just toss in the garbage. She put lipstick on its blue lips. Mascara on its long eyelashes. Blush. Perfume—a lot of perfume, to cover the smell. Some nice clip-on earrings. It would amaze nobody to find out she spent every night sitting on the sofa in her apartment, watching the television and chatting at it.

Just Cora and Betty. Chatting in French.

Still, nobody's calling Cora Reynolds a crackpot. Maybe just a soft touch.

County policy says they should've bagged the old dummy in black plastic and heaved it onto a top shelf in the evidence room. Forgetting her there. *Betty,* not Cora. Abandoned. Fermenting. Ignored with the numbered bags of dope and coke. The vials of crack and heroin balloons. All the guns and knives waiting to appear in some courtroom. All the seized baggies and balloons shrinking, getting smaller and smaller, until there's just enough left for a felony conviction. All those objects, used.

But, no, they broke the rules. They let Cora take the old dummy home.

Nobody wanted her to grow old alone.

Cora. She was the kind of person, she couldn't buy just one stuffed animal. Part of her job description was to buy a stuffed toy for each kid who came in to give a statement. Each kid taken into custody by the court. Any kid pulled for neglect and placed in a foster home. At the toy store, Cora would take one little plush monkey out of a bin full of animals . . . but it would look so alone in her shopping cart. So she'd choose a furry giraffe to keep it company. Then a stuffed elephant. A hippo. An owl. At some point, there would be more animals in her shopping cart than in the display bin. And the animals left behind each had an eye missing, an ear frayed, a seam split open. Stuffing poked out. These were the animals no one would want.

Nobody felt how Cora's heart dropped off a cliff at that moment. That long fall from the tip-top of the world's tallest rollercoaster, that feeling left Cora just skin. Just a skin tube with a tight hole at each end. An object.

Those little tigers smudged with dirt, trailing loose threads. The stuffed reindeers crushed flat. They filled her apartment, those torn pandas and stained little owls and Breather Betty. Just a different type of evidence room.

It's what human beings do . . .

But poor, poor Cora. Now she's trying to cut off people's tongues. To infect them with parasites. Obstruct justice. She's stealing public property. Nobody's talking about misappropriation of office supplies: pens, staplers, copy paper.

It's Cora who orders the office supplies. She collects everyone's time card on Friday. She hands out the paychecks on Tuesday. Submits all the expense reports to Accounting for reimbursement. Answers the phone: "Child and Family Case Services." She gets a cake and sends a card around the department when it's somebody's birthday. That's her job.

Nobody had a problem with Cora Reynolds before the little girl and boy arrived from Russia. Really, the problem was, Cora never sees a little kid, a freckle-faced, pigtailed little girl, unless somebody's fucked her.

Every rapscallion little boy, every scamp in bib overalls with a slingshot stuck in his back pocket, Cora's only meeting him because he's been forced to suck cock. Every kid's gap-toothed smile, here it's a mask. Every grass-stained knee, a clue. Every bruise, an indicator. Every wink or squeal or giggle, there's a blank to check for it on the victim-intake form. It's Cora's job, keeping track of those interview forms. Keeping track of the kids, each case file, any ongoing investigation. Until what happened, Cora Reynolds was the best office manager ever.

Still, what happens here is just damage control. You can't unfuck a kid. Once you bang a kid, there's no getting that genii *out* of the bottle. That kid's pretty much wrecked for good.

No, most kids come in here quiet. Stretch-marked. Already middle-aged. Not smiling.

Kids come here, and the first step is the evaluation interview with an *anatomically detailed* doll. This is different from an *anatomically correct* doll, but plenty of folks get them confused. Cora did. Got them confused.

Your typical anatomically *detailed* doll is made of cloth, sewn like a stuffed animal. It has strands of yarn for hair. The big difference between it and Raggedy Ann is the details: A floppy stuffed penis and balls. Or a lacy cloth vagina. A drawstring pulled tight in back to make a puckered anus. Two buttons sewn to the chest for nipples. These dolls are something the intake kids can use to play-act. To demonstrate what Mommy or Daddy or Mommy's new boyfriend did.

The kids stick their fingers in the dolls. Drag the dolls by their yarn hair. Hold the dolls by the neck and shake them until their stuffed heads flop. They hit and lick and bite and suck the dolls, and it's Cora's job to sew the nipples back on. Cora will find two new marbles when the little felt scrotum gets yanked too hard.

Everything done to the kids gets done to those dolls.

Nobody just stumbles into this line of work.

Threads come loose from too many molested children molesting the dolls. Too many diddled little boys suck that same pink felt penis. Too many little girls have forced a finger, two fingers, three fingers into that same satin-lined vagina. Ripping it at the top and bottom. Little hernias of cotton batting were bulging out. Under their clothes, the dolls were smudged and dirty. Sticky and smelling bad. The fabric was rubbed into pills and snagged with scars where threads were gone.

This little rag doll girl and boy the whole world gets to abuse.

And of course, Cora did what she could to keep them clean. She stitched them back together. But one day she went on the Internet to find another pair. A new pair.

Somewhere were women who made their career stitching tiny pocket-shaped vaginas or coin-purse scrotums. These kids, the women dressed in flowered calico dresses and bib overalls. But this time, Cora wanted something durable. She got on the Internet. She ordered a new pair, from some maker she'd never heard about before. This time, she confused anatomically *detailed* with *correct*.

Anatomically correct, she asked for, boy and girl dolls. Lowest price possible. Durable. Easy to clean.

A search engine offered her two dolls. Made in the former Soviet Union. With flexible arms and legs. Anatomically correct. Because these were the lowest-priced, and because that was the county purchasing policy, she placed the order.

Later, nobody ever asked why she ordered those dolls. When the box arrived, brown cardboard and big as a four-drawer file cabinet, when the delivery guy wheeled it up on a cart and left it next to her desk, when he made her sign his clipboard, then it was Cora first figured this might be a mistake.

The moment they opened the box, when they saw what was inside, it was too late.

It was Cora and a county detective, pulling the metal staples and then digging through the mats of bubble wrap, digging until they found a foot. A pink child's foot, five perfect toes poking up, out of the Styrofoam pellets and bubble wrap.

The detective wiggled one of the toes. He looked at Cora.

"These were the cheapest," Cora said. She said, "You don't get a lot of choice."

The foot was pink rubber, finished with clear, hard toenails. The skin smooth, without a freckle or mole or vein. At this, the detective put a hand around the ankle and lifted it to show a smooth pink knee. Then a pink thigh. Then a shower of white packing peanuts. Bubble wrap popping and falling away. And a naked pink little girl hung from the detective's fist near the ceiling. Her blond hair fell in curls, brushing the floor. Her bare arms hung down at either side of her head. Her mouth hung open, a silent gasp, showing white teeth small as pearls, and the smooth pink roof of her mouth. A little girl the age for Easter-egg hunts and First Communion and Santa's lap.

With one ankle in the detective's hand, the girl's other leg sagged, bent at the knee. Between her legs, spread there, not just anatomically correct but . . . perfect, was the girl's pink vagina. The darker pink lips of it, curving inside.

Still in the box, looking up at her, looking up at them all, was a naked little boy.

A printed brochure fluttered to the floor.

Then Cora's arms were around the girl, hugging her pillow softness, clutching for a sheet of wrapping paper to put around the little body.

The detective smiled, shaking his head, squeezing his eyes shut, and saying, "Great job at *procurement,* Cora."

Cora held the girl, one hand cupped to hide the pink buttocks. One hand cupped to hold the blond head to Cora's chest, and she said, "This is a mistake."

The brochure said the dolls were soft molded silicone, the kind used for breast implants. They could be left under an electric blanket and would hold the heat for hours of pleasure. Their skin covered a skeleton of fiberglass with steel joints. Their hair was inserted, strand by strand, planted into the skin of their scalp. They had no pubic hair. The male doll had an optional foreskin that you could roll onto the head of its penis. The girl doll had a replaceable plastic hymen you could send away for. Both dolls, the brochure said, had deep tight throats and rectums, *for vigorous oral or anal entry.*

The silicone had a memory and would return to its original shape, no matter what you did. Their nipples could be tugged to five times their original length without tearing. The labia, scrotums, rectums could be stretched to *accommodate almost any desire.* The dolls, the brochure said, could take *years of violent, strenuous enjoyment.*

For clean-up, you just used soap and water.

Leaving the dolls in direct sunlight might fade their eyes and lips, the brochure said in French, Spanish, English, Italian, and what looked like Chinese.

The silicone was guaranteed odorless and tasteless.

At lunch, Cora went out to buy a little dress and a little pair of pants and shirt. When she got back to her desk, the box was empty. Styrofoam peanuts and bubble wrap popped under her every step. The dolls were gone.

In the ward room, she asked the dispatcher if he knew anything. The dispatcher shrugged. In the break room, a detective said that maybe someone needed them for a case. He shrugged and said, "That *is* what they're for . . ."

Outside, in the hallway, she asked another detective if he'd seen them.

She asked, where were they, the kid dolls?

Her teeth were edged together. The spot between her eyes ached from her brows bunching in the middle. Her ears felt blood-hot. Melting, glowing hot.

She found the dolls in the director's office. Sitting on the sofa. Smiling and naked. Freckle-faced and ashamed of nothing.

Director Sedlak was tugging at a nipple on the boy's chest. With her fingers, her thumb and index finger, just the dark-red fingernails, the director twisted and pulled at the pink nipple. With her other hand, the director trailed her fingertips up and down between the girl's legs, saying, "Damn, that feels real."

To the director, Cora said she was sorry. She leaned down to brush some hair off the boy's forehead, and said she had no idea. She crossed the girl's arms across her pink nipples. Then, she crossed her plastic legs at the knee. She put both the boy's hands spread open in his lap. Both dolls just sat there, smiling. They both had blue glass eyes, blond hair. Shining porcelain teeth.

"Sorry for what?" the director said.

For wasting county funds, Cora said. For buying something this expensive sight-unseen. She thought she was getting a good deal. Now the county would be stuck using the old rag dolls for another year. The county was stuck, and these dolls would have to be destroyed.

And Director Sedlak said, "Don't be silly." She combed her fingernails through the girl's blond hair, saying, "I don't see a problem." Saying, "We can use these."

But the dolls, Cora said, they were too real.

And the director said, "They're rubber."

Silicone, Cora said.

And the director said, "If it helps, just think of each one as a seventy-pound condom . . ."

That afternoon, even as Cora pulled the new clothes onto the boy and girl, detectives came by her desk, asking to check them out. For intake interviews. For investigations. Asking to reserve them for some hush-hush off-site evaluation. For overnight, to use them early the next morning. For the weekend. The girl, preferably, but if she wasn't available, then the boy. By the end of that first day, both the dolls were booked solid for the next month.

If someone wanted a doll right away, she'd offer the old rag dolls.

Most times, the detective said he'd wait.

All this flood of new cases, but nobody submitted a single new case file to her.

For almost that whole month, Cora only saw the boy and girl for a moment, only long enough to hand them over to the next detective. Then the next. And the next. And it was never clear who did what, but the little girl arrived and departed, one day with her ears pierced, then her belly button, then wearing lipstick, then reeking with perfume. The boy arrived, at some point, tattooed. A chain of thorns around his little calf muscle. At another point, with his nipples pierced by little silver rings. Then his penis. At some point, his blond hair smelling sour.

Smelling like marigold flowers.

Like the bags of marijuana in the evidence room. That room full of guns and knives. The bags of marijuana and cocaine that always weighed a little less than they should have. The evidence room always the next stop for a detective after he checked out one of the dolls. The girl tucked under one arm, he'd be fumbling with a bag of evidence. Tucking something into his pocket.

In the director's office, Cora showed the expense receipts that detectives would submit for reimbursement. One receipt for a hotel room, the same night the detective had taken the girl home for an interview the next morning. The hotel room was a stakeout, the detective had said. Another detective the next night, the girl again, one hotel room, one room-service meal. An adult movie ordered on the television. Another stakeout, he said.

Director Sedlak had just looked at her. Cora standing there, leaning over the director's wooden desk, shaking so hard the receipts fluttered in Cora's fist.

The director just looked at her and said, "What's your point?"

It was obvious, Cora said.

And, sitting behind her wooden desk, the director just laughed and laughed.

She said, "Consider this tit for tat."

"All those women," the director says, "all chanting and protesting against *Hustler* magazine, saying porno turns a woman into an object . . . Well," she says, "what do you think a dildo is? Or donor sperm from some clinic?"

Some men may only want pictures of naked women. But some women only want a man's dick. Or his sperm. Or his money.

Both sexes have the same problem with intimacy.

"Stop fussing about some damned rubber dolls," Director Sedlak told Cora. "If you're jealous, go out and buy yourself a nice vibrator."

Again, it's what human beings do . . .

Nobody could see where this was headed.

That same day, Cora went to lunch and bought some Superglue.

And the next go-round, when the dolls came back to her, before she handed them off to another man, Cora squeezed Superglue inside the girl's vagina. Inside both the kids' mouths, sealing their tongue to the roof of their mouth. To seal their lips together. Then she squeezed glue inside them both, in back, to weld their butts shut. To save them.

Still, the next day, a detective was asking: Did Cora have a razor blade he could use? An X-Acto knife? A switchblade?

And when she asked, Why? What did he need it for?

Then he says, "Nothing. Never mind. I'll find something in the evidence room."

And the next day, the girl and boy were both cut open, still soft but covered with scars. Carved open. Dug out. Still smelling like glue, but more and more smelling like the ooze inside Breather Betty at home, leaking spots on Cora's sofa.

Those spots, Cora's cat would sniff at for hours. Not lick, but sniff like Superglue. Or evidence-room cocaine.

It's then Cora goes to lunch and buys a razor blade. Two razor blades. Three razor blades. Five.

The next go-round, when the girl gets back to her desk, Cora takes her into the bathroom and sits her on the edge of a sink. With a tissue, Cora scrubs the rouge off her pink cheeks. Cora washes and combs the girl's limp blond hair. With the next detective already knocking at the locked bathroom door, Cora tells the girl, "I'm sorry. I'm sorry. I'm sorry . . ." Saying, "You're going to be okay." And Cora tucks a razor blade up, deep inside the soft silicone vagina. Into the hole hollowed out by some man with his knife. Tilting the girl's head back, Cora tucks another razor down deep inside her silicone throat. The third razor blade Cora tucks just inside the girl's hacked-out, whittled-open butt.

When the boy arrives back at her desk, just dropped there, flopped facedown over the arm of her desk chair, Cora takes him into the bathroom with the last two razor blades.

Tit for tat.

The next day, a detective comes in, dragging the girl by her hair. He drops her on the floor beside Cora's desk. Taking a pad and pen from his inside jacket pocket, he writes: "Who had her yesterday?"

And, lifting the girl from the floor, smoothing her hair, Cora tells him a name. A random name. Another detective.

His eyes narrow and, shaking his head, the man holding his pen and paper says, "Tha thon-atha-bith!" And you can see how the two halves of his tongue are held together with black stitches.

The detective who brings back the little boy is limping.

All five razor blades are gone.

It's after that, Cora must talk to somebody at the county health clinic.

Nobody knows how she got that biohazard sample from the lab.

After that, every man in the department, he's pinching his ball skin through his pants. Lifting one elbow the way a monkey would, to scratch the hair under that arm. In their heads, they ain't had sex with anybody. No way could this be crab lice.

Maybe about this time, a detective's wife comes downtown. Finding the little leak spots of blood you get with crab lice. A splatter of red pepper you find in your tightie whities or the inside of your white T-shirt, anywhere clothes come up against body hair. Little specks of blood, blood, blood. Maybe the wife finds it in her hubby's shorts. Maybe she finds it in her own. These are college-gone, suburban, and shopping-mall people with no real crab-lice experience. Now all their itching makes sense to her.

And now this wife, she's pissed off, bad.

And no way could any wife know this is the rubber-doll version of getting crabs from a toilet seat. No doubt the story her husband would tell. But that's all Cora could rustle up from County Health. You can't keep spirochetes alive on silicone. You can't pass hepatitis unless you got broken skin. Blood. Saliva. No, the dolls are real, but not *that real*.

Any wife lets this go, and next week he'll bring home herpes to her and the kids. Gonorrhea. Chlamydia. AIDS. So she's all over Cora, asking: "Who's my husband banging on his lunch hour?"

One good look at Cora, her hair-spray hairstyle and pearls and knee-high nylons and pants suit, and no wife would cast blame in that direction. Cora with old tissues tucked up the sleeve of her cardigan sweater. Cora with a dish of hard ribbon candy on her desk. The *Family Circus* cartoons pinned to her cork bulletin board.

Still, nobody's saying Cora Reynolds is unattractive.

Then the wife sees Director Sedlak with her red-red fingernails.

Nobody was not amazed when Cora got called in for a little sit-down.

Nobody could tell Cora Reynolds her days were numbered.

The director, she sits Cora across from her big wooden desk. The director's office with its high-up window. The director sitting, outlined in the sunshine and the view of cars in the county parking lot. With the fingers of one hand, she waves Cora to lean closer.

"It was a tough call," the director says, "deciding if my entire team is crazy, or if you are . . . overreacting."

Nobody felt how Cora's heart dropped off a cliff at that moment. She sat, frozen. It's what we do: turn ourselves into objects. Turn objects into ourselves.

Those millions of people, all over the world, still trying to save Breather Betty. Maybe they should just mind their own business. Maybe it is too late.

It's the kids, the director says, who tear up the dolls. It always has been. Abused kids abuse what they can. Each victim will find a victim. It's a cycle. She says, "I think you should take some time off."

If it helps, just think of Cora Reynolds as a 120-pound condom . . .

Nobody says that last part. But nobody has to.

Nobody tells her to go home and get set for the worst.

As part of keeping her job, Cora will have to return the Breather Betty doll she's reported to have taken. She's to relinquish the stuffed toys she purchased with county funds. She's to surrender her keys to the health room. Immediately. And make the room and the anatomically correct dolls available to all staff members. First come, first served. Immediately.

How Cora felt, it was like coming to your first stoplight after driving a million billion miles, too fast, wearing no seat belt. Resignation mixed with tired relief. Cora, just a skin tube with a hole at either end. It was a terrible feeling, but it gave her a plan.

The next day, coming into work, nobody sees her duck into the evidence room. In there were knives that smelled of blood and Superglue, there for anyone to take.

Already, a line is forming beside her desk. All of them waiting for the last detective to bring back a kid. Either kid. They both look the same, silicone-face down.

Cora Reynolds, she's nobody's fool. Nobody pushes *her* around.

A detective arrives with the boy hanging under one arm, the girl hanging under his other arm. The man heaves them both on the desk, and the crowd surges forward, clutching the pink silicone legs.

Nobody knows who are the real crazy people.

And Cora, she's holding a gun, the evidence tag still hanging off it on a string. The case number written there. She waves the gun at the two dolls.

"Pick them up," she says. "And come with me."

The little boy wears just his white underpants, dark with grease in the seat. The girl, a white satin slip, stiff with stains. The detective scoops them both, the weight of two kids, with just one arm and hugs them to his chest. Their nipple rings and tattoos and crab lice. Their stink of dope smoke and what drips from Breather Betty.

Waving with the gun, Cora walks him toward the office door.

The men stalking her, circling her, Cora works the detective backward down the hall, dragging the girl and boy past the director's office, past the health room. To the lobby. Then the parking lot. There, the detectives wait while she unlocks her car.

With the boy and girl sitting in her back seat, Cora hits the gas, spraying the men with gravel. Before she's even through the gate in the chain-link fence, you can hear sirens on their way.

Nobody knew Cora Reynolds would be so ready. Breather Betty was already in the car, riding shotgun, with a scarf tied over her red hair, dark sunglasses on her rubber face. A cigarette hanging between her red-red lips. This French girl returned from the dead. Rescued and seat-belted to keep her torso upright.

This person made into an object, now made back into a person.

The crippled stuffed animals, the ratty tigers and orphaned bears and penguins, they're all lined up in the car's rear window. The cat among them, asleep in the sun. All of them waving good-bye.

Cora hits the freeway, her back tires fishtailing, already doing twice the posted speed limit. Her four-door brown sedan already pulls a kite's tail of police cruisers, their lights flashing blue and red. Helicopters. Angry detectives in unmarked county cars. Television camera crews, each in a white van with a big number painted on the side.

Already there's no way Cora can't win.

She has the girl. She has the boy. She has the gun.

Even if they run out of gas, nobody will fuck her kids.

Even if the troopers shoot out her tires. Even then, she'll shoot up their silicone bodies. Cora will blow off their faces. Their nipples and noses. She'll leave them nothing any man would stick his dick into. She'll do the same to Breather Betty.

And she'll shoot herself. To save them.

Please understand. Nobody says what Cora Reynolds did was right.

Nobody is even saying Cora Reynolds was sane. But she still won.

This is just what human beings do—turn objects into people, people into objects. Back and forth. Tit for tat.

This is what the police will find if they get too close. The children mutilated. All of them dead. The animals soaked with her blood. Them all dead, together.

But until that moment, Cora has a full tank of gas. She has a bag full of evidence-room cocaine to keep her awake. A bag of sandwiches. A few bottles of water and the cat, purring asleep.

She has nothing but a few hours of freeway between her and Canada.

But, more than all that, Cora Reynolds has her family.

Mother Nature slips into some kind of black coat. It's a military uniform or an ice-skating costume, black wool with a double row of brass buttons up the front. A black velvet majorette with her split nose scabbed together with dark red. She gets her arms through each long sleeve, then says, "Button me up?" to Saint Gut-Free.

She wiggles what's left of her hands, and says, "I don't have the fingers I need."

Her fingers are just stubs and knuckles. Only her index fingers are left for dialing telephones after she's famous. Punching buttons on a cash machine. Fame already reducing her from something with three dimensions to something flat.

Mother Nature, Saint Gut-Free, Reverend Godless, we're all dressing in black before we carry Mr. Whittier down to the subbasement. Before we play this next important scene.

Never mind that our funeral is just a rehearsal. We're just stand-ins for the real funeral, to be played by movie stars in front of cameras after we're discovered. By doing this, wrapping Mr. Whittier and tying his body into a bundle, then delivering him to the subbasement for a ceremony—this way we'll all have the same experience. We'll all be telling the same tragic story to the reporters and police.

If Mr. Whittier is stinking or not, it's hard to tell. Miss Sneezy and Reverend Godless carry the silver bags of spoiled food, each bag leaking a trail of stink juice. Trailing drips and spots of stink, they carry the bags across the lobby to the restrooms and flush them down the toilet.

"Not being able to smell," Miss Sneezy says, and sniffs, hard, "it helps."

This works fine, one bag at a time. Until Reverend Godless tries to hurry, when the smell gets choking-bad. Dry-heaves-bad. The stink soaks into their clothes and hair. The first time they try to flush two bags together, the toilets start to clog and overflow. Another toilet clogs. Already, the water is flooding out, swamping the blue carpet in the lobby. The bags, stuck in some main sewer pipe, they soak up water, swelling the way the turkey Tetrazzini killed Mr. Whittier, clogging the main pipe so even the toilets that look fine, they back up.

None of the toilets will work. The furnace and water heater are broken. We still have boxes of food, rotting. Mr. Whittier is not our biggest problem.

According to Sister Vigilante's calendar watch and Miss America's grown-out brown roots, we've been here about two weeks.

As he does the last of her brass buttons, Saint Gut-Free leans in to kiss Mother Nature, saying, "Do you love me?"

"I pretty much have to," she says, "if the romantic subplot is going to work."

Dead Lord Baglady sparkling on her finger, Mother Nature wipes the back of one hand across her lips, saying, "Your saliva tastes terrible . . ."

Saint Gut-Free spits in his palm and licks the spit back into his mouth. He sniffs his empty hand, saying, "Terrible, how?"

"Ketones," Mrs. Clark says to nobody. Or to everybody.

"Sour," Mother Nature says. "Like a lemon-and-airplane-glue aromatherapy candle."

"It's starvation," Mrs. Clark says, tying a gold silk rope around the bundle of Mr. Whittier. "As you burn up your body fat, the acetone concentration increases in your blood."

Saint Gut-Free sniffs his hand, the snot rattling inside his head.

Reverend Godless lifts one arm to sniff underneath. There, the damp taffeta is darker black with sweat, in his pores, the memory of too much Chanel No. 5.

Lugging a body up- and downstairs, we're wasting our valuable body fat.

Still, we should have a gesture of mourning, says Sister Vigilante, still clutching her Bible. With Mr. Whittier wrapped and being carried to the subbasement, rolled tight in a red velvet curtain from the imperial-Chinese promenade, and tied with gold silk ropes from the lobby, we should stand around him to talk profound. We should sing a hymn. Nothing too religious, just whatever will play best.

We draw straws to see who has to weep.

More and more, we leave room open in every group for Agent Tattletale's camera. We speak so the Earl of Slander's tape recorder will get every word. The same tape or memory card or compact disk getting used, over and over. We erase our past with our present, on the gamble that the next moment will be sadder, more horrible or tragic.

More and more, something *worse* needs to happen.

Mr. Whittier's been dead for days or hours. It's hard to tell since Sister Vigilante started turning the lights on and off. At night, we hear someone walking around, great booming footsteps, a giant coming down the lobby stairs in the dark.

Still, something *more terrible* needs to happen.

For market share. For dramatic appeal.

Something *more awful* needs to happen.

From his dressing room, backstage, we carry Mr. Whittier across the stage and up the center aisle of the auditorium. We carry him through the blue velvet lobby and down the stairs to the orange-and-gold Mayan foyer in the first basement.

Sister Vigilante says her watch keeps resetting itself. That's a classic sign of a haunting. The Baroness Frostbite claims she found a cold spot in the Gothic smoking room. In the Arabian Nights gallery, you can see your breath steaming in the cold air above the cushion where Mr. Whittier used to sit. The Countess Foresight says it's the ghost of Lady Baglady we hear walking around after lights-out.

Following behind in the funeral procession, Director Denial: "Has anybody seen Cora Reynolds?"

Sister Vigilante says, "Whoever took my bowling ball, give it back and I *promise* not to kick your ass . . ."

Leading the procession, cradling the lump that would be Mr. Whittier's head, Mrs. Clark says, "Has anyone seen Miss America?"

After this is over, it would never work to shoot the movie here. After we're discovered, this place will become a landmark. A National Treasure. The Museum of Us.

No, whatever production company will just have to build sets to copy each of the big rooms. The blue velvet French Louis XV lobby. The black mohair Egyptian auditorium. The green satin Italian Renaissance lounge. The yellow leather Gothic smoking room. The purple Arabian Nights gallery. The orange Mayan foyer. The red imperial-Chinese promenade. Each room a different deep color, but all with the same gold accents.

Not rooms, Mr. Whittier would say, but settings. We carry his wrapped body through these echoing big boxes where people become a king or an emperor or duchess for the price of a movie ticket.

Locked in the office behind the lobby snack bar, that little closet of varnished pine walls with its ceiling sloped under the lobby staircase, there the filing cabinets are packed solid with printed programs and invoices, booking schedules and time-clock punch cards. Those sheets of paper turning to dust along their edges, printed across the top of each page it says: Liberty Theater. Some are printed: Capital Theater. Some printed: Neptune Vaudeville House. Others printed: Holy Convention Church. Others: Temple of Christian Redemption. Or: Assembly of Angels. Or: Capital Adult Theater. Or: Diamond Live Burlesque.

All these different places, they all had this same address.

Here, where people have knelt in prayer. And knelt in semen.

All the screams of joy and horror and salvation still contained and stifled inside these concrete walls. Still echoing in here, with us. Here, our dusty heaven.

All these different stories will end with our story. After the thousand different realities of plays and movies, religion and strippers, this building will become, forever, the Museum of Us.

Every crystal chandelier, the Matchmaker calls it a "peach tree." The Gothic smoking room, Comrade Snarky calls it the "Frankenstein Room."

In the Mayan foyer, Reverend Godless says the orange carvings are bright as a runway spotlight shining through the silk petals of a tulip sewn to a vintage Christian Lacroix bustle . . .

In the Chinese promenade, the silk wallpaper is a red dye that's never been in the daylight. Red as the blood of a restaurant critic, says Chef Assassin.

In the Gothic smoking room, the wing chairs are covered in a rich yellow leather that's never bleached a moment in the sun. Not since it covered a cow, says the Missing Link.

The walls of the Italian Renaissance lounge are dark green, streaked and clotted with black, a coat of paint that turns to malachite stone if you look hard enough.

In the Egyptian auditorium, the walls are plaster and papier-mâché, carved and molded into the pyramids, the sphinx. Giant seated pharaohs. Pointed-nose jackals. Rows and rows of big-eyed hieroglyphics. Above all this dangle the fronds of fake palm trees made from ribbons of black paper sagging with mold. Above the dusty treetops, the black plaster of the night sky is studded with a heaven of electric stars. The Big Dipper. Orion. The constellations, just stories people make up so they can understand that night sky. These stars, hazy behind clouds of cobweb.

Black mohair covers the seats, scratchy as dried moss on tree bark. The carpets are black, worn to the gray grid of canvas down the center of each aisle.

The trim in all the rooms is gold. Gold paint, bright as neon piping. Everything black in the auditorium, every seat-back and carpet-edge, it's outlined in this same bright gold.

If you want hard enough, the trim is real gold. Every room depends on your faith.

The group of us in our fairy-tale silk and velvet and dried blood, we're black moving against the blackness. In dim light, Mr. Whittier must seem to float in his red velvet cocoon, wound around with gold rope. No longer a character, Mr. Whittier has become a prop. Our puppet. A constellation we can put stories on to say we understand.

Her face behind a lace handkerchief, Comrade Snarky says, "I don't know why we should be crying." She's breathing through the old perfume of the lace, trying to escape the stink. She says, "My character wouldn't be crying." She says, "I'll swear by the rose tattooed on my ass, that old man raped me."

Here, the funeral parade stops. At this point, Comrade Snarky is a victim among victims. The rest of us—just her supporting cast.

Mrs. Clark, leading us, she looks back and says, "He what?"

And from behind his camera, Agent Tattletale says, "Me, too. He raped me first."

Saint Gut-Free says, "Well, what the hell . . . He poked me, too."

As if poor skinny Saint Gut-Free had *enough* ass left to poke.

And Mrs. Clark says, "This is not funny. Not in the least."

"Tough," the Matchmaker tells her. "It's wasn't funny, either, when you raped me."

Shaking his ponytail, the Duke of Vandals tells the Matchmaker, "You couldn't *pay* to get raped."

And Mother Nature laughs—blowing scabs and blood all over.

The devil is dead. Long live the devil.

Here is our funeral for Satan. Mr. Whittier, he's the demon who'll make all our past sins look like nothing by comparison. The story of his crimes will leave us buffed and polished to the virgin-white color of victim.

More sinned against than sinning.

Still, his being dead leaves a job opening at the bottom that no one wants.

So, in the movie version, you'll see us weeping and forgiving Mr. Whittier while Mrs. Clark cracks the whip.

The devil is dead. Long live the devil.

We wouldn't last a moment without someone to blame.

Up the black-carpet aisle of the auditorium, through the red Chinese promenade, down the blue French stairs, we carry Mr. Whittier. Through the bright orange of the Mayan foyer, there Mother Nature pushes some white wig hair off her forehead, her brass bells jingling. She's wearing a pile of gray curls left over from some opera. The curls hang, wet from the sweat on her face, and Mother Nature says, "Is anybody else hot?"

The Duke of Vandals is panting with his shoulder under the weight of Mr. Whittier, panting and pulling at the collar of his tuxedo jacket.

Even the red silk bundle feels damp with sweat. The airplane-glue smell of ketones. Starvation.

And Reverend Godless says, "It's no wonder you're hot. Your wig's on backward."

And the Matchmaker says, "Listen."

Below us, the subbasement is dark. The wood stairs, narrow. Beyond that dark, something rumbles and growls.

Something *mysterious* needs to happen.

Something *dangerous* needs to happen.

"It's the ghost," says the Baroness Frostbite, the greasy pucker of her mouth sagging open.

It's the furnace, running full-blast. The blower pumping hot air into the ducts. The gas burner chugging. The furnace that Mr. Whittier destroyed.

Somebody's fixed it.

From somewhere in the dark, a cat screams, just one time.

Something needs to happen. So we start down the wood stairs with Mr. Whittier's body.

All of us sweating. Wasting even more energy in this impossible new heat.

Following the body down, into the dark, Mother Nature says, "What do you know about wearing wigs?" With the stumps of both hands, her diamond ring flashing, she twists the gray wig around on her head, saying to Reverend Godless, "A big lug like you, what do you know about a vintage Christian Lacroix anything?"

And the Reverend Godless says, "A Lacroix tulip-skirt bustle?" He says, "You'd be surprised."

Babble

A Poem About Reverend Godless

"Until Genesis, chapter eleven," says the Reverend
    Godless, "we had no war."
    Until God set us to fight each other, for the rest of
        human history.

Reverend Godless onstage, his eyebrows are plucked and
    shaped
    into twin-penciled arches, with, underneath each,
    a rainbow of sparkle eye shadow in shades from red to
        green.
And on one bare bicep muscle, bulging,
    below the spaghetti strap of a red-sequined evening
        gown,
    tattooed there is a skull face with, under the chin, these
        words:
Death Before Dishonor.

Onstage, instead of a spotlight, a movie fragment:
    A travelogue that shows churches, mosques, and
        temples.
    Religious leaders in jeweled robes
    waving to crowds from bulletproofed town cars.

Reverend Godless, he says, "On a plain in the land of
Shinar, all people toiled together."
All humanity with a shared vision,
a great noble dream they worked side by side to fulfill
in this time before armies and weapons and battles.
Then God looked down to see their tower, the people's
shared dream,
inching up, just a little too close for comfort.
And God said, "Behold, they are one people . . . and this is
only the beginning
of what they will do . . . Nothing that they propose to do
will now be impossible for them . . ."
His words, in His Bible. The Book of Genesis, chapter
eleven.

"So our God," says Reverend Godless, his bare arms and
calf muscles stippled
with the black marks of a shaved hair growing back in
each pore,
he says, "Our all-powerful God got so scared He
scattered the human race
across the face of the earth,
and shattered their language to keep His children apart."

Part female impersonator, part retired U.S. Marine, the
Reverend Godless,
sparkling in his red sequins, says,
"An almighty God this insecure?"
Who pits his children against each other, to keep them
weak.
He says, "This is the God we're supposed to worship?"

Punch Drunk

A Story by the Reverend Godless

Webber looks around, his face pushed out of shape, one cheekbone lower than the other. One of his eyes is just a milk-white ball pinched in the red-black swelling under his brow. His lips, Webber's lips are split so deep in the middle he's got four lips instead of two. Inside all those lips, you can't see a single tooth left.

Webber looks around the jet's cabin, the white leather on the walls, the bird's-eye maple varnished to a mirror shine.

Webber looks at the drink in his hand, the ice hardly melted in the blast of the air conditioning. He says, too loud on account of his hearing loss, he almost shouts, "Where we at?"

They're in a Gulfstream G550, the nicest private jet you can charter, Flint says. Then Flint digs two fingers into a pants pocket and hands something across the aisle to Webber. A little white pill. "Swallow this," Flint says. "And drink your drink, we're almost there."

"Almost where?" Webber says, and he drinks the pill down.

He's still twisted around to see the white leather club chairs that recline and swivel. The white carpet. The bird's-eye maple tables, polished until they look wet. The white suede couches that line the cabin. The matching little throw cushions. The magazines, each one big as a movie poster, called *Elite Traveler,* with a cover price of fifty dollars. The 24-carat gold-plated cup holders and the faucets in the bathroom. The galley with its espresso machine and halogen light bouncing bright off the lead-crystal glassware. The microwave and fridge and ice machine. All this flying along at fifty-one thousand feet, Mach zero-point-eight-eight, somewhere above the Mediterranean Sea. All of them drinking Scotch whiskey. All of this nicer than anything you'll ever be inside. Anything short of a casket.

Webber's nose, he tilts his drink back, sticks his big red-potato nose into the cold air, and you can see up inside each nostril. See how they don't really go anywhere, not anymore. But Webber says, "What's that smell?"

And Flint sniffs and says, "Does *ammonium nitrate* ring a bell?"

It's the ammonium nitrate their buddy Jenson had ready for them in Florida. Their buddy from the Gulf War. Our Reverend Godless.

"You mean, like, fertilizer?" Webber says.

And Flint says, "Half a ton."

Webber's hand, it's shaking so hard you can hear the ice rattle in his empty glass.

That shaking, it's just traumatic Parkinson's is all. Traumatic encephalopathy will do that to you, where partial necrosis of brain tissue takes place. Neurons replaced by brain-dead scar tissue. You put on a curly red wig and false eyelashes, lip-synch to Bette Midler at the Collaris County Fair and Rodeo, and offer people the chance to punch your face at ten bucks a shot, and you can make some real money.

Other places, you'll need to wear a curly blond wig, squeeze your ass into a tight sequined dress, your feet in the biggest pair of high heels you can find. Lip-synch to Barbra Streisand singing that "Evergreen" song, and you'd better have a friend waiting to drive you to the emergency room. Take a couple Vicodins beforehand. Before you glue on those long pink Barbra Streisand fingernails;

after them you can't pick up anything smaller than a beer bottle. Take your painkillers first, and you can sing both the A and B sides of *Color Me Barbra* before a really good shot puts you down.

As a fund-raiser, our first idea was "Five Bucks to Punch a Mime." And it worked, mostly in college towns. The aggie schools. Some towns, nobody went home without some of that Clown White smeared across their knuckles. Clown White and blood.

Problem is, the novelty wears off. Renting a Gulfstream costs bucks. Just buying the gas and oil to fly from here to Europe costs about thirty grand. One way, it's not so bad, but you never want to go into a charter place saying you only plan to fly the plane one way—talk about your red flags.

No, Webber would put on that black leotard, and folks would already be salivating to hit him. He'd paint his face white, step into his invisible box, start miming away, and the cash would just flow in. Colleges mostly, but we did good business at county and state fairs, too. Even if folks took it as some kind of minstrel show, they'd still pay to knock him down. To make him bleed.

For roadhouse bars, after the mime routine petered out, we tried "Fifty Bucks to Punch a Chick." Flint had this girl who was up for it. But after, like, one shot to the face, she was saying, "No way . . ."

On the floor, sitting in the peanut shells on the floor and holding her nose, this girl says, "Let me go to flight school. Let me play the pilot, instead. I still want to help."

We still had, must've been half the bar standing in line with their money. Divorced dads, dumped boyfriends, guys with old potty-training issues, all of them wanting to take their best shot.

Flint says, "I can fix this up." And he helps his girl to her feet. Taking her by the elbow, he leads her into the ladies' room. Going in with her, Flint holds up his hand, fingers spread, and he says, "Give me five minutes."

Just out of the army like that, we didn't figure how else to make that kind of money. Not legal-wise. The way Flint saw it, there's no law yet says folks can't pay to sock you.

It's then Flint comes out of the ladies' room, wearing the girl's Saturday-night wig, all her makeup used up on his big clean-shaved face. He's unbuttoned his shirt and tied the shirttails together over his gut with paper towels stuffed in to make boobs. With whole tubes of lipstick smeared around his mouth, Flint, he says, "Let's do this thing . . ."

Folks standing in line, they're saying fifty bucks to punch some guy is a cheat.

So Flint, he says, "Make it ten bucks . . ."

Folks still hang back, look around for some better way to waste their cash.

It's then Webber's gone over by the jukebox. Dropped in a quarter. Pressed a couple buttons, and—magic. The music starts, and for the length of one exhale, all you can hear is every man in the bar letting out a long groan.

The song, it's the wailing song from the end of that *Titanic* movie. That Canadian chick.

And Flint, with his blond wig and big clown mouth, he steps up on a chair, then up on a table, and starts singing along. With the whole bar watching, Flint gives it everything he's got, sliding his hands up and down the sides of his blue jeans. His eyes closed, all you can see there is his shimmering blue eye shadow. That red smear, singing.

Right on time, Webber reaches up to offer Flint a hand down. Flint takes it, ladylike, still lip-synching. You can see now, his fingernails painted candy-red. And Webber whispers to him, "I plugged in five bucks' worth of quarters." Webber helps Flint down to face the first man in line, and Webber says, "This song's the only thing they're going to hear all night."

From Webber's five bucks, they made almost six hundred that night. Not a fist left that bar not beat deep, tattooed blue and red and eyeliner-green with the makeup from Flint's face. Some guys, they'd hit him until that hand got tired, then get back in line to use their other.

That wailing *Titanic* song, it almost fucking killed Flint. That and the guys wearing big honking finger rings.

After that, we had a rule about no rings. That, and we'd check to see you weren't palming a roll of dimes or a lead fishing weight to make your fist do more damage.

Of all the folks, the women are the worst. Some of them ain't happy 'less they see teeth fly out the other side of your mouth.

Women, the drunker they get, the more they love, love, love to slug a drag queen. Knowing it's a man. Especially if he's dressed and looking better than they are. Slapping was fine, too, but no scratching.

Right quick, that market opened up. Webber and Flint, they started skipping dinner. Drinking lite beer. Any new town, you'd catch one of them standing sideways to a mirror, looking at his stomach, his shoulders pulled back and his butt stuck out.

Every town, you'd swear they each had another damn suitcase. This suitcase for dressy dresses, evening dresses. Then garment bags so's they wouldn't wrinkle as much. Bags for shoes and wig boxes. A big new makeup case for each of them.

It got so their getups were cutting into the bottom line. But say a word about it and Flint would tell you, "You got to spend it to make it."

That's not even adding up what they spent for music. Hit or miss, they found most people want to slug you if you play the following record albums:

Color Me Barbra
Stoney End
The Way We Were
Thighs and Whispers
Broken Blossoms
Or *Beaches*. Really, especially *Beaches*.

You could put Mahatma Gandhi into a convent, cut off his nuts, shoot him full of Demerol, and he'd still take a shot at your face if you played him that "Wind Beneath Your Wings" song. Least-wise, that was Webber's experience.

None of this is what the military trained them for. But, coming home, you don't find any want ads for munitions experts, targeting specialists, missions point-men. Coming home, they didn't find much of any kind of job. Nothing that paid near what Flint was getting, his legs peeking through the slit down the side of a green satin evening gown, his toes webbed with nylon stockings and poking out the front of gold sandals. Flint stopped just long enough between songs and slugs to put more foundation over his bruises, his cigarette ringed with red from his lips. His lipstick and blood.

County fairs were good business, but motorcycle runs came a close second. Rodeos were good, too. So were boat shows. Or the parking lots outside those big gun-and-knife conventions. No, they never had to look too far for a good-paying crowd.

Driving back to the motel one night, after Webber and Flint had left most of their makeup smeared on the blacktop outside the Western States Guns and Ammo Expo, Webber pulls the rearview mirror around to where he's riding shotgun in the front seat. Webber rolls his face around to see it from the mirror at every angle, and he says, "I can't be up to this much longer."

Webber, he looks fine. Besides, how he looks don't matter. The song matters more. The wig and lipstick.

"I was never what you'd call *pretty*," Webber says, "but least-ways I always kept myself looking . . . *nice*."

Flint's driving, looking at the chipped red paint on his fingernails holding the steering wheel. Nibbling down a torn nail with his chipped teeth, Flint says, "I was thinking about using a stage name." Still looking at his fingernails, he says, "What do you all think of the name *Pepper Bacon?*"

About by now, Flint's girl, she was off in flight school.

That's just as well. Things was sliding down hill.

For instance, just before they got set up and ready, in the parking lot outside the Mountain States Gem and Mineral Show,

Webber looks at Flint and says, "Your goddamn boobs are too big . . ."

Flint's wearing a halter kind of long dress, with straps that tie behind his neck to keep the front up. And, yeah, his boobs look big, but Flint says it's the new dress.

And Webber says, "No, it ain't. Your boobs been growing for the past four states."

"All your carping," Flint says, "it's just cuz they're bigger than yours."

And Webber says, real quiet out the corner of his lipstick mouth, he says, "Former Staff Sergeant Flint Stedman, you're turning into a sloppy goddamn cow . . ."

Then it's sequins and wig hair flying every which way. That night, they raked in a total of zero cash. Nobody wants to slug a mess like that, already all scratched up and bleeding. Eyes all bloodshot and mascara all smeared from crying.

Looking back, that little cat fight damn near scuttled their mission.

The reason this country can't win a war is because we're all the time fighting each other instead of the enemy. Same as in the Congress not letting the military do their job. Nothing ever getting settled that way. Webber and Flint, they ain't bad people, just typical of what we're trying to rise above. Their whole mission is to settle this terrorism situation. Settle it for good. And doing that takes money. To keep Flint's girl in school. To get their hands on a jet. Get the drugs they'll need to knock out the regular lease-company pilot. That all takes solid cash money.

The truth be told, Flint's tits were getting a little on the scary side.

Flying here, reclining on white leather at fifty-one thousand feet, they're headed south along the Red Sea, all the way to Jedda, where they'll hang a left.

The other guys in the air right now, all of them headed for their own assigned targets, you have to wonder how they made their money. What pain and torture they went through.

You can still see where Webber got his ears pierced, and how pulled down and stretched out they still look from those dangle earrings.

Looking back, most of the wars in history were over somebody's religion.

This is just the attack to end all wars. Or at least most of them.

After Flint got control of his tits, they toured from college to college. Anywhere people drank beer with nothing to do. By now, Flint had a detached retina floating around, making him blind in that eye. Webber had a 60-percent hearing loss from his brain getting bounced around. Traumatic brain lesions, the emergency room called it. They were both of them a little shaky, needing both hands to hold a mascara wand steady. Both of them too stiff to work the zipper up the back of his own dress. Wobbly on even their medium heels. Still, they went on.

When it came time, when the jet fighters from the United Arab Emirates would come to shadow them, Flint might be too blind to fly, but he'd be in the cockpit with everything he'd learned in the air force.

Here, in the white leather cabin of their Gulfstream G550, Flint has kicked off both his boots, and his bare feet show toenails still painted titty-pink. You can still smell a hint of Chanel No. 5 perfume mixed with his BO.

One of their last shows, in Missoula, Montana, a girls steps out of the crowd to tell them they're hateful bigots. That they're encouraging violent hate crimes being acted out against the gender-conflicted members of our otherwise peaceful pluralistic society . . .

Webber standing there, cut off in the middle of singing "Buttons and Bows," the spiffy Doris Day version, not the cheesy Dinah Shore version, he's wearing a strapless blue satin sheath with all his chest hair, his shoulder and arm hair billowing from wrist to wrist like a lush boa of black feathers, and he asks this girl, "So you wanna buy a punch or not?"

Flint's one step away, at the head of the line, taking people's money, and he says, "Take your best shot." He says, "Half price for chicks."

And the girl, she just looks at them, tapping one of her feet in its tennis shoe, her mouth clamped shut and pulled way over to one side of her face.

Finally, she says, "Can you fake-sing that *Titanic* song?"

And Flint takes her ten bucks and gives her a hug. "For you," he says, "we can play that song all night long . . ."

That was the night they finally topped out the fifty grand for the mission.

Now, outside the jet, you can see the torn brown-and-gold coastline of Saudi Arabia. The windows of a Gulfstream are two, three times the size of the little porthole you get on a commercial jetliner. Just looking out, at the sun and ocean, everything else mixed together from this high up, you'd almost want to live. To scrub the whole mission and head home, no matter how bleak the future.

A Gulfstream carries enough fuel to fly 6,750 nautical miles, even with an 85-percent headwind. Their target was only going to take 6,701, leaving just enough jet fuel to trigger their luggage, their suitcases plus the bags and bags that Jenson loaded in Florida, where they landed because the pilot started to feel sick. This is after they got him a cup of coffee. Three Vicodins ground and mixed in black coffee would make most people dizzy, groggy, sick. So they landed. Offloaded the regular pilot. Onloaded the bags. Mr. Jenson humping the ammonium nitrate. And here was Flint's girl, Sheila, fresh out of flight school and ready to take off.

In the open doorway to the cockpit, you can see Sheila slip her earphones down to rest around her neck. Looking back over one shoulder, she says, "Just heard on the radio. Somebody dove a jet full of fertilizer into the Vatican . . ."

Go figure, Webber says.

Looking out his window, kicked back in his white leather recliner, Flint says, "We got company." Off that side of the plane, you can see two jet fighters. Flint gives them a little wave. The profiles of the little fighter pilots, they don't wave back.

And Webber looks at the ice melting in his empty glass and says, "Where are we going?"

From the cockpit, Sheila says, "We've had them since we made the turn inland at Jedda." She puts her headphones back over her ears.

And Flint leans across the aisle to pour the empty glass full of Scotch, again, and Flint says, "Does Mecca ring a bell, old buddy? The Al-Haram?" He says, "How about the Ka'ba?"

Sheila, one hand touching the earphone over one ear, she says, "They got the Mormon Tabernacle . . . the National Baptist Convention Headquarters . . . the Wailing Wall and the Dome of the Rock . . . the Beverly Hills Hotel . . ."

Nope, Flint says. Disarmament didn't work. The United Nation didn't, either. Still, maybe this will.

With their friend, Jenson, our Reverend Godless, to be the sole survivor.

Webber says, "What's in the Beverly Hills Hotel?"

And Flint drains his glass and says, "The Dalai Lama . . ."

That girl in Missoula, Montana, Webber got her name and phone number that night. When it came time for them all to write out their last will and testaments, Webber left that girl everything he had in the world, including the Mustang parked in his folks' breezeway, his set of Craftsman tools, and fourteen Coach purses with the shoes and outfits to match.

That night, after she paid fifty bucks to kick Webber's ass, the girl looks at him with his blind white eye swollen almost shut, his lips split. He's three years older than her, but he looks like her grandma, and she says, "So why is it you're doing this?"

And Webber peels off the wig, all the strands and curls of blond hair stuck to the blood dried around his nose and mouth. Webber says, "Everybody wants to make the world a better place."

Drinking his lite beer, Flint looks at Webber. Shaking his head, he says, "You *fucker . . .*" Flint says, "Is that my wig?"

Not every day was filled with terror.

The Matchmaker called this one job "picking white peaches."

You drag two scrolly white sofas together, face to face, straight under the "tree." On this island of sofa, you build a "ladder" by piling together gold-carved little tables. Each table with its heavy, gray marble top veined pink. On top of those, you stack brittle, eggshell-delicate palace chairs, so you can climb higher and higher. Until you're looking down into the gray nest of everyone's dusty wig, everyone's face tilted back so far their mouths hang open against their neck. So high you can look down into the pit behind their collarbones and see the stair steps of their rib cage disappear into their dress or collar.

Everyone, our hands are wrapped in bloody rags. Gloves hang flapping-loose with fingers empty. Shoes are stuffed with balled-up socks to replace missing toes.

We call ourselves the People's Committee to Conserve the Daylight.

The Matchmaker, he takes down a "peach," wrapped in velvet to protect his hand, and he lowers it to skinny Saint Gut-Free. Who hands it to Chef Assassin, the chef with his big stomach hammocked in the waistband of his pants.

Agent Tattletale, with the video camera pressed to his face, he records the peach passed hand to hand.

The oldest peaches, the ones gone dark, you can see yourself reflected in them. The Matchmaker says it's the tungsten filament. As electricity passes through it, the thin wire would burst into flame. That's why each peach is filled with some inert gas. Most of them, argon. Some gas you can't breathe, it keeps the tungsten filament from burning. The very oldest filled with nothing. A vacuum.

The Matchmaker, with pink freckles across his cheeks, more pink freckles on his forearms where his sleeves are rolled back to each elbow, he tells us, "The melting point of tungsten is six thousand degrees Fahrenheit." The normal heat of a "peach" is enough to melt a frying pan. Hot enough to bring copper pennies to a boil. Four thousand degrees Fahrenheit.

Instead of bursting into flame, the tungsten filament evaporates, atom by atom. Some atoms bounce back, off the atoms of argon, and attach to the filament, again, in crystals small as perfect jewels. Other atoms of tungsten, they attach to the cooler inside of the glass "peach."

The atoms "condense," the Matchmaker says. Coating the inside of the glass with metal, turning the outside into a mirror.

Frosted black on the inside, this turns the lightbulbs into little round mirrors that make us look fat. Even skinny Saint Gut-Free with his pant legs and shirtsleeves always twisting and flapping around the bony stalk of each arm and leg.

No, not all our days were filled with murder and torture. Some were just this:

Comrade Snarky holds a peach, turning her face to see it from different angles in the curved glass. The fingers of her free hand, the fingertips pulling the slack skin back at the top of one ear. While she pulls, the dark hollow under that cheekbone is gone. "This is going to sound terrible," Comrade Snarky says. Her fingers release the skin, and that half her face turns back into shadowy sags and wrinkles. "I used to see photographs of those people behind barbed wire in death camps," she says. "Those *living skeletons*. And I always thought: 'Those people could *wear anything*.'"

The Earl of Slander reaches toward her, stretching his arm to collect her words in his hand-sized silver tape recorder.

Comrade Snarky hands the peach to the Baroness Frostbite . . .

Who says, "You're right." The Baroness Frostbite says, "That does sound awful."

And Comrade Snarky leans into the microphone and says, "If you're recording this, you are an asshole."

The Baroness Frostbite, with her teeth loose and rattling in her gums, each big white tooth tapering to show its thin brown root, she hands the peach to the Duke of Vandals.

The Duke, with his ponytail undone and hair hanging in his face. The Duke of Vandals, his jaw works in slow circles on the same wad of nicotine gum he's chewed since forever. His hair the smell of clove cigarettes.

The Duke hands the peach to Miss America, the black roots of her bleach-blond grown out to show how long we've been trapped here. Our poor pregnant Miss America.

Above us, the tree blinks dark for a moment. That moment, we don't exist. Nothing exists. The next moment, the power flashes back. We're back.

"The ghost," Agent Tattletale says, muffled through his video camera.

"The ghost," the Earl of Slander repeats into the tape recorder inside his fist.

Around here, every power surge, every cold draft or strange noise or food smell, we blame it on our ghost.

To Agent Tattletale, the ghost is a murdered private detective.

To the Earl of Slander, the ghost is a has-been child actor.

The brass branches of the tree. Each branch, loopy, bent, twisted as grapevines dipped in dull gold. Dripping with the glass and crystal "leaves" of the tree. The tinkling rustle as you reach inside. The burning smell of dust on each "ripe" peach, still glowing bright white. Too hot to touch without a handful of fabric, a scrap of velvet skirt or brocade waistcoat, to protect your hand. The other peaches, "rotten," gone dark and cold, frosted with dust, and draped with white strands of cobweb. The glass-and-crystal leaves, all white and silver and gray at the same time. As they turn, their edges still sparkle, a moment, a flash of rainbow, before they're no color again.

The branches, twisted and tarnished to dark brown. They each balance a black rice path of dried mouse shit.

Rocking his body, front to back, and holding his breath, the Matchmaker reaches around inside the tree and picks the peaches. He tosses each peach, still hot, down to where the Missing Link catches it in between two silk pillows. Our sports hero, the Missing Link. Mr. College Scholarship, with his single eyebrow thick as pubic hair. Mr. Champion Halfback, with his cleft chin big as two nuts in a sack.

From just this short toss, the peach is cool enough to touch. Mother Nature takes the peach from between the pillows and packs it into a hatbox of old wigs that Miss Sneezy carries, wrapped in both arms, in front of her waist.

Mother Nature, red henna designs smudge the back of her hands and outline the length of each finger. Her every head turn or nod, it rings the chain of brass bells around her neck. Her hair, the smell of sandalwood and patchouli and mint.

Miss Sneezy coughs. Poor Miss Sneezy is always coughing, her nose red and mashed toward one cheek from being wiped with her shirtsleeve. Her eyes bulging-big, swimming in tears, and shattered with red veins. Miss Sneezy coughs and coughs, tongue out, a hand on each knee, bent double.

Sometimes, the Matchmaker clutches the legs of chairs, the veined-marble edges of gold tables, to keep the ladder steady.

Sometimes, the Countess Foresight stands on her toes and holds the handle of a stiff, dusty broom in both hands, high over her head, and she pokes the tree, turning it enough to help you reach more of the "ripe" peaches. The ones still hot enough to boil copper. On her toes, her arms stretched out, you can see the security bracelet still sealed around her wrist. The tracking device dictated by the terms of her parole.

To the Countess Foresight, the ghost is an old-man antiques dealer, his throat slashed with a straight razor.

And with every peach the Matchmaker "picks," the tree goes a little darker.

To Saint Gut-Free, the ghost is an aborted two-headed baby, both heads with his skinny face.

To the Baroness Frostbite, the ghost wears a white apron around his waist and curses God.

Sometimes, Sister Vigilante taps the face of her black wristwatch, saying, "Three hours, seventeen minutes, and thirty seconds until lights-out . . ."

To Sister Vigilante, the ghost is a hero with the side of his face caved in.

To Miss Sneezy, the ghost is her grandmother.

Standing this high up, the Matchmaker says, you can see the ceiling as an empty frontier where no one has ever set foot. That same way—when you were little and you'd sit upside down on the sofa, with your legs against the back cushions and your back against the seat cushions, so your head would hang down the front—that way the old family living room became some strange new place. Upside down, you could walk out across that flat painted floor and look up at the new ceiling, padded with carpet and cluttered with the stalactites of furniture hanging down.

The way, the Duke of Vandals says, an artist will turn his painting upside down, for the same reason, or look at it reversed in a mirror, to see it the way a stranger might. As something he doesn't know. Something new and novel. The reality of someone else.

It's the same way, Saint Gut-Free says, a pervert will turn his pornography upside down to make it new and exciting for a little bit longer.

In this way, each tree of glass leaves and peaches is rooted to the ground by the braided trunk of a thick chain, that trunk covered with a sleeve of dusty red velvet for bark.

When the tree is almost dark, we move our ladder, chair by chair, sofa by sofa, to the next tree. When the "orchard" is bare, we go through the door to the next room.

The harvested peaches we pack away in a hatbox.

No, not every day we're trapped here is filled with kidnapping and humiliation.

The Earl of Slander slips a notepad out of his shirt pocket. He scribbles on the blue-lined paper, saying, "Sixty-two bulbs still viable. With twenty-two held in reserve."

Our last line of defense. Our last resort against the idea of dying alone, here, left in the dark with all the lights burned out. A world without a sun, the survivors left cold and clutching the pitch-dark. The damp wallpaper, growing slippery with mold.

Nobody wants that.

The ripe peaches you leave behind, as they go dark and rotten, and you build your furniture ladder again. You climb back up. Putting your head back into that canopy of glass and crystal leaves, that forest of tarnished brass branches. Dust and mouse turds and cobwebs. And you replace the dark peaches with a few peaches still ripe and burning bright-hot.

The dead peach in the Matchmaker's hand, it shows us not the way we are. More the way we were. The dark glass reflecting all of us, only fat in the curved side. The layer of tungsten atoms precipitated on the inside, the opposite of a pearl, the silver backing on a mirror. Blown glass, thin as a soap bubble.

Here's Mrs. Clark with her new wrinkles disguised behind a veil thick as chicken wire. Even starved-skinny, her lips still look silicone-fat, frozen mid–blow job. Her breasts swell, but full of nothing you'd want to suck. Her wig, powdery-white, it leans to one side. Her neck stringy and webbed with tendons.

Here's the Missing Link with the dark forest on his cheeks, the brush sunk into the deep canyons that run down from each eye.

Something needs to happen.

Something terrible needs to happen.

And—pop.

A peach has slipped and broke on the floor. A nest of glass needles. A mess of white slivers. The image of us as fat, now gone.

The Earl of Slander jots a line in his notepad and says, "Twenty-*one* viable lightbulbs held in reserve . . ."

Sister Vigilante taps her wristwatch and says, "Three hours and ten minutes until lights out . . ."

It's then Mrs. Clark says, "Tell me a story." Through her veil, looking up at the Matchmaker in his sparkling, crystal tree, her silicone lips say, "Tell me something to forget I'm so hungry. Tell me a story you could never tell anyone."

His hand twisting a peach, wrapped in a sticky scrap of dried-bloody velvet, the Matchmaker says, "There's a joke." High on his piled-up ladder of chairs, he says, "There's a joke my uncles only tell when they're drinking . . ."

The Earl of Slander holds up his tape recorder.

Agent Tattletale, his video camera.

The Consultant
A Poem About the Matchmaker

"If you love something," says the Matchmaker, "set it free."
    Just don't be surprised if it comes back with herpes . . .

The Matchmaker onstage, he slouches with his hands
    stuffed deep
    in the pockets of his bib overalls.
    His boots crusted with dried horse shit.
    His shirt, plaid. Flannel. With pearl snaps instead of
        buttons.

Onstage, instead of a spotlight, a movie fragment:
    of wedding videos where brides and grooms trade rings
    and kiss to run outside to blizzards of white rice.
All this trickles across his face, the Matchmaker's bottom lip
    stretched to pocket a chaw
    of chewing tobacco.

The Matchmaker says, "The girl I loved, she thought she
    could do better."
    This girl, she wanted a taller man, with a deep tan, long
        hair, and a bigger dick.
    Who could play the guitar.
    So she said "no" when he'd first kneeled down to propose.
So, the Matchmaker hired a whore named Steed, a male
    prostitute who advertised:

Long hair and a dick as thick as a can of chili. And who
    could learn
to play a few chords.
And Steed pretended to meet her by accident, at church.
    Then, again, at the library.
    The Matchmaker paying two hundred dollars per date,
    and taking notes as the whore told him how much the
        girl liked her nipples
    played with from behind. And how best to make her
        come two or three times.
Steed sent her roses. He sang songs. Steed fucked her in
    back seats and hot tubs,
    where he swore eternal love and devotion.
    Then didn't call her for a week. Two weeks. A month.
    Until he pretended to meet her by accident, at church
        again.
There, Steed said they were finished—because she was too
    slutty. Almost a whore.

"I swear," the Matchmaker says, "he called *her* a whore. The
    nerve of that guy . . ."
God bless him.

All of this, the Matchmaker's secret plan to give his girlfriend
    a premature, accelerated broken heart. Then catch her
        on the rebound.
His last meeting with Steed, he paid an extra fifty bucks for
    a blow job.
    Steed kneeling there, at work between his knees.
    This way, when his future wife had her well-researched,
        multiple orgasms,
    the man in her head would not be a total stranger to her
        husband,
    the Matchmaker.

There's a joke the uncles only tell when they're drunk.

Half the joke is the noise they make. It's the sound of someone hawking up spit from the back of his throat. A long, rasping sound. After every family event, when there's nothing left to do except drink, the uncles will take their chairs out under the trees. Out where we can't see them in the dark.

While the aunts wash dishes, and the cousins run wild, the uncles are out back in the orchard, tipping bottles back, leaning back on the two rear legs of their chairs. In the dark, you can hear one uncle make the sound: *Shooo-rook.* Even in the dark, you know he's pulled one hand sideways through the air in front of him. *Shooo-rook,* and the rest of the uncles laugh.

The aunts hear the sound and it makes them smile and shake their heads: Men. The aunts don't know the joke, but they know anything that makes men laugh so hard must be stupid.

The cousins don't know the joke, but they make the sound. *Shooo-rook.* They pull a hand through the air, sideways, and fall down laughing. Their whole childhood, all the kids did it. Said: *Shooo-rook.* Screamed it. The family's magic formula to make each other laugh.

The uncles would lean down to teach them. Even as little kids, barely on two legs, they'd mimic the sound. *Shooo-rook.* And the uncles would show how to pull one hand sideways, always from left to right, in front of your neck.

They'd ask—the cousins, hanging off the arm of an uncle, kicking their feet in the air—they'd ask, what did the sound mean? And the hand motion?

It was an old, old story an uncle might tell them. The sound was from when the uncles were all young men in the army. During the war. The cousins would climb the pockets of an uncle's coat, a foot hooked in one pocket, a hand reaching for the next pocket higher up. The way you'd climb trees.

And they'd beg: Tell us. Tell us the story.

But all an uncle would do is promise: Later. When they were grown up. The uncle would catch you under the arms and throw you over his shoulder. He'd carry a cousin that way, running, racing the other uncles into the house, to kiss the aunts and eat another slice of pie. You'd pop popcorn and listen to the radio.

It was the family password. A secret most of them didn't understand. A ritual to keep them safe. All the cousins knew was, it made them laugh together. This was something only they knew.

The uncles said the sound was proof that your worst fears might just disappear. No matter how terrible something looked, it might not be around tomorrow. If a cow died, and the other cattle looked sick, swelling with bloat and about to die, if nothing could be done, the uncles made the sound. *Shooo-rook.* If the peaches were setting in the orchard and a frost was predicted that night, the uncles said it. *Shooo-rook.* It meant the terror you were helpless to stop, it might just stop itself.

Every time the family got together, it was their greeting: *Shooo-rook.* It made the aunts cross-eyed, all these cousins making that silly sound. *Shooo-rook.* All the cousins waving one hand through the air. *Shooo-rook.* The uncles laughing so hard they stood leaning forward with one hand braced on each knee. *Shooo-rook.*

An aunt, someone married into the family, she might ask: What did it mean? What was the story behind it? But the uncles would shake their heads. The one uncle, her own husband, would slip his arm around her waist and kiss her cheek and tell her, honey bunch, she didn't want to know.

The summer I turned eighteen, an uncle said it to me, alone. And that time, he didn't laugh.

I'd been drafted to serve in the army, and no one could know if I'd ever come back.

There wasn't a war, but there was cholera in the army. There was always disease and accidents. They were packing a bag for me to take, just me and the uncle, and my uncle said it: *Shooo-rook.* Just remember, he said, no matter how black the future looks, all your troubles could be disappeared tomorrow.

Packing that bag, I asked him. What did it mean?

It was from the last big war, he said. When the uncles were all in the same regiment. They were captured and forced to work in a camp. There, an officer from the other army would force them to work at gunpoint. Every day, they expected this man to kill them, and there was nothing they could do. Every week, trains would arrive filled with prisoners from occupied countries: soldiers and Gypsies. Most of them went from the train, two hundred steps to die. The uncles hauled away their bodies. The officer they hated, he led the firing squad.

The uncle telling this story, he said every day the uncles stepped forward to drag the dead people way—the holes in their clothes still leaking warm blood—the firing squad would be waiting for the next batch of prisoners to execute. Every time the uncles stepped in front of those guns, they expected the officer to open fire.

Then, one day, the uncle says: *Shooo-rook.*

It happened, the way Fate happens.

The officer, if he saw a Gypsy woman he liked, he'd take her out of line. After that batch was dead, while the uncles hauled away the bodies, the officer would make this woman undress. Standing there in his uniform, crawling with gold braid in the bright sun, surrounded by guns, the officer made the Gypsy woman kneel in the dirt and open his zipper. He made her open her mouth.

The uncles, they'd seen this happen too many times to remember. The Gypsy would bury her lips in the front of the officer's pants. Her eyes closed, she'd suck and suck and not see him take a knife from the back of his belt.

The moment the officer came to orgasm he'd grab the Gypsy by her hair, holding her head tight with one hand. His other hand would cut her throat.

It was always the same sound: *Shooo-rook.* His seed still erupting, he'd push her naked body away before the blood could explode from her neck.

It was a sound that would always mean the end. Fate. A sound they'd never be able to escape. To forget.

Until, one day, the officer took a Gypsy and had her kneel naked in the dirt. With the firing squad watching, the uncles watching with their feet buried in the layer of dead bodies, the officer made the Gypsy open his zipper. The woman closed her eyes and opened her mouth.

This was something the uncles had witnessed so often they could watch without seeing it.

The officer gripped the Gypsy's long hair, wrapped it in his fist. The knife flashed, and there was the sound. That sound. Now the family's secret code for laughter. Their greeting to each other. The Gypsy fell back, blood exploding from under her chin. She coughed once, and something landed in the dirt next to where she died.

They all looked, the firing squad and the uncles and the officer, and there in the dirt was half a cock. *Shooo-rook,* and the officer had cut off his own erection stuck down the throat of this dead woman. The zipper in the officer's pants was still erupting with his seed, exploding with blood. The officer reached one hand to where his cock lay coated with dirt. His knees buckled.

Then the uncles were dragging away his body to bury it. The

next officer in charge of the camp, he wasn't so bad. Then the war was over, and the uncles came home. Without what happened, their family might not be. If that officer had lived, I might not exist.

That sound, their secret family code, the uncle told me. The sound means: Yes, terrible things happen, but sometimes those terrible things—they save you.

Outside the window, in the peach trees back of their house, the other cousins run. The aunts sit on the front porch, shelling peas. The uncles stand, their arms folded, arguing about the best way to paint a fence.

You might go to war, the uncle says. Or you might get cholera and die. Or, he says, and moves one hand sideways, left to right, in the air below his belt buckle: *Shooo-rook . . .*

It's Sister Vigilante who finds the body. She's coming down the lobby stairs, from the first-balcony foyer, from turning on the lights in the projection booth, when she stumbles over Miss America's pink exercise wheel gripped between two dead-white hands.

There, in the video camera's little viewing screen, the Duke of Vandals's stretched out at the foot of the lobby stairs, his fringed buckskin shirttails hanging out, his blond hair fanned out, facedown on the blue carpet. The pink plastic wheel is between his hands. One side of his face is stomped flat, the hair pasted down in every direction with blood.

The royalties to our story split one less way.

Sister Vigilante, she had the video camera. Getting around in the dark, Mr. Whittier had used a flashlight, but now the old batteries were as dead as him and Lady Baglady. Now Sister Vigilante used the camera spotlight, with its rechargeable batteries, to find her way up and down the stairs before dawn, and after dark.

"Subarachnoid hemorrhage," Sister Vigilante says, her words recorded as she pans the camera over the body. "With partial avulsion of the left cerebellar hemisphere." Saying, It's the most common sequela of massive head trauma. She zooms in for a close-up of the compound skull fracture, the bleed-ing inside the outer layers of the brain.

"As you press the skull in one spot," she says, "the contents swell around that location and burst the skull in a rough circle."

The camera roving over the sharp edges and dried red on the skull, Sister Vigilante's voice says, "The *outbending* is extensive . . ."

The camera comes up to show the rest of us, staggering into the lobby, yawning and squinting into the spotlight.

Mrs. Clark looks down at the sprawled buckskin body of the Duke, his cud of nicotine gum—plus all his teeth—knocked halfway across the lobby floor. And her inflated lips squeak out a lit-tle scream.

Miss America says, "The *bastard.*" She steps over to the body and kneels to pry the stiff, dead fingers off the black rubber grips of the exercise wheel. "He was trying to lose more weight than the rest of us," she says. "The evil shit was doing aerobics to look . . . *worse.*"

As Miss America wrestles and kicks at the stiff fingers, Mrs. Clark says, "Rigor mortis."

As Miss America pulls the body to one side, twisting the wheel to free it from the hands, as she pulls, the body turns faceup. The Duke of Vandals, his face is dark as a sunburn, but purple except for the tip of his nose. The tips of his chin and nose and the flat of his forehead are all blue-white.

"Livor mortis," Mrs. Clark says. The blood settles to the lowest points of the body. Except where the face pressed into the carpet: at those points the weight of the body kept the capillaries collapsed, so no blood could pool inside.

From behind the video camera, Sister Vigilante says, "You sure seem to know a lot about dead bodies . . ."

And Mrs. Clark says, "Just what did *you* mean by *partial avulsion of the left cerebellar hemisphere?*"

The video camera still panning the body, taping over the death of Mr. Whittier, the voice of Sister Vigilante says, "That means the brains are leaking out."

The pink wheel slips free from the Duke's hands, and the fingers seem to relax. Rigor mortis only goes away, Mrs. Clark says, as the body starts to decompose.

By now, Agent Tattletale has arrived, looking strange with both his eyes showing. Reverend Godless stands over the body. Mother Nature with her patchouli smell. The Matchmaker, his back teeth chewing around and round on a cheekful of spit and tobacco, he leans over for a better look.

The Matchmaker says, "Decomposition?"

And Mrs. Clark nods, frowning her silicone lips. After death, she says, the actin and myosin filaments of the muscles become complexed from the lack of adenosine-triphosphate production . . . She says, "You wouldn't understand."

"Too bad," Chef Assassin says. "If he wasn't so far gone, we might've had a big breakfast."

Mother Nature says, "You're kidding."

And the chef says, "No. Actually, I'm not."

The Matchmaker is pop-eyed, squatting next to the body, digging in the back pants pocket.

Rubbing her hennaed hands together and yawning, Mother Nature says, "How can you be so *awake*?"

And, opening his mouth, wide, pointing a finger at the brown mess inside, the Matchmaker says, "Chaw . . ." He pulls out the wallet, slips out the paper money, and tucks the wallet back into the pocket, saying, "Kiss me, and you'll perk up, too."

And, shaking her head, Mother Nature says, "No. Thanks."

"Little girl," the Matchmaker says. He spits a brown stream on the blue carpet, and he says, "you need to be a little sexier character, or no bankable actress is going to want to play you . . ."

And Saint Gut-Free pulls her away.

Sister Vigilante shuts off the camera and hands it back to Agent Tattletale.

To nobody. Or to everybody, Mrs. Clark says, "Who do you suspect?"

And Agent Tattletale says, "You."

Mrs. Clark. She got up late last night. She found the Duke of Vandals alone, doing this stomach exercise. She crushed his skull. End of official story.

"You ever wonder," Mrs. Clark says, "what you'll do after you sell your *old life*?"

And the Matchmaker licks the spit off his lips, saying, "What do you mean?" He hooks both thumbs behind the straps of his bib overalls.

"After you've sold *this* story," Mrs. Clark says, "will you just look for a new villain?" She says, "For the rest of your life, will you be looking for someone new to blame everything on?"

And Agent Tattletale smiles, saying, "Relax. There's no point blaming one of *us* for this. There are *victims*," he says, pointing a finger at his chest. "And there are *villains*," he says, pointing a finger at her. "Don't create shades of gray that a mass audience can't follow."

And Mrs. Clark says, "I did not kill this young man."

And the Agent shrugs. He shoulders his camera, saying, "You want audience sympathy at this point, you're going to have to campaign for it." His spotlight flickers bright, spotlighting her, and Agent Tattletale says, "Tell us one thing. Give us one good flashback to make the folks at home feel just a teeny bit sorry for you . . ."

The Nightmare Box

A Story by Mrs. Clark

The night before she disappeared, Cassandra cut off her eyelashes.

Easy as homework, Cassandra Clark takes a little pair of scissors out of her purse, little chrome fingernail-scissors, she leans into the big mirror above the bathroom sink and looks at herself. Her eyes half closed, and her mouth hanging open the way she puts on mascara, Cassandra braces one hand against the bathroom counter and uses the scissors to snip. Each long black lash falling, settling, fluttering down the sink drain, she doesn't even look at her mother reflected there, standing behind her in the mirror.

That night, Mrs. Clark hears her slip out of bed while it's still dark. In the one hour when there's no traffic in the street, she goes naked to the living room with all the lights off. There's the rumble of springs inside the old sofa. There's the rasp and—click—of a cigarette lighter. Then a sigh. A whiff of cigarette smoke.

After the sun's up, Cassandra's still there, sitting naked on the sofa with the curtains open and cars going past. All her arms and legs bunched tight around her in the cold air. In one hand, she's got the cigarette, burned down to the filter. Ashes on the sofa cushion beside her. She's awake and looking at the blank television screen. Maybe looking at herself reflected there, naked in the black glass. Her hair looks lumpy with tangles from not combing. Her lipstick from two days ago, it's still smeared across her cheek. Her eye shadow outlines the wrinkles around each eye. Her eyelashes gone, her green eyes looking dull and fake because you never see her blink.

Her mother says, "Did you dream about it?"

Mrs. Clark asks: does she want French toast? Mrs. Clark turns on the wall heater and gets Cassandra's robe off the back of the bathroom door.

Cassandra hugging herself in the cold sunshine, sitting knees-together, her breasts are pushed up by her arms. Flakes of gray cigarette ash are scattered on the top of each thigh. Flakes of gray ash settle into her pubic hair. Her feet twitch with tendons under the skin. Her feet flat and side by side on the polished wood floor, they're the only part of her not statue-still.

Mrs. Clark says, "Did you remember something?" Her mother says, "You had on your new black dress . . ." She says, "The short-short one."

Mrs. Clark goes to put the bathrobe around her daughter, tucking it up tight around her neck. She says, "It happened in that gallery. Across from the antique store."

Cassandra doesn't look away from her own dark reflection in the off television. She doesn't blink, and the bathrobe slips down, putting both her breasts back out in the cold.

And her mother says, what did she see?

"I don't know," Cassandra says. She says, "I can't say."

"Let me get my notes," Mrs. Clark tells her. She says, "I think I have this figured out."

It's when she comes back from the bedroom, her thick brown folder of notes in one hand, the folder open so she can pick through it with her other hand, when she looks around the living room, Cassandra's gone.

At that moment, Mrs. Clark's saying, "The way the Nightmare Box works is, the front . . ."

But Cassandra's not in the kitchen or the bathroom. Cassandra's not in the basement. That's their whole house. She's not out in the backyard or on the stairs. Her bathrobe is still on the sofa. Her purse and shoes and coat, none of them are gone. Her suitcase is still on her bed, half packed. Only Cassandra's gone.

At first, Cassandra said it was nothing. According to the notes, it was an art-gallery opening.

There in Mrs. Clark's notes, it says, "Random Interval Timer . . ."

Her notes say, "The man hung himself . . ."

It started on the night all the galleries open their new shows, and downtown was crowded with people, everyone still dressed up from the office or school and holding hands. Medium-young couples in dark clothes that wouldn't show the dirt from a taxi seat. Wearing the good jewelry they couldn't wear on the subway. Their teeth white, as if they never used teeth for anything except to smile.

They were all watching each other look at art before watching each other eat dinner.

It's all in Mrs. Clark's notes.

Cassandra had on her new black dress. The short-short one.

That night, she wanted a long glass of white wine, just to hold it. She didn't dare lift the glass, because her dress was strapless, so she kept her arms down at each side, holding her elbows close in. This flexed some muscle across her chest. Some new muscle she'd found playing basketball in school. It pushed her breasts so high her cleavage seemed to start at her throat.

That dress, it was black and stitched with black sequins and beads. It was a crust of rough black glitter with her breasts pink and meaty inside. A hard black shell.

Both her hands, the way her painted fingernails meshed together, they looked handcuffed around the stem of her wineglass. Her hair coiled and pinned up high, it was so heavy and thick. Strands and curls were coming undone, dangling, but she didn't dare reach up to fix it. Her bare shoulders, her hair coming apart, her high heels clenched the muscles of each leg, pushed her ass up, curving it out at the bottom of a long zipper.

Her perfect lipstick mouth. No red smeared on the glass she didn't dare lift. Her eyes looking huge under long eyelashes. Her green eyes the only part of her moving in the crowded room.

Standing and smiling in the center of an art gallery, she was the only woman you'd remember. Cassandra Clark, only fifteen years old.

This was less than a week before she disappeared, just three nights.

Sitting now in the warm spot and ashes Cassandra left on the sofa, Mrs. Clark looks through the folder of notes.

The gallery owner was talking to them, to them and the people gathered around.

"Rand," her notes say. The owner's name was Rand.

The gallery owner was showing them a box on three tall legs. A tripod. The box was black, the size of an old-time camera. The kind of camera where a man might stand behind, hunched under a sheet of black canvas to protect the glass plate coated with chemicals inside. The kind of Civil War camera that took your picture with a flash of gunpowder. A mushroom cloud of gray smoke that hurt your nose. When you first walked into the gallery, that's how it looked, this box on three legs.

The box was painted black.

"Lacquered," the gallery owner said.

It was lacquered black, waxed and smudged gray with fingerprints.

The gallery owner was smiling down the stiff, strapless front of Cassandra's dress. He had a thin mustache, plucked and trimmed perfect as two eyebrows. He had a little devil's beard that made his chin look pointed. He wore a banker's blue suit and a single earring, too big, too fake-bright to be anything but a real diamond.

The box was fitted along every seam with complicated moldings, ridges and grooves, that made it look heavy as a bank vault. Every seam hidden under detail and thick paint.

"Like a little coffin," somebody in the gallery said. A man with a ponytail, chewing gum.

On each side of the box were brass handles. You had to hold them both, the gallery owner told them. To complete a circuit. If you wanted to make the box work right, you held both handles. You pressed your eye to the brass peephole in the front. Your left eye. And you looked inside.

Person after person, a hundred people must've looked that night, but nothing happened. They held on and looked inside, but all they saw was their own eye reflected in the darkness behind the little glass lens. All they heard was a little sound. A clock, ticking. Slow as the drip . . . drip . . . drip . . . from a leaky faucet. This little ticking from inside the smudged, black-painted box.

The box felt sticky with its layer of grime.

The gallery owner held up one finger. He tapped his knuckle against the side of the box and said, "Some kind of Random Interval Timer."

It could run for a month, always ticking. Or it could run for another hour. But the moment it stopped, that would be the moment to look inside.

"Here," the gallery owner said, Rand said, and he tapped a little brass push-button, small as a doorbell, on the side of the box.

You hold the handles, and you wait. When the ticking stops, he said, you look and push the button.

On a little brass nameplate, a plate screwed to the top of the box, if you stood on tiptoes, you could read "The Nightmare Box." And the name "Roland Whittier." The brass handles were green from people holding tight, waiting. The brass fitting around the peephole was tarnished with their breath. The black outsides were waxed with grease from their skin rubbing, pressed close.

Holding the handles, you could feel it inside. The ticking. The timer. Steady and forever as a heartbeat.

The moment it stopped, Rand said, the push-button would trigger a flash of light inside. A single pulse of light.

What people saw then, Rand didn't know. The box came from the closed antique shop across the street. There it had sat for nine years and never stopped ticking. The man who owned it, the antiques dealer, he always told customers it might be broken. Or it was a joke.

For nine years, the box sat ticking on a shelf, until dust buried it. Until, one day, the dealer's grandson found it, not ticking. The grandson was nineteen years old, going to college to become a lawyer. This teenager without a hair on his chest, all day girls came into the shop to use their eyes on him. A good kid with a scholarship playing soccer, a bank account, and his own car, he had a summer job at the antique shop, dusting. When he found the box, it was silent—ready and waiting. He took the handles. He pressed the button and looked inside.

The antiques dealer found him, dust still smeared around his left eye. Blinking. His eyes focused on nothing. He just sat in a pile of dust and cigarette butts he'd swept up on the floor. The grandson, he never went back to college. His car sat at the curb until the city towed it away. Every day after that, he sat in the street outside the shop. Twenty years old, and he sits on the curb all day, rain or shine. You ask him anything and he just laughs. That kid, by now he should be a lawyer, practicing law, but now you can go visit him in some fleabag hotel. Public housing, on Social Security for a complete mental depression. Not drugs even.

Rand, the gallery owner, says, "Just a case of total crackup."

You go visit this kid, and he sits on his bed all day, cockroaches crawling in and out of his clothes, his pant legs and shirt collar. Each fingernail and toenail is grown long and yellow as a pencil.

You ask him anything: How he's doing? Is he eating? What did he see? And the kid still only laughs. Cockroaches moving around, lumps inside his shirt. His head circled with houseflies.

Another morning, the antiques dealer comes in to open his shop, and the dusty clutter is different. It could be someplace he's never been. Again, the box has stopped ticking. That always-quiet countdown. And the Nightmare Box sits there, waiting for him to look.

All morning, the dealer doesn't unlock the front door. People come and cup their hands against his window to peek inside. To look for something back in the shadows. For some reason why the shop isn't open.

In that same way, the antiques dealer could've peeked inside the box. To see why. To know what happened. What would take the spirit out of a kid, now twenty years old, a kid with everything to look forward to.

All morning, the antiques dealer watches the box not tick.

Instead of looking, the dealer scrubs the toilet bowl in the back. He hauls out a ladder and picks the dry, dead flies from each hanging light fixture. He polishes brass. Oils woods. He sweats until his starched white shirt is soft with wrinkles. He does everything he hates.

People from the neighborhood, his longtime customers, they come to the store and find the door locked. Maybe they knock. Then they go away.

The box waits to show him what for.

It's going to be somebody he loves who looks inside.

All his lifetime, this antiques dealer, he works hard. He finds good stock at a fair price. He carts it here and puts it on display. He wipes the dust from it. Most of his life, he's been in this one store, and already he's going to estate sales and buying back the same lamps and tables, selling them for the second and third times. Buying from dead customers to sell to live ones. His shop just inhaling and exhaling this same stock.

This same tide of chairs, tables, china dolls. Beds, cabinets, little knickknacks.

Coming in and going out.

All morning, the dealer's eyes keep coming back to the Nightmare Box.

He does his bookkeeping. All day, he fingers the ten-key adding machine, balancing accounts. Totaling and comparing long columns of numbers. Seeing the same stock, the same dressers and hat racks arrive and depart on paper. He makes coffee. He makes more coffee.

He drinks coffee until the can of grounds is empty. He cleans until everything in the shop is just his reflection in buffed wood and clean glass. The smell of lemon and almond oils. The smell of his sweat.

The box waits.

He changes into a clean shirt. He combs his hair.

He calls his wife and says how, for years, he's been hiding cash in a tin box under the spare tire in the trunk of their car. Forty years ago, when their daughter was born, the antiques dealer tells his wife, he had an affair with some girl who used to come in on her lunchtime. He says he's sorry. He tells her not to hold dinner for him. He says he loves her.

Next to the telephone, the box sits, not ticking.

The next day, the police find him. His accounts balanced. His shop in perfect order. The antiques dealer's taken an orange extension cord and knotted it to the coat hook on his bathroom wall. In the tiled bathroom, where any mess would be easy to clean up, he's knotted the cord around his neck and then just—relaxed. He's sunk down, slumped against the wall. He's choked, dead, almost sitting on the tiled floor.

On the display counter, in the front of the store, the box is ticking, again.

This history, it's all in Tess Clark's thick folder of notes.

It's then the box comes here, to Rand's art gallery. By then, it's kind of a legend, Rand tells the little crowd. The Nightmare Box.

Across the street, the antique store is just a big painted room, empty behind its front window.

It was right then, that night, Rand showing them the box, Cassandra's arms bunched in tight to hold her dress up, it was that moment somebody in the crowd said, "It's stopped."

The ticking.

It had stopped.

The crowd waited, listening to the quiet, their ears reaching out for any sound.

And Rand said, "Be my guest."

"Like this?" Cassandra said, and she gave Mrs. Clark the tall glass of white wine to hold. She lifted one hand to the brass handle on that side. She handed Rand her beaded little evening bag, her little clutch, with her lipstick and emergency cash inside. "Am I doing this right?" she said, and lifted her other hand to the opposite handle.

"Now," Rand said.

Mrs. Clark stood there, the mother, a little helpless with a full glass of wine in each hand, watching. Everything ready to spill or break.

Rand cupped his hand against the back of Cassandra's neck, the bare skin above her spine, where only a soft curl of hair fluttered down. At the top of her long-zippered ass. He pressed so her neck arched, her chin coming up a little and her lips moving open. Holding her neck in one hand and her purse in his other, Rand told her, "Look inside."

The box is quiet. Silent the way a bomb might be the moment before it goes off. Explodes.

Cassandra opens up the left side of her face, her eyebrow held high, her eyelashes on that side trembling, thick with black mascara. Her green eye, wet and soft, something between solid and liquid, she puts her eye against the little glass, the darkness inside.

The crowd around them. Waiting. Rand still holding the back of her neck.

One painted fingernail moves to the button and, Cassandra's face pressed to the black wood of the box, she says, "Tell me when."

The way you have to look inside, to make your face fit against the box, you have to turn your face a little to the right. You have to stoop a little, leaning too far forward. You have to hold both handles because this puts you off balance. Your weight, it has to rest against the box, pressing through your hands, balancing on your face.

Cassandra's face against the black, complicated corners and angles of the old box. The way she might be kissing it. The trembling curls of her hair. The sparkling dangle of each bright earring.

Her finger moves on the button.

And the ticking starts again, faint and deep inside.

What happens, only Cassandra sees it.

The random timer starts again for another week, another year. Another hour.

Her face stays there, pressed into the peephole, until her shoulders sag. She stands, her arms still hanging down, her shoulders go round and sloped.

Blink-blinking her eyes, fast, Cassandra steps back and shakes her face a little. Her eyes not meeting anyone's eyes, Cassandra looks around at the floor, at people's feet, her lips shut tight. The stiff front of her dress bags forward, gapping out away from her breasts with no bra inside. She reaches out and pushes herself back from the box.

She steps out of each high heel, standing flat-footed on the gallery floor, and the muscles in her legs disappear. The two rock-hard halves of her ass, they go soft.

A mask of loose hair hangs in her face.

If you're tall enough, you can see her nipples.

Rand says, "Well?" He clears his throat, pushing breath out through a long sound of spit and snot, and he says, "What did you see?"

And, still not looking at anyone, her eyelashes still pointing at the floor, Cassandra reaches a hand up and plucks the earring from each side of her head.

Rand reaches to give her the little beaded purse, but Cassandra doesn't take it. Instead, she hands him her jewelry.

Mrs. Clark says, "What happened?"

And Cassandra says, "Can we go home now?"

They listen to the box tick.

It's a couple days later she cut off her eyelashes. She flopped a suitcase open across the foot of the bed and she started putting things in, shoes and socks and her underwear, then taking things out. Packing and repacking. After she disappeared, the suitcase was still there. Half full or half empty.

Now all Mrs. Clark has are her notes, her thick folder full of notes about how the Nightmare Box must work. Somehow it must hypnotize you. It implants an image or an idea. A subliminal flash. It injects some message into your brain so deep you can't retrieve it. You can't resolve it. The box infects you this way. It makes everything you know wrong. Useless.

What's inside the box is some fact you can't unlearn. Some new ideas you can't undiscover.

Days after they went to the art gallery, now Cassandra's gone.

On the third day, Mrs. Clark goes downtown. Back to the gallery. Her thick brown folder of notes tucked under one arm.

The street door's unlocked and the lights are off. In the gray light from the windows, Rand is there, sitting on the floor in a dusting of cut hair. His little devil's beard is gone. His fat diamond earring, gone.

Mrs. Clark says, "You looked, didn't you?"

The gallery owner just sits there, sprawled, legs spread on the cold concrete, looking at his hands.

Mrs. Clark sits cross-legged on the floor next him and says, "Look at my notes." She says, "Tell me I'm right."

The way the Nightmare Box works, she says, is because the front is angled out on one side. It forces you to put your left eye against the peephole. It has a little glass fish-eye lens, set in a brass fitting, the same kind you'd find in anyone's front door. The way the front of the box is angled, the only way you can look is with your left eye.

"This way," Mrs. Clark says, "what you see, you have to perceive with your right brain."

Whatever you see inside, it's the intuitive, emotional, instinctual side of you, the right-brain part, that has to witness it.

Plus, only one person can look each time. What you suffer, you suffer it alone. What happens inside the Nightmare Box, it only happens to you. There's no one you can share it with. There's no room for someone else.

Plus, the fish-eye lens, she says, it warps what you see. It distorts.

Plus, she says, the name engraved on the brass plate—The Nightmare Box—it tells you that you'll be scared. The name creates an expectation that you fulfill.

Mrs. Clark sits and waits to be right.

She sits, watching for Rand to blink.

The box stands over them on its three legs, ticking.

Rand doesn't move except his chest, to breathe.

On his desk, near the back of the gallery, there's still Cassandra's jewelry. Her little beaded purse.

"No," Rand says. He smiles and says, "That's not it."

The ticking counts down, loud in the cold quiet.

You can only call the hospitals, asking if they have a girl with green eyes and no eyelashes. You can only call so many times, Mrs. Clark says, before they start not to hear you. To put you on hold. Make you give up.

She looks up from her thick stack of paper, her notes, and says, "Tell me."

The antique store, it's still empty across the street.

"This isn't what happened," Rand says. Still just looking at his hands, he says, "But this is how it felt."

One weekend, he had to go to a company picnic for a job he used to have. A job he hated. And as a joke, instead of food, he brought a wicker crate full of trained doves. To everyone, this was just another picnic basket, more pasta salad and wine. Rand kept the hamper under a tablecloth all morning, keeping it shaded and cool. Keeping the doves inside quiet.

He snuck them crumbs of French bread. He squeezed bits of corn polenta through holes in the wicker.

All morning, the people he worked with, they sipped wine or sparkling water and talked about corporate goals. Mission statements. Team building.

At the moment when it seemed they'd all wasted a beautiful Saturday morning, that moment when all the small talk comes to an end, Rand says that's when he opened the hamper.

People. These people who worked together every day. Who thought they knew each other. As this white chaos. This storm exploded up from the center of the picnic. Some people screamed. People fell back into the grass. They covered their faces with their open hands. Food and wine fell. Good clothes got stained.

It was the moment after when people saw it wouldn't hurt them. When people saw this was safe. It was the most lovely thing they'd ever seen. They fell back, too amazed to even smile. For the countless hours of that one long moment, they forgot everything important and watched the cloud of white wings twist up into the blue sky.

They watched it spiral. And the spiral open. And the birds, trained by many trips, follow each other away to someplace they knew every time was their real home.

"That," Rand says, "is what's inside the Nightmare Box."

It's something that goes beyond life-after-death. What's in the box is proof that what we call life isn't. Our world is a dream. Infinitely fake. A nightmare.

One look, Rand says, and your life—your preening and struggle and worry—it's all pointless.

The grandson crawling with cockroaches, the antiques dealer, Cassandra with no eyelashes wandering off naked.

All your problems and love affairs.

They're an illusion.

"What you see inside the box," Rand says, "is a glimpse of the real reality."

The two people still sitting there, together on the concrete gallery floor, the sunlight from the windows and the street noise, it all feels different. It could be somewhere they've never been before. It's right now the ticking from the box, it's stopped.

And Mrs. Clark was too afraid to look.

1.
2.
3.
4.
5.
6.
7.
8.
9.
10.
11.
12.
13.
14.
15.
16.
17.
18.
19.
20.
21.
22.
23.
24.

We have no food. No hot water. Pretty soon, we may be trapped here in the dark, Brailling our way from room to room, feeling, hand over hand, every moldy, soft patch of the wallpaper. Or crawling over the sticky carpet, our hands and knees crusted, heavy with dried mouse turds. Touching every stiff carpet stain, branched with arms and legs.

We have no heat, now that the furnace is broken, again—the way it should be.

Every so often, you hear Saint Gut-Free shout for help, but a shout soft as the last echo off a wall a long ways away.

The Saint calls himself the People's Committee for Getting Attention. All day, he's walking the length of every outside wall, banging on the locked metal fire-doors, screaming. But only banging with his open hand. And not yelling too loud. Just loud enough to say he tried. We tried. We made the best of the situation by being brave, strong characters.

We organized committees. We stayed calm.

We're still suffering, despite the ghost who snaked the sewer pipes one night and got the toilets to work. The ghost used pliers to turn the gas back on to the water heater, after Comrade Snarky threw away the valve handle. It even spliced the power cord to the washing machine and started a load of clothes.

To the Reverend Godless, our ghost is the Dalai Lama. To the Countess Foresight, it's Marilyn Monroe. Or it's Mr. Whittier's empty wheelchair, the chrome shining in his room.

During the rinse cycle, the ghost adds fabric softener.

With collecting the lightbulbs and shouting for help and undoing the ghost's good deeds, we have almost no time left over. Just keeping the furnace broken is a full-time job.

What's worse is, this is nothing we can put in the final screenplay. No, we have to look in pain. Hungry and hurting. We should be praying for help. Mrs. Clark should be ruling us with an iron fist.

None of this is going bad enough. Even our hunger is less than we'd want. A letdown.

"We need a monster," Sister Vigilante says, her bowling ball in her lap and her elbows propped on it. Using a knife to pry up her fingernails, wedging the knife tip under and rocking the blade side to side to pop each nail up, then pull it off, she says, "The basis of any horror story is, the building has to work against us."

Flicking away each fingernail, she shakes her head, saying, "It doesn't hurt when you think how much money the scars are worth."

It's all we can do not to drag Mrs. Clark out of her dressing room and force her at knife point to bully and torture us.

Sister Vigilante calls herself the People's Committee for Finding a Decent Enemy.

Director Denial limps around with both feet wrapped in silk rags. All of her toes hacked off. Her left hand is nothing, just a paddle of skin and bone, just the palm, with all the fingers and thumb hacked off, this paddle wrapped huge with rags. Her right hand is just her thumb and index finger. Between them, she holds a severed finger with her dark-red polish still on the nail.

Holding this finger, the Director walks from room to room, the Arabian Nights gallery to the Italian Renaissance lounge, her saying, "Here, kitty, kitty, kitty." Saying, "Cora? Come to Mama, Cora, my baby. Dinner's ready . . ."

Every so often, you hear the voice of Saint Gut-Free shouting soft as a whisper, "Help us . . . Someone, please, help us . . ." Then the soft clap of his hands patting the exit doors.

Extra soft and quiet, just in case someone is right outside.

Director Denial calls herself the People's Committee for Feeding the Cat.

Miss Sneezy and the Missing Link, they're the People's Committee for Flushing the Rest of the Ruined Food. With every bag they flush, they force down a cushion or a shoe, anything that will make sure the toilets stay clogged.

Agent Tattletale knocks at Mrs. Clark's dressing-room door, saying, "Listen to me." Saying, "You can't be the victim, here. We've voted you the next villain."

Agent Tattletale calls himself the People's Committee for Getting Us a New Devil.

The lightbulb "peaches" the Matchmaker picks, that he lowers to Baroness Frostbite . . . That she packs so careful into boxes padded with old wigs . . . At the end of every day, the Earl of Slander takes them to the subbasement and breaks them on the concrete floor. He throws them the exact same way he'll tell the world Mrs. Clark broke them.

Already, the rooms seem bigger. Dimmer. The colors and walls disappear into the dark. Agent Tattletale videotapes the broken bulbs and Sister Vigilante's thrown-away fingernails on the floor. Identical half-moon shards of white.

Despite the ghost, our life is almost bad enough.

To Sister Vigilante, the ghost is a hero. She says we hate heroes.

"Civilization always works best," Sister Vigilante says, picking the knife under another fingernail, "when we have a bogeyman."

Voir Dire

A Poem About Sister Vigilante

"Some man sued for a million bucks," Sister Vigilante says,
   "because of a dirty look."
   On her first day doing jury duty.

Sister Vigilante onstage, she holds a book to shield the
   front of her blouse.
   Her blouse, frilly-yellow and edged with white lace.
   The book, black leather with the title stamped in gold
      leaf across the cover:
   Holy Bible
On her face, black-framed eyeglasses.
   Her only jewelry, a charm bracelet of jiggling, trembling
      silver reminders.
   Her hairdo dyed the same deep black as her shoe
      polish. As her Bible.

Onstage, instead of a spotlight, a movie fragment:
   Each lens of her glasses, it glares with the reflected
      image of electric chairs
   and gallows. Grainy newsreel footage of prisoners
      sentenced to the gas chamber
   or the firing squad.
Where her eyes should be,
   no eyes.

That first day on jury duty, the next trial, a man tripped over
    a curb and sued
    the luxury car he fell against.
    Asking an award of fifty grand for being such a stupid
        butterfingers.
"All these people with no sense of physical coordination,"
    Sister Vigilante says.
    They all had excellent *blaming skills.*

Another man wanted a hundred grand from a homeowner
    who left the garden hose
    stretched across the backyard that tripped him,
    breaking his ankle,
    while he fled from the police in an otherwise totally
        unrelated case
    of rape.
This crippled rapist, he wanted a fortune for his pain and
    suffering.

There, up onstage, the silver charms flashing against the
    lace of her cuff,
    her Bible gripped between the fingers of both hands,
    her fingernails painted the same yellow as her frills,
    Sister Vigilante says she pays her taxes on time.
She never jaywalks. Recycles her plastic. Rides the bus to
    work.

"At that point," says Sister Vigilante, her first day of jury
    duty, "I told the judge"
    Some charm-bracelet version of:
    "Fuck this shit."
And the judge held *her* in contempt . . .

Civil Twilight

A Story by Sister Vigilante

It was the summer people quit complaining about the price of gasoline. The summer when they stopped bitching about what shows were on television.

On June 24, sunset was at 8:35. Civil twilight ended at 9:07. A woman was walking uphill on the steep stretch of Lewis Street. On the block between 19th and 20th Avenues, she heard a pounding sound. It was the sound a pile driver might make, a heavy stomping sound she could feel through her flat shoes on the concrete sidewalk. It came every few seconds, getting louder with each stomp, getting closer. The sidewalk was empty, and the woman stepped back against the brick wall of an apartment hotel. Across the street, an Asian man stood in the bright glass doorway to a delicatessen, drying his hands on a white towel. Somewhere in the dark between streetlights, something glass broke. The stomp came again and a car alarm wailed. The stomp came closer, something invisible against the night. A newspaper box blew over sideways, crashing into the street. The crash came again, she says, and the windows blew out of a glass telephone booth only three parked cars away from where she stood.

According to a small item in the next day's newspaper,

her name was Teresa Wheeler. She was thirty years old. A clerk at a law firm.

By then the Asian man had stepped back into the deli. He turned the sign around to say: Closed. Still holding the hand towel, he ran to the back of the store, and the lights went out.

Then the street was dark. The car alarm wailing. The stomp came again, so heavy and close by, Wheeler's reflection shimmered as the glass in the dark deli windows shook. A mailbox, bolted to the curb, it boomed loud as a cannon, then stood shaking, vibrating, dented and leaning to one side. A wooden utility pole shuddered, the cables draped across it rattling against each other, the sparks sprinkling down, bright summer fireworks.

A block downhill from Wheeler, the Plexiglas side of a bus shelter, the backlighted photograph of a movie star wearing just his underpants, the Plexiglas exploded.

Wheeler stood, stuck there flat against the brick wall behind her, her fingers worked into the joints between each brick, her fingertips touching mortar, clinging tight as ivy. Her head held back so hard that when she showed the police, when she told them her story, the rough brick had worn a bald spot in her hair.

Then, she said, nothing.

Nothing happened. Nothing had gone by in the dark street.

Sister Vigilante, telling this, she's worming a knife under each of her fingernails and prying off the nail.

Civil twilight, she says, is the period of time between sunset and when the sun is more than six degrees below the horizon. That six degrees equals about half an hour. Civil twilight, Sister Vigilante says, is different from nautical twilight, which lasts until the sun is twelve degrees under the horizon. Astronomical twilight goes until the sun is eighteen degrees below the horizon.

The Sister says, that something no one ever saw, downhill from Teresa Wheeler, it crumpled the roof of a car, waiting at a red light near 16th Avenue. The same invisible nothing wiped out the neon sign for The Tropics Lounge, crushed the neon tubing and folded the steel sign in half where it hung near a third-floor window.

Still, there was nothing to describe. Effect without cause. An invisible riot run amok on Lewis Street, all the way from 20th Avenue to somewhere near the waterfront.

On June 29, Sister Vigilante says, sunset was at 8:36.

Civil twilight ended at 9:08.

According to a guy working the box office of the Olympia Adult Theater, something rushed past the glass front of his ticket booth. This was nothing he could see. It was more the sound of air, an invisible bus going past, or an enormous exhale, so close it fluttered the paper money he had stacking in front of him. Just a high-pitched sound. At the edge of his sight, the lights of the diner across the street, they fluttered, blinked, as if something blotted out the whole world for an instant.

In the next breath, the ticket taker, he described the pounding sound first reported by Teresa Wheeler. A dog barked, somewhere in the dark. It was a walking sound, the kid in the box office would tell police. The sound of something taking huge steps. Just one huge foot he never saw swing past, only as far as one breath away.

On July 1, people were complaining about the water shortage. They were griping about city budget cuts and all the police getting laid off. Car prowls were on the rise. Spray-paint tagging and armed robbery.

On July 2, they weren't.

On July 1, sunset was at 8:34, with civil twilight ending at 9:03.

On July 2, a woman walking her dog found the body of Lorenzo Curdy, the side of his face caved in. Dead, Sister Vigilante says.

"Subarachnoid hemorrhage," she says.

The moment before he was hit, the man must've felt something, maybe the rush of air, something, because he put his hands up in front of his face. When they found him, both hands were buried, punched so deep in his face his fingernails had dug into his own crushed brain.

On a street, the moment you're between streetlights, there in the dark you'd hear it. The stomp. Some people called it a clomping sound. You might hear a second sound from closer, somewhere nearby, or, worse, the next victim would be you. People heard it coming, once, twice, closer, and they froze. Or they forced their feet, left, right, left, three or four steps into a close-by doorway. They crouched, cowering next to parked cars. Closer, the next stomp came, a crash and a car alarm wailing. It was coming down the street, sounding closer, getting loud and gaining speed.

In the pitch-dark, Sister Vigilante says, it would hit—bam—a bolt of black lightning.

On July 13, sunset at 8:33 with civil twilight over at 9:03, a woman named Angela Davis had just left work at a dry cleaner's on Center Street when nothing hit her square in the middle of her back, breaking her spine so hard it lifted her out of her shoes.

On July 17, when civil twilight ended at 9:01, a man named Glenn Jacobs stepped off a bus and started up Porter Street toward 25th Avenue. What nobody saw, it slammed into him so hard his ribcage collapsed. His chest punched in the way you'd crush a wicker basket.

July 25, civil twilight ended at 8:55. Mary Leah Stanek was last seen jogging along Union Street. She stopped to tie one tennis shoe and check her pulse against her wristwatch. Stanek pulled off the baseball cap she wore. She turned it backward and put it back on, tucking her long brown hair up under it.

She headed west on Pacific Street, and then she was dead. Her face torn loose from the skull and muscle underneath.

"Avulsion," Sister Vigilante says.

What killed Stanek, it was wiped clean of fingerprints. Clotted with blood and hair. They found the murder weapon wedged under a parked car down along 2nd Avenue.

It was a bowling ball, the police reported.

Those smudged, greasy-black bowling balls, you can buy them at any thrift shop for half a buck. You can pick and choose, they have bins of them. Somebody buying over a stretch of time, say one ball each year from every junk store in town, that person could have hundreds. Even in bowling alleys, it's simple to walk out with an eight-pound ball under your coat. A twelve-pound ball tucked in a baby stroller, a barely concealed weapon.

The police held a press conference. They stood in a parking lot and someone threw a bowling ball down, threw it hard against the concrete. And the ball bounced. It made the sound of a pile driver far away. It bounced high, taller than the man who threw it. It didn't leave a mark, and if the sidewalk were sloped, the police said, it would keep going, bouncing higher, faster, bouncing downhill in long strides. They threw it down from a third-story window in police headquarters, and the ball bounced even higher. The television news crews got it on tape. Every station played it that night.

The city council pushed for a law to paint all balls bright pink. Or neon yellow, orange, or green, some color you could see flying at your face down a dark side street late at night. To give people just a moment to dodge before—blam—their face is gone.

City fathers, they pushed for a law to make owning black balls a crime.

The police called it a *nonspecific-motive killer*. Like Herbert Mullin, who killed ten people to prevent southern-California earthquakes. Or Norman Bernard, who shot hobos because he thought it would help the economy. What the Federal Bureau of Investigation would call *personal-cause* killers.

Sister Vigilante says, "The police thought the killer was their enemy."

The bowling ball was a police cover-up, people said. The bowling ball was a red herring. A monster wannabe. The bowling ball was a quick fix to keep everybody calm.

On July 31, the sun was six degrees under the horizon at 8:49. That night, Darryl Earl Fitzhugh was homeless, sleeping on Western Avenue. Open across his face, Fitzhugh had a paperback copy of

Stranger in a Strange Land when his chest was crushed, both his lungs collapsed, and his heart muscle ruptured.

According to one witness, the killer came out of the bay, dragging itself over the lip of the seawall. Another witness saw the monster, dripping ooze, squeezing up from the storm sewer. These same people said the forensic evidence was consistent with a hard backhanded slap from a giant lizard walking on its hind legs. The ribcage collapsed was sure proof the victim was stepped on by some dinosaur throwback.

Something dashed past, other people said, something low to the ground, too fast to be an animal. Or it was a maniac run amok with a fifty-pound sledgehammer. One witness, she said we were being "smote" by God from the Old Testament. Swatted by something with a huge paw. Black as the black night. Silent and invisible. Everyone saw something different.

"What matters," Sister Vigilante says, "is, people need a monster they can believe in."

A true and horrible enemy. A demon to define themselves against. Otherwise, it's just us versus us.

Working the tip of the knife blade under another nail, she says, What's important is, the crime rate went down.

In times like that, every man is a suspect. Every woman, a potential victim.

Public attention went this same way during the White Chapel Murders. During Jack the Ripper. For that hundred days, the murder rate dropped 94 percent, to just five prostitutes. Their throats slashed. A kidney half eaten. Guts hung around the room on picture hooks. The sex organs and a fetus taken for a souvenir. Burglaries dropped by 85 percent. Assault by 70 percent.

Sister Vigilante, she says how nobody wanted to be the next victim of the Ripper. People locked their windows. More important, nobody wanted to be accused of being the killer. People didn't walk out at night.

During the Atlanta Child Murders, while thirty kids were stran-
gled, tied to trees, and stabbed, beaten, and shot, most of the city
lived in security and safety they'd never known.

During the Cleveland Torso Murders. The Boston Strangler. The
Chicago Ripper. The Tulsa Bludgeoner. The Los Angeles Slasher . . .

During these waves of murder, all crime dropped in each city.
Except for the showoffy handful of victims, their arms hacked away
and their heads found elsewhere, except for these spectacular sacrifices, each city enjoyed the safest period in its history.

During the New Orleans Ax Man Murders, the killer wrote the
local newspaper, the *Times-Picayune*. On the night of March 19, the
killer promised to kill no one in a house where he could hear jazz
music. That night, New Orleans was roaring with music, and no
one was killed.

"In a city with a limited police budget," Sister Vigilante says, "a
high-profile serial killer is an effective means of behavior modi-
fication."

With the shadow of this horrible bogeyman, with it stalking the
streets downtown, nobody beefed about the unemployment rate.
The water shortage. The traffic.

With the angel of death going door to door, people stayed
together. They quit bitching and behaved.

At this point in Sister Vigilante's story, Director Denial walks by,
calling and sobbing for Cora Reynolds.

It's one thing, the Sister says, a person getting killed, somebody
with a crushed ribcage trying to catch another breath before they
die, they heave and moan, their lips stretched wide, mouthing the
air. Somebody with a crushed-in ribcage, she says, you can kneel
next to them in the dark street with nobody around to watch. You
can see their eyes glaze over. But killing an animal, well, that's different. Animals, she says, a dog, it makes us human. Proof of our
humanity. Other people, they just make us redundant. A dog or cat,
a bird or a lizard, it makes us God.

All day long, she says, our biggest enemy is other people. It's people packed around us in traffic. People ahead of us in line at the supermarket. It's the supermarket checkers who hate us for keeping them so busy. No, people didn't want this killer to be another human being. But they wanted people to die.

In ancient Rome, Sister Vigilante says, at the Colosseum, the "editor" was the man who organized the bloody games at the heart of keeping people peaceful and united. That's where the word "editor" really comes from. Today, our editor plans the menu of murder, rape, arson, and assault on the front page of the day's newspaper.

Of course, there was a hero. By accident, August 2, sunset at 8:34, a twenty-seven-year-old named Maria Alvarez was leaving a hotel where she worked as the night auditor. She stood on the curb, stopped to light a cigarette when a man pulled her back. That same instant, the monster rushed past. This man had saved her life. The city applauded on television, but in their hearts, they hated him.

A hero, this messiah, they didn't want. The idiot bastard who saved a life that wasn't their own. What people wanted was a sacrifice every few days, something to throw in the volcano. Our regular offering to random fate.

How it ended is, one night the monster got a dog. A hairy rag of a little dog on the end of a leash, tied to a parking meter on Porter Street, it stood and barked as the pounding came closer. The closer the sound came, the more the dog barked.

A store window webbed into a puzzle of broken glass. A fire hydrant clanked to one side, cracked cast iron, hissing a white curtain of water. The edge of a windowsill explodes in a spray of gravel and concrete dust. A smacked parking meter, jiggling in place, rattling the coins inside. A steel "No Parking" sign flaps down, torn from its metal post. The metal post still humming from some invisible impact.

One more stomp and the barking stopped.

The monster seemed to disappear after that night. A week went by, and the streets were still empty after dark. A month went by, and the editors found some new horror to put on the front page of the newspaper. A war somewhere else. Some new kind of cancer.

On September 10, sunset was at 8:02. Curtis Hammond was leaving a group-therapy session he attended every week at 257 West Mill Street. He was pulling down the knot of his tie when it happened. He'd just opened his collar button. It was when he'd just turned to look up the street. He smiled at the warm air on his face, shut his eyes, and breathed in through his nose. A month before, everyone in town knew him from the front page of the paper. From the television news. He'd pulled a night auditor away from getting killed by the monster. From getting smote by God.

He was the hero we didn't want.

On September 10, civil twilight was at 8:34, and a moment later, Curtis Hammond turned toward a noise. His tie loose, he squinted into the dark. Smiling, his teeth shining, he said, "Hello?"

1.
2.
3.
4.
5.
6.
7.
8.
9.
10.
11.
12.
13.
14.
15.
16.
17.
18.
19.
20.
21.
22.
23.
24.

We find Comrade Snarky collapsed on the carpet in front of a tapestry sofa in the second-balcony foyer. Her face, blue-white, framed by the pillow of her crusty, gray wigs. The wigs piled and pinned together. None of her moving. Her hands are bones beaded together with tendon inside the flesh of her black velvet gloves. The cords of her thin neck look webbed with skin. Her cheeks and each closed eye look caved in, sunken and hollow.

She's dead.

Her eyes, the pupils stay the same pinhole size when the Earl of Slander thumbs her eyelids up. We check her arms for rigor mortis, her skin for stippling and settled blood, but she's still fresh meat.

Our royalties only have to split fourteen ways now.

The Earl of Slander thumbs the eyes shut.

Thirteen ways, if Miss Sneezy keeps coughing. Twelve ways, if the Matchmaker gets the courage to chop off his dick.

Now Comrade Snarky's a permanent member of the supporting cast. A tragedy the rest of us get to tell. How she was so brave and kind, now that she's dead. Just a prop in our story.

"If she's dead—she's food," Miss America says. She

stands at the top of the lobby stairs, one hand holding the golden railing. Her other hand holds her belly. "You know she'd eat you," she says. Clutching the railing, supported by fat cupids painted gold, Miss America says, "She'd want us to."

And the Earl of Slander says, "Roll her over, if that makes it easier. So you can't see her face."

So we roll her over, and Chef Assassin kneels on the carpet and digs the layers of skirts and petticoats, muslin and crinoline, up around her waist to show yellow cotton panties sagged across her flat, pale ass. He says, "You sure she's dead?"

Miss America leans down and slips two fingers against the side of Comrade Snarky's webbed neck, inside the high lace collar, pressing the blue-white skin. Chef Assassin watches this, kneeling there, holding his boning knife, one finger-long blade of steel. His free hand holds back the drift of white and gray lace, yellow muslin, the pile of petticoats and skirts. He looks at the blade and says, "Think we should sterilize this?"

"You're not taking out her appendix," Miss America says, her two fingers still tight against the side of the blue-white neck. "If you're worried," she says, "we can just cook the meat longer . . ."

In a way, the Donner Party was lucky, says the Earl of Slander, still scribbling in his notepad. So was the plane full of South American rugby players who crash-landed in the Andes in 1972. They were luckier than us. They had the cold weather on their side. Refrigeration. When somebody died, they had time to debate the finer points of acceptable human behavior. You just buried anybody dead in the snow until everyone was so hungry it didn't matter.

Here, even in the basement, even in the subbasement with Lady Baglady's and Mr. Whittier's and the Duke of Vandals' velvet-wrapped bodies, it's not freezing cold. If we don't eat now, before the bacteria inside Comrade Snarky begin their own chow-down, she'll be wasted. Swollen and putrefied. Poisoned so much no amount of turning around and around in the microwave oven will ever make her into food again.

No, unless we do this—butcher her, here and now, on these gold-and-flower carpets beside the tapestry sofas and crystal light-sconces of the second-balcony lobby, it will be one of us here, dead, tomorrow. Or the next day. Chef Assassin with his boning knife will be cutting our underwear up the back to show our withered-flat, blue-white butt and little-stick thighs. The back of each knee turned gray.

One of us, just meat about to go bad.

On one flat ass cheek, the panty fabric peels back to show a tattoo, a rose in full bloom. Just like she said.

Those rugby players lost in the Andes, it's from reading their book that Chef Assassin knows to carve up the buttocks first.

Miss America pulls her two fingers back from the cold neck, and she stands up. She blows on the fingers, warm breath, then rubs her hands together fast and stuffs them in the folds of her skirt. "Snarky's dead," she says.

Behind her, Baroness Frostbite turns toward the stairs that lead down to the lobby. Her skirts rustling and dragging, her voice trailing away, she says, "I'll get a plate or a dish you can use." She says, "How you present food is *so important*," and she's gone.

"Here," Chef Assassin says, "somebody hold this shit back off me." And he elbows the pile of skirts and stiff fabric that wants to fall where he has to work.

The Earl of Slander steps over the body, straddling it at the waist, looking at its feet. The legs disappear inside white socks rolled to halfway up each stringy calf bone wiggling with veins, the feet in red high heels. The Earl of Slander gathers the skirts in both arms and crouches down, holding them back. With a sigh, he sits down, his butt settling on Comrade Snarky's dead shoulder blades, his knees pointed up at the ceiling, his arms lost in the drift of her skirts and lace. The little-mesh microphone sticking out of his shirt pocket. The little RECORD light, glowing red.

And with one hand, the fingers spread, Chef Assassin holds the skin on one buttock tight. And with his other hand, he drags the knife down. As if he's drawing a straight line down Comrade Snarky's blue-white ass, a line that gets thicker and bolder the longer he draws it. Pulling the knife parallel with the crack of her ass. The line looks black against the blue-white skin, red-black until it drips, red, onto the skirts under her. Red on the blade of the boning knife. The red, steaming. Chef Assassin's hands red and steaming, he says, "Is a dead person supposed to *bleed* this much?"

Nobody says anything.

One, two, three, four, somewhere else, Saint Gut-Free whispers, "Help us!"

Chef Assassin's elbow is bobbing up and down as he saws, sawing the little blade in and out of the red mess. His original straight line lost in the red stew. The steam rising with the blood smell of Tampax, that women's-bathroom smell in the cold air. His sawing stops, and one hand lifts a scrap of something red. His eyes don't follow it. His eyes stay on the mess, red in the center of this snowdrift of petticoats. This big steaming flower, here on the carpet of the second-balcony foyer. Chef Assassin shakes the red scrap in his raised hand. What he can't look at, dripping and running with dark red. And he says, "Take it. Somebody . . ."

Nobody's hand reaches out.

Her rose tattoo, there, in the center of the scrap.

And, still not looking at it, Chef Assassin shouts, "Take it!"

A rustle of fairy-tale satin and brocade skirts, and Baroness Frostbite is back among us. She says, "Oh my God . . ."

A paper plate hovers under the dripping red scrap, and Chef Assassin drops it. On the plate, it's meat. A thin steak. The way a cutlet looks. Or those long scraps of meat labeled "strip steaks" in the butcher's case.

Chef Assassin's elbow is bobbing again, sawing. His other hand lifts scrap after dripping scrap out of the steaming red center of that huge white flower. The paper plate is piled high and starting to fold in half from the weight. Red juice spilling off one edge. The Baroness goes to get another plate. Chef Assassin fills that, too.

The Earl of Slander, still sitting on the back of the body, he shifts his weight, pulling his face away from the steaming mess. Not the nothing smell of cold, clean meat from the supermarket. This is the smell of animals half run-over and smearing a path of shit and blood as they drag their shattered back legs off a hot summer highway. Here's the messy smell of a baby the moment after it's born.

Then the body, Comrade Snarky, lets out a little moan.

It's the soft groan of someone dreaming in her sleep.

And Chef Assassin falls backward, both hands dripping. The knife left behind, jutting straight up from the flower's red center—until the dropped skirts flutter, lower, sift down to hide the mess. The Baroness drops the first paper plate, burdened with meat. The flower closing. The Earl of Slander springs to his feet, and he's off her. We, we're all standing back. Staring. Listening.

Something needs to happen.

Something needs to happen.

Then, one, two, three, four, somewhere else, Saint Gut-Free whispers, "Help us!"

The soft, regular foghorn of his voice.

From somewhere else, you hear Director Denial calling, "Here . . . kitty, kitty, kitty . . ." Her words stretched long and then broken by sobs, she says, "Come . . . to Mama . . . my baby . . ."

His hands webbed with gummy red, Chef Assassin flexes his fingers, not touching anything, just staring at the body, he says, "You told me . . ."

And Miss America crouching forward, her leather boots creak. She slides two fingers into the lace collar and presses the side of the blue-white neck. She says, "Snarky's dead." She nods at the Earl of Slander and says, "You must've forced some air out of her lungs." She nods at the meat spilled off the plate, now breaded with dust and lint on the foyer carpet, and Miss America says, "Pick that up . . ."

The Earl of Slander rewinds his tape, and Comrade Snarky's voice moans and moans the same moan. Our parrot. Comrade Snarky's death taped over the Duke of Vandals' taped over Mr. Whittier's taped over Lady Baglady's death.

How Comrade Snarky died was probably a heart attack. Mrs. Clark says it's from a shortage of thiamine, what we call vitamin B_1. Or it could've been a shortage of potassium in her bloodstream, causing muscle weakness and, again, a heart attack. That was how Karen Carpenter died in 1983, after years of anorexia nervosa. Fainted dead on the floor like this. Mrs. Clark says it was no doubt a heart attack.

Nobody really dies of starvation, Mrs. Clark says. They die of pneumonia brought on by malnutrition. They die of kidney failure brought on by low potassium. They die of shock caused by bones broken by osteoporosis. They die of seizures caused by lack of salt.

However she died, Mrs. Clark says, that's how most of us will. Unless we eat.

At last, our devil commands us. We're so proud of her.

"Easy as skinning a chicken breast," Chef Assassin says, and he drops another lump of meat on the dripping paper plate. He says, "Christ Almighty, I do love these knives . . ."

"To become a household word," says Chef Assassin, "all
  you need is a rifle."
    This he learned early, watching the news. Reading the
    paper.

Chef Assassin standing onstage, he wears those black-and-
  white-checkered pants
    that only professional cooks get to wear.
    Billowing big, but still stretched tight to cover his ass.
His hands, his fingers, a patchwork of scabs and scars.
    Shiny old burns.
    His white shirtsleeves rolled up,
    and all the hair singed off the muscle of his forearms.
    His thick arms and legs that don't bend
    so much as they *fold* at the knee and elbow.

Onstage, instead of a spotlight, a movie fragment flickers:
    where two close-up hands, the fingernails clean and the
      palms perfect
    as a pair of pink gloves,
    they skin a chicken breast.
    His face, a round screen, lost under a layer of fat, his
      mouth lost under the pastry brush

of a little mustache,
Chef Assassin says, "That's my backup plan."

The Chef says, "If my garage band never gets a record
    contract—"
    if his book never finds a publisher—
    if his screenplay never gets a green light—
    if no network picks up his pilot episode—
The Chef, his face worms and twitches with those perfect
    hands:
    skinning and boning,
    pounding and seasoning,
    breading and frying and garnishing,
    until that piece of dead flesh looks too pretty to eat.

A gun. A scope. Good aim and a motorcade.
    What he learned as a kid, watching the news on
        television, every night.
"So I'm not forgotten," the Chef says.
    So his life isn't wasted.
He says, "That's my Plan B."

To Mr. Kenneth MacArthur
Manager of Corporate Communications
Kutting-Blok Knife Products, Inc.

Dear Mr. MacArthur,

Just so you know, you make a great knife. An excellent knife.

It's tough enough doing professional kitchen work without tolerating a bad knife. You go to do a perfect potato *allumette,* that's thinner than a pencil. Your perfect cheveu cut, that's about as big around as a wire—that's half as thick as a potato chip. You make your living cutting carrots *brunoisette* with hot sauté pans already waiting with butter, people yelling for those potatoes cut *minunette,* and you learn quick the difference between a bad knife and a Kutting-Blok.

The stories I could tell you. Time and time again, how your knives have pulled my ass out of the fire. You chiffonade Belgian endive for eight hours, and you might get some idea what my life is like.

Still, it never fails, you can *tourné* baby carrots all day, carving each one into a perfect orange football, and the one you screw up, that carrot lands on the plate of some failed cook, some nobody with a community-college degree in hospitality services, just a piece of paper, who now thinks he's a restaurant critic. Some prick who hardly knows how to chew and swallow, and he's writing in next week's paper how the chef at Chez Restaurant is lousy at *tourné*-ing carrots.

Some bitch no caterer would even hire to flute mushrooms, she's putting in print how my *bâtonnet* parsnips are too thick.

These sellouts. No, it's always easier to nitpick than actually to cook the meal.

Every time somebody orders the *dauphinoise* potatoes or the beef Carpaccio, please know that someone in our kitchen says a little prayer of thanks for Kutting-Blok knives. The perfect balance of them. The riveted handle.

Sure, knock wood, we would all like to make more money for less work. But selling out, turning critic, setting yourself up as a know-it-all, and taking cheap shots at the people still trying to make their living peeling calf tongue . . . paring away kidney fat . . . pulling off liver membrane . . . while those critics sit in their nice clean offices and type their gripes with nice clean fingers—that's just not right.

Of course, this is just their opinion. But there it is, showcased next to real news—famines and serial killers and earthquakes— there it's given the same-sized type. Somebody's gripe that their pasta wasn't quite al dente. As if their opinion is an Act of God.

A negative guarantee. The opposite of an advertisement.

To my mind, those who can, do. Those who can't, gripe.

Not journalism. Not objective. Not reporting, but judging.

These critics, they couldn't cook a great meal if their life depended on it.

It's with this in mind I started my project.

No matter how good you are, working in a kitchen is a slow death by a million tiny knife cuts. Ten thousand little burns. Scalds. Standing on concrete all night, or walking across greasy or wet floors. Carpal tunnel, nerve damage from stirring and chopping and spooning. Deveining an ocean of shrimp under ice water. Knee pain and varicose veins. Wrist and shoulder repetitive-motion injuries. A career of perfect *calamares rellenos* is a lifelong martyrdom. A lifetime spent turning out the ideal *ossobuco alla milanese* is a long, slow death by torture.

Still, no matter how thick-skinned you are, getting picked apart in public by some newspaper or Internet writer does not help.

Those online critics, they're a dime a dozen. Everybody with a mouth and a computer.

That's what all my targets have in common. It's a blessing the police don't work a little closer together. They might notice a freelance writer in Seattle, a student reviewer in Miami, a Midwestern tourist posting his opinion on some travel Web site . . . There is a pattern to my sixteen targets, so far. Yes, and there's my years of motivation.

There's not much difference between boning a rabbit and a snarky Web-site blogger who said your *costatine al finocchio* needed more Marsala.

And thanks to Kutting-Blok knives. Your forged *tourné* knives do both jobs beautifully, without the hand and wrist fatigue you might get using a less expensive, stamped paring knife.

Likewise, cleaning a skirt steak and skinning the little weasel who posted an article about how your beef Wellington was ruined with too much foie gras, both jobs go fast and effortless thanks to the flexible blade of your eight-inch filleting knife.

Easy to sharpen and easy to clean. Your knives are a blessing.

It's the targets that always turn out to be such a disappointment. No matter how little you expect when you meet these people in person.

All it takes is a little praise to arrange a get-together. Imply the kind of sexual partner they might want. Better yet, imply you're the editor of a national magazine, looking to take their voice worldwide. To exalt them. Give them the glory they so richly deserve. Lift them to prominence. All that attention crap, offer them half that and they'll meet you in any dark alley you can name.

In person, their eyes are always so small, each eye like a black marble stuck into a fat man's bellybutton. Thanks in part to Kutting-Blok knives, they look better, cleaned and dressed and trimmed. Meat, ready for some good use.

After you've pulled the cold viscera out of a hundred guinea hens, it's no big deal, slitting the belly of a freelance writer who wrote in some regional entertainment guide that your escarole-feta turnovers were too chewy. No, the Kutting-Blok ten-inch French knife makes even that task as easy as gutting a trout or salmon or any round fish.

It's odd, the parts that stand out in your mind. A look at someone's thin, white ankle, and you can see who she must've been as a girl in school, before she learned to make her living by attacking food. Or another critic, who wore his brown shoes polished bright as the caramel crust on a crème brûlée.

It's this same attention to detail that you put into every knife.

This is the care and attention I used to put into my kitchen work.

Still, no matter how careful I am, it's just a matter of time before the police will catch me. With this in mind, my only fear is that Kutting-Blok knives will become linked in the public mind with a series of deeds that people might misunderstand.

Too many people will see my preference as a kind of endorsement. Like Jack the Ripper doing a television commercial.

Ted Bundy for Such & Such Brand rope.

Lee Harvey Oswald pitching Such & Such Brand rifle.

A kind of negative endorsement, true. Maybe even something that would hurt your market share and net sales. Especially in the upcoming retail Christmas season.

It's standard procedure at all major newspapers, the moment they hear about a big jetliner disaster—a midair collision, a hijacking, a runway crash—they know to pull all the big display advertisements for airlines that day. Because, within minutes, every airline will call to cancel their ad, even if it means paying full price for a space they won't use. A space filled at the last moment with a freebie promo ad for the American Cancer Society or Muscular Dystrophy. Because no airline wants to risk being associated with the day's bad, bad news. The hundreds dead. Being linked that way in the public mind.

It takes very little effort to recall what the so-called Tylenol Murders did for that product's stock. With seven people dead, just the 1982 recall of their product cost Johnson & Johnson $125 million.

That kind of negative endorsement, it's the opposite of an advertisement. Like what critics do with their snide reviews, printed only to show how clever and bitter they've become.

The details of each target, including the knife used, it's all still so fresh in my mind. It would take very little effort for the police to make me confess, to make it public record, the wide variety of your excellent knives I've used and for what purpose.

Forever after, people will refer to the "Kutting-Blok Knife Murders" or the "Kutting-Blok Serial Killings." Your company is so much better known than anonymous little me. You have a knife in so many kitchens, already. It would be a horrible shame to see your generations of quality and hard work wrecked because of my project.

Please bear in mind, food critics don't buy many knives. Knock on wood, but industry sympathy in this case might well be with me. Me, a grass-roots hero. You never know.

Any small investment you can make, it will benefit us both.

The more resources you can provide me to evade capture, the less likely it will be that this unfortunate fact is ever known to the average knife-consumer. A gift of as little as five million dollars would allow me to emigrate and live unnoticed in another country, far, far outside your market demographic. That money will guarantee your company a steady rise into a bright future. For me, the money will allow me to retrain in a new field of work, a new career.

Or, for as little as one million dollars, I will switch to Sta-Sharp knives—*and if arrested will swear I've used only their substandard products throughout my project* . . .

One million dollars. How's that for brand loyalty?

To contribute, please run a display advertisement this upcoming Sunday, in your local daily newspaper. Upon seeing that ad, I will contact you about accepting your help. Until then, I must continue with my work. Otherwise, you can expect another target.

Thank you for considering my request. I look forward to hearing from you, soon.

In this world, where so few people will devote their lives to producing a product of lasting quality, I applaud you.

> I remain, as always, your biggest fan,
> Richard Talbott

1.
2.
3.
4.
5.
6.
7.
8.
9.
10.
11.
12.
13.
14.
15.
16.
17.
18.
19.
20.
21.
22.
23.
24.

Behind the lobby snack bar, the microwave oven dings, once, twice, three times, and the light inside shuts off. Chef Assassin pops open the door, and takes out a paper plate covered with a sheet of paper towel. He lifts the towel, and steam mushrooms into the cold lobby air. On the plate, a few long curls of meat still pop and spit, steaming in their pools of melted grease.

Chef Assassin sets the plate on the snack bar's marble countertop and says, "Who wants thirds?"

Standing around the lobby, here and there, tucked into the shadow of alcoves and niches, in the coat-check window and usher's stand, Mrs. Clark and Miss America, Countess Foresight and the Earl of Slander, all of us stand, chewing. Grease shines bright on our chins and the tips of our fingers. Each of us holds a damp paper plate in one hand. Chewing.

"Quick, before they get cold," Chef Assassin says. "These have Cajun spices. It's to hide the flowery smell."

It's the smell of Comrade Snarky's perfume or bath powder, maybe her lace handkerchief, something sweet with the smell of roses. Chef Assassin says two-thirds of your sense of taste is based on how a food smells.

Miss America steps over and holds out her plate. Chef

Assassin puts a brown curl of meat in his own mouth, then plucks it out with his fingers, fast. "It's still hot," he says, and blows on it. With his other hand, he drops little curls of meat on Miss America's plate.

Her plate full, Miss America disappears to stand, almost hidden, behind the coat-check counter. The wall and racks of wooden hangers behind her. The hangers all empty except for the little numbered brass tag on each one.

The lobby air is rich with cookout smells, fatty bacon smells, hamburger smells, burned-fat and grease-fire smells. And all of us stand here chewing. Nobody says: Should we go get more? Nobody says: We need to wrap what's left and haul it to the subbasement before it becomes a public-health issue . . .

No, we stand here, licking our fingers.

Each of us writing and rewriting our story of this moment. We're inventing how Mr. Whittier butchered Comrade Snarky. And what her ghost did, for revenge.

Nobody sees her come down the stairs. Nobody hears her walking down the carpet from the second-balcony foyer. Nobody looks up until she says, "You have food?"

It's Comrade Snarky. In her heaped layers of fairy-godmother ball gowns. Her piled-on layers of shawls and wigs. She stands at the wide foot of the lobby's grand staircase, her blue-white hands lost in the folds of her skirt. Her eyes lead the rest of her into the room, her eyes and nose pulling her forward. "What are you cooking?" She says, "Give me some . . ."

Nobody says anything. All our mouths stuffed full. We're picking at shreds of meat stuck between our teeth.

Comrade Snarky sees the paper plate of curled brown meat, steaming there on the snack-bar counter.

Nobody thinks to stop her.

Comrade Snarky lurches across the blue lobby, falling once on the pink marble floor, her skirts dragging, then reaching up to grab the edge of the snack-bar countertop and pull herself to her feet. Standing there, her face and the pile of her wigs collapse onto the plate of meat.

Behind her, coming down the blue-carpeted stairs, are her footprints in blood.

The on-again, off-again ghost of here.

All any of us can see is her towering gray curls as they bob and bounce over the paper plate on the marble countertop. The seat of her dress is blooming, bigger and bigger, with a huge red flower. Then her wigs pull back, and all of her turns away from the empty plate. A brown curl of meat still clutched in one blue-white hand, Comrade Snarky licks her lips and says, "God, it's so tough and bitter."

Somebody needs to say something. To be . . . kind.

Skinny Saint Gut-Free, he says, "I don't usually eat meat, but *that* was . . . quite delicious." And he looks around.

Holding up the stop sign of one greasy palm, his eyes shut, Chef Assassin says, "I warn you . . . do *not* criticize my cooking . . ."

The rest of us nod our heads yes. Delicious. The rest of us, our plates are empty. We all swallow, still chewing. Our tongues sliding over our teeth for any leftover film of oil. Of fat.

Comrade Snarky crosses to the tapestry sofas in the center of the lobby, dead center, under the frozen sparkle of the biggest crystal chandelier. Her hands lift a blue velvet pillow, gold tassels hanging from the four corners, and she moves it to one end of a sofa. Her feet kick out of her shoes. Her white stockings stained red. She goes to sit down, to lie back on the sofa with her head on the pillow. And Comrade Snarky, she winces. Her face pulls together, tight for a minute, then relaxes. She reaches behind her, feeling up, underneath the wet layers of her skirts and petticoats. She leans forward as if to stand, and her eyes fall on the footprints of blood that have followed her across the blue carpet from the stairs to the snack bar to the sofa.

We all look at the blood spilling out of her shoes.

Still chewing, her jaw going around and around, a cow with its cud, Comrade Snarky looks at us.

Trying to digest this scene.

When her hand comes out from the back of her skirt, she's holding Chef Assassin's boning knife. The blade still clotted and varnished with blood.

Chef Assassin steps forward from behind the snack bar. His hand open, and wiggling his greasy fingers at her, he says, "I'll take that. It's mine."

And Comrade Snarky stops chewing. And swallows.

"I . . . ," she says.

Comrade Snarky looks at the knife and the curl of meat she still holds.

On the snack of meat, there's a rose tattoo she's never seen before. Except maybe in a mirror. Only now it's lightly browned.

The Earl of Slander, his face is hidden as he licks his paper plate.

Comrade Snarky says:

"I only fainted . . ."

She says:

"I fainted . . . and you ate my ass?"

She looks at the empty, greasy paper plate still sitting on the snack bar, and she says:

"You fed me my own ass?"

Mother Nature belches behind her open hand, and says, "Beg pardon."

Chef Assassin holds out his hand for the knife, a thin circle of red showing under one thumbnail. He looks up to see a thousand-thousand tiny versions of Comrade Snarky sparkling in the dusty chandelier crystal. In her hand, the thousand-thousand Cajun-cooked roses.

Countess Foresight turns away but keeps watching her own, smaller version of this reality, a movie- or television-sized version of Comrade Snarky reflected in the wide mirror behind the snack bar.

All of us seeing our own version of Comrade Snarky. All with our own story about what's going on. All of us sure that our version is what's real.

Checking her wristwatch, Sister Vigilante says, "Eat up. It's only one hour before lights-out."

All those smaller versions of Comrade Snarky, they all swallow hard. Their blue-white cheeks bulge. Their throats cinch shut, gagging on the taste of their own bitter skin.

Each of us turning our reality into a story. Digesting it to make a book. What we see happen, already a movie screenplay.

The Mythology of Us.

Then, right on cue, the full-sized Comrade Snarky sitting on the tapestry sofa, she slides to the floor. Her eyes still open a little to stare up at the chandelier. To lie in a heap of velvet and brocade on the pink marble floor. It's then she's dying. One hand still holding the boning knife. One hand still holding the brown curl of her fried butt.

The tapestry sofa blotted with dark red where she'd sat down. The blue velvet pillow still dented from her head. Comrade Snarky will not be the camera behind the camera behind the camera. We hold the truth about her in our hands. Wedged between our teeth.

Her voice a whisper, Comrade Snarky says, "I guess . . . I deserved . . ."

And after a moment of rewind, from the Earl of Slander's tape recorder, her voice again says, "deserved this . . . deserved this . . ."

Anticipation

A Poem About Comrade Snarky

"I lost my virginity," Comrade Snarky says, "through my ear."
    So young, she still believed in Santa Claus.

Comrade Snarky onstage, her knuckles rest on her hips,
    her arms bent
    so her leather elbow patches poke out at each side.
    Her laced-up, steel-toed boots planted wide apart.
    Her legs in baggy camouflage pants, tied around each
      ankle.
She leans so far forward, her chin casts a shadow
    down the front of her army-surplus olive-drab field jacket.

Onstage, instead of a spotlight, a movie fragment:
    the footage of protest signs and picket lines, the bullhorn
      shapes of mouths
    yelling, all their way open.
    All teeth and no lips.
    Mouths open so far, the effort shuts their eyes, tight.

"After the judge awarded joint custody," Comrade Snarky
    says, "my mother told me . . ."
    In the middle of the night,
    while you're fast asleep with your head on the pillow,

if your father ever tiptoes into your room:
you, come tell me.
Her mother said, "If your father ever tugs down your pajama
bottoms and fingers you . . ."
You, come tell me.
If he takes a fat, heavy snake out from the zipper in the
front of his pants—that hot, sticky club that smells bad—
and tries to force this in your mouth . . .
You, come tell me.

"Instead of all that," Comrade Snarky says, "my father took
me to the zoo."
He took her to the ballet. He took her to soccer practice.
He kissed her good night.

The colors of sit-down strikes, the shapes of civil
disobedience still marching,
marching, marching,
across her face,
Comrade Snarky says,
"But, for the rest of my life, I was always ready."

Speaking Bitterness

A Story by Comrade Snarky

From the minute he sat down, we tried to explain . . .

We don't allow men. This is a women-only safe space. The purpose of our group is to nurture and empower women with a sense of privacy. To allow women to speak freely without being questioned or judged. We need to exclude men because they inhibit women. Male energy intimidates and humiliates women. To men, a woman is either a virgin or a slut. A mother or a whore.

When we ask him to get out, of course he plays dumb. He says to call him "Miranda."

We respect his choice. The effort and desire he's put into attaining the physical appearance of being female. But this space, we tell him in a gentle, sensitive way, this space is only for women *born* women.

He was born Miranda Joyce Williams. He says this and snaps open his little pink lizard-skin pocketbook. He takes out a driver's license. With a long, pink fingernail he slides the license across the table, tapping where there's a letter "F" under the category of sex.

The state may recognize his new gender, we tell him, but we choose not to. Many of our members suffered childhood traumas regarding men. They fear being reduced to their

bodies. Being used as objects. These are issues he could never understand, being born male.

He says: I was born female.

Somebody in the group says, "Can you show us your birth certificate?"

"Miranda" says: Of course not.

Someone else says, "Are you menstruating?"

And "Miranda" says: Not this minute.

He's playing with a rainbow-colored scarf tied around his neck,
twisting and pulling it. Preening in a caricature of female nervous
behavior. He's playing with the sparkling, shimmery scarf draped
around his shoulders, letting it fall down behind him, to hang from
his elbows. He's combing his fingers through the long fringe at each
end. He pulls a little more scarf to one side, then the other. He
crosses his legs, one knee over the other. Then the bottom one on
top. He lifts and folds the fur coat in his lap. Turning it, he pets the
fur with one open hand, his fingernails together, painted pink and
bright as jewelry.

His lips and shoes and handbag, his fingernails and watchband,
they're all as pretty-pink as a redhead's asshole.

Someone in the group gets up, glaring. She says, "What's the
goddamn point?" Cramming her knitting and bottled water into
her tote bag, she says, "I look forward to this all week. Now it's
ruined."

"Miranda" just sits there, his eyes tented under long, thick
lashes. His eyes floating in blue-green pools of eyeliner. He tubes
red lipstick onto his lipstick. He smears blusher on top of his
blusher. Mascara on his mascara. His cropped blouse rides up on his
chest. The pink silk of it seems to hang off the two points of his nipples, each breast roughly the same size as his face, both ballooning
off the tanned ripples of his rib cage. His stomach showing, tight
and tanned, it's a male stomach. He's a total sex-doll fantasy, the
kind of woman only a man would become.

For a rap group, "Miranda" says he expected a little more rap.

We just look at him.

This silly man. This "Miranda." Here's every male fantasy brought to life in a kind of Frankenstein monster of stereotypes: The perfect big round breasts. The hard muscle of long thighs. The mouth, a perfect pout, greasy with lipstick. The pink leather skirt too short and tight for anything but sex. He speaks with the breathy voice of a little girl or a movie starlet. A huge gush of air for what little sound comes out. It's the kind of whispery voice *Cosmopolitan* magazine teaches girls to use, to make listening men lean closer.

We just sit here, nobody talking, nobody sharing. You just can't be honest, knowing there's a penis under the table. Even in the middle of Frida Kahlo and Georgia O'Keeffe posters . . . apple-cinnamon candles . . . the bookstore's calico cat.

Okay, "Miranda" says, then I'll start.

"Miranda," his bleached hair is piled beauty-parlor tall, stiff with spray, and wired with bobby pins.

There's this guy at work who "Miranda" fell just train-wreck in love with. The guy won't flirt back. He's just this totally cute number, a slick-haired junior sales associate who drives a Porsche. He's married, but "Miranda" knows there's sheer animal interest on the guy's side. This one time after work, "Miranda" says, the guy came over and put his hand—

And we all just stare.

The guy put his hand on "Miranda's" arm and asked about going out for a drink.

"Miranda's" arms are thin, tanned muscle with no jiggle to them. Smooth as tan plastic. He giggles. "Miranda" actually giggles. He rolls his eyes at the ceiling.

"Miranda" says how the sales associate from work drove the two of them to this very dark bar, the kind where you'd go to not be noticed by—

This is so like a male, all this me, me, me stuff, all night.

We come here to get away from men, from husbands who won't

pick up dirty socks. Husbands who slap us around, then cheat on us. Fathers disappointed that we're not boys. Stepfathers who diddle us. Brothers who bully us. Bosses. Priests. Traffic cops. Doctors.

Most time, we don't allow cross talk, but somebody in the group says, "Miranda?"

And "Miranda" stops yakking.

We tell him that consciousness raising is rooted in complaint. What so many people call a bitch session. In communist China, in the years after Mao's revolution, an important part of building a new culture was allowing people to complain about their past. At first, the more they complained, the worse the past would seem. But by venting, people could start to resolve the past. By bitching and bitching and bitching, they could exhaust the drama of their own horror stories. Grow bored. Only then could they accept a new story for their lives. Move forward.

This is why we come here every Wednesday night, to this bookstore backroom without windows, to sit in folding metal chairs around a big square table.

The revolution called this "Speaking Bitterness."

"Miranda" shrugs his shoulders. His eyebrows raised, he shakes his head and says he doesn't have any horror stories. He sighs and smiles and bats his eyes.

And someone in the groups says, "Then we don't want you here."

The whole idea of men creating perfect robot women for their own pleasure, it happens every day. The most "beautiful" women you see in public, none of them are for real. They're just men perpetuating their perverted stereotype of women. Just the oldest story in the world. There's a penis on every page of *Cosmopolitan* magazine if you know where to look.

"Miranda" says how we're not very welcoming.

And somebody says, "You're not a woman."

We meet in the women-only safe gathering space behind the Wymyn's Book Cooperative. No way do we want our space polluted by oppressive phallic yang energy.

Being a woman is special. It's sacred. This isn't just some club you can join. You don't just get a shot of estrogen and show up here.

"Miranda" says: You just need a little makeover. To pretty yourself up.

Men, they just don't get it. Being a woman is more than just wearing makeup and high heels. This kind of sex mimicry, this gender parroting, is the worst insult. A man thinks, all he has to do is put on lipstick and cut off his dick and that makes him a sister.

Someone gets up from her chair. Someone else gets up, and they both start around the table.

"Miranda" asks: What are they planning?

And a third woman, standing, says, "A major makeover."

"Miranda's" pink fingernails go to her pocketbook. He takes out a canister of hot-pepper spray and says he's not afraid to use it. He puts a silver rape whistle between his pink lips.

Someone else goes around the table to stand too close to him, his hand clutched white around the pepper spray. Then somebody in the group says, "Let's see your tits . . ."

In our group, we don't have a leader. The rules of consciousness raising don't allow cross talk. No one can challenge the experience of another member. Everyone gets a turn to talk.

"Miranda," the silver rape whistle drops out of his mouth. His Paris lips blown up with collagen. The pout of a fashion model saying, "Thursday."

"Miranda" says we have to be joking.

It's so typical, men want all the perks of being female, but none of the bullshit.

Somebody else says, "No, really. Show us . . ."

We're all female, here. It's not like we haven't seen tits before. Somebody standing close, she reaches toward the top button on "Miranda's" pink blouse. The blouse is pink silk, tented over his breasts. It's cropped to show his smooth, flat stomach, and hangs in folds above his belted skirt. His pink lizard-skin belt is no bigger than a dog collar.

One of his pink hands slaps the woman away. When no one else makes a move, then "Miranda" lets out a little sigh. With all of us watching, he undoes the top button, himself. His pink fingernails open the next button down. Then the next. He's looking back at us, looking from woman to woman, until all the buttons are done and the blouse gaps open. Inside is a pink satin bra embroidered with roses and trimmed with lace. His skin is airbrush-pink, centerfold-clear, without the moles or hairs or red bug-bites you see on real skin. Around his neck, a pearl necklace points straight down into his big ass-crack cleavage.

The bra is the kind that hooks open in the front, and "Miranda" waits a beat, holding the clasp and looking from woman to woman.

And somebody in the group says, "How much estrogen do you have to shoot up to keep a rack on you that big?" Somebody else whistles. The rest of the group whispers together. The breasts are too perfect. Both the same size and not too far apart. They look engineered.

The pink fingernails twist, and the bra falls open. The bra falls open, but the breasts stay up, firm and round, with nipples pointed at the ceiling. The exact set of breasts a man would choose.

Someone standing close, she reaches out a hand and makes a grab. Her hand squeezes flesh. Thumbing the nipple, she says, "Every-body. You've got to feel this—God, it's so gross." Her hand squishes, then lets go. Squishing again, she says, "It's like . . . I don't know . . . bread dough?"

"Miranda" twists to get away, his body pulling back against his chair.

But the hand clutching his breast, the fingers grip hard, and the woman says, "Don't."

Someone else says, "I wouldn't mind having hooters that nice."

They have to be silicone. Another hand reaches into the open blouse and grabs the second breast, rolling it, forcing it up against the pearl necklace, so we can look for a surgical scar underneath.

"Miranda" sits there, his arms bent forward at the elbow, each hand still holding half the pink bra, holding it open while we look. He starts to bring the bra back together, to seal things back inside.

And someone still groping a titty says, "Not yet."

The driver's license still on the table in front of us, the big "F" printed under "sex."

Someone else says, "Fake boobies don't prove nothing."

Someone else says, "My husband's got bigger ones than that."

Hands from around behind "Miranda," they pull the scarf off his shoulders, pulling the pink blouse back and down until it slips off his arms. His skin glows, clear as the pearl earring in each ear. His nipples pink as the lizard-skin pocketbook, he lets this happen.

Somebody throws the blouse off into a corner of the room.

And somebody else says, "Let's see your pussy."

And "Miranda" says: No.

It's obvious. This poor, sad, misguided fuck, he's using us. The way a masochist goads a sadist. The way the criminal wants to be caught. "Miranda" is begging for it. This is why he's shown up here. It's why he's dressed this way. He knows this shorty-short skirt, these big casaba boobs, they drive a real woman wild. In this case, "no" does mean "yes." It means "Yes, please." It means, "slap me."

"Miranda," he says: You're making a big mistake.

And everybody laughs.

We say how consciousness raising means coming to terms with your genitals. Other meetings we've had, we've all brought hand mirrors and squatted over them. We've all shared a speculum and studied the difference between the cervix of a virgin and a mother. We've had speakers from the women's health cooperative here to demonstrate period extraction with the Karman Cannula. Yes, all this, right here on this wooden table. Together, we've shopped for sex toys and studied the G-spot.

A little pushing, and "Miranda" is up on the table. Even on his hands and knees, his breasts still look round and solid, not stretched and hanging down. Six inches of zipper, and his skirt slides down his skinny ass. He's wearing pantyhose: more proof he's not a real woman.

The women in the group, we look at each other. To have a man here taking orders. Some of us were molested. Some of us, raped. All of us, ogled, groped, undressed by male eyes. It's our turn, and we don't know where to begin.

Somebody rolls the pantyhose down, off his ass. Somebody else says, "Arch your back."

Nobody's surprised at how "Miranda's" labia look. The skin too frilly. The wet-flower look a stylist works hard to get in *Playboy* or *Hustler*. Still, the flesh doesn't look soft enough, and the color's too pale, not pink or light brown. Surgical scar tissue. The pubic hair trimmed and waxed down to a thin stripe. Perfumed. Not the way a pussy is supposed to look. The longer we look, the more we agree it's not real.

Somebody pokes at "Miranda" with a car key. Not ever a finger. Somebody pokes at the folds of her skin and says, "I hope you didn't pay a lot for this . . ."

Another member of the group says we should see how deep it goes.

Whatever he is, "Miranda" is crying. Caught up in his little drama, all his eye makeup and blusher mixed with his foundation and coming down his cheeks to each corner of his mouth. He's almost naked with his stretched pantyhose webbed between his ankles, his feet still in gold-elegant high-heeled sandals. His blouse is gone and his pink lace bra is open and hanging off his shoulders. His firm, round breasts shiver with each sob. He's on the conference table this way. His fur coat on the floor, kicked off into a corner. His blond hair falling down. His own little horror story.

Somebody tells "Miranda" to shut up. Shut up and turn over.

Somebody takes him by an ankle. Someone takes the other ankle, and they twist his legs until he lets out a little shriek and turns over. Now on his back, his feet are still pulled wide apart, each gold sandal gripped by a different set of hands.

This isn't a woman. Maybe if someone from the planet Mars only ever saw a woman in *Cosmopolitan,* this is what they'd create. We point out how the clitoris must be the penis whittled down. Somebody describes how the artificial vaginal vault is just the penis, gutted and stuffed inside, a section of mucus-producing lower intestine spliced in for depth. Where the cervix should be, they use the skin salvaged from the empty scrotum.

"Waste not, want not," somebody says.

Someone gets a little flashlight out of her tote bag and says, "I've got to see this."

Somebody else says, "All this fuss. It proves he's never had a pelvic."

In hindsight, they should've just gone home. Oh, it's all so politically enlightened until somebody gets hurt.

Still, here they meet week after week, rapping about who didn't get what job. Who's stuck under what glass ceiling. Who feels her breasts undressed by the eyes of gas-station attendants and construction workers. All they ever do is talk. Here at last is their chance to strike back.

It's a team-building exercise.

They ask, Why is he here? Is he a spy?

Experts say a woman makes only sixty cents for every dollar a man makes doing equal work. He makes all this extra dough, and this is how he blows it. Makeup and plastic tits. Any real woman's gonna have stretch marks. Gray hairs. Cheesy cellulite thighs.

They ask, what did he expect to find?

Somebody is digging with her fingers. Someone holds the flashlight, pushing it forward.

The group asks, did he expect a gang of man-hating bulldykes getting together for some hot girl-on-girl rug munching?

The flashlight, the little halogen lightbulb must be hot, because he's squealing, squirming so hard it takes all of them to hold him down. To hold his legs apart and force him open for a look.

Someone says, "What's it look like?"

The rest of the group wait for their turn.

"Miranda" thrashing on the table, the group leans over him, his pearl necklace breaks and goes rolling everywhere. The pins drop out of his hair. His breasts bounce and jiggle, two mounds of gelatin.

And someone pinches one by the nipple, tweaking it and saying, "Shake 'em, sexy mama."

Someone else says, "We just want to see where you put your balls, bitch."

It's an interesting juxtaposition. A fascinating sociopolitical power relationship, being fully clothed and examining a naked person held down, wearing only his high heels and jewelry.

The two women digging between his legs, they stop. Someone says, "Wait."

The one holding the little flashlight says, "Hold him still," and she leans in, forcing the flashlight deeper. She asks him, "Is this what you wanted to happen?"

"Miranda," spread-eagled on the table, he sobs, trying to bring his knees together. To roll to one side and curl into a ball.

"Miranda" is sobbing, saying: No. Saying: Please stop. Saying: It hurts.

Oh, it hurts. Boo-hoo. You're hurting me.

The woman with the flashlight, she looks the longest time, squinting and frowning, twisting the flashlight and poking it around. Then she stands straight and says, "The batteries are dead," and towers there, looking down on "Miranda," his legs still spread open in front of her.

The woman looks down at the table smeared with makeup and tears, the pearls scattered on the floor, and she says for us to let go. She swallows nothing, her eyes touching all over the body on the table. Then she sighs and tells "Miranda" to get up. Get up and get dressed. Get dressed and get out. Get out and not to come back.

Someone says maybe the flashlight's just turned off and asks to look at it.

And the woman puts her flashlight in her tote bag and says, "Don't."

Someone says, "What did you see?"

We saw what we wanted to see, the woman says. We all did.

The woman with the flashlight, she says, "What just happened here?" She says, "How did we *get this way*?"

From the minute he sat down, we tried to explain. We don't allow men. This is a women-only safe space. The purpose of our group . . .

1.
2.
3.
4.
5.
6.
7.
8.
9.
10.
11.
12.
13.
14.
15.
16.
17.
18.
19.
20.
21.
22.
23.
24.

To some of us, the nights are too long. To some, the days. The lights come on when Sister Vigilante raises the sun, but at sunrise today, it's a smell that pulls us out of bed. The perfect dream of a smell that pulls us out of our dressing rooms, into the hallway. Us, zombie-walking, pulled along by the nose.

Director Denial steps into the hall, falling halfway to the floor before her hands brace against the wall opposite her open door. Wedged against the wall to stay upright, she says, "Cora? Kitty, kitty?"

In the hallway, Reverend Godless struggles with both hands to zipper his matador pants, the pants that fit yesterday. "The ghost," he says, "must be shrinking our clothes."

The choker of brass bells cuts into the skin of Mother Nature's neck, so tight that every time she swallows you hear them jingle. "Damn," she says, "I shouldn't have had that extra helping of Comrade Snarky."

Out of the next door comes the Missing Link, his head tipped back so far his nostril hair is the tallest part of him. He sniffs and steps past Director Denial and Reverend Godless. Still sniffing the air, his nostrils flared into big black-hairy holes, he takes another step toward the stage and the auditorium beyond.

Director Denial says, "Cora . . ." and slides to the floor.

Out of another door comes Mrs. Clark, saying, "We'll need to wrap up Comrade Snarky today. She needs to go with Mr. Whittier."

From the floor, Director Denial says, "Cora . . ."

"Fuck that cat," Miss America says. Wearing a long Mandarin Chinese coat, embroidered with dragons, she leans in the doorway to her dressing room, her spidery hands clutching the doorframe. Her face is pale around the black smear of her mouth as Miss America says, "My head is killing me," rubbing her face with one open hand.

Miss America shrugs the Mandarin coat off one shoulder and snakes out a thin white arm. She lifts the arm over her head, the hand limp, dark hair sprouting in her armpit. She says, "Feel my lymph nodes. They're huge."

Up and down her thin, bare arm run long red scratches. Cat scratches, running close together. Trails and miles of cat scratch marks.

Looking up-close at her face, the Missing Link says, "You look terrible." He says, "Your tongue is black."

And Miss America drops her arm to hang limp along the doorframe. Her thick, black tongue licking her lips, leaving her lips black, she says, "I was so hungry. Last night, I ate all my lipsticks."

Stepping over Director Denial, she says, "What is that smell?"

You can smell breakfast toast and eggs fried in grease. A greasy-fat smell. A shared hallucination of our hunger. It's the smell of escargots and lobster tails. The smell of English muffins, dripping.

The Earl of Slander follows the Missing Link follows Mrs. Clark follows Sister Vigilante. We're all following the smell across the stage and up the center aisle toward the lobby.

Miss Sneezy blows her nose. Then she sniffs the air and says, "It's butter."

The smell of hot butter.

The ghost in every movie theater.

It's the greasy ghost of Comrade Snarky, what we'll have to smell every time we use the microwave. We're breathing her spirit. Her sweet buttery stink will haunt us.

The only other smell is Mother Nature's breath, from eating a bayberry aromatherapy candle.

Halfway up the center aisle, we stop.

Faint and outside, we hear hail falling. Or machine-gun fire. Or a drumroll.

A blizzard of snaps and bangs come on top of each other. This fast, faint rattle comes from the lobby.

Us, standing there in the black plaster center of the Egyptian auditorium, with the dusty, spiderwebbed stars dim above us, we clutch the gold-painted back of the black seats for support. We stand and listen.

And the gunfire, the hailstorm, it stops.

Something exciting needs to happen.

Something amazing needs to happen.

In the blue velvet lobby, the microwave oven dings once, twice, three times.

The ghost of Comrade Snarky.

Still tugging at her necklace, Mother Nature slides down into the rough black mohair of a seat.

Saint Gut-Free looks at Reverend Godless, who looks at the Matchmaker, who looks at the Earl of Slander taking notes, who nods, Yes. And they start up the aisle, the rest of us a step behind them. Agent Tattletale's camera spotlight following them.

Through the auditorium doors, the French velvet lobby is empty. Shadows hide behind every palace chair and sofa. The light from the few bulbs we left, it's not bright enough to show the walls on the far side of the room. The doors to the lobby bathrooms are propped open, and the tile floor inside shines with water from the toilets. Here and there, melted lumps of toilet paper are stranded in the puddle.

On top of the toilet smell, the smell of rotten turkey Tetrazzini, the smell of Comrade Snarky's cooked ass, you can still smell . . . butter.

Through the smoked glass of the microwave door, you can see something white almost filling the oven.

It's the Missing Link who yelps. Our hairy man-animal. He yelps and slams both hands down on the snack bar so hard he swings his legs up to one side and vaults over it. Behind the snack bar, he yanks open the microwave, and grabs what's inside.

He yelps, again, and drops it.

By then, the Baroness Frostbite is vaulted over the marble counter of the snack bar.

The Countess Foresight rushes over to see.

Mother Nature says, "It's popcorn." Her bells ringing with every word.

Another yelp comes from behind the counter, and the something white bounces high up into the air. Hands follow it, volleyball-slapping it, a white paper ball, keeping it out of the reach of any one person. In the camera spotlight, it becomes a spinning, steaming white moon.

Miss Sneezy is laughing and coughing. Countess Foresight, crying behind her sunglasses. All of us, reaching for it. Stretching to catch the spinning, greasy, hot smell of it.

The Matchmaker shouts, "We can't." Waving his arms, he shouts, "We can't eat any!"

The paper ball batted between hands, it spins and bounces near the ceiling.

And Countess Foresight shouts, "He's right." She shouts, "We could be rescued, today!"

One man-animal jump, and the Missing Link has both hands on the bag.

The Link passes to the Countess, who passes to the Matchmaker, who runs for the bathroom.

The rest of us—the Saint and Miss America and the Sister and the Baroness—we race after, screaming and weeping. Behind us all,

Agent Tattletale follows after with the camera, saying, "Please don't let's fight. Please don't fight. Please . . ."

The Earl of Slander, already rewinding his tape recorder to hear the drumroll sound of the popcorn still hot in the microwave oven. Then the little "ding" that says it's ready.

Behind the snack bar, only Chef Assassin and Mrs. Clark are left.

To Mother Nature, her friend Lentil is our ghost. To Miss Sneezy, the ghost is her English teacher with cancer. The same way we ruined the food, our ghost might be the combined work of any two or three people. Of us.

From the bathroom, you hear a toilet flush. The toilet flushes, again. A chorus of moans echo from the tile inside the open bathroom door. A fresh sheet of water fans out the doorway, lapping at the edge of the lobby's blue carpet.

The water, spotted here and there with melted paper. Paper and popcorn. Another gift from our ghost.

Still staring into the open microwave oven, Mrs. Clark says, "I still can't believe we killed her . . ."

Still sniffing the buttered air, Agent Tattletale says, "It could've been worse."

In the wash of water backed up from the toilet, washed up and stranded on the lobby carpet, you can see fur. Tabby-cat fur. A thin black leather collar. Some pencil-thin bones.

By now, Director Denial has followed us from her dressing room. She's just in time to see the little-toothed skull, picked clean by someone and then coughed up by the toilet.

Engraved on the collar, a tag that says "Miss Cora."

Looking away from the expression on Director Denial's face, watching her reflected small in the mirror behind the snack bar, Mrs. Clark says, "How? How could killing anyone get any worse?"

American Vacations

A Poem About Agent Tattletale

"Americans do drugs," says Agent Tattletale, "because they
   don't do leisure very well."
Instead, they do Percodans, Vicodins, OxyContin.

Agent Tattletale onstage, one hand holds his video camera
   as a mask
   to hide half his face.
   The rest of him, off-the-rack in a brown suit. Brown
      shoes.
   A mustard-yellow vest. His straight brown hair combed
      back.
   A yellow bow tie and a white button-down dress shirt.
There, the white of his shirt shimmers,
   patterned with movie actors.

Instead of a spotlight, Agent Tattletale is a screen for stock
   footage:
   a shot of some theater audience.
   Rows and rows of people, all of them,
   their crowds of hands all clapping without a single
   sound.

Onstage stands Agent Tattletale, favoring his left leg,
   leaning a little more to the right all the time.

Instead of one eye, that spot filled by the red
RECORD
light of the video camera, watching.
Instead of an ear, on that side the built-in
microphone. To hear nothing but himself.

Agent Tattletale, he says, "Americans are the world's best at
doing their work."
And studying and competition.
But we suck when it comes time to relax.
There's no profit. No trophy.
Nothing at the Olympic Games goes to the Most Laid-
Back Athlete.
No product endorsements for the World's Laziest
anything.

His camera eye on auto-focus, he says, "We're great at
winning and losing."
And nose grindstoning,
but not accepting. Not shoulder shrugging and tolerance.

"Instead," he tells himself, "we have marijuana and
television. Beer and Valium."
And health insurance.
To refill, as needed.

Crippled

A Story by Agent Tattletale

Right this minute, Sarah Broome's looking at her best wooden rolling pin. She swings it, testing how heavy it feels. The hard slap of it against her open palm. She's moving around cans and bottles on the shelf above her washing machine, shaking the jug of bleach to hear how much is left.

If she could hear, if she'd just listen, I'd tell her it's okay to kill me. I'd even tell her how.

My rented car is just down the road, maybe one song away if you're listening to the radio. Maybe two hundred steps if you count steps when you're scared. She could hike down and drive it back. A dark-red Buick, covered with dust by now from cars going past on the gravel. She could park it close enough to this toolshed or garden shed or whatever she's got me locked inside.

In case she's outside, near enough to hear, I shout, "Sarah? Sarah Broome?"

I shout, "You've got nothing to feel bad about."

Me locked here inside, I could coach her. Walk her through it. Tell her how. Next, she'll need to get a screwdriver and loosen the clamps that hold the tinfoil accordion duct to the back of the clothes dryer. Then she can use this same clamp to anchor one end of the duct around the tailpipe of my car. Those ducts, they stretch out, longer than you'd expect. My gas tank is almost full. Maybe she's got a power drill to put some holes in the wooden side of the shed, or in the door. Being a woman, she can drill where it won't show later.

How nice her place looks is important. Seeing how it's everything she has.

"Her life used to be mine," I say. "I can see the way she thinks things are."

She can tear off strips of duct tape to hold the hose against the shed. To speed up killing me, she could throw a plastic tarp over the top half of the shed, then wrap it tight to the sides with rope. Turn this into a tight little smokehouse. In five hours, she'll have two hundred pounds of beefstick summer sausage.

Most people, they've never killed a chicken, much less a human being. People, they have no idea how tough this is going to be.

I promise to just breathe deep.

The report from the insurance company, it says her name is Sarah. Sarah Broome, she's forty-nine years old. A senior baker in a commercial bakery for seventeen years, she used to throw a sack of flour up on one shoulder, heavy as a ten-year-old boy, she could balance the flour there while she ripped out the pull-string at the front edge and poured the flour, little by little, into a spinning mixer. According to her account, on her last day at work the floor was still wet from mopping the night before. The lighting wasn't too good, neither. The weight of the flour tipped her over backward, bouncing her head on the rolled-steel edge of a table, resulting in memory loss, migraine headaches, and general weakness that left her unfit for any kind of labor.

The CAT scans showed nothing. The MRIs, nothing. The X-rays, nothing. But Sarah Broome never went back to work.

Sarah Broome, married three times. No kids. She gets a little Social Security. A little company settlement money every month.

She gets twenty-five milligrams of OxyContin to treat the chronic pain that follows her spine from her brain and radiates down both arms. Some months, she'll ask for Vicodins or Percodans.

Not three months after her settlement, she moved here, to the middle of nowhere, with no neighbors.

Right this minute, sitting here inside her shed, my right foot looks put on backward. The knee's got to be broken, the nerves and tendons inside twisted halfway around. Everything below that knee, numb. It's too dark to see, but where I sit smells cow-shitty. The slick feel of plastic must be bags of composted steer manure ready for her new garden plot. Leaning against the walls are a shovel, a hoe, a garden rake.

Poor Sarah Broome, right this minute, she's looking at her power tools. She's sick with the idea of sinking a skill saw into me. Instead of sawdust, the spinning blade spraying a wet rooster-tail of blood and flesh and bone. Well, that's if she has an extension cord long enough. She's reading the labels on paint cans, slug bait, cleaning fluid, looking for the skull and crossed bones. The green frowny face of Mr. Yuck. She's calling the local Poison Control hotline, asking how much barbecue lighter fluid a man would have to drink to die. When the poison expert asks why, then Sarah hangs up, fast.

How I know this is . . . ten years ago I was running kegs of beer between a distributor and too many little bars and taverns. These were places too small to have a loading zone, so you double-parked. Or you parked in the suicide lane, between lanes of fast traffic cutting past you in both directions. I humped kegs. I stacked cases of bottled beer on a handcart and waited for a gap in traffic big enough to run through. Always behind schedule, until, by complete accident, a keg rolled off the rack and creamed me out flat on the pavement.

After that, I got a place almost this nice. A rusted Winnebago motor home that wasn't going anywhere, parked next to a one-hole shithouse, along a wide spot in a gravel road through the woods. I had a four-banger Ford Pinto with a manual transmission to get me into town. A pension for being totally disabled, and all the time in the world.

The rest of my life, all I had to do is keep my car running. I stayed high on so much Vicodin that just taking a walk in the sun felt as good as any massage. As good as a massage with a hand job, even.

Just watching the birds at the birdfeeder. The hummingbirds. Putting out peanuts, stoned and laughing as the squirrels fight the chipmunks, it's a good enough life. The American dream of living without an alarm clock. Without having to punch a time clock or wear a damn hairnet. A dream life, where you don't need to ask some asshole's permission before you can go take a crap.

No, until this afternoon, Sarah Broome had nothing to do but read paperback books from the library. Watch the hummingbirds. Pop those little white pills. A kind of dream vacation that's never supposed to end.

What sucks is, crippled or not, you've got to at least act crippled. You have to limp, or hold your head stiff on your neck to show you can't turn it. Even with painkillers pulsing through you, this is the kind of play-acting that starts you feeling terrible. You fake any symptom long enough, and you'll start to hurt for real. You limp around, and then your knee really does start to ache. You sit around and turn into a big fat hunchback.

The American dream of leisure, it gets boring fast. Still, you're paid to be a cripple. Sitting with your television. Laying in a hammock, watching the damn animals. If you don't work, you don't sleep. Day and night, you're half awake, bored.

Daytime television, you can tell who's watching by the three kinds of commercials. Either it's clinics for drying out drunks. Or it's law firms who want to settle injury suits. Or it's schools offering mail-order vocational degrees to make you a bookkeeper. A private detective. Or a locksmith.

If you're watching daytime television, this is your new demographic. You're a drunk. Or a cripple. Or an idiot. After the first couple weeks, being a sloth sucks ass.

You don't have the money to travel, but it doesn't cost anything to turn a shovelful of dirt. Work on your car. Plant a vegetable garden.

One night, after it's dark, a cloud of mosquitoes and deer flies are thick around my porch light. Me in my Winnebago with a mug of hot tea and some Vicodin in my bloodstream, I look up from my book to watch the bugs outside the windows. That's when the sound comes. It's a man's voice, shouting from somewhere in the dark, back up in the woods.

It's somebody shouting for help. Please. Help. He's slipped and hurt his back. Fallen out of a tree, he tells me.

In the middle of the night, here he's dressed in a brown suit with a mustard-yellow vest, wearing brown leather wingtip shoes, and he says he's bird-watching. A pair of binoculars hang from a strap around his neck. That's what they teach in correspondence school. If you're caught by the suspect, say you're a bird-watcher. I offer to carry his briefcase. Then we each put an arm around the other and run a slow, slow, three-legged race back toward the porch light of my motor home.

Almost there, the man sees my old shithouse and asks, can we stop a minute. He really needs to drop a load, he says. I help him inside the door.

Soon as the door's shut and his belt buckle hits the wood floor, I pop open his briefcase. Inside is a lot of paper. And a video camera. The side of the camera pops open, and inside is a tape. When I pick it up, when I snap the camera shut, the tape starts to play by itself, and the little viewing screen lights up.

On the screen, a little man takes a rear wheel and tire off a beat-up old Pinto.

It's me, rotating my tires. Me, knocking lug nuts loose and jockeying the wheels off and on my car.

Nothing else. No bird-watching. After a little buzz of static, the screen shows a tiny version of me, shirtless and lifting a full tank of propane. I carry the tank to the front of the Winnebago, where I change it for an empty.

If Sarah is anything like me, right this minute, she's picking a bread knife out of a kitchen drawer. If she gives me a few Vicodins in a glass of water, maybe she could knock me out. Right now, she's looking close-up, almost cross-eyed, at the serrated edge of the knife, at how sharp it is. It's so easy to section a chicken, cutting a throat couldn't be worse. She's maybe put an old towel over my face, that way she could pretend I was just a loaf of bread. Just slicing bread, or a meatloaf, until she sawed through a vein, then the heart still pushing blood, the big surge after surge after surge of blood. Right this minute, she's putting the knife back in the drawer.

It could be she's got an electric carving knife she got for a wedding present, half her lifetime ago, and she's never used. It's still in the fancy printed box with the little pamphlet about how to carve a turkey . . . bone a ham . . . slice a leg of lamb.

Nothing about how to dismember a detective.

What you have to consider is, maybe I wanted to get caught.

Mean evil me, spying on poor Sarah Broome and her family of cats.

What you have to consider is, maybe *she* wanted to get caught. We all need a doctor to yank us out of our perfect womb. We piss and moan, but we appreciate God kicking us out of Eden. We love our trials. Adore our enemies.

In case Sarah Broome is close by, I yell, "Please, don't beat yourself up over this . . ."

There's no lock to keep somebody inside a shithouse, so I wrapped a rope around the whole thing, three times, tight, and tied a triple granny knot. Inside, the man was grunting, dropping his mess into the hole he sat on. Slapping the mosquitoes and deer flies that swarmed up from the dark, he was too busy to hear me tie the knot and take his briefcase into my motor home for a little look.

In the detective's briefcase, there's a computer-printout spreadsheet of names next to disabilities next to an address for each one. Here's guys with carpal-tunnel syndrome. Guys with nonspecific soft-tissue damage to their lower backs. Chronic pain in their cervical vertebrae. Listed here is the disability provider, the insurance company. Here's the painkillers prescribed in each case.

And on that spreadsheet, there I am: Eugene Denton.

Inside the briefcase, a rubber band wraps a thick stack of business cards, all of them saying: Lewis Lee Orleans, Private Investigator. And a phone number.

When I dial the phone number, a cell phone inside the briefcase begins to ring.

Outside, Lewis Lee Orleans is hollering for me to help open the shithouse door.

If it would help Sarah Broome feel better about killing me, I'd tell her how the detective, he cried. His sobs muffled behind both hands, he told me he had a wife at home and three kids. Little kids. But he didn't wear a wedding ring, and inside his wallet were no pictures.

People say they can feel getting looked at. Being watched has the same feeling as ants crawling up your pant leg. Not me. That afternoon, I rotated my tires, checked the wear on my brake pads. Changed my oil, going from winter 10-10 weight to summer 10-40 weight. Here on the little video screen, here was me with a full case of motor oil, dragging it out from under the motor home and lugging it under one arm. Totally disabled me, the poor delivery driver who swore in court I couldn't lift my arms high enough to brush my teeth. A crippled invalid who deserved to be put out to pasture for the rest of my natural life. Here, shirtless on camera, the sweat from my armpit soaking a dark-brown shadow on the case of oil, I could pass for a circus strongman.

Living outdoors in good weather, not eating much, sleeping long nights, this tanned little muscle man could be me when I was nineteen years old.

This was the best life I'd ever known, and the man trapped in my shithouse was about to wreck it all.

Most big disability cases, they're always in appeal. The workers'-comp insurance folks, they want years to trail their man. To get just five minutes of good clear video that shows him lift a rototiller into the back of his pickup truck. They play that tape in court, and it's: Case closed. Disability denied. The plaintiff, one minute he's set for life, a good-enough chunk of cash every month, medical benefits covered, plus all the Vicodins and Percocets, all the OxyContin he needs to stay sweet the rest of his days. The defense team plays that tape in court—the rototiller going into his truck bed—and he's got nothing.

He's forty-five or fifty years old, and he's accused of insurance fraud. No chance he's getting anything but minimum wage the rest of his life. No benefits. No free time until he's sixty-something years old and qualifies for relief.

Right this minute, to Sarah Broome even life in prison for murder looks good compared to falling behind in her property taxes, losing her car, and pushing a shopping cart on the street.

When I was in her shoes, all I had on hand was a case of four bug bombs. The Winnebago where I lived had a wasp nest underneath. The directions on each bug bomb said to shake well and then break the tip off a little nozzle on top. The bomb would spray out poison smoke until it was empty.

The label said it would kill anything.

The poor detective. I climbed up a ladder and dropped all four of those bombs down the shitter vent pipe. After that, I clapped a hand over the pipe to stop any leaking out. Me up there, Adolf fucking Hitler, dropping poison gas and listening to my detective cough and beg for air. Just the sound of him gagging up wet puke, then the glop of it hitting the wood floor in chunks, just the sound alone almost made me hurl. The sulfur smell of bug spray and the puke smell. Those bug bombers kept hissing until white whiffs curled out from every little crack and nail hole. Gasoline-smelling smoke puffed from each side of the shithouse as the detective threw himself at the walls, then the door, trying to break out. Beating his arms to bruised pulp inside the shoulder pads of his good brown suit. Wearing himself out.

Sitting here, my leg aching from the waist down, waiting for Sarah Broome to play problem solver, there's so much I want to tell her. How the insecticide only made the detective and me both sick. How it felt, hitting somebody in the side of his head with a lug wrench. How, the first dozen times you hit, it only makes a mess. Even swinging with both hands, you're pounding hair and blood, not really breaking much bone. How the blood gets the lug wrench so slippery you can't hold it, and you've got to go find something clean to finish the job.

If I wasn't disabled before killing that Mr. Lewis Lee Orleans, I was after. Killing somebody is hard work. Hard, messy work. Hard, messy, noisy work, with him bellowing loud, his words making no more sense than a cow on the killing floor.

How I figure is, even if I didn't kill my Mr. Nosy Detective, the long cold night would have. The deer flies and shock from his broken leg would have. Dead is dead, and this way neither of us had to suffer. Not much.

Even if I never got caught, killing the detective spoiled my taste for being crippled. Now I knew people were watching, I'd seen the spreadsheet, another detective would come spying on me someday.

So, if you can't beat them, join them.

On television, the next commercial for a correspondence school, I called them up. They teach you how to stake out a suspect. How to dig through a garbage can for evidence. In six weeks, I had a paper to say I was a private investigator. After that, I had my own spreadsheet of deadbeats to go spy on. To make my own whistle-blowing little "stalk-umentaries," I call them.

You get out by getting smart and turning in your fellow cripples. Most cases, you don't even have to appear in court. Just turn in your expense report for the motel, the rental car, the restaurant meals, and you get your check in the mail. Plus the commission.

Leading up to right now. I've been following Ms. Broome for five days of nothing. When you're shooting a stalk-umentary, you're pretty much married to your subject. To the post office to pick up her mail. To the library for another book. To the grocery store. Even if she sits in the trailer all day, the curtains shut, watching television, then I'd be parked down the gravel road, slouched down low, stretched across the front seat of my rented car so I could lean back on a pillow propped against the inside of the passenger door. So I could keep an eye out. Even if nothing's going to happen.

It's a marriage.

All afternoon, slapping mosquitoes up on the hillside behind her trailer, I was squatted down, hidden back in the bushes. Watching her through the viewfinder on my video camera, I was waiting for my chance to hit the RECORD button. All Sarah had to do was bend over and pick up a white tank of propane. Just five minutes of her unloading heavy bags of cat food from her old hatchback car, and this job would be done. Nothing left to do but check in my rental car and catch the next plane home.

Of course, I'm sitting here in her shed because I tripped and fell. She came and found me, after it got dark, after the mosquitoes were worse than anything—gunshots, knife wounds—she could ever do to me. I had to yell for help, and she put one arm around my waist and half carried me this far. She set me here. To rest a minute, she said.

Nobody's saying I'm too original. I'm a bird-watcher, I tell her. This area is famous for the red-crested hairy plover. This time of year the blue-necked pheasant comes here to mate.

She's got my video camera, fooling with the little playback screen pulled out, and she says, "Oh, please. Show me." The camera makes a buzz, a click, and the red PLAY light blinks on, bright. She watches the screen, smiling, stoned.

I tell her, No. I reach for the camera, to take it back, but too fast. I tell her, No. Too loud.

And Sarah Broome, she steps away, pulling her elbows and her hands holding the camera out of my reach. Light from the little screen flickering soft as candlelight on her face, she smiles and keeps watching.

She keeps watching, but her face relaxes, her smile drooping, her cheeks sagging into jowls.

It's footage of her lifting sacks of steer manure, slippery white plastic bags packed with cow crap. Each bag printed in black letters: Net Weight Fifty Pounds.

Her eyes still pinned on the little screen, all the muscles of her face squeeze together in the middle. Her eyebrows. Her lips. Here's the five minutes that will end life as she knows it. My short stalkumentary that's going to put her back into blue-collar slavery.

It could be her back healed. It could be she faked it all, but what's clear is, she's no invalid. With the arms on her, she could wrestle alligators for a living.

Sarah Broome, I just want to tell you I understand. Right this minute, while you read the back of a box of rat poison, I want you to know—that first week of being totally crippled, completely helpless and disabled, it was hands-down the best week of my adult life.

Here's the dream of every farmer. Every railroad brakeman and waitress who ever took a week's vacation to go camping. One lucky day, a freight train takes a corner too fast and derails, or they step in a spilled milkshake, and they end up living down some no-name gravel road. Happy cripples.

It's maybe not the Good Life, but it's the Good-Enough Life. The washer and dryer sitting on a covered deck next to the trailer. Everything painted metal, pimpled and blistered with rust.

If she'd just listen, I could tell Ms. Broome just where to find my carotid artery. Or where on my head to connect when she swings the sledgehammer.

No, Sarah Broome just tells me to wait a spell. She shuts the doors to the shed and leaves me sitting here inside. A padlock snaps.

Right this minute, she's sharpening a knife. She's looking through her clothes, her slacks and blouses, jeans and sweaters, looking for an outfit she'll never again want to wear.

Waiting for her, I'm yelling for her not to feel bad. I'm yelling that what she's doing is all right. It's the only perfect way for all of this to end.

Standing behind the lobby snack bar, Agent Tattletale tells us, "Turns out, she was smarter than me, that Sarah Broome."

Instead of killing him, she left the video camera recording. She got the story of his past on tape. The murder of Lewis Lee Orleans. And after she'd hidden the tape, she drove him to the hospital.

"That," the Agent tells us, "is what I'll take for a happy ending . . ."

Some stories, Mr. Whittier would say, you tell them and you use them up. Other stories, they use you up.

Miss America is clutching her belly in both hands, squatting on the yellow seat of a wing chair in the Gothic smoking room, rocking forward and back with a shawl around her shoulders. If her belly looks big, or if she's just overdressed, we can't tell. She rocks, her arms and hands lined with the swollen red welts and scabs from cat scratches. She says, "You ever hear of CMV, cytomegalovirus? It's deadly to pregnant women, and cats carry it."

"If you feel bad about that cat," the Missing Link says, "you should."

Holding her belly and rocking, Miss America says, "It was either that cat or me . . ."

We're all of us sitting in the "Frankenstein Room," in front of the yellow-and-red glass fireplace, watching each other. Making mental note of each gesture and line of dialogue. Taping over every moment, every event, every emotion with the next.

Sitting in a yellow leather wing chair, the Missing Link turns to the Countess Foresight in the next chair and says, "So? Who did you kill to get here?"

Everyone pretends not to know what he means.

Each of us trying to be the camera, not the subject.

"Doesn't it seem like we're all hiding out from something?" the Missing Link says. With his long nose, his awning of a single dense eyebrow, his beard, he says, "Why else would people walk through that door with Whittier—a man they don't really know?"

On the yellow silk wallpaper, between the tall, pointed windows of stained glass with the eternal twilight of fifteen-watt lightbulbs behind them, on the yellow wallpaper, Saint Gut-Free has drawn hash marks to count off our days so far. With just the thumb and forefinger he has left on one hand, he holds a pastel crayon and makes one mark for every day Sister Vigilante turns on the power.

On the fit-stone floor, Agent Tattletale rolls back and forth with the pink exercise wheel, trying to lose more weight.

The furnace is broken—again. The water heater, too. The toilets, stuffed and choked with popcorn and dead cat. The washing machine and dryer are both hairy with yanked and hacked-off wires.

People piss in a bowl and carry it to a sink. Or they hike their skirt and piss in the dark corner of some huge, grand room.

Us in our fairy-tale wigs and velvet, killing each day in these echoing cold chambers, in the stink of piss and sweat, this is what fancy court life was like for the aristocracy a couple centuries ago. All those palaces and castles that look clean and elegant in today's movie version, in reality—brand-new, they were stinking and cold.

According to Chef Assassin, the kitchens in French châteaux were so far from the royal dining rooms that the food would arrive at dinner cold. That's why the French invented their zillion thick sauces, as blankets to keep food hot until it arrived at the table.

Us, we've found all the scavenger-hunt items: the bowling ball, the exercise wheel, the cat.

"Our humanity isn't measured by how we treat other people," the Missing Link says. Fingering the layer of cat hair on his coat sleeve, he says, "Our humanity is measured by how we treat animals."

He looks at Sister Vigilante, who looks at her wristwatch.

In a world where human rights are greater than at any time in history . . . in a world where the overall standard of living is at a peak . . . in a culture where each person is held responsible for their life—here, the Missing Link says, animals are fast becoming the last real victims. The only slaves and prey.

"Animals," the Missing Link says, "are how we define humans."

Without animals, there would be no humanity.

In a world of just people, people will mean nothing . . .

"Maybe that's how the folks at the Villa Diodati kept from killing each other, all those rainy days, trapped indoors," the Missing Link says.

By having their big collection of dogs and cats and horses and monkeys, to make them behave like human beings.

Looking at Miss America, her eyes red and her face sweating with fever, the Missing Link says how, in the future, the people protesting outside clinics—those people holding picket signs that show smiling babies, those people cursing and spitting on expectant mothers—in that miserable, crowded world, the Link says, "Those folks will rail against the few selfish women who still choose to give birth . . ."

In that future world, the world outside here, the only animals will be the ones in zoos and movies. Anything not human will just be a flavor for dinner: chicken, beef, pork, lamb, or fish.

Miss America clutches her belly and says, "But I needed to eat."

"Without animals," the Missing Link says, "there will be humans, but no humanity."

Looking at her engagement ring, the fat diamond of Lady Baglady sparkling on her thin finger, Mother Nature says, "What you said about protesting babies . . . it's so terrible, you sound like Comrade Snarky."

The fourth ghost of here.

"I agree," says Saint Gut-Free, watching Mother Nature. "Babies are . . . wonderful."

Mother Nature and the Saint—still our romantic subplot.

Then the Missing Link lifts his hands and shakes back the sleeves of his coat. With an index finger pressed to each temple, he says, "Then I'm channeling her." Channeling Comrade Snarky. And, channeling Mr. Whittier, he's saying that human beings need to accept the wild-animal side of their nature. We need some way to exhaust our fight-or-flight reflexes. Those skills we learned over the past thousand generations. If we ignore our need to hurt and get hurt, if we deny that need and let it pile up, that's when we get wars. Serial killers. School shootings.

"You're saying we have wars," Saint Gut-Free says, "because we have a low threshold for boredom?"

And the Missing Link says, "We have wars because we deny that low threshold."

Agent Tattletale videotapes the Earl of Slander, who tape-records the Missing Link, all of us looking for a telltale bit of physical business we can relay to an actor, on a set, someday. Some detail to make our version of the truth more real.

Reaching one hand up, underneath the layers of her skirts, Miss America lets her eyes roll down to stare at nothing on the carpet. While the fingers of her hand work under her skirts, her breathing, the rise and fall of her chest, it stops.

When she brings out her hand, the fingers shine, wet with something clear. Not blood. She brings her hand to her nose and inhales the smell. Frowning, her skin pulls together into deep wrinkles between her blue eyes.

Poor Director Denial has stopped crying, oh, forever ago. Since then, she just sits, watching Miss America. Following her from room to room. Waiting.

"You have a bacterial infection," the Missing Link says, looking at the scratches on Miss America's arms. "*Bartonella bacterium,* an infection of the lymph nodes." And he stops talking long enough for people to take note. Letter by letter, he spells, "B-A-R-T . . . ," while the Earl of Slander scribbles.

"And if I'm not mistaken," the Link says, sniffing the air, "your water's just broke . . ."

Miss Sneezy coughs into her fist, and against the quiet, the sound of the pen scribbling on paper is loud as thunder.

When Miss America's wet hand goes to her nose, Director Denial's eyes follow it.

Each of us, the camera behind the camera behind the camera.

Brushing the loose fur from his coat sleeves, without looking up, the Missing Link says, "The common name for your disease is 'cat-scratch fever.' "

"I have a migraine headache," Miss America says, and she wipes her wet fingers on her shawl. Lifting handfuls of her skirt, she topples forward out of her chair. She pulls her shawl up, higher around her scratched neck. On her feet, Miss America starts toward the stairs, saying, "I'm going to my room."

The leather seat of her chair is dark. Wet. With water, not blood.

As Miss America disappears, dropping lower and lower as she steps down the stairs, only then does Director Denial move.

As soon as Miss America is out of sight, Director Denial starts after her.

And the rest of us watch, and write this down. The way the Director's hands each hold a fistful of her uniform, a Clara Barton–long skirt and bib apron with a red cross on the chest and a folded nurse-cap pinned to the top of her wig, her fingers grip the skirt so tight they look blue. The way her chin tucks to her chest so her eyes roll up to see out from under the shelf of her brow. Her mouth is shut so tight, the muscle at each corner of her jaw is balled up, big. Without a sound louder than our pens on paper, Director Denial starts off after Miss America.

The rest of us sit, waiting for the scream.

Something gristly needs to happen.

Something ghoulish needs to happen.

The mythology of us—only with the royalties split one less way.

Agent Tattletale flops on the floor, resting on his side, panting and shiny with sweat. His caftan showing billowy harem pants underneath, his wig pulled down low and warm on his head. To the Missing Link, he says, "To test your own theory," Agent Tattletale says, "who did you kill to get here?"

Evolution

A Poem About the Missing Link

"What will you do today?" asks the Missing Link. "How will
  you justify it?"
  That mountain of dead animals and ancestors on which
    you stand.

The Missing Link onstage, his eyes stare out, yellow eyes,
  from deep in the shade of his brow bone.
  His eyes and nose, they're crowded into the clearing, the
    small open space
  between the hair bushy on his forehead and the forest of
    his beard.
His hands hang too near his knees,
  his knuckles hanging with black curls.

Onstage, instead of a spotlight, a movie fragment:
  The sixteen-millimeter footage of a monster covered with
    red fur,
  tall as a man on horseback, with a pointed top to its
    head,
  running away from the camera.
  A sunny day along a river, with pine trees as a backdrop.
This documentary monster, superimposed over the Missing
  Link,

her red-furry breasts swinging,
she turns to look back.

Onstage, the Missing Link says, "Every breath you take is
because something has died."
Something or someone lived and died so you could have
this life.
This mountain of dead, they lift you into daylight.
The Missing Link, he says, "Will the effort and energy and
momentum of their lives . . ."
How will it find you?
How will you enjoy their gift?
Leather shoes and fried chicken and dead soldiers are only
a tragedy
if you waste their gift
sitting in front of the television. Or stuck in traffic. Or
stranded at some airport.

"How will you show all the creatures of history?" says the
Missing Link.
How will you show their birth and work and death were
worthwhile?

Dissertation

A Story by the Missing Link

It turns out this wasn't a real date.

Sure, it was beer in a tavern with a pretty-enough girl. A game of pool. Music on the jukebox. A couple hamburgers with fried eggs, French fries. Date food.

It was too soon after Lisa's death, but this felt good. Getting out.

Still, this new girl, she never looks away. Not at the football game on the television above the bar. She misses every pool shot because she can't even watch the cue ball. Her eyes, it's like they're taking dictation. Making shorthand notes. Snapping pictures.

"Did you hear about that little girl getting killed?" she says. "Wasn't she from the reservation?" She says, "Did you ever know her?"

The rough cedar walls of the bar are smoked from years of cigarettes. Sawdust is thick on the floor to soak up the tobacco spit. Christmas lights string back and forth across the black ceiling. Red, blue, and yellow. Green and orange. Some of the lights blinking. Here's the kind of bar where they don't mind you bringing your dog or wearing a gun.

Still, despite appearances, this is less of a date than an interview.

Even when this girl's stating a fact, it comes out as a question:

"Did you know," she says, "that Saint Andrew and Saint Bartholomew tried to convert a giant with a dog's head?" She's not even trying to line up her next shot, saying, "The early Catholic church describes the giant as twelve feet tall with a dog's face, the mane of a lion, and teeth like the tusks of a wild boar."

Of course she misses, but she won't let up. Just: yak, yak, yak.

"Have you ever heard the Italian term *lupa manera*?" she says.

Bent over the pool table, she muffs another easy shot, the two-ball straight in line for a corner pocket. All the time, she's saying, "Have you heard of the French Gandillon family?" Saying, "In 1584, the entire family was burned at the stake . . ."

This girl, Mandy Somebody, she's around campus for the past couple months, since Christmas break maybe. Short skirts and boots with pointed heels sharp as a pencil. Not any sort of clothes a girl could even buy around here. At first, she hung around the anthro office mostly. In "World Peoples 101," she was the graduate TA, and it's there her staring routine really started. Then she's hanging around the English department, asking about the prelaw program. Every day, she's there. Every day, she says hello. Still, always spying. Her eyes snapping pictures. Jotting down notes.

Being: Mandy Somebody, Secret Agent.

Major eye contact goes on through all winter term, and this week she says, "You want to get a bite?" Her treat. Still, even with hamburgers, the Christmas lights, and beer, this is no date.

Now, scratching on the six-ball, she says, "I'm a better anthropologist than I am a pool player." Chalking her cue, she says, "Do you know the word *varulf*? How about a man named Gil Trudeau? He was the guide to General Lafayette during the American Revolution?" Still grinding that little blue chalk cube on the tip of her cue, Mandy Somebody says, "Or have you heard the French term *loup-garou*?"

All the time, her eyes, watching. Measuring. Looking for some answer. A reaction.

It's the anthropology part of her that wants to meet and go out. She moved here from New York City, all that way just to meet guys from the Chewlah Reservation. Yeah, it's racist, she says. "But it's *good* racist. I just think Chewlah guys are hot . . ."

Over hamburgers, Mandy Somebody leans forward, both elbows on the table, one hand cupped to hold her chin, her other hand fingering an invisible design on the greasy tabletop. She says guys from the Chewlah tribe do all look alike.

"Chewlah men all have a big dick and balls for their face," she says.

What she means is, Chewlah men have square chins that stick a little too far out. They have cleft chins so deep it could be two balls in a sack. Chewlah guys always need a shave, even right after they shave.

That constant dark shadow, Mandy Somebody calls it "Five-Minute Shadow."

Guys from the Chewlah Reservation, they only have one eyebrow, a bush of black thatch, thick as a stand of pubic hair on the bridge of their nose, then trailing away to almost reach their ears on either side.

Between this clump of black curls and their bristly sack of low-hanging chin, there's that Chewlah nose. One long swell of tube, flopped down the middle of their face. A nose so thick and half hard, the fat head of it hides their mouth. A Chewlah nose hangs so long it overlaps their nutsack chin, just a bit.

"Those eyebrows hide their eyes," Mandy says. "The nose hides the mouth."

When you meet a guy from the Chewlah tribe, all you see at first is pubic hair, a big half-hard dick hanging down, and the two balls hanging a little behind it.

"Like Nicolas Cage," she says, "but more so. Like a dick and balls."

She eats a French fry and says, "That's how to tell if any guy's good-looking."

The table is gritty with the salt she's dumped on her French fries. She pays for everything with a color of American Express card the bartender has never seen before. Titanium or uranium.

It's her dissertation that brought her out here. You can only bear to build a case like this, in Manhattan, in the middle of all those anthropology graduate students, giggling, you can only tolerate that so long before your advisers start coaching you to do some field-work. In her field, cryptozoology. The study of extinct or legendary animals, like Bigfoot, the Loch Ness Monster, vampires, the Surrey Puma, Mothman, the Jersey Devil. Animals that might or might not exist. It was her adviser's idea she should come here, to visit the Chewlah Reservation, to study the culture and do a little forensic legwork. To build the case for her thesis.

Her eyes jumping up and down, looking for a reaction, some con-firmation.

"God," she says, tongue out, fake-gagging, "does that make me come across like some wannabe Margaret Mead?"

Her original plan was to *live* on the Chewlah Reservation. She'd rent a house or something. Her mom and dad are both doctors and want her to follow her dream, not turn out the way they have, no matter how much it costs them. Even talking about herself, Mandy Somebody asked questions. Talking about her parents, she says, "Why don't they change careers? Is that sad or what?"

Her every sentence ending with that question mark.

Her eyes, blue or gray, then silver eyes, still always watching. Her teeth take a bite of her hamburger, even though by now it must be cold. Like eating something dead.

She says, "That girl who died . . ."

Then, "What do you think happened?"

Her dissertation is about how the same giant mysterious crea-tures occur in all regions around the world. Those giants they call Seeahtiks in the Cascade Mountains around Seattle. They're called Almas in Europe. Yetis in Asia. In California, they're the Oh-mah-ah. In Canada, Sasquatch. In Scotland, Fear Liath More, the famous "Gray Men" that roam the mountain Ben Macdhui. In Tibet, the giants are Metoh-kangmi, or Abominable Snowmen.

All of those just different names for hairy giants that wander through the forest, the mountains, sometimes glimpsed by hikers or loggers, sometimes photographed, but never captured.

A cross-cultural phenomenon, she calls it. She says, "I hate the generic term: Bigfoot."

All of these different legends grew up in isolation, but they all describe towering, hairy monsters that stink to high heaven. The monsters are shy, but attack if provoked. In one case, from 1924, a group of miners in the Pacific Northwest shot at what they thought was a gorilla. That night, their cabin on Mount Saint Helens was pounded by a group of these same hairy giants, throwing stones. In 1967, a logger in Oregon watched as another shaggy giant pulled one-ton rocks out of the frozen ground and ate the ground squirrels hibernating under them.

The biggest proof against these monsters is, none have ever been captured. Or found dead. With all the hunters in the wilderness these days, people on motorcycles, it would seem one would bag a Bigfoot.

The bartender comes by the table, asking who wants another round? And Mandy Somebody shuts up talking, like what she's saying is a big state secret. With him standing there, she says, "Run a tab."

When he steps away, she says, "Do you know the Welsh term *gerulfos*?"

She says, "Do you mind?" Twisting herself to one side, putting both hands into her purse on the seat beside her, she takes out a notebook wrapped with a rubber band. "My notes," she says, and rolls off the rubber band, looping it around one wrist for safe keeping.

"Have you heard about the race the ancient Greeks called the *cynocephali*?" she says. With her notebook open, she reads, "How about the *vurvolak*? The *aswang*? The *cadejo*?"

This is the second half of her obsession. "All these names," she says, staking a finger on the open page of her notebook, "people all over the world believe in them, going back thousands of years."

Every language in the world has a word for werewolves. Every culture on earth fears them.

In Haiti, she says, pregnant women are so terrified that a were-wolf will eat a newborn, those expectant mothers drink bitter coffee mixed with gasoline. They bathe in a stew of garlic, nutmeg, chives, and coffee. All this to taint the blood of their baby and make it less appetizing to any local werewolf.

That's where Mandy Somebody's thesis comes in.

Bigfoot and werewolves, she says, they're the same phenomenon. The reason science has never found a dead Bigfoot is because it changes back. These monsters are just people. It's only for a few hours or days each year they change. Grow hair. Go *berserk,* the Dan-ish used to call it. They swell up, huge, and need room to roam. In the forest or in the mountains.

"It's kind of like," she says, "their menstrual cycle."

She says, "Even males have these cycles. Males elephants go through their *must* cycle every six months or so. They reek of testos-terone. Their ears and genitals change shape, and they're cranky as hell."

Salmon, she says, when they come upstream to spawn, they change shape so much, their jaw deforming, their color, you'd hardly recognize them as the same species of fish. Or grasshoppers becoming locusts. Under these conditions, their entire bodies change size and shape.

"According to my theory," she says, "this Bigfoot gene is related either to hypertrichosis or to the humanoid *Gigantopithecus,* thought to be extinct for a half-million years."

This Ms. Somebody just yak, yak, yaks.

Guys have listened to worse shit, trying to get a piece of ass.

That first big word she says, hypertrichosis, it's some inherited disease where you get fur growing out of every pore on your skin and end up working as a circus side show. Her second big word, *Gigantopithecus,* was a twelve-foot-tall ancestor of humans, discov-ered in 1934 by some doctor named Koenigwald while he was researching a single huge fossilized tooth.

One finger tapping the open page of her notebook, Mandy Somebody says, "Do you realize why the footprints," and she taps her finger, "photographed by Eric Shipton on Mount Everest in 1951," and she taps her finger, "they look exactly like the footprints photographed on Ben Macdhui in Scotland," and she taps her finger, "and exactly like the footprints found by Bob Gimlin in northern California in 1967?"

Because every lumbering hairy monster, worldwide, is related.

Her theory is, people around the world, isolated groups of people, carry a gene that changes them into these monsters as part of their reproductive cycle. The groups are isolated, they stay alone on tracts of wilderness, because nobody wants to become a towering, shaggy half-animal in the middle of, say, Chicago. Or Disneyland.

"Or," she says, "on that British Airways flight, halfway between Seattle and London . . ."

She's referring to a flight last month. The jet crashed somewhere near the North Pole. The pilot's last communication said something was tearing through the cockpit door. The steel-reinforced, bulletproof, blast-resistant cockpit door. On the flight recorder, the black box, the last sounds include screams, snarls, and the pilot's voice screaming, "What is it? What's going on? What are you? . . ."

The Federal Aviation Administration says no guns, knives or bombs could possibly have been carried aboard the flight.

The Homeland Security Office says the crash was most likely caused by a single terrorist, high on massive amounts of some designer drug. The drug gave him or her superhuman strength.

Among the dead passengers, Mandy Somebody says, was a thirteen-year-old girl from the Chewlah Reservation.

"This girl was headed for"—she pages through her notes—"Scotland."

Her theory is, the Chewlah tribe was sending her overseas before puberty hit. So she could meet and maybe marry someone from the Ben Macdhui community. Where, tradition holds, giants with gray fur roam the slopes above four thousand feet.

Mandy Somebody, she's full of theories. The New York Public

Library has one of the nation's largest collections of books about the occult, she says, because a coven of witches once ran the library.

Mandy Somebody, she says how the Amish keep books of every Amish community on earth. An inventory of every member of their church. So as they travel or immigrate they can always be among, live among, mate among their own kind.

"It's not so outlandish to expect these Bigfoot people keep the same kind of inventory books," she says.

Because the change is always temporary, that's why searchers have never found a dead Bigfoot. And that's why the idea of werewolves occurs in all cultures, over all of human history.

The one piece of movie footage, shot by a man named Roger Patterson in 1967, shows a creature walking upright, covered with fur. A female with a pointed head and enormous breasts and buttocks. Her face and breasts and butt, her entire body covered with shaggy red-brown hair.

That few minutes of film, which some call a fraud, and others call undeniable proof, that's probably just somebody's Aunt Tilly going through her cycle. Running around eating berries and bugs, just trying to steer clear of folks until she changes back.

"That poor woman," Mandy says. "Imagine millions of people seeing a film of you naked on your worst 'bad hair' day?"

Probably, the rest of that woman's family, every time that footage is on television, they probably call her into the living room and tease her.

"What looks like a monster to the world," Mandy says, "it's just home movies to the Chewlah tribe."

And she waits a little window of time, maybe for a reaction. For laughter or a sigh. A nervous twitch.

About the girl on the flight, Mandy Somebody says, imagine how she must have felt. Eating her little in-flight meal, but still hungry. Hungrier than she'd ever felt before. Asking the flight attendant for snacks, leftovers, anything. Then realizing what was about to happen. Until then, she'd only heard the stories how Mom and Dad would hike off into the woods for a few nights, eating deer, skunks, salmon, everything they could catch. Going wild for a few nights, and coming home exhausted and maybe pregnant. Imagine this girl getting up to hide in the airplane bathroom, but it's locked. Occupied. She stands there in the aisle, just outside the bathroom door, getting hungrier and hungrier. When the door at last comes open, the man inside says, "Sorry," but it's too late. What's outside that door isn't human anymore. It's just hunger. It shoves him back into the little plastic bathroom and locks them both inside. Before the man can scream, what had been a thirteen-year-old girl snaps her teeth around his windpipe and rips it out.

She eats and eats. Tearing off his clothes, the way you'd peel an orange, to eat more of the juicy flesh inside.

While the passengers in the main cabin drift off to sleep, this girl eats and eats. Eats and grows. And maybe then a flight attendant sees the sticky wash of blood coming from underneath the locked bathroom door. Maybe the flight attendant knocks and asks if everything is all right. Or maybe the Chewlah girl eats and eats and is still hungry.

What comes out of that locked bathroom, soaked in blood, it's nowhere near done eating. What bursts out, into the darkened main cabin, grabbing handfuls of face and shoulder, it walks down the cabin aisle the way you'd walk down a buffet, grazing, nibbling. That packed jetliner must've looked like a fat heart-shaped box of chocolates to its hungry yellow eyes.

U-pick human heads on this all-you-can-eat flying smorgasbord.

The captain's last radio transmission, before the cockpit door tore open, he shouted, "Mayday. Mayday. Somebody's eating my flight crew . . ."

Mandy Somebody stops here, her eyes almost full round circles, one hand pressed to her rolling chest as her breathing tries to catch up with all her talk. Her breath, the smell of beer.

From the street, the door opens and a lot of guys walk into the bar, all of them dressed in the same color of bright orange. Their sweatshirts. Vests. Orange coats. A sports team, but really a road crew. On the television above the bar is a commercial to join the navy.

"Can you imagine?" she says.

What will happen if she can prove all this true? If just someone's race will make them a weapon of mass destruction? Will the government order everyone with this secret gene to take drugs to suppress it? Will the United Nations order them all into security quarantine? Concentration camps? Or will they all be tagged with radio transmitters, the way park rangers tag dangerous grizzly bears and track them?

"It's just a matter of time," she says, "don't you think, before the FBI comes to conduct interviews on the reservation?"

Her first week here, she drove out to the reservation and tried to talk to people. The plan was to rent a place and observe everyday life. Soak up the details of Chewlah culture, how people earned their living. Collect an oral account of their legends and history. She drove out there, armed with a tape recorder and five hundred hours of tapes. And no one would sit and talk. There were no houses or apartments or rooms to rent. She wasn't there an hour before the council sheriff told her about some curfew that required she be off the reservation by sunset. What with the length of the drive, he told her she'd best start on her way back right then.

They kicked her out.

"My point is," Mandy Somebody says, "I could've prevented all this."

The girl's feeding frenzy. The crashed jetliner. The FBI only a few days from arriving here. Then the concentration camps. The ethnic cleansing.

Since then, she's hung out at the community college, trying to date a Chewlah guy. Asking questions and waiting. But not waiting for an answer. She's waiting for the applause. Waiting to be right.

That word she said before, *varulf*, it's Swedish for "werewolf." *Loup-garou* is French. That man, Gil Trudeau, the guide to General Lafayette, he was the first werewolf mentioned in American history.

"Tell me I'm right," she says, "and I'll try to help you."

If the FBI gets here, she says, this story will never see the light of day. All the people with the suspected gene will just disappear into government custody. For the public welfare. Or there will be some official accident to resolve the situation. Not genocide, not officially. But there's a good reason why the government went so hard on some tribes, wiping them out with smallpox blankets, or sticking them away on distant reservations. True, not all tribes carried the Bigfoot gene, but a century ago, how could you identify the ones at risk?

"Tell me I'm right," Mandy Somebody says, "and I can get you on the *Today* show in the morning."

Maybe even the A Block . . .

She'll break the story. Create public sympathy. Maybe get Amnesty International involved. This can be the next big civil-rights battle. But global. She's already identified the other communities, tribes, groups around the world most likely to carry her theoretical monster gene. Her breath, the smell of beer, saying "monster" loud enough so the orange road-crew guys look over.

She's got guys all over the world she could be flirting with. Even if this date is a bust, she'll find somebody who'll tell her what she wants to hear.

That werewolves and Bigfoot exist. And that he's both.

Guys have listened to worse shit, trying to get a piece of ass.

Even Chewlah guys with their dicks on their face.

Even me. But I tell her, "That thirteen-year-old, her name was Lisa." I say, "She was my little sister."

"Oral sex," Mandy Somebody says, "is *not* out of the question . . ."

Any guy would be an idiot not to take her home to the reservation. Maybe introduce her to the folks. The whole fam-damnly.

And, standing, I tell her, "You can see the reservation—tonight—but I really need to make a phone call first."

1.
2.
3.
4.
5.
6.
7.
8.
9.
10.
11.
12.
13.
14.
15.
16.
17.
18.
19.
20.
21.
22.
23.
24.

In Miss America's dressing room, in the gray concrete and bare pipes, kneeling beside the one twin bed, Mrs. Clark is saying how having a child isn't always the dream you might imagine.

The rest of us, we're in the hallway to spy. We're all afraid we'll miss some key event and be forced to take another person's word.

Miss America curled on her bed, curled on her side with her face to the gray concrete wall, she doesn't have any lines in this scene.

And, kneeling beside her, Mrs. Clark's huge, dry breasts shelved on the edge of the bed, she says, "You remember my daughter, Cassandra?"

The girl who looked into the Nightmare Box.

Who cut off her eyelashes and then disappeared.

"When she disappeared is the first time I noticed Mr. Whittier's advertisement," she says. Tucked in a book, in the bedroom she'd left behind, Cassandra had written on a sheet of blank paper: *Writers' Retreat. Abandon Your Life for Three Months.*

Mrs. Clark says, "I *know* Mr. Whittier has done this before."

And Cassandra was here—trapped in this place—the last time.

Kids, she says. When they're little, they believe everything you tell them about the world. As a mother, you're the world almanac and the encyclopedia and the dictionary and the Bible, all rolled up together. But after they hit some magic age, it's just the opposite. After that, you're either a liar or a fool or a villain.

With the rest of us scribbling, you can almost not hear for the noise of our pens on paper. We're all writing: *either a liar or a fool.*

From the Earl of Slander's tape recorder, we hear, ". . . or a villain."

All Mrs. Clark really knows is, after Cassandra was gone for three months, they found her. The police found Cassandra.

Kneeling beside Miss America's bed, she says, "I agreed to help Whittier because I wanted to know what happened to my child . . ." Mrs. Clark says, "I wanted to know, and she would never tell me . . ."

Poster Child

A Story by Mrs. Clark

Three months after Cassandra Clark disappeared, she walked back. A morning commuter driving inbound on the state highway saw a girl limping, almost naked, along the gravel shoulder. The girl seemed to be wearing a dark loincloth and dark gloves and shoes. She had on some kind of bib or a black kerchief tied around her neck and hanging down to cover her chest. By the time the driver had turned his car around and phoned for the police, by then the sun was bright enough to see the girl was actually naked.

Her shoes and gloves, her loincloth and bib were just dried blood, dried thick and black and swarming, buzzing, busy with black flies. The flies crawling on her, thick as black fur.

The girl's head was scraped and scabbed. Ragged tufts of hair sprouted behind her ears and around the crown of her bare head.

She limped because the two small toes had been amputated from her right foot.

The bib, that layer of blood on her chest, that fur of flies, at the hospital emergency room the doctors swabbed it with alcohol and found a game of tic-tac-toe carved in the skin above her breasts. The X player had won.

When they swabbed her hands, they found the smallest

finger missing from both. On the rest of her fingers, the nails had been pried up and torn away, leaving the fingertips swollen and purple.

Under the dried blood, her skin was blue-white. The girl's face was the bony knobs of her chin, her cheekbones, and the ridge of her nose. At the temples and above her jawline, the skin sagged into shadowed holes.

Inside the curtained walls of the emergency room, Mrs. Clark leaned over the chrome rails of her daughter's bed and said, "Baby, oh, my sweet baby . . . who did this to you?"

Cassandra laughed and looked at the needles stuck in her arms, the clear plastic tubes stuffed into her veins, and she said, "The doctors."

No, Mrs. Clark said, who cut off her fingers?

And Cassandra looked at her mother and said, "You think I'd let *someone else* do this to me?" Her laughter stopped, and she said, "I did this to myself." And that was the last time Cassandra ever laughed.

The police, Mrs. Clark said, they found evidence. They found slivers of wood, thin as needles, embedded in the walls of her vagina. And her anus. The police forensics people dug slivers of glass out of the cuts on her chest and arms. Mrs. Clark told her daughter that not talking wasn't an option.

They needed to know every detail Cassandra could remember.

The police said that whoever had done this would kidnap another victim. Unless Cassandra could face her fear and help them, her attacker would never be found.

In bed, in the sunlight from a window, Cassandra lay propped up on pillows and watched birds soar back and forth in the blue sky.

Her fingers wrapped big in white bandages, her chest padded with bandages, her pencil-hand only moved to draw the birds, flying back and forth. A sketch pad propped against her knees.

Mrs. Clark said, "Cassandra, honey? You need to tell the police everything."

If it would help, a hypnotist would come to the hospital. The caseworkers would bring *anatomically detailed* dolls to use in the interview.

And Cassandra still watched the birds. Sketching them.

Mrs. Clark said, "Cassandra?" and put her hand over one of Cassandra's white-wrapped hands.

And Cassandra looked at her mother and said, "It won't happen again." Looking back at the birds, Cassandra said, "At least not to me . . ."

She said, "I was a victim of myself."

Outside, in the parking lot, the television news crews were setting up their satellite feeds, each van aligning the broadcast dish on its roof. Ready for the toss from the studio anchor. The on-location talent, holding a microphone and inserting an IFD in her ear.

For three months, the town where they lived had stapled posters to telephone poles. Each poster showing a photo of Cassandra Clark in her head-cheerleader uniform, smiling and shaking her blond hair. For three months, the police had questioned kids at the high school. Detectives had interviewed people who worked at the bus station, the train station, the airport. The local television and radio stations ran public-service announcements that gave her weight as 110 pounds, height five foot six, green eyes, and shoulder-length hair.

Search-and-rescue dogs sniffed her cheerleading skirt and followed a scent trail as far as a bus-stop bench.

State troopers in powerboats dragged every pond and lake and river within a day's drive.

Psychics phoned to say the girl was safe. She had eloped and gotten married. Or she was dead and buried. Or she was sold into white slavery and smuggled out of the country to live in the harem of some oil magnate. Or she'd had a sex change and would be coming home as a boy, soon. Or the girl was trapped in a castle or some kind of palace, locked inside with a group of strangers, all of them cutting themselves. That psychic wrote two words on a sheet of paper and sent them to Mrs. Clark. Folded inside the paper, the shaky pencil lines said:

Writers' Retreat

After three months, all the yellow ribbons that people had tied to their car antennas were faded to almost white. Flags of surrender.

Nobody paid much attention to the psychics, there were so many of them.

For every Jane Doe the police found, burned or rotted or mutilated beyond identification, Mrs. Clark held her breath until dental records or DNA testing showed she wasn't Cassandra.

By the third month, Cassandra Clark was smiling and shaking her hair on the side of milk cartons. By then, the candlelight prayer vigils had stopped. The reward fund at the local bank branch was the only part of the case still drawing any interest.

Then—a miracle—and she was limping naked along the highway.

In her hospital bed, her skin looked purple with bruises. Her head was shaved bald. The plastic band around her wrist, it said: C. Clark.

The county medical examiner swabbed her for penis cells—which he said are long-shaped, unlike the round-shaped vaginal cells. They swabbed her for semen. The team of detectives vacuumed her scalp and hands and feet for foreign skin cells. They found fibers of blue velvet, red silk, black mohair. They swabbed the inside of her mouth and cultured the DNA in petri dishes.

Police counselors came and sat at her bedside, saying how important it was that Cassandra talk out all her pain. That she speak her bitterness.

The television and radio crews, the newspaper and magazine reporters sat in the parking lot, shooting their stories with her hospital window in the background. Some stepping back to film crews filming crews filming crews filming her window. To show what a circus this had become, as if that was the final truth.

When the nurse brought sleeping pills, Cassandra shook her head no. Just by shutting her eyes, she fell asleep.

After Cassandra wouldn't talk, the police fell on Mrs. Clark, telling her about the total cost to the taxpayer for their investigation. The detectives shook their heads and said how angry and betrayed they felt, working this hard, caring this much about a girl who didn't give a rat's ass about the pain and hardship she was causing her family, her community, and her government. She had everyone weeping and praying. Everyone hated the monster who'd tortured her, and they all wanted to see him caught and put on trial. After all their searching and effort, they deserved that much. They deserved to see her on the stand, weeping while she described how the monster had cut off her fingers. Carved her chest. Shoved a wood stake up her starving ass.

And Cassandra Clark just looked at the detectives lined up alongside her bed. All their faces, all their hate and rage focused on her because she wouldn't hand over another target. A bona-fide real demon. The devil they needed so bad.

The district attorney threatened to sue Cassandra for obstruction of justice.

Her mother, Mrs. Clark, among those glaring faces.

Cassandra smiled and told them, "Can't you see, you're addicted to conflict." She says, "This is my happy ending." Looking back to the window, to the birds flying past, she says, "I feel terrific."

Still in the hospital, she asked for a goldfish in a bowl. After that, she lay propped up in bed, watching it swim around and around, sketching it. The same way her mother watched program after television program every night.

The last time Mrs. Clark went to visit, Cassandra looked away from the fish only long enough to say, "I'm not like you anymore." She said, "I don't need to brag about my pain . . ."

And after that, Tess Clark didn't visit.

1.
2.
3.
4.
5.
6.
7.
8.
9.
10.
11.
12.
13.
14.
15.
16.
17.
18.
19.
20.
21.
22.
23.
24.

In her dressing room, Miss America is screaming.

In bed, her skirts pulled up and her stockings down, Miss America screams, "Don't let that witch take my baby . . ."

Kneeling next to the bed, toweling the sweat from America's forehead, the Countess Foresight says, "It's not a baby. Not yet."

And Miss America screams, again, but not in words.

In the hallway outside the dressing-room doorway, you can smell blood and shit. It's the first bowel movement any of us has had in days, maybe weeks.

It's Cora Reynolds. A cat reduced to a flavor. To crap.

"She's there, waiting," Miss America says, panting, biting her fist. Pain pulling her knees up to her chest. Cramps turning her onto her side, curled in the mess of sheets and blankets.

"She's waiting for the baby," Miss America says. Tears turning her pillow dark gray.

"It's not a baby," the Countess Foresight says. She wrings water from a rag and leans over to wipe away sweat. She says, "Let me tell you a story."

Wiping Miss America's face with water, she says, "Did you know? Marilyn Monroe had two miscarriages?"

And for a moment, Miss America is quiet, listening.

From our own rooms, putting pen to paper, we're all listening. Our ears and tape recorders tilted toward the heating ducts.

From the hallway outside the door, in her Red Cross nurse uniform, Director Denial shouts, "Should we start boiling water?"

And, kneeling beside the bed, the Countess Foresight says, "Please."

Again from the hallway, Director Denial's head and white nurse-hat leans in through the open doorway, and she says, "Chef Assassin wants to know . . . how soon should he put in the carrots?"

Miss America screams.

And the Countless Foresight shouts, "If that's a joke, it's *not* funny . . ."

The invisible carrot, the story left over from Saint Gut-Free.

And from the hallway, Chef Assassin shouts, "Calm down. Of course it's a joke." He says, "We don't *have* any potatoes or carrots . . ."

Shortsighted

A Poem About the Countess Foresight

"An electronic tracking sensor," says the Countess
Foresight, shaking her plastic bracelet.
A condition included in the terms of her recent parole
from prison.

The Countess Foresight onstage, she's folded inside the
webs of a black lace shawl.
A turban of blue velvet wrapped around her head.
A ring with different-colored stones on every finger.
Her turban, pinned in front with a polished black stone,
onyx or jet or sardonyx,
some stone that absorbs everything. Reflects nothing.

Onstage, instead of a spotlight, a movie fragment:
The shadows of dead movie stars, the residue of
electrons bounced off them
a hundred years ago.
Those electrons passed through a film of cellulose,
to change the chemical nature of silver oxide
and re-create chariot races, Robin Hood, Greta Garbo.

"Radar," says the Countess. "Global positioning systems.
X-ray imaging . . ."

Two hundred years ago, these would get you burned as
    a witch.
    A century ago, at least laughed at. Called a fool or a liar.
Even today, if you predict the future or read the past from
    indicators
    not everyone can recognize . . .
    it's the prison or the asylum you'll eventually call home.
The world will always punish the few people with special
    talents
    the rest of us don't recognize as real.

A psychologist at her parole hearing called her crime "acute
    stress-induced psychosis."
    An "isolated, atypical episode."
    A crime of passion.
    That would never, ever, ever happen again.
    Knock wood.
At that point, she'd served four years of a twenty-year
    sentence.
    Her husband was gone with her kids in tow.

Two hundred years from today, when what she saw, and
    read, and knew,
    when it all makes sense.
    By then, the Countess will be nothing but a prisoner
        number.
    A case file.
    The ash of a witch.

Something's Got to Give

A Story by the Countess Foresight

Claire Upton phones from a bathroom stall in the back of an antique store. From behind a locked door, her voice echoes off the walls and floor. She asks her husband: How tough is it to get into a video surveillance camera? To steal a security videotape? she says, and starts to cry.

This is the third or fourth time Claire's been to this shop in the past week. It's one of those shops where you have to leave your purse with the cashier to get inside. You have to check your coat, too, if it has deep, roomy pockets. And your umbrella, because some people might drop small items, combs, jewelry, knickknacks, inside the folds. A sign next to the old-man cashier, written with black felt-tipped pen on gray cardboard, it says: "We don't like you stealing from us!"

Taking her coat off, Claire said, "I'm not a thief."

The old-man cashier looked her up and down. He clicked his tongue and said, "What makes you the exception?"

He gave Claire half a playing card for each item she left behind. For her purse, the ace of hearts. For her coat, the nine of clubs. Her umbrella, the three of spades.

The cashier eyed Claire's hands, the lines of her breast pockets and pantyhose, for bulges that might be something stolen. Behind the front counter, all over the store, hung little signs telling you not to shoplift. Video cameras watched every aisle and corner, showing it on a little screen, stacked with other screens, a bank of little television monitors where the old-man cashier could sit behind the cash register and watch them all.

He could watch her every move, in black and white. He'd know where Claire was at any moment. He'd know everything she touched.

The shop was one of those antique-selling cooperatives where a lot of small dealers band together under one roof. The old-man cashier was the only person working that day, and Claire was his only customer. The store was big as a supermarket, but broken up into small stalls. Clocks everywhere made a wallpaper of sound, a din of tick, tick, ticking. Everywhere were brass trophies tarnished dark orange. Cracked and curled leather shoes. Cut-glass candy dishes. Books fuzzy with gray mold. Wicker rocking chairs and picnic hampers. Woven straw hats.

A cardboard sign, taped to the edge of a shelf, said: "Lovely to Look At, Delightful to Hold, But If You Should Break It, Consider It SOLD!"

Another sign said: "See it. Try it. Break it. BUY IT!"

Another sign says, "You break it here . . . YOU TAKE IT HOME!"

Even with the security cameras watching her, Claire treats an antique shop as a psychic petting zoo. A museum where you can touch each exhibit.

According to Claire, everything ever seen in a mirror is still there. Layered. Everything ever reflected in a Christmas ornament or a silver tray, she says she can still see it. Everything shiny is a psychic photo album or a home movie of the images that occurred around it. In an antique store, Claire can fondle objects all afternoon, reading them the way people read books. Looking for the past still reflected there.

"It's a science," the Countess Foresight says. "It's called *psychometry*."

Claire will tell you not to pick up a silver-handled carving knife because she can still see the reflection of a murder victim screaming in its blade. She can see the blood on the policeman's glove as he pulls it out of someone's dead chest. Claire can see the darkness of the evidence room. Then a wood-paneled courtroom. A judge in black robes. A long wash in warm, soapy water. Then the police auction. This is all still reflected in the blade. The next reflection is right now, you standing here in an antique store ready to pick up the knife and take it home. You just thinking it's pretty. Not knowing its past.

"Anything pretty," Claire will tell you, "it's only for sale because no one wants it."

And if no one wants something pretty and polished and old, there's a terrible reason why.

With all the shoplifting video cameras watching her, Claire could tell you all about surveillance.

When she went back to get her coat, she gave the old-man cashier his three playing cards cut in half. The ace of hearts. The nine of clubs. The three of spades.

From behind his cash register, the old man said, "Were you looking to buy something?" He hands her purse across the counter, nodding his head toward the bank of little televisions. The proof he'd been watching her touch everything.

It's then she sees it, in a glass case behind the old man, in a curio cabinet crowded with salt and pepper shakers and porcelain thimbles, surrounded by junk jewelry, there's a jar full of murky white liquid. Inside the haze, a tiny fist, lined with four perfect fingers, was just touching the glass.

Claire points past the old man, looking from him to the curio case, and she says, "What's that?"

The man turns to look. He takes a ring of keys from a hook behind the counter and goes back to open the cabinet. Reaching in, past the jewelry and thimbles, he says, "What would you say it is?"

Claire couldn't say. All she knows is, it gives off an incredible energy.

As the old man carries the jar toward her, the dirty white liquid sloshes inside. The top is white plastic, screwed down and sealed with a band of tape striped red and white. The old man sets one elbow on the counter in front of Claire, holding the jar near her face. With a twist of his wrist, he turns the jar until she can see a small dark eye looking out. An eye and the outline of a small nose.

A moment later, the eye is gone, sunk back into the murk.

"Guess," the old man says. He says, "You'll never guess." He lifts the jar to show the glass underside, and pressed there are a tiny pair of gray buttocks.

The old man says, "You give up?"

He sets the jar on the counter, and on top of the white plastic lid is a peeling label. Printed in black ink, it says: "Cedars–Sinai Hospital." Below that, handwritten in red ink, the rest is smeared. Some words. A date, maybe. Too smudged to read.

Looking at it, Claire shakes her head.

Reflected in the side of the glass jar, she can see years back, decades back: A room lined with green tile. A woman with both bare feet hooked to either side, draped in blue cloth. The woman's legs hooked in stirrups. Above an oxygen mask, Claire can see the woman's white-blond hair, growing out, already a little brown at the roots.

"It's the real deal," the old man says. "We tested the DNA against some certified hair. Markers all matched."

You can still buy her hair on the Internet, the man says. The bleached-blond scraps and trimmings.

"According to you bra-burners," the old man says, "it ain't a baby—just tissue. Could be her appendix."

Reading the glass, the layers of picture there, Claire can see: A lamp on a bedside table. A telephone. Prescription pill bottles.

"Whose hair?" Claire says.

And the old man says, "Marilyn Monroe's." He says, "If you're interested, it's not cheap."

This is a movie relic, the old man says. A sacred relic. The Holy Grail of movie memorabilia. Better than the ruby slippers from *The Wizard of Oz* or the sled named "Rosebud." Here's the baby Monroe lost while shooting *Some Like It Hot,* when Billy Wilder made her run down the train-station platform, take after take, wearing high heels.

The man shrugs. "Got it from a guy—told me the real story how she died."

And Claire Upton just stared, watching the movie of old reflections in the jar's curved side.

Here's a souvenir, a relic like the hand of a saint, mummified and adored in the rock-crystal case of some Italian cathedral. Or a lock of hair. Or this is another person, dead. The little boy or girl that might've saved Monroe's life.

The old man says, "Everything has a cash value on the Internet."

According to the man who sold it to him, Monroe got herself murdered. The summer of 1962, she'd been fired from the production of *Something's Got to Give.* George Cukor was bad-mouthing her, and the studio execs were pissed about how she'd jumped ship from the production to go sing at Kennedy's birthday bash. Her thirty-sixth birthday had just come and gone. The Kennedys were shutting her out. She was getting old with nobody, nothing. Her career over, and Liz Taylor eating up the public's attention.

"So she tries to get smart," the old man says.

Monroe gets *Life* magazine on her side, reeling them in to do a big feature on her. She talks Dean Martin into quitting *Something's Got to Give* when the studio replaces her with Lee Remick. And she calls a little meeting. At her place in Brentwood, a very little meeting with just the tip of every movie-studio iceberg. Every studio that owns a movie she's been in.

"Smart girl like her," the man says, "and you'd think she'd keep a gun on hand. Something to defend herself with."

With all the studio top brass sitting around her Mexican table, Monroe drinks champagne and tells them she plans to kill herself. Unless they give her back the last movie, and sign her to a new million-dollar contract, she'll overdose. Simple as that.

"Studio people," he says, "they don't scare that easy."

Those sharks, they got the best of her already in the can. Monroe's just getting older, and the public is bored with her looks. Killing herself would gold-plate every movie of hers they had in their vaults. They told her: Go ahead, lady.

"The guy who sells me the jar, here," the old man says, "he heard that direct from a big shot at the meeting."

Monroe getting high on champagne. The studio dragons in their chairs. She had their blessing. It must've broke her heart.

"Then," the old man says, "she gets smart with them."

She's changing her will, she says. True, she's got terrible profit-sharing deals, but she pulls a little from any re-release of her old stuff. Those films in the vaults, someday they'll sell to television. And they'll keep selling, especially if she's done suicide. She knows that. So do they.

Dead, she'll be sexy forever. People will love that studio-owned image of her forever. Those old films are money in the bank, unless . . .

The old man says, "Here's where her last will and testament comes in."

She'll set up a foundation: The Marilyn Monroe Foundation. And all income from her estate will feed into it. And that foundation will distribute every penny to the causes she'll name. The Ku Klux Klan. The American Nazi Party. The North American Man/Boy Love Association.

"Maybe some of those didn't exist back then," the old man says, "but you get the general idea."

When the American public knows that a few cents of every ticket to one of her shows, maybe even a nickel, goes to Nazis . . . No box office. No television sponsors. Those films will be worth—nothing.

No naked picture of her will be worth anything. Marilyn Monroe will become America's Lady Hitler.

"She'd made her image, she told the studio heads. And she could damn well break it," the old man said.

The jar sitting on the counter between them, Claire looked up from watching it and said, "How much?"

The old man looked at his wristwatch. He said he'd never sell it except he's getting old. He'd like to retire and not sit here all day getting robbed blind.

"How much?" Claire said, her purse on the counter, open, and her gloved hands digging out her wallet.

And the man said, "Twenty thousand dollars . . ."

It's five-thirty, and the store closes at six.

"Chloral hydrate," the old man told her. Knockout drops, is how the guy killed her. That August night he found her half asleep on pills, he just tipped a bottle down her throat. Of course, a Mickey Finn shows up in the liver during autopsy, but everybody said she'd got the stuff in Mexico. Even her doctor who'd wrote the script for her pills, he said Mexico. Even he said suicide.

Twenty thousand dollars.

And Claire said, "Let me think." Still watching the white murk inside the jar, she pushed back from the counter, saying, "I need to . . ."

The old man snapped his fingers for her purse and coat and umbrella. If she was going to wander the store, he'd hang on to them.

Without even taking the playing cards, Claire handed her things over the counter.

Claire Upton, she could look at a polished trophy and see a young man still reflected there, smiling and beaded with sweat, holding a tennis racquet or a golf club. She can watch him getting fat, married, with kids. After that, the trophy shows nothing but the inside of a brown cardboard box. Then the trophy comes out, held by another young man. This one, the son of the first.

But that jar, it felt like a bomb waiting to go off. A murder weapon trying to confess. Just putting your finger on it, you'd feel a jolt. An electric shock. Some kind of warning.

While she wandered through the shop, he was watching her in the video monitors.

In the dark lenses of old sunglasses for sale, she watches a man wrestle a woman to the ground and kick her feet apart.

In the gold-tone tube of an old lipstick, she can see a face crushed inside a nylon stocking, two hands around the neck of someone in bed, then the same hands scooping the spare change, the wallet, and keys off the dresser beside the lipstick. The witness.

Claire Upton and the old-man cashier, they're alone in the shadowy store with pillows of yellowed lace. Needlepoint dishtowels. Counted cross-stitch pot holders. Silver-plate brush sets tarnished dark brown. Mounted deer heads holding wide racks of antlers.

In the steel blade of a straight razor, the handle, chromium, scrolled and heavy—reflected there, Claire can see her future.

There, among the shaving mugs and horsehair brushes. Tall stained-glass church windows. Beaded evening bags.

Alone in the shop with Marilyn Monroe's lost child. Alone in this museum of things that no one wanted. Everything dirty with the reflection of something terrible.

Telling the story now, locked in the bathroom stall, Claire says how she picked up the razor and kept walking, down every aisle, always peeking at the blade to see if it showed her the same scene.

Telling her story now, sitting in the bathroom at the back of the antique store, Claire says it's not easy, being a gifted psychic.

The truth is, Claire's not easy to be married to. Over dinner at a restaurant, she may be listening, then her entire body will shudder. One hand will fly to cover her eyes, and her head will rear back and twist away from you. Still shaking, she'll peek out at you from between her fingers. A beat later, she'll sigh and put one hand against her mouth in a fist, biting the knuckle but looking at you without a word.

When you ask her what's wrong . . .

Claire will say, "You don't want to know. It's too awful."

But when you press her to tell . . .

Claire will say, "Just promise me. Promise you'll stay away from all cars for the next three years . . ."

The truth is, even Claire knows she can be wrong. To test herself, she picks up a polished silver cigarette-case. And reflected there is her future: her holding the straight razor.

When it's closing time, she walks to the front of the shop, just in time to watch the old man turn the sign from "Open" to "Closed." He was pulling down the shade that covered the window in the front door. The shop display window was cluttered with egg cups. Chenille bathrobes and bedspreads. Perfume bottles shaped like Southern belles wearing hoop skirts. Dead butterflies framed behind glass. Rusted birdcages. Railroad lanterns with shades of red or green glass. Folding silk fans. No one on the street could see inside.

The old-man cashier says, "Made up your mind?" The jar is back, locked in the glass cabinet next to his register. In the white murk, only a dark eye and the shell of a tiny ear show through.

Reflected in the jar's curved side, distorted there, while the old man had told the story of Monroe's murder, Claire had seen something else: A man tipping a small bottle between two lips. A face rolling back and forth against a pillow. The man wiping the lips with his shirtsleeve. His eyes settling on the bedside table. The phone and lamp and the jar.

In Claire's vision, the man's face comes closer. His two hands reach out, huge, until they wrap the jar in darkness.

That reflected face, it's the old-man cashier, without his wrinkles. With lots of brown hair.

Behind the counter, the jar just sits there, throbbing with energy. Glowing with power. A sacred relic trying to tell her something important. A time capsule of stories and events wasted here, locked in a glass case. More compelling than the best television series. More honest than the longest documentary. A primary history source. A real player. The child sits there, waiting for Claire to rescue it. To listen.

Wanting justice. Revenge.

Still watched by the security cameras, Claire holds up the straight razor. She says, "I want to buy this, but I don't see a price on it . . ."

And the old man leans over the counter for a closer look.

Outside the shopwindows, the street is empty. The security video monitors show the store, every aisle and corner, empty.

In the monitor, the old man falls backward, smashing the glass curio cabinet behind him, then sliding to the floor in a mess of broken glass and blood. The jar tipping, then falling, then broken.

Calling now, from a bathroom stall, Claire Upton tells her husband, "It was a doll. A plastic baby doll."

Her purse and coat and umbrella spattered with sticky red.

On the phone, she says, "Do you know what this means?"

And again, she asks how best to destroy a video camera.

The Baroness Frostbite leans closer, a steaming bowl of something liquid cupped in her hand, and she says, "No carrots. No potatoes. Now, drink it."

And, curled on her bed, in the camera spotlight, Miss America says, "No." She looks at the rest of us crowded outside the doorway, Director Denial included, then Miss America turns away to face the concrete wall, saying, "I know what that is . . ."

The Baroness Frostbite says, "You're still bleeding."

Leaning into the room, Director Denial says, "You need to eat something soon or you'll die."

"Then let me die," Miss America says, her face muffled in the pillow.

All of us in the hallway, listening. Recording. Witnesses.

The camera behind the camera behind the camera.

The Baroness Frostbite leans closer with the soup. In the rising steam of it, her mutilated lips reflected in the shimmering hot grease that floats on top, the Baroness says, "But we don't want you to die."

Still facing the wall, Miss America says, "Since when? The rest of you, you'll only have to split the story one less way."

"We don't want you to die," the Reverend Godless says, from the doorway, "because we don't have a freezer."

Miss America turns to look at the bowl of hot soup. She stares at our faces, leaned halfway into her dressing room. The teeth inside our mouths, waiting. Our tongues, swimming in drool.

Miss America says, "Freezer?"

And the Reverend Godless makes a fist and knocks on his forehead, the way you'd knock on a door, saying, "Hello?" He says, "We need you to stay alive until the rest of us are hungry again."

Her baby was the first course. Miss America will be the main course. Dessert is anybody's guess.

The tape recorder in the Earl of Slander's hand, it's ready to tape over her last scream with her next. Agent Tattletale's camera is focused to videotape over everything so far, in order to catch our next big plot point.

Instead, Miss America asks, Is this how it will go? Her voice shrill and shaky, a bird's song. Will this be just one horrible event after another after another after another—until we're all dead?

"No," Director Denial says. Brushing cat hair off her sleeve, she says, "Just some of us."

And Miss America says she doesn't mean just here, in the Museum of Us. She means life. Is the whole world just people eating up other people? People attacking and destroying each other?

And Director Denial says, "I know what you meant."

The Earl of Slander writes that down in his notepad. The rest of us, nodding.

The Mythology of Us.

Still holding the soup, looking at her own reflection in the grease on top, the Baroness Frostbite says, "I used to work in a restaurant, in the mountains." She dips a spoon into the bowl and brings it steaming toward Miss America's face.

"Eat," the Baroness says. "And I'll tell you how I lost my lips . . ."

Absolution

A Poem About the Baroness Frostbite

"Even if God won't forgive us," says the Baroness Frostbite,
    "we can still forgive Him."
    We should show ourselves to be bigger than God.

The Baroness onstage, she tells most people, "Gum
    disease,"
    when they look too long at what's left
    of her face.
Her lips are only the ragged edge of her skin,
    greased red with lipstick.
    Her teeth, inside:
    the yellow ghost of every cup of coffee,
    and every cigarette in her middle-aged life.

Onstage, instead of a spotlight, a movie fragment:
    The shifting, falling color of snow flurries.
    No two of the tiny blue shadows the same shape or size.
The rest of her is goosedowned, quilted and insulated,
    her hair tucked under a knitted hat,
    but never again
    warm enough.

Standing center stage, the Baroness Frostbite says, "We
    should forgive God . . ."

For making us too short. Fat. Poor.

We should forgive God our baldness.

Our cystic fibrosis. Our juvenile leukemia.

We should forgive God's indifference, His leaving us
behind:

Us, God's forgotten Science Fair project, left to grow
mold.

God's goldfish, ignored until we're forced to eat our own
shit off the bottom.

Her hands inside mittens, the Baroness points to her face,
saying, "People . . ."

They assume she was once gorgeously beautiful.

Because now she looks so—bad.

People, they need some sense of justice. A balancing act.

They assume cancer, her own fault, something she
deserved.

A disaster she made happen herself.

So she tells them, "Floss. For God's sake, floss before bed
every night."

And every night the Baroness, she forgives other people.

She forgives herself.

And she forgives God for those disasters that just seem to
happen.

Hot Potting

A Story by the Baroness Frostbite

"Come February nights," Miss Leroy used to say, "and every drunk driver was a blessing."

Every couple looking for a second honeymoon to patch up their marriage. People falling asleep at the steering wheel. Anybody who pulled off the highway for a drink, they were somebody Miss Leroy could maybe talk into renting a room. It was half her business, talking. To keep people buying another next drink, and another, until they had to stay.

Sometimes, sure, you're trapped. Other times, Miss Leroy would say, you just sit down for what turns out to be the rest of your life.

Rooms there at the Lodge, most people, they expect better. The iron bed frames teeter, the rails and footboards worn where they notch together. The nuts and bolts, loose. Upstairs, every mattress is lumpy as foothills, and the pillows are flat. The sheets are clean, but the well water up here, it's hard. You wash anything in this water, and the fabric feels sandpaper-rough with minerals and smells of sulfur.

The final insult is, you have to share a bathroom down the hall. Most folks don't travel with a bathrobe, and this means getting dressed just to take a leak. In the morning, you wake up to a stinking sulfur bath in a white-cold cast-iron claw-foot tub.

It's a pleasure for her to herd these February strangers toward the cliff. First, she shuts off the music. A full hour before she even starts talking, she turns down the volume, a notch every ten minutes, until Glen Campbell is gone. After traffic turns to nothing going by on the road outside, she turns down the heat. One by one, she pulls the string that snaps off each neon beer sign in the window. If there's been a fire in the fireplace, Miss Leroy will let it burn out.

All this time, she's herding, asking what plans these people have. February on the White River, there's less than nothing to do. Snow-shoe, maybe. Cross-country ski, if you bring your own. Miss Leroy lets some guest bring up the idea. Everybody gets around to this same suggestion.

And if they don't, then she brings up the notion of hot potting.

Her stations of the cross. She walks her audience through the road map of her story. First she shows herself, how she looked most of her life ago, twenty years old and out of college for the summer, car camping up the White River, begging for a summer job, what back then was the dream job: tending bar here at the Lodge.

It's hard to imagine Miss Leroy skinny. Her skinny with white teeth, before her gums started to pull back. Before the way they look now, the brown root of each tooth exposed, the way carrots will crowd each other out of the ground if you plant the seed too close together. It's hard to imagine her voting Democrat. Even liking other people. Miss Leroy without the dark shadow of hair across her top lip. It's hard to imagine college boys waiting an hour in line to fuck her.

It makes her seem honest, saying something funny and sad like that, about herself.

It makes people listen.

If you hugged her now, Miss Leroy says, all you'd feel is the pointy wire of her bra.

Hot potting, she says, is, you get a gang of kids together and hike up the fault side of the White River. You pack in your own beer and whiskey and find a hot-springs pool. Most pools stand between 150 and 200 degrees, year-round. Up at this elevation, water boils at 198 degrees Fahrenheit. Even in winter, at the bottom of a deep icy pit, the side of snowdrifts sloping into them, these pools are hot enough to boil you alive.

No, the danger wasn't bears, not here. You wouldn't see wolves or coyote or bobcat. Downriver, yes, just one click away on your odometer, just one radio song down the highway, the motels had to chain their garbage cans shut. Down there, the snow was busy with paw prints. The night was noisy with packs howling at the moon. But here, the snow was smooth. Even the full moon was quiet.

Upriver from the Lodge, all you had to worry about was being scalded to death. City kids, dropped out of college, some stay around a couple years. Some way, they pass down the okay about which pools are safe and where to find them. Where not to walk, there's only a thin crust of calcium or limestone sinter that looks like bedrock but will drop you through to deep-fry in a hidden thermal vent.

The scare stories, they pass along also. A hundred years back, a Mrs. Lester Bannock, here visiting from Crystal Falls, Pennsylvania, she stopped to wipe the steam from her smoked glasses. The breeze shifted, blowing hot steam in her eyes. One wrong step, and she was off the path. Another wrong step, and she lost her balance, landing backward, sitting in water scalding hot. Trying to stand, she pitched forward, landing facedown in the water. Screaming, she was hauled out by strangers.

The sheriff who raced her into town, he requisitioned every drop of olive oil from the kitchen at the Lodge. Coated in oil and wrapped in clean sheets, she died in a hospital, still screaming, three days later.

Recent as three summers ago, a kid from Pinson City, Wyoming, he parked his pickup truck and out jumped his German shepherd. The dog splashed dead center, jumping into a pool, and yelped itself to death mid–dog paddle. The tourists chewing their knuckles, they told the kid, don't, but he dove in.

He surfaced just once, his eyes boiled white and staring. Rolling around blind. No one could touch him long enough to grab hold, and then he was gone.

The rest of that year, they dipped him out with nets, the way you'd clean leaves and dead bugs out of a swimming pool. The way you'd skim the fat off a pot of stew.

At the Lodge bar, Miss Leroy would pause to let people see this a moment in their heads. The bits of him left all summer skittering around in the hot water, a batch of fritters spitting to a light brown.

Miss Leroy would smoke her cigarette.

Then, like this is something she's just remembered, she'd say, "Olson Read." And she'd laugh. Like this is something she doesn't think about part of every minute, every hour she's awake, Miss Leroy will say, "You should've met Olson Read."

Big, fat, virtuous, sin-free Olson Read.

Olson was a cook at the Lodge, fat and pale white, his lips too big, blown up with blood and squirming red as sushi against the sticky-rice-white skin of his face. He watched those hot pools. The way he'd kneel beside them all day, watching it, the bubbling brown froth, hot as acid.

One wrong step. One quick slide down the wrong side of a snow-drift, and just hot water would do to you what Olson did to food.

Poached salmon. Stewed chicken and dumplings. Hard-boiled eggs.

In the Lodge kitchen, Olson used to sing hymns so loud you could hear them in the dining room. Olson, huge in his flapping white apron, the ties knotted and cutting into his thick, deep waist, he sat in the bar, reading his Bible in the almost-dark. The beer-and-smoke smell of the dark-red carpet. If he joined your table in the staff break room, Olson bowed his head to his chest and said a rambling blessing over his baloney sandwich.

His favorite verb was "fellowship."

A night when Olson walked into the pantry and found Miss Leroy kissing a bellhop, just some liberal-arts dropout from NYU, Olson Read told them kissing was the devil's first step to fornication. With his rubbery red lips, Olson told everyone he was saving himself for marriage, but the truth was, he couldn't give himself away.

To Olson, the White River was his Garden of Eden, the proof his God did beautiful work.

Olson watched the hot springs, the geysers and steaming mud pots, the way every Christian loves the idea of hell. The way every Eden had to have its snake. He watched the scalding water steam and spit, the same way he'd peek through the order window and watch the waitresses in the dining room.

On his day off, he'd carry his Bible through the woods, through the clouds and fog of sulfur. He'd be singing "Amazing Grace" or "Nearer My God to Thee," but only the fifth or sixth verses, the parts so strange and unknown you might think he made them up. Walking on the sinter, the thin crust of calcium that forms the way ice sets up on water, Olson would step off the boardwalk and kneel at the deep edge of a spitting, stinking pool. Kneeling there, he'd pray out loud for Miss Leroy and the bellhop. He'd pray to his Lord, our God Almighty, Maker of Heaven and Earth. He'd pray for the immortal soul of each busboy by name. He'd inventory the sins of each hotel maid out loud. Olson's voice rising with the steam, he prayed for Nola, who pinned up the hem of her skirt too high and committed the act of oral sex with any hotel guest willing to cut loose a twenty-dollar bill. The tourist families standing back, safe on the boardwalk behind him, Olson begged mercy for the dining-room waiters, Evan and Leo, who assaulted each other with lewd acts of sodomy every night in the men's dorm. Olson wept and shouted about Dewey and Buddy, who breathed glue from a brown paper bag while they washed the dishes.

There at the gates of his hell, Olson yelled opinions into the trees and sky. Making his report to God, Olson walked out after the dinner shift and shouted your sins at the stars so bright they bled together in the night. He begged for God's mercy on your behalf.

No, nobody very much liked Olson Read. Nobody any age likes a tattletale.

They'd all heard the stories about the woman wrapped in olive oil. The kid cooked to soup with his dog. And Olson especially would listen, his eyes bright as candy. This was proof of everything he held dear. The truth of this. Proof you can't hide what you've done from God. You can't fix it. We'd be awake and alive in Hell, but hurting so bad we'd wish we could die. We'd spend all eternity suffering, someplace no one in the world would trade us to be.

Here, it would be, Miss Leroy would stop talking. She'd light a new cigarette. She'd draw you another beer.

Some stories, she'd say, the more you tell them, the faster you use them up. Those kind, the drama burns off, and every version, they sound more silly and flat. The other kind of story, it uses you up. The more you tell it, the stronger it gets. Those kind of stories only remind you how stupid you were. Are. Will always be.

Telling some stories, Miss Leroy says, is committing suicide.

It's here that she'd work hard to make the story boring, saying how water heated to 158 degrees Fahrenheit causes a third-degree burn in one second.

The typical thermal feature along the White River Fault is a vent that opens to a pool crusted around the edge with a layer of that crystallized mineral. The average temperature of thermal features along the White River being 205 degrees Fahrenheit.

One second in water this hot, and pulling your socks off will pull off your feet. The cooked skin of your hands will stick to anything you touch and stay behind, perfect as a pair of leather gloves.

Your body tries to save itself by shifting fluid to the burn, to dissipate the heat. You sweat, dehydrating faster than the worst case of diarrhea. Losing so much fluid your blood pressure drops. You go into shock. Your vital organs shut down in rapid succession.

Burns can be first-degree, second-, third-, or fourth-degree. They can be superficial, partial-thickness, or full-thickness burns. In superficial or first-degree burns, the skin turns red without blistering. Think of a sunburn and the subsequent desquamation of necrotic tissue—the dead, peeling skin. In full-thickness, third-degree burns, you get the dry, white leather look of a knuckle that bumps the top heating element when you take a cake out of the oven. In fourth-degree burns, you're cooked worse than skin deep.

To determine the extent of a burn, the medical examiner will use the "Rule of Nines." The head is 9 percent of the body's total skin. Each arm is 9 percent. Each leg is 18 percent. The torso front and back are each 18 percent. One percent for the neck, and you get the whole 100 percent.

Swallowing even a mouthful of water this hot causes massive edema of the larynx and asphyxial death. Your throat swells shut, and you choke to death.

It's poetry to hear Miss Leroy spin this out. Skeletonization. Skin slippage. Hypokalemia. Long words that take everybody in the bar to safe abstracts, far, far away. It's a nice little break in her story, before facing the worst.

You can spend your whole life building a wall of facts between you and anything real.

A February just like this, most of her life ago, Miss Leroy and Olson, the cook, were the only people in the Lodge that night. The day before dropped three feet of new snow, and the plows hadn't come through yet.

The same as every night, Olson Read takes his Bible in one fat hand and goes tramping off into the snow. Back then, they had coyotes to worry about. Cougar and bobcat. Singing "Amazing Grace" for a mile, never repeating a verse, Olson tramps off, white against the white snow.

The two lanes of Highway 17, lost under snow. The neon sign saying *The Lodge* in green neon, free-standing on a steel pole anchored in concrete with a low brick planter around the base of it.

The outside world, like every night, is moonlight black and blue, the forest just dark pine-tree shapes stretched up.

Young and thin, Miss Leroy never gave Olson Read a second thought. Never realized how long he was gone until she heard the wolves start to howl. She was looking at her teeth, holding a polished butter knife so she could see how straight and white her teeth looked. She was used to hearing Olson shout each night. His voice shouting her name followed by a sin, real or imagined, it came from the woods. She smoked cigarettes, Olson shouted. She slow-danced. Olson screamed at God on her behalf.

Telling the story now, she'll make you tweeze the rest out of her. The idea of her trapped here. Her soul in limbo. Nobody comes to the Lodge planning to stay the rest of their life. Hell, Miss Leroy says, there's things you see happen worse than getting killed.

There's things that happen, worse than a car accident, that leave you stranded. Worse than breaking an axle. When you're young. And you're left tending bar in some little noplace for the rest of your life.

More than half her life ago, Miss Leroy hears the wolves howl. The coyotes yip. She hears Olson screaming, not her name or any sin, but just screaming. She goes to the dining-room side door. She steps outside, leaning out over the snow, and turns her head sideways to listen.

She smells Olson before she can see him. It's the smell of breakfast, of bacon frying in the cold air. The smell of bacon or Spam, sliced thick and hissing crisp in its own hot fat.

At this point in her story, the electric wall heater always comes on. That moment, the moment the room's got as cold as it can get. Miss Leroy knows that moment, can feel it make the hair stand up on her top lip. She knows when to stop a second. To leave a little way of quiet, and then—voom—the rush and wail of warm air out of the heater. The fan makes a low moan, far away at first, then up-close loud. Miss Leroy makes sure the barroom's dark by now. The heater comes on, the low moan of it, and people look up. All they can see in the window is their own reflection. Their own face not recognized. Looking inside at them is a pale mask full of dark holes. The mouth is a hanging-open dark hole. Their own eyes, two close-together staring black holes through to the night behind them.

The cars parked just outside, they look a hundred cold miles away. Even the parking lot looks too far to walk in this kind of dark.

The face of Olson Read, when she found him, his neck and head, this last 10 percent of him was still perfect. Beautiful even, compared to the peeling, boiled-food rest of his body.

Still screaming. As if the stars give a shit. This something left of Olson, dragging itself down this side of the White River, it stumbled, knees wobbly, staggering and coming apart.

There were parts of Olson already gone. His legs, below his knees, cooked and drug off over the broken ice. Bit and pulled off, the skin first and then the bones, the blood so cooked inside there's nothing going off behind him but a trail of his own grease. His heat melting deep in the snow.

The kid from Pinson City, Wyoming, the kid who jumped in to save his dog. Folks say that when the crowd pulled him out his arms popped apart, joint by joint, but he was still alive. His scalp peeled back off his white skull, but he was still awake.

The surface of the seething water, it spit hot and sparkling rainbow colors from the kid's rendered fat, the grease of him floating on the surface.

The kid's dog boiled down to a perfect dog-shaped fur coat, its bones already cooked clean and settling into the deep geothermal center of the world, the kid's last words were, "I fucked up. I can't fix this. Can I?"

That's how Miss Leroy found Olson Read that night. But worse.

The snow behind him, the fresh powder all around him, it was cut with drool.

All around his screams, fanned out around behind him, Miss Leroy could see a swarm of yellow eyes. The snow stamped down to ice in the prints of coyote feet. The four-toe prints of wolf paws. Floating around him were the long skull faces of wild dogs. Panting behind their own white breath, their black lips curled up along the ridge of each snout. Their little-root teeth meshed together, tight, tugging back on the rags of Olson's white pants, the shredded pant legs still steaming from what's boiled alive inside.

The next heartbeat, the yellow eyes are gone and what's left of Olson is what's left. Snow kicked up by back feet, it still sparkles in the air.

The two of them, in the warm cloud of bacon smell, Olson pulsed with heat, a big baked potato sinking deeper into the snow beside her. His skin was crusted now, puckered and rough as fried chicken, but loose and slippery on top of the muscle underneath, the muscle twisting, cooked, around the core of warm bone.

His hands clamped tight around her, around Miss Leroy's fingers, when she tried to pull away, his skin tore. His cooked hands stuck, the way your lips freeze to the flagpole on the playground in cold weather. When she tried to pull away, his fingers split to the bone, baked and bloodless inside, and he screamed and gripped Miss Leroy tight.

He was too heavy to move. Sunk there in the snow.

She was anchored there, the side door to the dining room only twenty footprints away in the snow. The door was still open, and the tables inside set for the next meal. Miss Leroy could see the dining room's big stone mountain of a fireplace, the logs burning inside. She could watch, but it was too far away to feel. She swam with her feet, kicking, trying to drag Olson, but the snow was too deep.

Instead of moving, she stayed, hoping he would die. Praying to God to kill Olson Read before she froze. The wolves watching with their yellow eyes from the dark edge of the forest. The pine-tree shapes going up into the night sky. The stars above them, bleeding together.

That night, Read Olson told her a story. His own private ghost story.

When we die, these are the stories still on our lips. The stories we'll only tell strangers, someplace private in the padded cell of midnight. These important stories, we rehearse them for years in our head but never tell. These stories are ghosts, bringing people back from the dead. Just for a moment. For a visit. Every story is a ghost. This story is Olson's.

Melting snow in her mouth, Miss Leroy spit the water into Olson's fat red lips, his face the only part of him that she could touch without getting stuck. Kneeling there beside him. The devil's first step to fornication. That kiss, the moment Olson had saved himself for.

For most of her life, she never told anyone what he yelled. Holding this inside was such a burden. Now she tells everyone, and it's no better.

That boiled, sad thing up the White River, it screamed, "Why did you do this?"

It screamed, "What did I do?"

"Timber wolves," Miss Leroy says, and she laughs. We don't have that trouble. Not here, she says. Not anymore.

How Olson died, it's called myoglobulinaria. In extensive burns, the burned muscles release the protein myoglobulin. This flood of protein into the bloodstream overwhelms each kidney. The kidneys shut down, and the body fills with fluid and blood toxins. Renal failure. Myoglobulinaria. When Miss Leroy says these words, she could be a magician doing a trick. They could be a spell. An incantation.

This way to die takes all night.

The next morning, the snow plow came through. The driver found them: Olson Read dead and Miss Leroy asleep. From melting snow in her mouth all night, her gums were patched with white. Frostbite. Read's dead hands were still locked around hers, protecting her fingers, warm as a pair of gloves. For weeks, the frozen skin around the base of each tooth, it peeled away, soft and gray from the brown root, until her teeth looked the way they do. Until her lips were gone.

Desquamating necrotic tissue. Another magic spell.

There's nothing out in the woods, Miss Leroy would tell people. Nothing evil. It's just something so sad and alone. It's Olson Read not knowing, still, what he did wrong. Not knowing where he's at. So terrible and alone, even the wolves, the coyotes are gone from up that end of the White River.

That's how a scary story works. It echoes some ancient fear. It re-creates some forgotten terror. Something we'd like to think we've grown beyond. But it can still scare us to tears. It's something you'd hoped was healed.

Every night's scattered with them. These wandering people who can't be saved but won't die. You can hear them at night, screaming out there, up this side of the White River Fault.

Some February nights, there's still the smell of hot grease. Crisp bacon. Olson Read not feeling his legs but still getting tugged back. Him screaming. His fingers hooked claws into the snow, getting tugged back into the dark by all those clenched little teeth.

1.
2.
3.
4.
5.
6.
7.
8.
9.
10.
11.
12.
13.
14.
15.
16.
17.
18.
19.
20.
21.
22.
23.
24.

According to Mrs. Clark, the average person burns sixty-five calories per hour while asleep. You burn seventy-seven calories each hour awake. Just walking slow, you burn two hundred. Just to stay alive, you need to eat 1,650 calories each day.

Your body can only store about twelve hundred calories of carbohydrates—most of them in your liver. Just being alive, you burn through all your stored calories in less than one day. After that, you burn fat. Then muscle.

This is when your blood fills with ketones. Your serum-acetone concentrations soar, and your breath starts to smell. Your sweat stinks of airplane glue.

Your liver and spleen and kidneys shrink and atrophy. Your small intestine swells from disuse and fills with mucus. Ulcers open up holes in the wall of your colon.

As you starve, your liver converts muscle to glucose to keep your brain alive. As you starve, your hunger pains disappear. After that, you're just tired. More and more, you're confused. You stop noticing the world around you. You quit keeping yourself clean.

Once you burn through 70 to 94 percent of your body fat, and 20 percent of your muscle, you die.

For most people, this takes sixty-one days.

"My daughter, Cassandra," Mrs. Clark says, "she never did tell me what happened."

Most of what we know about starvation, Mrs. Clark says, comes from watching prisoners in Northern Ireland on hunger strikes.

While starving, sometimes your skin fades to pale blue. Sometimes it turns dark brown. A third of the starved swell—but only the ones with pale skin.

On the wall in the Gothic smoking room, Saint Gut-Free has counted off forty days' worth of hash marks. Forty stripes of his pencil.

Our story, the true-life epic of our brave survival in the face of cruel, cruel torture, well, the royalties get split only thirteen ways. Now that Miss America's bled to death.

Most of us have quit trying to break the furnace after it's been fixed by the ghost. Still, we don't wash our clothes. Some days, from lights-on to lights-out, we lie in bed in our dressing rooms, backstage. Each of us, reciting our story to our self.

If we have the strength, we might borrow a knife from Chef Assassin and hack our hair off at the scalp. Another humiliation inflicted on us by Mr. Whittier. Here's another way to make our *after* picture more terrible compared to the *before* pictures of us, right now being stapled to telephone poles or printed on milk cartons.

The Reverend Godless breaks the leg off a chair and twists the wood inside his ass, to get some slivers for the police to find. A fine idea, provided by Mrs. Clark's daughter, Cassandra.

After dark, we hear footsteps. Doors creak open. The ghost footsteps of here. Mr. Whittier. Lady Baglady. Comrade Snarky and Miss America.

Since what the ghost did to the Duke of Vandals, we all lock our doors after lights-out. No one wanders except in twos or threes, every witness with another witness, to stay safe. Everybody carries one of Chef Assassin's knives.

After she came home, Mrs. Clark says, her daughter never did gain back much weight. Cassandra's fingernails grew back, but she never painted them. Her hair grew back, but Cassandra would only wash it and keep it combed. She never curled it, piled it into hair-dos, tinted it. Of course her missing teeth never grew back.

She wore a size nothing. No hips. No chest. Just knees and shoulders and death-camp cheekbones. Cassandra could've worn anything, but every day was just the same of two or three long dresses. No jewelry. No makeup. She was so almost not there, it would take just a spoiled slice of lunchmeat to kill her. Just a handful of sleeping pills stirred into her oatmeal. If she would eat.

But of course Mrs. Clark took her to a dentist. Paid money for a good partial denture. Offered to pay for implants to replace the teeth. The withered breasts. She did research on anorexia nervosa.

Mrs. Clark lied and said she looked pretty, thin. Cassandra was never outside long enough to be anything but pale blue.

No, Cassandra just went to school, where nobody talked to her. Everyone talked about her, the stories of her torture getting more horrible every term. Even the teachers let their terrible imaginations run wild. Around the neighborhood, everyone stopped Mrs. Clark to pat her hand and say how sorry they felt. As if Cassandra had been found dead.

All the people who had canvassed, searched with the police dogs, they quit pressing for details. They got tired of Mrs. Clark telling them, "I don't know. I don't know. I don't *know* . . ."

Cassandra's first year back in school, her grades went up. She didn't try out for cheerleader. She didn't play basketball or soccer. She didn't do anything but read and come home. She watched the birds in the sky. She watched her goldfish swim.

Still, Cassandra wouldn't wear the partial denture even when Mrs. Clark begged and threatened—threatened to hurt herself. Mrs. Clark could burn her arm with cigarettes and her daughter would just sit by and watch. Breathing in the smell.

Cassandra would just listen. While Mrs. Clark begged her and yelled at her, asking Cassandra to *please* make an effort to be pretty.

To be popular. To talk to a counselor. Get back into the swim of life. Anything. All Cassandra did was listen.

"My own daughter," Mrs. Clark says, "and she was friendly as a houseplant."

A robot that got straight A's through her senior year but didn't go to the prom. Didn't date. Didn't have any girlfriends. A Nightmare Box that ticked away, high up on some shelf.

"She sat through every day," Mrs. Clark said, "the way people sit in church."

Silent. Straight-backed. Bright-eyed. But not singing, never offering any detail about what went on inside her head. Cassandra would just watch and listen. Not the girl her mother had known, but someone else. A statue that looked down from behind an altar. A statue carved in a cathedral a thousand years ago. In Europe. A statue that knew it was carved by Leonardo da Vinci. That's how Cassandra looked to people.

Mrs. Clark says now, "It drove me crazy."

Other times, it was like living with a robot. Or a bomb. Some days, Mrs. Clark waited for whatever cult or nutcase to call and ask for Cassandra on the phone. Some nights, Mrs. Clark slept with a knife under her pillow and her bedroom door locked.

Nobody knew what this silent girl might become. She'd lived through something the rest of them could never imagine. So much torture and horror that she didn't need to tell people about it. She'd never need drama or joy or pain ever again.

You could walk into a room, turn on the television, eat a bag of popcorn, and only then notice she was sitting beside you on the couch.

Really, she was *that* kind of spooky. Cassandra was.

One dinner, just the two of them at the kitchen table, Mrs. Clark asked, did Cassandra remember the Nightmare Box? Did that night in the gallery have anything to do with her disappearing?

And Cassandra said, "It made me want to be a writer."

After that, Mrs. Clark couldn't sleep. She wanted her daughter gone. Into college. In the army. In a convent. Anywhere. Just gone.

And, one day, Mrs. Clark called the police to say Cassandra was missing.

Of course she'd looked all over the house. Mrs. Clark knew the way Cassandra could disappear into the wallpaper or the stripes of the sofa fabric. But she really was gone.

With all the faded yellow ribbons still flapping from everyone's car, those flags of surrender, Cassandra Clark had disappeared, again.

If there's any trick to doing a job you hate . . . Mrs. Clark says it's to find a job you hate even more.

After you find a bigger task to dread, the little chores will be a breeze. Here's another reason to have a devil on hand. It does make all the little demons more . . . bearable. Another Mrs. Clark extension to the theories of Mr. Whittier.

We love drama. We love conflict. We need a devil or we'll create one.

None of that is bad. It's just the way human beings operate. Fish gotta swim, birds gotta fly.

After her daughter disappeared the second time, Mrs. Clark dipped a cotton swab in a can of mineral oil and sealed the grout between each bathroom tile. It took most of a weekend.

She ran a dust cloth along the narrow length of each miniblind.

All those tedious jobs, for the time being they were made bearable by the telephone call that might come. The police detectives calling to say they'd found the remains. Or, worse, they'd found Cassandra alive.

That girl robot who could sit all day, painting the blue

jays that screeched outside her window. Or watching that damned goldfish swim around and around its bowl.

That . . . stranger with her toes and fingers gone.

What Mrs. Clark didn't know is, the police had found Cassandra. A Cub Scout came out of the woods, not talking. Quiet with a secret, the discovery he'd found. Out looking in the woods, following a little stream up a canyon, climbing over rocks where the water pooled behind before it tipped over and dug out a pool there, this Cub Scout was looking for a hole big enough it might hold trout. Green moss crested and ebbed around the rocks, and trees stood with branches holding each other back. In that shade, there was Cassandra Clark stretched out on one side, her hands folded under the side of her thin, pale face as if she were asleep. Cassandra, naked on a bed of this thick, soft moss, under where the leaves from a hawthorn tree hung down in a curtain all around.

The Scout tells someone adult, who calls the sheriff. Before dark, a string of detectives have followed the creek up that canyon. By dark, they've gone home, a crowd of people not talking about what they saw that day at work.

None of them call Mrs. Clark. At home, waiting, she turns each mattress in the house. She washes the second-floor windows. She dusts the top edge of baseboards. Every job too miserable most times, is nothing compared to just waiting. She cleans the fireplace, the telephone never so far away she can't grab it on the first ring.

This second disappearance, no one tied yellow ribbons to anything. Nobody went door-to-door, searching. Or lit prayer candles. No psychics called.

Not even the television stations dropped by while Mrs. Clark cleaned and cleaned.

That's another night Cassandra waited in that canyon, across a stream, and halfway up a rocky slope, a long carry from any forest-service logging road. No footprints marked the path, and her bare feet looked clean, as if she'd been carried.

By then, it was too late to measure the potassium in her aqueous humor. Her arms could bend, so she'd been dead longer than two days. Rigor mortis had come and gone.

That first team of detectives, they hung a microphone in the curtain of hawthorn branches. The same way they'd mike a murder victim's grave after a recent funeral. Because the killer has to come back. The killer has to talk, to tell this story until it's used up.

Other stories, they use you up.

To the only audience a killer can risk having, his victim.

Cassandra on her bed of moss. The microphone hanging above her, connected to a tape recorder and a transmitter broadcasting to a sheriff's deputy perched on rocks across the canyon. Far enough away he can swat mosquitoes without giving himself away. The headphones over his ears. Sitting on the ground, crawling with ants. All the time, listening.

In his earphones, birds sing. The wind blows.

You'd be amazed how many of the killers come back to say goodbye. They've shared something, the killer and the victim, and the killer will come to sit at the grave and talk about old times.

Everyone needs an audience.

In the deputy's earphone, black flies buzz, here to lay their eggs around the damp edge of Cassandra's eyelids, her blue lips opened just a crack. The flies lay eggs inside her nose and anus.

At home, Mrs. Clark has wrestled the refrigerator away from the kitchen wall so she can vacuum the compressor coils on its back.

On the bed of moss, Cassandra's blood has settled to the lowest side of her, leaving the parts you can see, her breasts and hands and face, looking painted white. Her eyes open and sticky-dry from the sucking tongues of insects. Her blond hair. Her hair rolls out yellow and thick from the back of her head, but dull, the way hair looks cut off and dead on the floor in a barbershop.

Her cells are digesting themselves, still trying to do some job. Desperate for food, the enzymes inside start eating through the cell walls, and the yellow within each cell starts to leak out. Cassandra's pale skin starts to slip, sliding slack over the muscle underneath.

Puckering and wrinkling, the skin on her hands looks loose-baggy as cotton gloves.

Her skin is marked with bumps beyond counting, a field of what could be tiny knife scars, every bump moving, grazing between skin and muscle. Every bump the larva of a black fly. Eating the thin layer of subcutaneous fat, tunneling just under her skin. The entire surface of her, of her arms and legs, a constellation of moving lumps.

In the deputy's headphones, the buzz of flies gives way to the crackle of grubs tunneling forward one bite at a time.

At home, a step from the silent telephone, Mrs. Clark sorts Christmas decorations in the choking dust of the attic, throwing out and repacking. Labeling each box.

The bacteria breathed inside Cassandra's lungs, the bacteria in her guts and mouth and nose, they split and split and split without white blood cells to stop them. They gobble the subcutaneous fat and the yellow protein leaking from her ruptured cells. Their numbers explode, bloating her pale stomach until her shoulders are forced back. Her legs are splayed open. Cassandra's belly swells tight, pregnant with the gas inside, the universe of bacteria eating and reproducing.

Her tongue swells, forcing her jaws apart and jutting out between lips swollen big as bicycle tires. The bacteria tunnel through the top of her mouth, breaking into the cranial vault, where her brain waits, soft and edible.

At home, Mrs. Clark carries the phone from room to room, scrubbing walls and washing the glass filled with dead houseflies covering each ceiling light.

After another day, Cassandra's brain would bubble, red and brown, out her ears and nose. The soft mass of it would melt and bubble out the sockets where her eyes have collapsed.

The microphone picks up the sound. Think of popcorn muted inside a microwave oven. Imagine slipping into hot water filled with bubble bath, the steady sound when all those bubbles burst. It's the sound of hard rain on a concrete patio. Hail hitting the roof of a car. That's the sound of maggots, by this time thick as white rice. The microphone picks up a rip and a squeal, the sound of skin coming apart and Cassandra's guts going flat.

Meat-eating beetles arrive. Mice and magpies. Birds sing in the forest, each string of notes bright as colored lights. A woodpecker listens with his head cocked to hear insects inside a tree. He knocks to peck a hole.

The skin sinks down, draped over bones, as Cassandra's guts leak away. Soaking into the ground. Leaving just this shadow of skin, this framework of bones mired in a puddle of her own mud.

In the sheriff deputy's earphones, the mice munched the beetles. Snakes arrived to swallow the squealing mice. Everything looking to be last in the food chain.

At home, Mrs. Clark sorted through the papers in her daughter's room, inside her desk drawers. The letters written on pink stationery. The old birthday cards. And, written in pencil, copied in Cassandra's handwriting on a sheet of lined notebook paper, the ragged perforations running up one side, a note said:

Writers' Retreat: Abandon your life for three months . . .

And she flushed her daughter's goldfish down the toilet, still alive. Then Mrs. Clark pulled on her winter coat.

That night, in the deputy's headphones, a woman's voice said, "Is this where you went? This *writers' retreat,* is this where they tortured you?"

It was the voice of Mrs. Clark saying, "I'm sorry, but you should've stayed missing. When you came back, you weren't the same." She says, "I loved you so much more when you were gone . . ."

Tonight, telling her story to the rest of us in the blue velvet lobby, Mrs. Clark says, "I did it with sleeping pills." Sitting halfway up the wide blue stairs, she says, "The moment I saw the microphone hanging there, I ran."

That night in the canyon, she could already hear the sheriff's deputy crashing through the brush, coming to arrest her.

She never went back to that clean house, with all those jobs she hated to do, done.

With nothing in the world but her winter coat and her purse, Mrs. Clark called the phone number on Cassandra's handwritten note. She met Mr. Whittier, and she met the rest of us.

Her eyes moving from our bandaged hands and feet to our ragged hair to our hollow cheeks, Mrs. Clark says, "I never was his . . . anything. I never loved Whittier."

Mrs. Clark says, "I just wanted to know what happened to my daughter."

Really, it was Mr. Whittier who killed the girl she'd given birth to.

She says, "I only ever wanted to know *why*."

1.
2.
3.
4.
5.
6.
7.
8.
9.
10.
11.
12.
13.
14.
15.
16.
17.
18.
19.
20.
21.
22.
23.
24.

The Matchmaker is alone in the Italian Renaissance lounge when we find him. Most days, while the lights are on, he just stands there at the long, black wood table with his zipper open and the meat cleaver in one hand. In his eyes: to chop or not to chop.

"Shooo-rook," the sound from his family ritual.

Proof that one day your worst fear might just disappear. No matter how terrible something looks, it might not be around tomorrow.

The Matchmaker, he's stopped asking the rest of us to swing the cleaver. Why should we help him hog the future spotlight? No, if he wants to be mutilated so bad—let him do it himself.

The table, each leg is carved to look like different sizes of balls, all balanced or beaded together in a straight line. The balls that touch the floor or the tabletop look the same size as apples. The ball in the middle of each leg is the size of a watermelon. All four legs, the same greasy black color. Long and narrow as a coffin, the table looks carved out of black wax. Long and flat, and smudged, so it reflects nothing.

Same as always, the Matchmaker stands there, hatchet

ready. His chin pressed to his chest. His eyes watch his dick poke out his open zipper the way a cat would watch a mouse hole.

The Italian Renaissance lounge is the same old green satin wallpaper since the white van dropped us in the alley. Since forever ago. The green satin looking wet. Slick. The edge of gold paint outlines every carved chair-back and baseboard molding and bracket that holds an electric candle to a green satin wall.

Sunk into little caves in the wall, little open closets or green satin niches, inside there stand statues of naked people so padded with muscle and breast they look fat. These are statues taller than most people and standing on plaster pedestals painted the black-green you want to be malachite stone. Some holding spears and shields. Others stick out their white plaster butts, standing with their feet close together and their lower backs arched. Muscle or butt, from their feet up, their plaster is smudged with fingerprints, or scarred, gouged down to clean white by fingernails, but only as far as people can reach. Only about waist-high.

We come up the stairs from the imperial-Chinese promenade, rushing from the red to green, and today the Matchmaker has his dick flopped out.

Panting, coughing, with one hand on his chest, the Reverend Godless says, "They're coming, people . . . You can hear them in the alley, outside."

From behind his camera, Agent Tattletale says, "If you're cutting it off, cut it off *now*."

And, cleaver in hand, the Matchmaker says, "What?"

The poor Matchmaker, compared to the bug-eyed, big-nosed, sunk-cheeked rest of him, his dick looks big as a statue. He's the last one of us still intact. So dirty he's pasted to the inside of his shirt, his tight skin looks cracked and shattered with the veins and arteries vined around his bony hands. Veins bunch and worm under the skin of his forehead. Tendons jump and twitch, webbed with the skin of his neck.

"Some people outside," the Missing Link says, his mouth hidden behind the fat end of his nose, tucked somewhere above the big nut-sack of his hairy chin. He says, "They're drilling the lock. We're about to be *famous*."

Well, all of us—except the Matchmaker, the man with no scars to show, no signs he did anything but not eat.

The table all around the gray head of his dick, the wood is criss-crossed with practice swings, every chop at a new angle. The chopped wood gone pulpy with our blood. The pulp pounded to slivers and splinters and knocked off, onto the floor.

Our ears and toes and fingers fed to the cat. Cora Reynolds fed to Miss America. Miss America and her child fed to us. That food chain, complete.

Every one of us fighting to be the last one in that chain.

The camera behind the camera behind the camera.

The Earl of Slander, he holds up one hand, wiggling the three bloody fingers still there, the fingernails torn off, missing, and he says, "Hurry and give me the chopper." He says, "I still have time to suffer some more."

Chef Assassin flops down in a gold palace chair and kicks off his shoes. Grabbing each sock by the toe, he stretches it longer, longer, longer, until it snaps off his foot. Looking at his toes, he says, "Me first. I got way too many toes left."

The poor Matchmaker standing with his hips pressed into the black wood edge of the table, his dick flopped out, he says, "Don't rush me." Sweat pumping out the pinholes of his forehead, he says, "You guys had your chance to suffer. It's my turn now."

"Then *suffer* already," the Chef says. He snaps his leftover fingers, saying, "Or give me my cleaver back. That *is* my cleaver . . ." He stands there, his hand out.

The Earl steps up to the table, his hands holding out the tape recorder, the little-mesh microphone ready to tape over the past with the single sound of the chop. The Earl of Slander, he says, "Be a *man*."

He says, "Here's your *last chance*. Be a man and whack off that dick."

The Missing Link, his shirt open, his chest nothing but dark hair and the ladder of his rib bones, he says, "When that door swings open, it's going to be too late for any of us." He says, "So *hurry*."

And the Matchmaker looks at himself reflected in the big blade of the cleaver. He holds the blade out toward the Reverend Godless and says, "Help me?"

The Reverend takes the cleaver. Gripping the handle in both hands, he hiss-slashes the air with it.

The Matchmaker sighs, deep, in and out, and he pushes his hips against the table. "Don't tell me when, just do it," the Matchmaker says.

And the Reverend says, "Remember." He says, "I'm doing this *only* as a favor."

The Matchmaker shuts his eyes. He cups both hands over the top of his head, his fingers basket-wove together.

And . . . then . . . and: *Shooo-rook.* The cleaver's stuck in the black wood of the table. The table done-jumped and humming, and something's shot across to drop off the other side. Something blurred pink and pushed along fast by a hot geyser of blood. The zipper still exploding with steaming-wet red, the Matchmaker reaches a hand after the gone object. To catch it. Then his knees buckle.

Both his hands grab the table edge, but the fingers slip. His chin hits the tabletop and his teeth hard-click together. After that, both the Matchmaker and his penis are under the table. Both of them, just gray meat.

Our poor Matchmaker, now just a prop we can build into our story. Our new puppet. His family story about death camps and blows jobs, now it's our story.

The Missing Link ducks under the table. He stands, and in his open hand is the gray cut-off dick, most of it wrinkled skin from changing size and shape with every hard-on. Just regular pink meat at the cut end . . .

"Dibs," the Link says. He sniffs it, once, twice, his nose tipped up and his nostrils flared and almost touching the meat. He shrugs, saying, "Everything we cook in that microwave is going to taste like popcorn . . ."

Even the Link knows that eating a dead man's severed penis will get him extra prime-time exposure on every late-night talk show in the world. Just to describe how it tasted. After that will be the product endorsements for barbecue sauce and ketchup. After that, his own novelty cookbook. Radio shock-jock shows. After that, more daytime game shows for the rest of his life.

A victim, someone with the missing toes and fingers to prove they suffered, they'll have the world's okay to be in always-bad taste.

And with arms out, hands up, stopsigns, Miss Sneezy says, "You can't."

Watching from their green satin niches, our audience is all the naked statues.

"Watch me," the Missing Link says, and tilts his head back, his mouth gaped open at the green ceiling. Holding his arm straight up, he drops the fleshy blob down his tongue. Past his teeth, whole, he swallows.

He swallows again and his eyes bulge. He swallows again and his hairy face swells, red. Eyes tight, shaking-shut under his one eyebrow. His hands grab around his throat and tears spill down his hot cheeks. The Link holds his throat, not breathing, Frankenstein-lurching one step, then another step, then another step around the room.

His panic-red face yawns, his werewolf teeth and lips making words with no sound. He drops to his knees on the bloody green carpet and makes each hand into a fist. Kneeling, he pounds, slugging himself in the stomach. All of his effort—the crying, the slugging, the begging—silent.

Nothing for the Earl to tape-record past the Link saying, "Watch me."

On his knees, the Missing Link leans to one side. He falls, to lie there, silent, his eyes still tight-puckered shut, his fists still buried in his gut.

Chef Assassin looks at the Earl, who looks at Miss Sneezy, who sniffs and says, "The people coming to rescue us, they might be able to save him . . ."

And the Reverend Godless shakes his head.

Downstairs right now, nobody's drilling the lock in the alley door. No rescue team. No one's arrived to save us. We lied because we were tired of the Matchmaker hogging the cleaver.

After now, we have two less ways to split the money. Only eleven of us left.

Coming up the stairs, her skirt bunched and pulled high in both hands, the Baroness Frostbite comes trudging. With her pink, scar-frilly lips, she's smiling, until she sees the Matchmaker on the floor, most of his clothes soaked black with blood. Next to him, the Missing Link, with his eyes dead-tight, rigor-mortis-shut, in his hairy gray face.

Her greasy pucker gaping, slack-open, the Baroness says, "Which one of you shits killed the Matchmaker?"

None of us, we tell her. It was him. After all this time, he cut off his dick.

And the poor Link, he choked to death trying to hog down the cut-off dick.

The Missing Link—the last link on that food chain. Well, the last link if you don't count the microbes and bacteria Mrs. Clark talked about eating her daughter.

Already, we can figure how this scene will sound on radio. Already, we're wondering if you can say "penis" on broadcast television. This scene alone will be more than most whole-truth books deliver, and just we saw it. The real-life dress rehearsal for a movie star someday choking to death on another star's cut-off dick.

You, choking to death from having your throat stuffed with penis, that's the kind of scene that wins the Academy Award.

Only us and maybe the Baroness saw.

Excepting that our version will say Mrs. Clark cut off the penis and forced the Link to eat it whole. The truth is so easy when everyone agrees who to blame.

"Not to be a killjoy," says the Baroness Frostbite, "but we'll need a new villain."

The devil is dead—we need a new devil.

The Baroness, she sashays over to the dark wood table and both-hands the cleaver from deep in the chopped mess. She says someone's killed Mrs. Clark.

"Whoever it was," the Baroness says, "they can't be very hungry right now."

The killer ate most of her left leg. The rest of her is backstage in her dressing room, stabbed in the stomach to death.

Chef Assassin shakes his fist at the Earl of Slander and says, "You stupid, greedy *fuck*."

And the Earl says, "Wait." He says, "Listen . . ."

We get quiet, and you can hear his stomach. The Earl's stomach is kicking and growling with the ghost of Miss America's stewed baby. No way was it him.

Still, Mrs. Clark—our whip-cracking, thumb-screwing she-devil, is dead. What's left of her, it's now just leftovers.

Our next order of business will be to elect our new devil.

After we have dinner.

It's over dinner, Miss Sneezy blows her nose. She sniffs and coughs and says she really, really needs to tell us a story . . .

The Interpreter

A Poem About Miss Sneezy

"My grandma made money," Miss Sneezy says, "by saying 'I
Love You.' "
As many ways as possible. For people who could not.

Miss Sneezy onstage, the cuffs of her sweater sleeves
sprout
the scraps and ruffles of dirty tissues stuffed there.
Those tissues, yellow and matted with nasal discharge.
Her nose running, bright with snot and blood, and her eyes
busy with red lightning and watering down each cheek.

Onstage, instead of a spotlight, a movie fragment:
a scene from some medical drama, showing doctors and
hospital staff
in white coats, holding test tubes,
busy finding a cure.

Between sniffing her nose and coughing, Miss Sneezy says,
"Until she died, my grandma made money saying 'Happy
Birthday' for people."
Saying, "Deepest Sympathy."
Saying, "Congratulations." And "We're so Proud of You!"
And "Merry Christmas."

As many ways as possible, her grandma said, "Happy
    Anniversary."
    "Happy Father's Day"
    and "Happy Mother's Day"
for a greeting-card company.

Between blowing her nose and stuffing the tissue back into
    her sleeve, Miss Sneezy says,
    "My grandma's job was to interpret what other people
        had no words to say."
    But every "Happy Birthday,"
    really, every card, she wrote with Miss Sneezy in mind.
    Her grandma's ideal target audience.
And the card rack is her bank account, her left-behind trust
    fund of future best wishes
    for her granddaughter.
So, after she was dead, her Miss Sneezy could come and
    find the right "I Love You"
    or "Happy Valentine's" for that moment of the distant
        future.
    Long, long after her grandma was dead.

"Still," Miss Sneezy says, "there's one card, one special
    occasion she never covered."
    There needs to be a card that says: I'm sorry.
    Please, Grandma.
    Please, forgive me.
    I didn't mean to kill you.

Evil Spirits

A Story by Miss Sneezy

The intercom comes on. First is a crackle of static, then a woman's loud voice, saying, "Good news, girlfriend." Coming out of the little wire-mesh speaker, it's Shirlee, the night guard, her voice saying, "Chances look good you might get laid in this lifetime . . ."

Just admitted this week, Shirlee says is another Type 1 Keegan virus carrier. This new resident, he's asymptomatic, and, better yet, he has got a huge dick.

Shirlee, she's as close to a best friend as it gets here.

You know that boy who had to live in the plastic bubble because he was immune to nothing? Well, this place is the opposite. The folks who live here, on Columbia Island, the permanent residents, they carry around bugs that would kill the world. Viruses. Bacteria. Parasites.

Me included.

The government types, the navy brass, they call this place The Orphanage. This is according to Shirlee. It's called The Orphanage because—if you're here—your family is dead. Chances are, your teachers are dead. All your old friends are dead. Anybody who knew you, they're dead and you killed them.

You know the government is a little over a barrel. Sure, they could kill these folks—to protect the public interest—

but these folks are innocent. So the government pretends it can find a cure. It keeps folks locked away here, drawing their blood every week to test. Providing clean sheets every week, and three square meals each day.

Every drop of piss that comes out of them, the government sterilizes it with ozone and radiation. Their every exhale is filtered and scrubbed with ultraviolet light before that air goes back into the outside world. The residents of Columbia Island, they don't get head colds. They never rub elbows with anybody who might give them the flu. Except for the fact they're each carrying their own personal potentially world-pandemic plagues, they're the healthiest batch of folks you could ever not want to meet.

And it's the navy's job to make sure you never do.

Most of what I know comes from Shirlee, my nighttime guard. Shirlee says being locked up here, it's not much to complain about. She says people in the outside world have to work all day, every day, and still don't get half of what all they want.

These days, Shirlee tells me to order up a set of hot rollers. To pretty myself up, some. For my new groom-to-be. This new guy, the Type 1 Keegan virus carrier.

Here, you just go to the computer and type a list of what you'd like. If the budget allows, it's yours. The biggest hurdle is when you get too much stuff. Books. Music CDs. Movie DVDs. They can shovel it in here, but after you touch it, the stuff is toxic. The bigger problem is how to burn it down to sterile ash.

To get around this, Shirlee has you ask for stuff that *Shirlee wants*. Shirlee loves old-time Elvis Presley shit. Buddy Holly shit. I put that on the list, and Shirlee pockets the music when it arrives. No muss. No fuss. And no big accumulation of toxic crap in the room.

The navy folks, they say they can't expense poetry books. If some public watchdog saw an item like *Leaves of Grass* on some Freedom of Information document, there would be hell to pay. So Shirlee buys my books out of her own pocket. And I pay her off with Elvis CDs I order but don't want. Most nights, Shirlee wants to educate me about current events, like who's dropping bombs on what country and who's the new boy singer every girl wants to fuck.

Instead, I want to know the stuff Shirlee can't say. The stuff I've started to forget—like how does rain feel on your skin? Or stuff I never knew—like how to French-kiss?

We talk back and forth through an intercom. This means pushing a button when you speak, then letting go to hear the other person. Even now, when I try to imagine Shirlee's face, all I can picture is the little wire-mesh speaker on the wall next to the bed.

All the time, Shirlee's asking, how did I get here?

And I tell her: It was all my dad's brilliant idea.

Shirlee's always after me to shave my legs. Order a tanning bed. Ride my stationary bicycle a thousand miles to nowhere. Shirlee tells me, her voice from the wire-mesh speaker says, "You only lose it once."

Me, I'm twenty-two years old and still a virgin. Until today, it looked pretty certain I'd always be a virgin.

Still, I'm not too much a social retard. Residents get to watch television. They get to surf the Internet. Of course, you can't send any messages out. You can lurk in chat rooms, reading all the action, but you can't contribute. You can read the postings on a bulletin board, but you can't respond. No, the government needs to keep you a National Security secret.

And Shirlee, her voice from the wire-mesh speaker, she says, "How did your old man get you put here?"

It was my senior year in high school when people around me started to die. They died the same way my folks had died ten years before.

My high-school English teacher, Miss Frasure, one day she's holding a paper I wrote, telling the whole class how good it is, the next day she's wearing sunglasses inside. Saying the light hurts her eyes. She's chewing those orange-flavored aspirin the school nurse gives out to girls on the rag. Instead of teaching, she turns out the lights and shows the class a movie called *How to Field Dress Wild Game.*

The movie's not even in color. It's just the only reel of film left on the shelf in the audiovisual room.

That's the last day they see Miss Frasure.

The next day, half the kids I know ask the school nurse for those orange-flavored aspirin. Instead of English class, we get sent to the school library for an hour of quiet study. Half the class say they can't focus their eyes to read a book. Behind a bookshelf, I let a boy named Raymon kiss me on the mouth. As long as he keeps saying I'm beautiful, I let him put one hand up inside my shirt.

The next day, Raymon doesn't come to school.

On the third day, my grandma goes to the emergency room, saying her head hurts so bad that everything looks black around the edges. She's going blind. I skip school to sit in the hospital waiting room. I'm reading a copy of *National Geographic* magazine, the pages all soft with wrinkles, sitting in a plastic chair crowded around with crying babies and old people, when a man comes into the waiting room wheeling a gurney. He's wearing white coveralls and a gauze surgical mask.

The man has a buzzed haircut, and through the gauze mask he tells the whole room to get out. They need to evacuate this part of the hospital, he says. I go to ask if my grandma's okay, and the man grabs me around one skinny arm. The man's wearing latex gloves. While the old people and crying babies hurry down the hallway, edging past the gurney, this man holds me in the waiting room, asking if I'm Lisa Noonan, age seventeen, currently residing at 3438 West Crestwood Drive.

From the gurney, the man takes a blue bundle sealed in clear plastic and tears it open. Inside is a blue container suit, all plastic and nylon with zippers sewn up and down the front and back of it.

I ask again, about my grandma.

And the man with the gurney shakes out the blue container suit. He says to put it on, and we'll go see Grandma in Intensive Care. The suit, he says, is for my grandma's protection, and he holds it by the shoulders so I can step inside. A container suit is three layers of plastic, each layer sealed with zippers. It has built-in gloves and feet and a pointed hood with a window of clear plastic to see out. The most outside zipper goes up the back and locks, so you're trapped inside.

When I step out of my tennis shoes, the man picks them up with his latex gloves and seals them inside a plastic bag.

At school, the rumor was Miss Frasure's had a CAT scan that showed a brain tumor. The tumor was the size of a lemon, filled with some piss-yellow fluid. According to gossip, the tumor was still growing.

Just before I pull the hood shut, the gurney man gives me a little blue pill and says to let it dissolve under my tongue.

The pill tastes sweet. So sweet my mouth fills with spit I have to swallow.

The man says to get up on the gurney. He says to lay down with my head on the little white paper pillow, and then we'll go see my grandma.

I ask, is she going to be okay? My grandma, she raised me since I was eight years old. She's my mom's mom, and she came across the country to get me after my mom and dad both died. By then, I was laid out on the gurney, and the man was wheeling it down the hospital corridor. Through open doors, you could see all the beds were empty, the sheets thrown back to show the dents where sick people had been. In some rooms, the televisions still played music or people talking. Next to some beds, lunch trays still sat, steam rising off the tomato soup.

The man wheeled the gurney so fast the ceiling tiles started to blur, so fast that, laying there, I had to shut my eyes or I'd get sick.

The hospital public-address system kept saying, "Code Orange, East Wing, second floor . . . Code Orange, East Wing, second floor . . ."

Still, I was swallowing the sticky-sweet taste of that pill.

That little blue pill, Shirlee says just two of those would be a fatal overdose.

When I woke up, it was here, in this room with this view of Puget Sound, this wide-screen television, this clean, beige-tile bathroom. The intercom in the wall beside the bed. Some of my clothes and music from my room at home, they were packed in boxes sealed with shrink-wrap plastic. A camera had to be watching me, because, the moment I sat up in bed, the intercom said, "Good morning."

My grandma was dead. Raymon was dead. Miss Frasure, my English teacher—dead. That was four Christmases back, but it might as well be a black-and-white TV rerun I watched a hundred years ago.

At The Orphanage, you lose track of time. According to the chart, I'm twenty-two years old. Old enough to drink beer, and I've only ever kissed a dead boy.

One, two, three days, and my life was over. I didn't even graduate from high school.

You build up a viral load to the point you can transmit the Type 1 Keegan virus, and don't expect you'll get a lawyer. Or a caseworker. Or an ombudsman. You end up on Columbia Island, and you can expect to stay in a decent hotelish room like at a franchise hotel, a Ramada Inn or a Sheraton, but for the rest of your life. The same room. The same view. The same bathroom. Room-service food. Cable-television movies. A brown bedspread. Two pillows. One brown recliner chair.

There's people locked up here, people who did just one wrong thing. They sat next to the wrong stranger on an airplane. Or they took a long elevator ride with another person they never even spoke to—then all they did was not die. There's lots of ways you can spend the rest of your life locked up here. Here being a little island in the middle of Puget Sound, in the state of Washington, the Columbia Island Naval Hospital.

Most of the people here, they arrived when they turned seventeen or eighteen years old. The staff doctor, Dr. Schumacher, says we were exposed to something when we were little, some virus or parasite that took years to build in our system. The day it hit the right viral load or blood-serum level, the people around us started to die.

That's when the Centers for Disease Control would notice a cluster of deaths, and the teams come throw you in a container suit and cart you here for the rest of your natural life.

Each resident at Columbia Island carries something different, Shirlee says. A unique strain of killer virus. Or a fatal parasite or bacteria. That's why they're, each of them, isolated. So they don't kill each other.

Still, Shirlee says, they get heat in the winter. Air conditioning in the summer. They get all their meals cooked for them, fish and vegetables, or ice cream, club sandwiches, anything within budget.

Come the hottest days of August, and Shirlee says the air conditioning alone makes her glad she works here.

Shirlee calls each resident a "blood cow." In every resident suite, two long rubber arms come through the wall from under a mirror. The arms are this bulletproof kind of long rubber glove. Every couple of days, a light comes on behind the mirror to show a lab tech sitting there, he or she will reach through the wall with the rubber arms and take a blood sample, place the sample in a little airlock, then retrieve it safely on the other side.

It's when the light comes on, when the mirror in your suite turns into a window, then you can see the camera that's always there. Always watching. Recording you.

Shirlee, it's part of her job to herd the blood cows outside for some exercise.

Every few days, the staff lets the cows put on container suits. Inside the suit, all you can smell is powdery latex. Pick a flower or lay down in the grass, and all you can feel is latex. Inside the sealed hood, all you can hear is your own breathing. The other hospital residents, they throw around a Frisbee, always knowing the exact number of minutes they have left before Shirlee herds thems back inside. They're always aware of the sharpshooters with rifles, in case a resident wades into the water to make a break for freedom. Wearing a container suit with its self-contained oxygen system, you could walk the mucky bottom of Puget Sound all the way to downtown

Seattle. The dark-blue shapes of ships crisscrossing the water, high above your head.

In case you're wondering how I got out . . .

"After that long underwater walk," Miss Sneezy says, "my sinuses have never been the same." And she wipes her nose sideways with one sleeve.

Out on Columbia Island, all of them outside on the hospital lawn, throwing a Frisbee back and forth, wearing their baggy blue container suits, they could've been a gang of stuffed animals. All blue, from head to foot. Sweating inside the layers of rubberized nylon and latex. Running and catching, all the time framed in the scope of some navy guy's rifle. It doesn't sound fun, but you want to cry when it's time to go back inside, to spend your life alone in your room.

The other residents, one girl has green eyes. A guy has brown eyes. With the container suits on, all you can see is somebody's eyes. The boy with the brown eyes, Shirlee says he's the other Type 1 Keegan carrier.

The new guy with the huge dick. She's seen it through his two-way mirror.

Shirlee says, next time I talk to Dr. Schumacher, I should ask about starting a breeding program. To see if we can give birth to a generation of babies immune to Type 1 Keegan. Another scary possibility is, this boy and me, we have different strains of the virus, and we'd just kill each other.

Or we'd have a healthy baby . . . and we'd kill it with our germs.

"Slow down," Shirlee says. "Forget babies. Forget dying." She says what's important is getting me deflowered.

This boy and me, the two of us locked up in a room, together. Both of us virgins. The video camera behind the mirror, watching, the staff hoping we'll breed a cure the government can patent. Those crafty drug-company people. Still, a cure wouldn't be bad.

And sex, that wouldn't be bad, either.

Shirlee says sometime The Orphanage should have a dance for the residents, but just the image of those baggy blue container suits, clutching each other and swaying to some pop music on a dance floor . . . nobody wants to see that.

Most times when I see Dr. Schumacher, I don't tell the doctor jack shit. The way I figure, I only have so many memories, and I don't want to use them up. Most of my best memories are of saving the world from evil space aliens or escaping on a jet boat from sexy Russian spies, but those aren't real memories. Those were movies. I forget how the girl doing that is a movie star.

Framed on the wall in my room, a sign says: Busy = Happy.

Shirlee says this same sign is in every resident's room. The light-bulbs in each room are full-spectrum lightbulbs that simulate nat-ural sunlight, generating vitamin D in people's skin and keeping their mood up. Shirlee says the official term for each room is "resi-dent suite." Mine, for example, is "Resident Suite 6-B." On all my charts and records, officially, I'm known as Resident 6-B.

As a parallel study, Shirlee says the data collected on residents here will be used to predict how people might live better in iso-lated, self-contained outer-space colonies.

Yeah, some days, Shirlee is full of useful information.

"Think of yourself," Shirlee says, "as an astronaut living in a Ramada Inn on a planet only six miles southwest of Seattle."

Shirlee, her voice coming over the intercom at night, she'll ask about my dad, how did my father get me put here. Then Shirlee will let go the button on her side, waiting for me to speak.

My old man, he didn't know enough for a college degree, but he knew how to make money. He knew guys who'd wait until the day you left on a week's vacation, then they'd move in with a crew and cut down a two-hundred-year-old black-walnut tree. They'd limb it and section it, right there in your front yard. They'd tell the neigh-bors you'd hired the work done. By the time you got home, your tree would be cut and milled and curing in some factory a dozen states away. By then it might even be black-walnut furniture.

This is the kind of smarts that scares the crap out of college people.

My old man, he had his maps. His treasure maps, he called them.

These treasure maps, they were from the 1930s, from the Great Depression. What people called the Works Project Administration, the government hired folks to go around and take notes about every abandoned cemetery in every county. Every state. Back when lots of these little cemeteries were going under the plow or about to be forgotten under blacktop. These old pioneer cemeteries, they were all that was left of towns that had disappeared from maps a hundred years before. Boom towns now crumbled and blown away. Or burned to ashes by forest fires. Gold mines that played out. Railroad spurs that shut down. All's that would be left is the little cemetery, a patch of weeds and fallen-down old headstones. The old man's treasure maps were the WPA maps, showing where to find each patch, how many graves it held, how the headstones would look.

Every summer I was out of school, me and the old man would follow these maps up into Wyoming or Montana, into the desert or the hills, where whole towns had vanished. Towns like New Keegan, Montana, where nothing's left except the tombstones. It was the kind of stuff that garden stores paid big money for in the city. In Seattle or Denver. San Francisco or Los Angeles. A load of hand-carved granite angels. Or sleeping dogs or little white marble lambs. People wanted something old and crusted with moss to put in their brand-new garden, to make their place look ancient. To look like they'd always had tons of money.

In New Keegan, not one of the tombstones had writing you could still read.

"Shaving cream," my Dad told me. "Shaving cream or chalk. Goddamn fucking graveyard freaks."

He told how people who loved to study tombstones, to read a faint inscription worn away by time and acid rain, they'd wipe shaving cream across the face of the tombstone. They'd shave off the extra with a piece of cardboard, leaving just the white in the engraving. This made the words and dates easy to read and photograph. What sucked is, shaving cream contains stearic acid. The residue these people left would eat the stone. Other tombstone junkies, they'd rub chalk on a tombstone, coloring the whole surface so the faint, engraved epitaph would stand out as darker. This chalk dust was plaster of Paris or gypsum, and rubbing it worked the dust into the invisible cracks and fissures of the tombstone. The next time it rained . . . the gypsum dust would soak up water and swell to twice its original size. The same way ancient Egyptians used wood wedges to split stone blocks for the pyramids, the swollen chalk dust would slowly explode the whole front off a tombstone.

All that stuff about stearic acid and gypsum and the Egyptian pyramids, it proves my dad wasn't an idiot.

He'd tell me, all these well-meaning cemetery folks, all they did was destroy what they claimed to love.

Still, it was nice, that last, best day with my dad on that hillside that used to be New Keegan, Montana. The hot sunshine baking the dead grass. The kind of brown lizards that would leave their squirming tail behind if you caught one.

If we could've read the headstones, we'd see how almost the entire town had died in one month. The first cluster of what doctors would call the Keegan virus. Rapid-onset viral brain tumors.

My dad sold that load of angels and lambs to a garden store in Denver. Driving home, he was already chewing aspirin and swerving the pickup truck all over the road. Him and my mom were both dead in the hospital before my grandma arrived.

After that, life calmed down for ten years. Until Miss Frasure and her brain tumor the size of a lemon. Until my viral load built up to make me infectious.

These days, the government can't kill me and they can't cure me. All they can do is damage control.

That new boy, with the dick, he's going to feel how I did when I first arrived: His family dead. Maybe half his school dead, if he was popular. Sitting alone in his room every day, he'll be scared, but full of hope for the cure the navy promised.

I can show him the ropes. Calm him down. Help him adjust to life here at The Orphanage.

That last good day of my life, my dad drove his pickup all the way from Montana to Denver, Colorado, where he knew a store that sold antique garden shit. Cast-iron deer and concrete birdbaths crusted with moss. Most of this stuff was stolen. This store guy gave him cash, and helped unload the angels off the truck. The store guy had a kid, a little boy who came out the back door of the store and stood in the alley to watch the work.

Talking to Shirlee over the intercom, I would press the button and ask if this new resident . . . did he have curly red hair and brown eyes?

Was he about my age? I'd ask if he was from Denver, and did his dead folks use to run a garden-antique store?

The ghost light is our only campfire left. Our last chance. The glaring-bare bulb on a tall stand, center stage. The safety valve made to keep old gaslight theaters from exploding, or the light always left on inside a new theater to keep any ghost from calling the place home.

We're sitting around the light, the circle of people still here, sitting on the stage, from where you can see only the gold-paint outline of each auditorium chair, the brass rail snaking along the front edge of each balcony, the cobweb clouds that hover across the dead electric-night sky.

In the dark rooms behind rooms, the Matchmaker and the Missing Link are dead in the Italian Renaissance lounge. In the subbasement below the basement, Mr. Whittier and Comrade Snarky and Lady Baglady and the Duke of Vandals are rotting-dead. In their dressing rooms, backstage, are Miss America and Mrs. Clark. All of their cells digesting each other into runny yellow protein. The bacteria in their guts and lungs going wild with bloat.

This leaving just eleven of us, sitting in our circle of light.

Our world of only humans, a world without humanity.

Agent Tattletale has been tiptoeing around, breaking lightbulbs. So have the Countess Foresight and Director Denial.

Each of us, we were sure, the only one at work. Each of us wanting to make our world just a little more dark. None of us aware we all had this same plan. Victims of our low threshold for boredom. Victims of ourselves. Maybe it's our being so hungry, some form of delusion, but here's all we have left.

This one lightbulb. The ghost light.

Here is light without heat, so we're bundled in pea coats and furs and bathrobes, our heads sagging under piled-up wigs and door-wide hats. All of us, ready.

When that alley door opens, we'll be famous. When we hear the lock turn, then the sliding rollers squeal, then the click-click and click-click of someone trying the light switch, then we'll have our story ready to sell. Our death-camp cheekbones ready for our best-profile close-up.

We'll say how Mr. Whittier and Mrs. Clark fooled us into coming here. They trapped us and held us hostage. They bullied us to write books, poems, screenplays. And when we wouldn't, they tortured us. They starved us.

Sitting cross-legged in our circle on the wood boards of the stage, we can't move in the layers of velvet and quilted tweed keeping us warm. It takes all our energy to repeat our story to each other: How Mrs. Clark ripped the unborn baby from Miss America and stewed it in front of its dying mother. How Mr. Whittier wrestled the Matchmaker to the floor and hacked off his penis. Then how Whittier stabbed Mrs. Clark and choked down so much of her thigh he split open. Us, we're practicing the word *peritonitis*. Under our breath, we practice *inguinal hernia*. We say *cheveu-cut potatoes*.

That's how both villains died, leaving us behind to starve.

It's been a lot of marks on the wall with Saint Gut-Free's pencil. Those hash marks, his only masterpiece. The landlord or rental agent or someone should be coming to check. Maybe a man from the power company coming to shut off the service for unpaid bills.

In the quiet, any flip of a switch will sound gunshot-loud.

A click makes us turn. The clatter of metal on metal turns our heads to look in the same direction. Toward the wings and, beyond that, the alley door.

There's a squeal, and the dark explodes.

In light this bright, after so long in the dark, everything we can see is only black and white. Only glaring shape-outlines we have to blink against.

The light is bolder, eye-shutting stronger than any lightbulb.

It's not the alley door. The stage explodes into daylight-bright, a solid fat beam of sunrise from somewhere overhead. The light so bright we squint and cup hands into shields to block it. This new day so sunny it throws our shadows out long behind us. Our shadows hunched and cowering against the brown water stains on the movie screen behind us.

Outlined on the movie screen, you can see our tilted wigs. Our bodies look so spidery thin, Comrade Snarky would tell us we could wear *anything*.

It's the movie projector with no film, the projector's bulb shining on us, a huge spotlight. Bright as a lighthouse. This sun shines from almost midnight on the rear wall of the theater.

None of us can stand yet. All we can do is duck our heads and look away.

The projector is so bright the ghost light looks burned out. Dim as a birthday candle on a summer day.

"Our ghost, again," says the Baroness Frostbite.

Saint Gut-Free's two-headed baby.

The Countess Foresight's antiques dealer.

Agent Tattletale's gassed and hammered private detective.

Miss Sneezy yawns, saying, "Another good scene for our story."

Like the popcorn. And the furnace being fixed. Our clothes getting washed and folded. Everything paranormal, every miracle is just another special effect.

Saint Gut-Free turns to Mother Nature and says, "Now that we're a romantic subplot . . . how about you give me that foot job?"

Agent Tattletale says, "After we're outside, I'm staying high for a month . . ."

The Reverend Godless says, "I'm burning every church I find . . ."

Each of us, just a lump of fabric, fur, and hair.

Director Denial says, "I'm buying Cora Reynolds a headstone . . ."

Back from the walls beyond the bright light, the place it hurts to look, from that far away, echo back the words ". . . headstone . . . headstone . . ."

All of us, still trying to get the last word. Rewinding his tape recorder, the Earl of Slander plays the words "headstone . . . headstone . . ." And the recorded echo, it echoes. An echo of an echo of an echo.

Echoing, until a voice from far away, from behind the sun, says, "You're playing to an empty house."

It's a voice from beyond the grave. It's the same as our story about Comrade Snarky coming back from the dead, staggering down the lobby stairs to beg for a bite of her own rose tattoo. Against the bright light, nobody sees our ghost come down the center aisle of the auditorium. Nobody hears him walking down toward the stage on the black carpet. Nobody can tell what's coming closer in the bright glare until the voice says, again, "You're playing to an empty house . . ."

It's old trembling, teenaged Mr. Whittier. Our dying skater punk. Our spotted little devil.

Walking. A cadaver in tennis shoes. A stereo headset looped around the back of his withered neck.

"Listen to yourselves," he says. Shaking his head, his few hairs swinging, he says, "You're so busy telling your stories to each other. You're always turning the past into a story to make yourselves right."

What Sister Vigilante would call our *culture of blame.*

It never changes, he says. The other group he brought here, it ended this same way. People fall so in love with their pain, they can't leave it behind. The same as the stories they tell. We trap ourselves.

Some stories, you tell them and you use them up. Other stories . . . and Whittier gestures at our skin and bones.

"Telling a story is how we digest what happens to us," Mr. Whittier says. "It's how we digest our lives. Our experience."

Mr. Whittier would say. This little boy dying of old age.

For a ghost he looks good. His spotted scalp, combed. His necktie knotted under his chin. His fingernails clean, shaky white half-moons. So very much the grown-up.

"You digest and absorb your life by turning it into stories," he says, "the same way this theater seems to digest people." With one hand, he points to a carpet stain, this dark stain sticky and growing mold, branched with arms and legs.

Other events—the ones you can't digest—they poison you. Those worst parts of your life, those moments you can't talk about, they rot you from the inside out. Until you're Cassandra's wet shadow on the ground. Sunk in your own yellow protein mud.

But the stories that you can digest, that you can tell—you can take control of those past moments. You can shape them, craft them. Master them. And use them to your own good.

Those are stories as important as food.

Those are stories you can use to make people laugh or cry or sick. Or scared. To make people feel the way you felt. To help exhaust that past moment for them and for you. Until that moment is dead. Consumed. Digested. Absorbed.

It's how we can eat all the shit that happens.

Mr. Whittier would say.

Looking at Mr. Whittier, the Countess Foresight says, "Satan." And her word hisses soft as the voice of a snake.

From Sister Vigilante, clutching her Bible, comes, "Devil . . ."

Hearing this, Mr. Whittier just sighs and says, "How we do love to have our evil enemies . . ."

"Here you go," Chef Assassin says, and he tosses a paring knife so it clatters across the stage and stops at Mr. Whittier's black shoes.

The Chef says, "Get some fingerprints on *that*. When they pry open that door, you'll be the most hated man in America."

"Correction," Mr. Whittier says. "The most hated *juvenile offender,* dude . . ."

"You might recognize that knife," Agent Tattletale says. His camera next to him, so heavy he can't lift it.

Her parole-officer security bracelet, it's gone. Her hand starved so small, so bony, the bracelet slipped off, Countess Foresight says, "You butchered me with that knife."

"And slit my nose," says Mother Nature, tilting her head back to show the scabbed scars. The diamond of Lady Baglady, it rattles so loose on her finger she has to make a fist not to lose it.

And Mr. Whittier looks from her split nose to the Earl of Slander's bloody-bandaged hands to the rind of scar tissue that used to be Reverend Godless's ear. He claps his hands, once, loud, in front of his chest, and says, "Well, the good news is . . . your three months are finished." He fishes in the front pocket of his trousers and brings out a key, saying, "You're all free to go."

The lock is still stuffed with a thin shard of plastic fork. No way can you put in a key.

"Last night," Mr. Whittier says, and he shakes the key in the air, "your friendly ghost picked the lock clean. I assure you, it works fine."

All of us, we're still sitting in our circle, some of us stuck to the stage boards by our own dried blood. Our clothes, the fabric of our gowns and cassocks and jodhpurs, it glues us to the spot.

Mr. Whittier leans down a little to offer his hand to Miss Sneezy, and he says, "And the Red Death held illimitable dominion over all . . ." Wiggling his fingers for her to take, he says, "Shall we go now?"

And she doesn't take the hand. Miss Sneezy says, "We saw you die . . ."

And Mr. Whittier says, "You've seen a lot of people die."

The dried-turkey Tetrazzini split his stomach from the inside. He died screaming. We wrapped his dead body in red velvet and carried him to the subbasement.

"Not quite," Mr. Whittier says. With Mrs. Clark's help, they faked his death so he could watch events run their course. All he did was watch—the last camera—even when Mrs. Clark died, stabbing herself for sympathy—but doing too good a job. Even when Director Denial found the body and ate half a leg. All Mr. Whittier did was watch.

Director Denial lifts her head from her chest. She belches and says, "He's right."

Again, Mr. Whittier stoops to offer his spotted hand to Miss Sneezy. He says, "I can give you all the love you want. If you can overlook our difference in age."

Her being twenty-two. Him being thirteen—fourteen next month.

The Earl of Slander says, "You're not going to rescue us. We're staying here until we're found."

We always do this, Mr. Whittier says. For the same reason our children's children's children's children will always have war and famine and disease. Because we love our pain. We love our drama. But we will never, ever admit that.

Miss Sneezy reaches to take the hand.

And Mother Nature says, "Don't be stupid." From her pile of rags and hair, she says, "He knows you're infected with that . . . brain virus." She laughs, her brass bells ringing, and scabs everywhere, and she says, "How can you possibly believe he really loves you?"

Miss Sneezy looks from the Mother to the Saint to Mr. Whittier's hand.

"You have no choice," Mr. Whittier tells her. "If you need to be loved."

And Saint Gut-Free says, "He doesn't love you." The Saint, his face is nothing but teeth and eyes as he says, "Whittier only wants to destroy the rest of the world."

Still reaching toward Miss Sneezy, Mr. Whittier shakes the key in his other hand, saying, "Shall we go?"

If we can forgive what's been done to us . . .

If we can forgive what we've done to others . . .

If we can leave all of our stories behind. Our being villains or victims.

Only then can we maybe rescue the world.

But we still sit here, waiting to be saved. While we're still victims, hoping to be discovered while we suffer.

Shaking his head, clucking his tongue, Mr. Whittier says, "Would it be so bad? To be the last two people in the world?" His hand slips around, wraps around, tight around Miss Sneezy's limp fingers, and Mr. Whittier says, "Why can't the world end the same way it started?" And he pulls Miss Sneezy to her feet.

Proof

Another Poem About Mr. Whittier

"How would you live?" asks Mr. Whittier.
    If you could not die.

Mr. Whittier onstage, he stands straight,
    on two feet, not stooped.
    Not trembling.
The stereo earphones looped around his neck,
    leaking loud drum-and-bass music.
Both feet in tennis shoes, the laces untied and one foot
    tapping.

Onstage, instead of a movie fragment, a spotlight,
    not a fragment of some old story projected to hide him.
A spotlight shines so hard it erases his wrinkles.
    Washes away his age spots.

And, watching him, we were God's children he held
    hostage, to make God show
    Himself.
    To force God's hand.
    And if we suffered enough, if we died . . . if Whittier could
      just torture us,
    starve us,

maybe we would hate him from even beyond this life.
Hate him so much, we'd come back for revenge.

If we died in enough pain, cursing old Mr. Whittier, then he
   begged for us to come back.
   To haunt him.
   To give him proof of a life after death.
   Our ghosts, our hate would prove the Death of Death.

Our role, when he finally told us: We were only here to
   suffer and suffer,
   and suffer and suffer,
   and suffer and die.
   To create just one ghost—fast.
   To comfort old, old dying Mr. Whittier—before he died.
   That was his real plan.

Leaning over us, he says, "If death meant just leaving the
   stage long enough
   to change costume and come back
   as a new character . . .
Would you slow down? Or speed up?
   If every life is just a basketball game or a play that
      begins and ends
   while the players go on to new games, new
      productions . . .
In the face of that fact, how would you live?

Dangling the key between two fingers, Mr. Whittier says,
   "You can stay here."
   But when you die, then come back
   just for a moment.
To tell me. To save me. With proof of our eternal life.

To save us all,
please, tell someone.
To create real peace on earth.
Let us all be—
Haunted.

For their last family vacation, Eve's dad herded them all
into the car and said to get comfortable. This trip could
take a couple hours, maybe more.

They had snacks, cheese popcorn and cans of soda and
barbecue potato chips. Eve's brother, Larry, and she sat in
the back seat with their Boston terrier, Risky. In the front
seat, her dad turned the key to start the engine. He turned
the ventilation to high and opened all the electric windows.
Sitting next to him, Eve's future ex-stepmom, Tracee, said,
"Hey, kids, listen to this . . ."

Tracee waved a government pamphlet called *It's Great to
Emigrate.* She flipped it open, bending the spine backward
to crack it, and started to read out loud. "Your blood uses
hemoglobin," she read, "to carry oxygen molecules from
your lungs to the cells in your heart and brain."

Maybe six months ago, everybody got this same pamphlet in the mail from the Surgeon General. Tracee slipped
her feet out of her sandals and put her toes up on the dash-
board. Still reading out loud, she said, "Hemoglobin actually *prefers* to bond with carbon monoxide." The way she
talked, as if her tongue were too big, it was supposed to
make her sound girly. Tracee read, "As you breathe car

exhaust, more and more of your hemoglobin combines with carbon monoxide, becoming what's called *carboxyhemoglobin.*"

Larry was feeding cheese popcorn to Risky, getting the bright-orange cheese powder all over the car seat between him and Eve.

Her dad switched on the radio, saying, "Who wants music?" He looked at Larry in the rearview mirror and said, "You're going to make that dog sick."

"Great," Larry said, and fed Ricky another piece of bright-orange popcorn. "The last thing I'll see is the inside of the garage door, and the last song I'll hear will be something by the Carpenters."

But there's nothing to hear. There's been nothing on the radio for a week.

Poor Larry, poor goth rocker Larry, with black makeup smeared around his white-powdered face, his fingernails painted black and his long stringy hair dyed black, compared to real people with their eyes pecked out by birds, real dead people with their lips peeling back from their big dead teeth, compared to real death, Larry could just be a really sad-faced clown.

Poor Larry, he'd stayed in his room for days after the final *Newsweek* cover story. The headline, big and bold, it said: "It's Hip to Be Dead!"

All those years of Larry and his band dressing like zombies or vampires in black velvet and dragging dirty shrouds, stomping around graveyards all night wrapped in rosary necklaces and capes, all that effort wasted. Now even soccer moms were emigrating. Old church ladies were emigrating. Lawyers wearing business suits were emigrating.

The last issue of *Time* magazine, the cover story said: "Death Is the New Life."

Now poor Larry, he's stuck with Eve and his dad and Tracee, the whole family emigrating together in a four-door Buick parked in a suburban split-level ranch-house garage. All of them breathing carbon monoxide and eating cheese popcorn with their dog.

Still reading, Tracee says, "As less hemoglobin is available to carry oxygen, your cells begin to suffocate and die."

There was still television on some channels, but all they played was the video sent back by the space mission to Venus.

It was the stupid space program that had started all this. The manned mission to explore the planet Venus. The crew sent back their video of the planet surface, the face of Venus as this garden paradise. After that, the accident wasn't because of chipped insulation panels or broken O-rings or pilot error. It wasn't an accident. The crew just chose not to deploy their landing parachutes. Fast as a meteor, the outer hull of their spacecraft burst into flame. Static and—The End.

The same way that World War II gave us the ballpoint pen, the space program had proved the human soul was immortal. What everybody called the Earth was just a processing station that all souls had to pass through. A step in some kind of refining process. Like the cracking tower used to turn crude oil into gasoline or kerosene. As soon as human souls had been refined on Earth, then we would all incarnate on the planet Venus.

In the big factory of perfecting human souls, the Earth was a kind of tumbler. The same as the kind people use to polish rocks. All souls come here to rub the sharp edges off each other. All of us, we're meant to be worn smooth by conflict and pain of every kind. To be polished. There was nothing *bad* about this. This wasn't suffering, it was *erosion.* It was just another, a basic, an important step in the refining process.

Sure, it sounded nuts, but there was the video sent back by the space mission that crashed itself on purpose.

On television, all they played was the video. As the mission's landing vehicle orbited lower and lower, dipping down inside the cloud layers covering the planet, the astronauts sent back this footage of people and animals living as friends, everyone smiling so hard their faces seemed to glow. In the video the astronauts sent back, everyone was young. The planet was a Garden of Eden. The landscape of forests and oceans, flower meadows and towering mountains, it was always springtime, the government said.

After that, the astronauts refused to deploy the parachutes. They drove straight down, pow, into the flowers and sweet lakes of Venus. All that was left was this grainy, hazy few minutes of video they sent back. What looked like fashion models wearing glittery tunics in a science-fiction future. Men and women with long legs and hair, sprawled, eating grapes on the steps of marble temples.

It was heaven, but with sex and booze and God's complete permission.

It was a world where the Ten Commandments were: Party. Party. Party.

"Beginning with headache and nausea," Tracee reads from her government pamphlet, "symptoms include a faster and faster pulse as your heart tries to get oxygen to your dying brain."

Eve's brother, Larry, he never really adjusted to the idea of eternal life.

Larry used to have this band, called Wholesale Death Factory. He had this one groupie slut called Jessika. They used to tattoo each other with a sewing needle dipped in black ink. They were so cutting-edge, Larry and Jessika, the very margin of the marginalized. Then death got to be so mainstream. Only it wasn't suicide anymore. Now it was called "emigration." People's dead, rotting bodies aren't corpses, not anymore. The stinking, bloated piles of them, heaped around the base of each tall building, or poisoned and sprawled on bus-stop benches, now these were called "luggage." Just left-behind luggage.

The way people had always looked at New Year's Eve as some kind of line drawn in the sand. Some kind of new beginning that didn't ever really happen. That's how people saw emigration, but only if *everyone* emigrated.

Here was actual proof of life after life. According to government estimates, as many as 1,760,042 human souls were already freed and living a party lifestyle on the planet Venus. The rest of humanity would have to live on through a long series of lifetimes, of suffering, before they were refined enough to emigrate.

Going around, eroding in the Big Rock Tumbler.

Then the government had its big brainstorm:

If all of humanity died at once, then there would be no wombs and no way to reincarnate souls here on Earth.

If humanity went extinct, then we'd all emigrate to Venus. Enlightened or not.

But . . . if only one breeding couple was left behind, the birth of a child could call back a soul. From just a handful of people, the whole process could start again.

Until a couple days ago, you could watch on television as the emigration movement dealt with people who were still noncompliant. You could watch the backward populations that weren't enrolled in the movement, you could see them being forced to emigrate by Emigration Assistance Squads, dressed all in white, carrying clean white machine guns. Whole screaming villages, carpet-bombed to relocate them to the next step in the process. Nobody was going to let a pack of Bible-waving hillbillies keep the rest of us here, here on dirty old planet Earth, the less-than-hip planet, not when we could all hurry on to the next great step in our spiritual evolution. So the hillbillies were poisoned to save them. The African savages were nerve-gassed. The Chinese hordes were nuked.

We'd pushed fluoride and literacy on them, we could push emigration.

If just one hillbilly couple stayed behind, you could become their filthy, ignorant baby. If just one rice-paddy band of Third World tribesmen didn't emigrate, your precious soul could be called back to live—swatting flies and eating spoiled mush studded with brown rat-turds under their sweating-hot Asian sun.

And, yes, sure, this was a gamble. Getting everyone to Venus, together. But now that death was dead, humanity really had nothing to lose.

That was the headline on the last issue of the *New York Times:* "Death Is Dead."

USA Today called it "The Death of Death."

Death had been debunked. Like Santa Claus. Or the Tooth Fairy.

Now life was the only option . . . but now it felt like an endless . . . eternal . . . perpetual . . . trap.

Larry and his rocker slut, Jessika, had been planning to run away. Hide out. Now that death had been co-opted by the mainstream, Larry and Jessika wanted to rebel by staying alive. They'd have a litter of kids. They'd fuck up the spiritual evolution of all humanity. But then Jessika's folks had spiked the milk in her breakfast cereal with ant poison. The End.

After that, Larry went downtown every day to hunt for painkillers in the abandoned pharmacies. Taking Vicodins and breaking windows, Larry said, that was enough enlightenment for him. All day, he'd be stealing cars and driving them through abandoned china shops, coming home stoned and dusted with the white talcum powder from exploded driver-side air bags.

Larry said he wanted to make sure this world was good and used up before he moved on to the next one.

As his little sister, Eve, told him, Grow up. She told him Jessika wasn't the last slutty goth rocker chick in the world.

And Larry had just looked at her, stoned and blinking in slow motion, and he'd said, "Yeah, Eve. Jesse pretty much was . . ."

Poor Larry.

That's why, when their dad said to pile into the car, Larry only shrugged and climbed in. He got in the back seat, carrying Risky, their Boston terrier. He didn't bother to fasten his seat belt. They weren't going anywhere. Not anywhere physical.

Here was the New Age spiritual equivalent of any fix-all idea, from the metric system to the euro. To polio vaccinations . . . Christianity . . . reflexology . . . Esperanto . . .

And it couldn't have come at a better time in history. Pollution, overpopulation, disease, war, political corruption, sexual perversion, murder, and drug addiction . . . Maybe they weren't any worse than they'd been in the past, but now we had television carping about them. A constant reminder. A culture of complaint. Of bitch, bitch, bitch . . . Most people would never admit it, but they'd been bitching since they were born. As soon as their head popped out into that bright delivery-room light, nothing had been right. Nothing had been as comfortable or felt so good.

Just the effort it took to keep your stupid physical body alive, just the finding food and cooking it and dishwashing, the keeping warm and bathing and sleeping, the walking and bowel movements and ingrown hairs, it was all getting to be too much work.

Sitting in the car, as the vents blow smoke in her face, Tracee reads, "As your heart beats faster and faster, your eyes close. You lose consciousness and black out . . ."

Eve's dad and Tracee, they'd met at the gym and started doing couples bodybuilding. They won a contest, posing together, and got married to celebrate. The only reason we didn't emigrate months ago is, they were still at their contest peak. Never had they looked so good, felt so strong. It broke their hearts to find out that having a body— even a body of ripped, defined muscle with only 2 percent body fat— was like riding a mule while the rest of humanity was zipping around in Lear jets. It was smoke signals compared to cell phones.

Most days, Tracee would still be pedaling her stationary bicycle, alone in the gym's big empty aerobics room, pedaling to disco music while she yelled encouragement to a spinning class not there anymore. In the weight room, Eve's dad would be lifting weights, but limited to machines or lighter free weights, since no one was around to spot him. Worse than that, there was nobody around for Dad and Tracee to compete against. Nobody for them to pose for. Nobody for them to beat.

Eve's dad used to tell this joke:

How many bodybuilders does it take to screw in a lightbulb?

It takes four. One bodybuilder to screw in the bulb, and three others to watch and say, "Really, dude, you look *huge*!"

With her dad and Tracee, it took hundreds of people applauding, watching them up onstage, pose and flex. Still, you couldn't deny it, no matter how perfected with vitamins and collagen and silicone, the human body was obsolete.

What's funny is, the other thing Eve's dad used to say was: "If everyone jumped off a bridge, would you do it, too?"

Experts advised this was the only point in history when we could make mass emigration happen. We'd needed the space program to give us proof of the next life. We needed the mass media to take this proof around the world. We needed our weapons of mass destruction to ensure full compliance.

If there were any future generations, they wouldn't know what we knew. They wouldn't have the tools we had to make this happen. They'd just live their horrible, miserable physical lives, eating rat turds, ignorant that we could all live in pleasure on Venus.

Of course, a lot of people pushed to just nuclear-blast the non-compliant, but vaporizing every little tribal island in the South Pacific, that left our missile silos empty. The radiation didn't migrate the way you would hope. A nuclear winter settled over Australia, only for a couple months. Rain fell, and there was a huge fish die-off, but the weather and the tides had a shitty way of cleaning up our poisoned mess. All this emigration potential wasted, since Australia was 100 percent compliant in the first six months.

All of our nerve gas and deadly viruses, all our nuclear and conventional bombs, they were all a disappointment. We weren't even close to erasing humanity. People hunkered in caves. People roamed on camels over vast, empty deserts. Any of these stupid, backward people could fuck. A sperm meets an egg, and your soul gets sucked back to live another tedious lifetime, eating, sleeping, getting sunburned. On Earth: Planet Hurt. Planet Conflict. Planet Pain.

For the Emigration Assistance Squads, with their clean white machine guns, the Top-A priority targets were noncompliant females between the ages of fourteen and thirty-five. All other females were Top-B priority targets for assistance. All noncompliant males were Top-C priority. If bullets were running out, a white-suited team might leave a whole village of men and old women alive to grow old and emigrate naturally.

Tracee always worried about being a Top-A priority target, about getting machine-gunned on her way to the gym. But most of the squads were in the countryside or the mountains, places where backward baby-having people might hide.

The stupidest stupid people could completely sidetrack your spiritual evolution. It just wasn't fair.

Everybody else, millions of souls, they were already at the party. On the Venus video, you could catch the faces of famous people who'd suffered enough on Earth and didn't have to come back for another life. You'd see Grace Kelly and Jim Morrison. Jackie Kennedy and John Lennon. Kurt Cobain. Those were ones Eve could recognize. They were all at the party, looking young and happy, forever.

Among the dead celebrities roamed animals extinct on Earth: passenger pigeons, duck-billed platypuses, giant dodos.

On the television news, big-name celebrities were applauded the moment they emigrated. If these people, movie stars and rock bands, could emigrate for the greater good of all humanity, these people with money and talent and fame, with everything to keep them here, if they could emigrate, everyone could.

In the last issue of *People* magazine, the feature story was the "Celebrity Cruise to Nowhere." Thousands of the best-dressed, most beautiful people, fashion designers and supermodels, software moguls and professional athletes, they boarded the *Queen Mary II* and sailed off, drinking and dancing, racing north across the Atlantic Ocean, looking, full speed ahead, for an iceberg to ram.

Chartered jetliners slammed into mountaintops.

Tour buses careened off towering ocean cliffs.

Here in the United States, most people went to Wal-Mart or Rite Aid and bought the Going Away Kits. The first generation of kits were barbiturates packaged inside a head-sized plastic bag with a drawstring for around your neck. The next generation of kits were a cherry-flavored chewable cyanide pill. So many people were emigrating right there in the store aisle—emigrating without paying for their kits—that Wal-Mart put the kits behind the customer-service desk with the cigarettes and made you pay first before they'd hand one over. Every couple minutes, an announcment over the public-address speakers asked customers to be courteous and not to emigrate while on store property . . . Thank you.

Early on, some people pushed what they called the French Method. Their idea was just to sterilize everyone. First by surgery, but this took too long. Then by exposing people's genitals to focused radiation. Still, by that time all the doctors had emigrated. Doctors were among the first to jump ship. Doctors, true, yes, death was their enemy, but without it they were lost. Brokenhearted. Without doctors, it was janitors shooting folks with radiation. People got burns. The power grid failed. The End.

By then, all the beautiful, cool people had emigrated with cyanide in champagne at glamorous "Bon Voyage Parties." They'd held hands and jumped from skyscraper penthouse parties. People already a little world-weary, all the movie stars and super-athletes and rock bands. The supermodels and software billionaires, they were gone after that first week.

Every day, Eve's dad would come home saying who was gone from his office. Who in the neighborhood had emigrated. It was easy to tell. Their front lawn would get too tall. Their mail and newspapers would pile up on the doorstep. Their curtains were never open, their lights never came on, and you'd walk past and catch a whiff of something sweet, some kind of fruit or meat rotting inside the house. The air buzzed with black flies.

The house next door, the Frinks' house, was like that. So was the house across the street.

For the first few weeks, it was fun: Larry going downtown to pound his electric guitar alone on the stage of the Civic Theater auditorium. Eve getting to use the entire shopping mall as her own private closet. School was out, and it would never, ever start back up.

But their dad, you could tell he was already over Tracee. Their dad was never good at the part after the romantic start. Normal times, this was when he'd start to cheat. He'd find some new squeeze at his office. Instead, he was watching the Venus footage on television, paying close attention, his nose almost touching the parts where you could make out people, groups of those beautiful supermodel people, piled together naked or linked in a long daisy chain. Licking red wine off each other. Humping without reproduction or disease or God's damnation.

Tracee, she was making a list of celebrities she wanted to be best friends with once the family arrived. At the top of her list was Mother Teresa.

By now even harried moms were rounding up their kids, shrieking for everybody to hurry up and drink their poisoned milk and get their asses the hell to the next step of spiritual evolution. Now even life and death would be phases to rush through, the way teachers hurried kids from grade to grade to graduation—no matter how much they did or didn't learn. A big rat race to enlightenment.

In the car now, her voice getting deep and rough from breathing the smoke, Tracee reads, "As the cells of your heart valves begin to die, the two halves, called *ventricles,* get sloppy, pumping less and less blood through your body . . ."

She coughs and reads, "Without blood, your brain stops functioning. Within minutes you'll emigrate." And Tracee shuts the pamphlet. The End.

Eve's dad says, "Good-bye, planet Earth."

And the Boston terrier, Risky, barfs up cheese popcorn all over the back seat.

The smell of dog barf, and the sound of Risky gobbling it up, are even worse than the carbon monoxide.

Larry looks at his sister, the black makeup smeared around his eyes, his eyes blinking in slow motion, he says, "Eve, take your dog outside to puke."

In case the family's gone when she gets back, her dad says there's a Going Away Kit on the counter in the kitchen. He tells Eve not to hang around too long. They'll be waiting for her at the big party.

Eve's future ex-stepmom says, "Don't hold the door open and let out any smoke." Tracee says, "I want to emigrate, not just be brain-damaged."

"Too late," Eve says, and tugs the dog outside to the backyard. There, the sun is still shining. Birds build nests, too dumb to know this planet is out of fashion. Bees crawl around inside the open roses, not knowing their whole reality is obsolete.

In the kitchen, on the counter next to the sink, is a Going Away Kit, the plastic blister card of cyanide pills. It was a new flavor, lemon. A family pack. Printed on the cardboard backing is a little cartoon. It shows an empty stomach. A clock face counts off three minutes. And then your cartoon soul would wake up in a world of pleasure and comfort. The next planet. Evolved.

Eve punches one out, a bright-yellow pill printed with a smiling happy-face in red. It didn't matter if they'd used that toxic kind of red dye. Eve punches out all the pills. All eight, she takes into the bathroom and flushes down the toilet.

The car's still running inside the garage. Through a window, standing on a lawn chair, Eve can see the heads slumped inside. Her dad. Her future ex-stepmom. Her brother.

In the backyard, Risky is nosing at the crack under the garage door, sniffing the fumes from inside. Eve tells him, No. She calls him back away from the house, back into the sunshine. There, with the neighborhood quiet except for the birds, the buzz of the bees, the backyard already looks messy and needs mowing. With no roar of lawn mowers and airplanes and motorcycles, the birds singing sound as loud as traffic used to.

After she lays down in the grass, Eve pulls up the bottom of her shirt and lets the sun warm her stomach. She closes her eyes and rubs the fingertips of one hand in slow circles around her bellybutton.

Risky barks, once, twice.

And a voice says, "Hey."

A face sticks over the fence from the backyard next door. Blond hair and pink pimples, a kid named Adam from school. From before all the schools shut down. Adam's fingers grip the top edge of the wood fence, and he pulls himself up until both elbows rest along the top. His chin hooked on his two hands, Adam says, "Did you hear about your brother's girlfriend?"

Eve shuts her eyes and says, "This sounds weird, but I really miss death . . ."

Adam kicks a leg sideways to hook his foot over the fence. He says, "Your folks emigrate yet?"

In the garage, the car's engine coughs and misses a beat on one cylinder. A ventricle getting sloppy. Inside the window glass, the garage air is shifting gray clouds of smoke. The engine misses again and goes quiet. Nothing inside moves. Eve's family, now they're just their own left-behind luggage.

And, spread out in the sunshine, feeling her skin turn tight and red, Eve says, "Poor Larry." Still rubbing circles around her belly-button.

Risky goes to stand next to the fence, looking up, as Adam hauls one leg, then the other over the top, then jumps down into the yard. Adam stoops to pet the dog. Scratching under the dog's chin, Adam says, "Did you tell them we're pregnant?"

And Eve, she doesn't say anything. She doesn't open her eyes.

Adam says, "If we get the whole human race started again, our folks will be *so pissed* . . ."

The sun is almost straight overhead. What sounds like cars is just wind blowing through the empty neighborhood.

Material possessions are obsolete. Money is useless. Status is pointless.

It would be summer for another three months, and there was a whole world of canned food to eat. That's if the Emigration Assistance Squad didn't machine-gun her for noncompliance. Top-A priority target that she is. The End.

Eve opens her eyes and looks at the white dot near the blue horizon. The Morning Star. Venus. "If I have this baby," Eve says, "I hope it's going to be . . . Tracee."

Mr. Whittier leads Miss Sneezy to the door. To the world, outside. The two of them, hand in hand. Here is our world without a devil, our Villa Diodati without any monster to blame. He's hauled the alley door open a little, open enough so a ray of real sunlight angles in from the alley. That bright slot, the opposite of the black slot we found when we arrived.

Miss Sneezy the same as Cassandra Clark, the bride of Mr. Whittier. The one he wants to save.

The projector bulb has burned out. Or burned so hot so long—with something *dramatic* always happening, something *horrible* always happening, something *exciting* always happening—it's tripped a circuit breaker.

The Baroness Frostbite is asleep in her pile of rags and lace, her greasy pink pucker, muttering. So is the Earl of Slander, sleep-talking, dream-rewinding the scenes in his head.

We all look to be asleep or unconscious or dreaming awake, muttering about how none of this is our fault. We're the prey. Everything here has been done to us.

Only Saint Gut-Free and Mother Nature whisper back and forth. He keeps sideways-eyeing the open door and the crack of light spilling inside. Mr. Whittier and Miss Sneezy, their dark skeletons outlined and dissolving in the glare of daylight.

The rest of us, dissolving into our costumes, into the carpet, into the floor.

Mother Nature keeps broken-record-saying, "Stop them . . . stop them . . ."

It would make a good-enough happy ending, Saint Gut-Free says. Those two young lovers walking out into the light of a bright new day. They could find help and save the group. The two of them could be victims and heroes.

But Mother Nature will only whisper, "Too early." They need to wait just a little longer. Being younger, they can afford to wait until a few more have died.

Mother Nature and Saint Gut-Free, they could outlive old Whittier and sick Miss Sneezy.

Looking around at the rest of us, you'd bet Agent Tattletale and Chef Assassin won't last another day. The Countess Foresight, her brocade chest has stopped moving up and down, and her lips have turned blue. Even the Reverend Godless, his plucked eyebrows have stopped trying to grow back.

No, the longer they can wait, the less ways the money will have to be split.

Her brass bells ringing, the red henna vines on her hands, Mother Nature slips off one of the Saint's shoes. Her fingers touching just the pleasure centers of his sole, she holds on, her touch rolling his eyes backward in his head.

No, Mother Nature and Saint Gut-Free can have it all. All the money, she says, still touching him down there. All the glory. All the pity.

His eyes rolled up, blind, white as hard-boiled eggs, his eyelashes flutter until he jerks his foot away, Saint Gut-Free saying:

"Mnye etoh nadoh kahk zoobee v zadnetze."

His pant legs and shirttails, they rip and stretch where they're glued to the stage with blood, and the Saint drags himself to his feet and says he's got to get out.

Not yet, says Mother Nature. Her voice a teeth-together, clenched hiss.

Saint Gut-Free takes a step and stumbles. His legs buckle, and he falls to his hands and knees. Crawling toward the open door, he says, "How can I stop them?"

And, reaching after him, Mother Nature catches her fingers hooked around his ankle and says, "Wait."

The path where the sunlight leads them to the door, there the concrete floor feels warm. The two of them crawling, they close their eyes, blinded by the brightness, feeling their way by where the floor is warmer, Brailling with their hands and knees until they find the doorframe with the fingertips they have left. They find the sunlight with the skin of their lips and eyelids.

In the alley's narrow blue sky, birds soar back and forth. Birds and clouds that aren't cobwebs. In a blue that isn't velvet or paint.

With his head stuck out the door, Saint Gut-Free says, "I know where we're at." Squinting, he says, "They're still here." He points with one hand, saying, "Miss Sneezy, wait . . ."

Mother Nature's fingers holding tight to his shirt and the waist of his pants, he keeps crawling, swimming, saying, "Please, stop."

Half out the door, his hands dragging him through the broken glass and trash of the alley, all of the beautiful garbage warm from the afternoon sun, Saint Gut-Free says, "Stop!"

While two figures stagger toward the alley's entrance: the girl close by, the old man almost a city block away, his arm raised as a taxi pulls to the curb.

Toward this, the Saint shouts, "Miss Sneezy!"

He shouts, "Wait!"

Miss Sneezy turns to look.

And . . . then . . . and . . . *Shooo-rook!*

The knife from the floor, the paring knife that Chef Assassin tossed at Mr. Whittier, Mother Nature's brought it with them.

That knife sticking out of Miss Sneezy's chest, it still shakes with each beat of her heart, shaking less and less as Mother Nature and Saint Gut-Free drag her back inside the door. Back into the dark.

The knife shakes less as they climb to their feet and wrestle the door shut, the metal rollers squealing. The sky, getting more narrow, until the birds and clouds and blue are gone.

In the alley, Mr. Whittier's voice shouts from closer and closer, for them to stop.

The knife shakes even less as Mother Nature says, "I told you: "Not yet."

And then the knife stands still. The coughing, sniffing, sneezing little person we've waited to see die from the day we arrived here—at last, dead.

We haven't so much saved the world as we've preserved our audience. Kept alive the people to watch us on television, read our books, go to our some-day movie. Our consumer base.

Saint Gut-Free holding the door shut, the lock clicks open from the outside. The knob rattling. The Saint clicks it locked, and again it clicks open.

The Saint clicks it shut, saying, "No." And the lock clicks open, turned by a key from the outside.

Back in the dark, back in the cold, Mother Nature pulls the sticky blade out of Miss Sneezy. Mother Nature sticks the blade into the lock and snaps it off.

The lock, ruined. The knife, ruined. Poor Miss Sneezy, with her red eyes and runny nose, reduced to being a prop in our story. A person made into an object. As if you cut open a rag doll with a silly name, and found inside: Real intestines, real lungs, a beating heart, blood. A lot of hot, sticky blood.

Now the story split another less way. What was done to us.

For now, we're still here. In our dim circle around the ghost light.

The voice of Mr. Whittier, he's wailing outside the steel door. His fists, pounding. Wanting to come inside. Not wanting to die alone.

For now we wait, repeating our story in the Museum of Us. In this, our permanent dress rehearsal.

How Mr. Whittier trapped us here. He starved and tortured us. He killed us.

We recite this: the Mythology of Us.

And someday soon, any day now, the world will come open that door and rescue us. The world will listen. Starting on that sun-glorious day, the whole world is going to love us.

The Poems

The Stories

About the Author

Chuck Palahniuk's six novels are the best-selling *Diary*, *Lullaby*, and *Fight Club*, which was made into a film by director David Fincher, *Survivor*, *Invisible Monsters*, and *Choke*. He is also the author of the best-selling nonfiction collection *Stranger Than Fiction* and the profile of Portland *Fugitives and Refugees*, published as part of the Crown Journeys series. He lives in the Pacific Northwest.